Punta Rosa

The Thomas Night Crime Novels

Punta Rosa

A Thomas Night Crime Novel
Book II

Paul Casper Scherer

Soul Attitude Press

Punta Rosa

Published by Soul Attitude Press

Pinellas Park, FL

www.soulattitudepress.com

3rd Edition: ISBN 978-1-946338-36-5

Printed in the United States of America

Dedication

To my wife
Cynthia Jeanne Petelle

Author's Note: On the meaning of Punta Rosa

"Punta" is a Spanish word meaning or describing a spot of land that expands from shore into a body of water. The word "Punta" is not meant to describe the female anatomy nor should the word "Punta" be mistaken for the slang word "puta". The word "Rosa" means "pink", or "like a rose".

Source: AZDictionary.com

Table of Contents

Introduction

If the reader has not read the prequel to the series titled "La Florida", the author suggests the reader take the time to read the text for the list of characters attached. The list of main characters will provide the reader a minimum of background information for this book.

This novel follows the law practice of Thomas Night, Esquire, in Florida and the countries of Belize and México in Central America in the late 1960s and early 1970s.

List of Main Characters

Francis Aloysius Barnes

"The Senator" - retired State Senator - his family owned Plantation #7 in North Ormond, Florida. The Senator, a widower, organized a company called Commercial Carrier Corporation (CCC) that owned timberland, saw mills and semi-trucks to deliver lumber to the Northeast US used to construct housing after WWII.

Francis Aloysius Barnes II

"Frank" - the Senator's son - married to Beatrice "Bea" O'Brien Barnes. Frank headed CCC, creating the biggest privately owned timberland and saw mill operation in the Southeast USA. Frank is the natural father of Jimmy and the adoptive father of Robert, Albert and Jenny Johnson-Barnes. He and Bea lived at the Homestead which was in Holly Hill. Frank's best friend and attorney is Thomas "Tom" Night. They attended college together and they created CCC.

Beatrice "Bea" O'Brien Barnes

Married Frank when she was 15 and Frank was 17. They had a child, Jimmy, who was born breach. His spine was injured by forceps used in the delivery and he suffered severe cerebral palsy as a result of oxygen deprivation during birth. Bea devoted her life to Jimmy and her adopted children, Bob, Little Al/Albert and Jenny. Bea also operated the dairy on the Homestead and developed the dairy into a large milk and cream processing facility that shipped dairy products by rail throughout the USA.

Thomas Night, Esquire

"Tom" was orphaned as a teen. Father, Mother and brother died from pneumonia as a complication of influenza in St. Petersburg, Florida. Tom was raised by two Aunts who were professors at Stetson University. Tom met Frank at Stetson. Tom studied law and his first clients were the Barnes Family and their businesses. He began his practice in Daytona Beach and then moved back to St. Petersburg and established a law firm.

Marlene James

"Marla" grew up in St. Petersburg, took business and secretarial courses in high school. Her first job was Tom's legal secretary. Marla was trusted by Tom and Frank and the Senator and she helped Tom and Frank's family and the businesses. For years she was Tom's girlfriend.

The adopted children

Robert (Bob), Albert (Little Al) and Jenny were born to Mary and Albert Johnson Senior (Big Al). Mary was schizophrenic. Big Al was an alcoholic. Bea convinced Mary to let her take Bob into her home to help her care for Jimmy then later after Mary became mentally ill and neither parent could care for the children, Frank and Bea adopted their children. The children all worked in the Barnes Family businesses.

New Characters

Anthony Arnold – treasure hunter

Thomas Night – Anthony Arnold's criminal attorney

Jorge Mendez – crewman on Anthony Arnold's dive boat

Pablo Mendez – Jorge Mendez's brother and Chief of Police of Cancún, Mexico

Rick Ibn – airplane pilot – owner of Aero Commander 500S, airplane

Jamie Sulby – passenger on Rick Ibn's plane

Winston Grey – ranch owner in Belize, drug trafficker

Fredrick and George – neighbors of Winston Grey

Andrew Prince – Solicitor General – chief legal officer in the Country of Belize

Anna Hernando, M.D. – doctor in Belize City

Joseph McDugal – the Bounty Hunter – employer of the two Mexican Wrestlers

Mexican Wrestlers –Santo and Diablo- masked Mexican wrestlers employed by the Bounty   Hunter to kidnap bail jumpers

Herbert John – Tom Night's solicitor in Belize

John Hale – State Attorney in Florida

Judge David Lucius – Florida Appellate judge

Judge Raymond Barrow – Florida trial judge

Jane McCormick – Judge Barrow's secretary

Harish Patel – Florida lawyer, represents Anthony Arnold's business interests

Darlene Street – lawyer who represents Tom Night in Florida

Jacob and Michael – members of Belize Mennonite Community in Spanish Lookout

Part I
Low Pressure System

Chapters 1 through 12

The storm hits Punta Rosa ... Anthony Arnold is captured by the Bounty Hunter ... Tom Night retrieves Anthony Arnold's dive boat ... Jorge Mendez is lost at sea ... The investigation into Jorge's disappearance from the dive boat ... The moon pool

Chapter 1

"I need to be sure Mr. Anthony will not know I was the one who ratted on him. That is my main concern."

Jorge Mendez was calling from a pay phone located outside a gas station on US 1 in Key Largo, Florida. Jorge was a crewman on one of two small ships that Anthony Arnold was motoring from the USA to Belize on the Yucatan in Central America. Jorge, a Mexican, was short, with a dark-skinned complexion and black, shiny hair. He was handsome with European features, but at the moment he was very nervous and frowning. He did not want to be seen speaking on the phone.

Anthony Arnold's two boats had tied up at a dock in a canal in Key Largo, Florida and the crew was loading the boats with fuel, ice, beer and food that Anthony purchased for the voyage from a marine supply house. It was a long trip to Belize and they intended to avoid land until they were in Mexican waters. The ships would encounter the Florida Straight with its volatile currents and storms that kicked up high seas. This time of year hurricanes and low pressure systems would also be a danger.

Neither boat was designed for rough seas. The M.V. Cap de l'Ile was an old coastal freighter on its last legs. The other vessel was newly constructed, designed especially for diving. It had a barge-like hull and an opening cut in the floor of the hull for a moon pool that allowed a diver to enter the water from inside the boat. Both boats were designed to operate near shore and in shallow water. In the ocean, if the seas were rough, the boats bounced like bobbers on a fishing line. The men were counting on calm weather.

Besides Anthony and Jorge there were two Honduran men who had agreed to help crew the small ships. Their pay was their passage, food and drink, together with a few pesos they would receive at the end of the voyage. They were content because they could re-enter Mexico without going through customs. The Hondurans said they were trying to get back home to their families in Central America. They appeared to be uneducated and had little knowledge of the modern world. Anthony thought they were probably criminals. They answered only to Spanish. Jorge was from Cancún, México and Spanish was his native language, but he could also speak English fluently. He had spent many years illegally in the United States.

Anthony was born in the USA. He was domiciled for all his 47 years in Pinellas County, Florida. The word "domiciled " is used to denote his official address. Most of his life he roamed throughout the country and Central America and he had no permanent homestead and he took his mail at his mother's house. He had too much fun when he was in his early 20's and was sentenced to jail for ten years for importation of marijuana. He learned to read Spanish from a lexicon and by reading Spanish pulp fiction novels. He tried to learn to speak the language fluently when he was in jail but never learned. State prison in Florida was segregated – blacks, whites, and Latinos. So, "Mr. Anthony", as he was known by the crew, could not speak Spanish fluently and had to rely on Jorge to speak to the Hondurans. Anthony Arnold had been in and out of prison all his life. He was a brilliant mechanic – boats, planes, cars. He could fix, design and construct anything with an engine. He was confident. He was strong, blond, tanned; always with a smile on his face which was scarred from acne when he was a teen.

***

Jorge was still on the phone. He was insistent. "Look I need to be assured that Mr. Anthony will not know I turned him in."

"He won't know. We couldn't stay in business if the people we arrested knew how we found them" said the Bounty Hunter. The

Bounty Hunter's business was arresting fugitives from courts in the United States.

"If something happens to me, how will I know you will pay my wife the fee for the information I want to sell?" asked Jorge. "I don't even know your real name."

"You have to trust us on that. We are offering you a lot of money, ten percent of the bail bond premium for the information, that's $17,500 US dollars. You got our phone number from someone, so you know our reputation. We will make payment for the information as we have agreed. We could only remain in business in the future if we make payment for the information we receive."

Seventeen thousand, five hundred US dollars was a huge sum of money in 1970. The reward Jorge would receive for information leading to Anthony's re-incarceration was 10% of the bail bond the insurance company had paid the court in Bushton, Florida, (the sum of $175,000). Under the terms of the appearance bond the insurance company paid the clerk to assure the court Anthony would appear for trial on a charge of theft of an airplane. Anthony was a no show and the company had to pay. The insurance company had a period of 30 days to catch Anthony and return him to the court and the money, less court costs, would be returned by the Clerk to the insurance company. The Bounty Hunter's job was to recapture Anthony Arnold.

"So tell me, where are you now?"

"We are in the Florida Keys at Key Largo," said Jorge.

"How long will you be there?"

"Not long. From here we head toward Isla Mujeres, México. But we don't intend to make port until we reach Punta Rosa."

"How do you know that?"

"Anthony has charts. I got a look at them." (See map 2)

"What is your route of travel?"

"We skirt the Florida Keys and then head west past the Dry Tortugas and then we go south from the Dry Tortugas heading for the east coast of the Yucatán," said Jorge.

"You do not stop in Isla Mujeres?" (See maps 1 and 4.) The Bounty Hunter was testing Jorge's knowledge of the Caribbean.

"Correct. We go south to Punta Rosa, México. We land in Punta Rosa and take on fuel there. The gas is cheap in México and that is the last Mexican port before Ambergris Caye in Belize. The fuel is very expensive in Belize."

"We have a man in Punta Rosa," said the Bounty Hunter. "He will contact us when you land. Do you know that there is a storm in the Caribbean Sea heading north?"

"We were told about the hurricane when we landed here in Key Largo. Mr. Anthony believes we will miss the storm. He is betting it goes north and then east toward the west coast of Florida. If that happens the storm will be behind us and all the shipping will be out of the area and we will be able to slip into México quietly."

"I hope you are successful." The phone was breaking up. "If Anthony changes his mind and decides to wait out the storm in Key Largo call us back. It would be easier to capture him in the States. Otherwise we will wait for our man's call from Punta Rosa. He has a marine radio and we can stay in touch. We can fly fast. If you see a black Lear jet overhead, that's our plane. Good luck to you."

"Thank you," said Jorge.

When Jorge got back to the ship, Anthony was working on the flying bridge of the dive boat. Jorge began to help and fell into the routine of stowing gear and lashing crates and cargo that would be exposed to the elements if their vessels were hit by the storm.

***

They had good luck for the first part of the trip and made it through the Florida Straight to the Dry Tortugas in calm seas. There was no fresh water on these keys or islands. The largest island was occupied by Fort Jefferson, built in the early 1800s. The occupants of Fort Jefferson had to rely on rain water and transport ships for potable water. The water was stored on the island in cisterns. Fort Jefferson had been built to protect Florida from a raid from an enemy who made a hostile approach by sea from the south. After the Civil War the fort became a prison. Its most famous inmate was Dr. Samuel A. Mudd, who treated the injury to John Wilkes Booth's ankle after Booth assassinated President A. Lincoln.

The fort was a tourist trap now. It did not have a ship's store or fuel. It was for day trips only and did not sell necessities, only souvenirs.

Arnold's ships passed the fort at night. The red brick structure was low on the horizon and, but for the lights on the ramparts, the fort would be invisible to a passing ship.

The weather held until they made the Straight of Cozumel (Mayan Riviera) just south of Isla Mujeres and they were heading south to Punta Rosa. The sky turned grey and the wind was from the east. The crew was peppered with stinging raindrops. The Isle of Cozumel with its high coast line protected the two vessels but once they passed the south end of the island the ships began to struggle with the wind. The boats had to bear southeast to keep south. But they were making progress and the men on the boats were confident they would make Punta Rosa before the storm would swamp their ships. Anthony had bet wrong that the storm would head north. All the signs were that it had first headed north and that it was now heading west in the direction of Punta Rosa.

Punta Rosa was located at the end of a strip of land that was about two miles wide and 30 miles long that extended south from the town of Vigia Chico. Vigia Chico was in the coastal wildlife preserve that surrounded the town. Punta Rosa was at the end of a dirt road. The dirt road was cut through the mangrove jungle and began at Cancún and passed the Mayan ruins at Tulum.

South of Punta Rosa there was nothing but water to the front and left of you and a vast mangrove swamp to the right until you arrived at Ambergris Caye in Belize.

Jorge was smiling when he saw the low buildings of Punta Rosa all tucked into the shoreline on a 20 foot high outcrop of lime rock on the shoreline. The promontory was probably the base of a Mayan lime rock tower or temple. Many towers had been built by the Mayans along the coast of the Yucatán. One could suppose that if the Mayans constructed a tower on the high spot at Punta Rosa and built a fire on top of the tower, the natives would have a lighthouse of sorts to use for navigation. To the west of the fishing village there was a small but deep bay that would offer a safe harbor in a storm.

Anthony, who was operating the dive boat, contacted Jorge by two way radio. Jorge was behind but in sight of the dive boat piloting the M.V. Cap de l'Ile. Anthony instructed him to go south past the port and tie up behind and to the west of the village in the bay at the Ship's Store. The men docked and topped off the fuel tanks and took on drinking water, beer and soft drinks. They did not remain tied up at the docks extending into the bay but instead, each vessel moved into the bay and set out a single large anchor hooked into the lime rock at the bottom of the bay. Tying to the bottom out in the bay would prevent the boats from colliding with the pilings around the docks if the storm hit. Once the boats were secured, a small craft came to them and carried them to the Ship's Store. This building was the largest on shore and was a combination warehouse, fuel depot, bar and restaurant.

December 30th, 1973.

Chapter 2

When the low pressure storm threatened, all the 20 or so residents of the fishing village named Punta Rosa wanted to huddle in the warehouse, named the "Ship's Store", because the building was new and strong, constructed to withstand a hurricane. It had been built on top of 30 foot long pine pilings. The pilings were sunk in holes that were dug ten feet deep into the highest point of the promontory. Then lime rock and sand were wedged around the poles and the sand was pounded tight against the pilings.

The pilings were set every four feet along the perimeter of the building and then the outside of the poles were covered with 8' by 4' sheets of ¾ inch marine plywood. There was a second wall of plywood inside the building so that the pilings were enclosed inside the plywood skins. The building was 48 feet long by 24 feet wide by 10 feet high at the eave of the roof. The roof was made of corrugated tin panels nailed on to manufactured rafters. The rafters were attached to the walls of the building with metal hurricane straps. There were screen windows cut in the walls but each window had a shutter that closed over the opening. The shutters were to be attached with screws to the wall over the screened windows if a heavy storm approached.

This was the first time the building had been tested by the full force of a hurricane.

The building had a floor made of 2" by 8" boards. The floor was constructed five feet off the ground. The idea was that if a storm pushed a surge of water over the promontory, the storm surge would flow under the floor of the building from the Caribbean Sea into the bay behind the building.

There was a kitchen inside the Ship's Store with a grill and oven and refrigeration unit. The oven and grill ran on propane gas and the refrigeration ran off a gas powered electric generator that also powered the lights and the fuel pumps for the diesel and gasoline tanks. The only system that was outside of the building were the toilets that were nothing more than outhouses built over the water of the bay on a dock about 100 yards from the Ship's Store.

The building was much more secure than the houses built by the residents of Punta Rosa. Their homes were simple shacks. They were idyllic until a storm hit and then they offered the owner little protection.

The owner and operator of the business was Felix Mercado, a Mexican national from Cancún. He and his wife and three children lived in an Airstream travel trailer that was parked to the west side of the store. The trailer was tied to the electricity and propane systems in the store. The trailer was not strapped to the building but it had been parked close to the leeward side of the building. The wind from the sea would be the most destructive if it came out of the West and the Ship's Store blocked the wind from the storm hitting the Airstream trailer directly.

Felix knew Jorge and his family. They grew up together in Cancún, Mexico and they recognized each other immediately. They struck up a conversation in Spanish as soon as they saw each other. Jorge was concerned about his wife and family. Felix offered Jorge the use of his ship to shore radio to call Cancún. Jorge's brother, Pablo Mendez, was the Cancún Police Chief and the police department was able to patch Jorge through to his brother while Pablo was in his police car.

Jorge learned from his brother that his family was safe. They had worried about him, knowing he was at sea with a storm in the Gulf. He told his brother, Pablo, he should be back within a week but he was safe now and would ride out the storm in Punta Rosa. Pablo told Jorge he would watch out for his wife and children until Jorge got home.

Jorge and his brother, Pablo, looked like twins but they had taken different journeys to middle age. Pablo was a respected and an important member of the Mexican Judiciary. Jorge was a criminal.

After he made the call, Jorge introduced Felix to Anthony. Felix offered to let Jorge, Anthony and the Hondurans stay inside the building with the other residents of the small community during the storm. Anthony was very appreciative and told Felix that he would purchase all of the remaining supplies needed for the trip south at the store because of the favor. Felix reminded Jorge and the rest of the crew that they should take advantage of the outhouses before they blew away.

Felix went to his radio to make another call to the States. He talked to the Bounty Hunter to tell him Anthony was there in the store and would be there until the storm passed.

Felix would be paid by the Bounty Hunter for the information. The Bounty Hunter was an American and flew a black Lear jet but no one knew his name or address, not even the people who worked closely with him. Everyone just called him the "Bounty Hunter".

Felix returned to the store and announced two rules for his neighbors and the others who would ride out the storm in his store. If anyone took a beer or food they were to write down the purchase in a tablet on the counter, and second, they were not to light the propane because the storm might cause a leak in the gas line and it could cause a fire.

Felix then went to the Airstream to be with his family. The Airstream was very comfortable. It was air-conditioned.

Chapter 3

On the way to the trailer, Felix approached an old Land Rover, a British, four wheel drive vehicle that was parked at the front of The Ship's Store. The engine was running and the fog lamps were turned on. The vehicle was equipped with a special air intake and exhaust system that allowed air to flow into the carburetor and out of the exhaust system through extension pipes so that the engine would continue to run even if the vehicle was in water mid-way up the driver's window (in water about four feet deep).

Felix could see a man in the driver's seat, which was on the right hand (English) side of the Land Rover. There was a passenger in the back. Both men were large and muscular. Felix knew them. They worked for the Bounty Hunter. They had been waiting for Anthony and his ships to arrive so they could kidnap Anthony.

Earlier in the day, once it was known the storm was on its way, the Bounty Hunter's men had prepared the vehicle's carburation and exhaust systems so they could safely drive in the storm. They intended to arrest Anthony and drive out from Punta Rosa on the old dirt trail past the Mayan ruins at Tulum and to the international airport in Cancún. Once they got Anthony to the airport, he would be tied up in a seat in the black Lear jet and the Bounty Hunter would fly Anthony to the States to prison for jumping bail.

Felix went over to the Land Rover and spoke to the men. "He's inside, but he should be out soon to use the baños (outhouse). He's wearing a blue wind breaker. He is six feet tall, slim build and he has blond hair. He's wearing dirty white shorts and a hat."

"Good," said the driver. "Thank you."

"Get him out quick." Felix was anxious. "You don't have to worry about the Mexican, Jorge, but there are two Hondurans with him. I don't know if they will try to help him or not, so get him when he is outside of the building and get him in the car quickly so no one sees you have him. In this wind no one inside will be able to hear him if he screams and yells for help."

"We will do as you wish," the driver said as he turned off the fog lamps and the engine.

***

The two men sat in the dark. It was cloudy and raining and the wind was howling. Both men smiled.

"It is wild." said the driver.

The rain was so heavy that it produced an effect like a white out in a blizzard. But it was not cold. It was hot and humid and the men were sweating heavily as they waited for Anthony to come out to be trapped.

***

The storm impacting Punta Rosa now contained steady gale force winds. Interspersed in the steady gale were gusts of hurricane force winds above 70 knots, but the wind was not yet sustained at hurricane force. When the men in the Land Rover last heard a weather bulletin, it was reported that the storm was not major but would reach hurricane strength.

The men were very familiar with the road from Punta Rosa to Cancún. Although it was narrow, it was about 15 feet above sea level. The surge of water from the storm was expected to hit at high tide but it was not expected to overtop the road except where there were sloughs cut through to drain the road. These ruts were dangerous because a driver of a vehicle would not see the rut due to the water on the road and the vehicle could break an axle if it fell into a deep rut while in motion. Also, the sloughs could be deep and fill with water and flood the engine or exhaust unless the vehicle was equipped with carburetor and exhaust extenders. The men had prepared for that possibility.

As the men waited for Anthony, they spent the time intently discussing their careers. They were "lucha libre", professional wrestlers, and were considering their managers suggestion that they wrestle in a "tres" (a three member tag team), rather than individually. They had wrestled as masked men. One was evil; a devil like the "Blue Demon", and one was an innocent like "El Santo". They sometimes wrestled each other. They liked to wear masks because they could trade off and sometimes one would be the good hombre and sometimes not. They could also trade off depending on their mood.

To be successful in their craft, the men knew they had to wrestle, putting their soul into the match. It was like a play. There was Drama and sometimes Comedy, but it was hard to be comedic if you were in pain. Most people think that wrestlers are acting and they do not feel pain when they jump off the top rope onto an opponent—but that is not true. High flying maneuvers can hurt, and the muscles can be sore afterward. If you wrestle someone who is inexperienced in the holds or in the routines performed during a competition you can be injured badly, particularly in your spine and your knees.

As they talked they became so engrossed in the subject of their future in wrestling that they almost missed Anthony. He appeared on the road as a figure in a blue jacket and shorts. He was hunkered down, hands in his pockets with a cap pulled low over his forehead. Anyone heading to the outhouse had to pass by the driver side of the Land Rover.

As Anthony passed the right side driver's door the driver opened the door. Anthony could not hear the door because of the noise of the wind, but he sensed movement to his rear and he turned. As Anthony turned, he took a step into an elbow that crashed into his chin. Down he went. The passenger in the back of the Rover got out and the wrestlers quickly cuffed Anthony's ankles and his wrists. They inserted a large mouth guard between his teeth so he would not be able to talk or bite and they covered his head with a hood and tied it below his chin at his neck. The hood had a piece of gauze in the front so that air would easily enter the hood. The men were familiar with the hood. They sometimes wrestled wearing hoods. They knew Anthony would be able to breath but the fact that he was blinded by the hood would scare and intimidate him into submission. He would do as they said to do.

***

From the Airstream trailer, Felix had been watching and he became nervous because it seemed to be forever before Anthony exited the building for the outhouse. Felix was worried that the people in the building were maybe using a bucket for a toilet because no one came out to the outhouses. But then Anthony appeared and Felix watched through a break in the rain as the men restrained him and subdued him and secured him in the vehicle quickly. They were very professional, thought Felix.

The head lights on the Land Rover ignited and the vehicle made a U-turn and headed north up the road.

Felix went back in the building to check on his property. All the systems were working. No one had used the propane; it was still shut off at the tank. There was a tablet on the counter and each beer that had been consumed was noted in the tablet.

Felix made one more call to the USA to confirm that the wrestlers had Anthony and the Land Rover was headed back to the airport in Cancún. The wind was now roaring and seemed constant. Felix asked the Bounty Hunter if he had any information about the storm. He was told it was predicted that the eye was heading north of Punta Rosa but that was all that was known because there was no official weather observer in the path of the storm. The reports relied on ships at sea and military radar. This area of México was sparsely populated. Felix knew that it was good for him and his family that they were south of the eye of the storm. Based on the report, the Ship's Store would not take a direct hit from the storm, but the wrestlers and their prisoner were in for a ride.

***

As the wrestlers had proceeded north, they were forced to drive more slowly as the intensity of the wind increased.

The road was built on a long peninsula that was only a mile or two wide. The road engineers had tried to place the road on the part of land that was the highest above sea level. Initially the Rover moved at the normal speed for the old dirt road, but that was only 35 mph. The wind was from the right and rear of their vehicle. As they approached the point where they were three quarters of the way between Punta Rosa and the Mayan Ruins to the north, their speed was down to 15 mph and they had about 15 miles to go to the ruins. The wind was strong and from the right, with each gust rocking the vehicle. Their calculation was that they would be forced to come to a dead stop in an hour or so because they would not be able to see to drive and stay on the road. But, in an hour, if they could average 15 mph, they hoped they would be at Tulum and safety.

As they got closer to Tulum the road had been built closer to the sea so there was very little vegetation between them and the ocean. The tide was ebbing when they first arrived at the Ship's Store but now the tide had changed. It was high tide and a surge of water was being pushed in front of the storm.

Tulum was about 40 feet above sea level and the wrestlers could drive into the center of the plaza of the ruin and park their Rover behind the rim of the temple walls that protected the ruin from the sea. If they could get to Tulum they would probably be safe and they could ride out the storm. If they could not reach Tulum they would probably be trapped in a location on the road which was only 15 feet above sea level and the sea surge would swamp the road, push the vehicle into the sea, and they would drown.

***

The Ship's Store had been constructed five feet above the top of the promontory, and the ground was about 20 feet above sea level. An hour after the wrestlers left Punta Rosa the sea had been pushed up the beach and the waves were washing under the building. The outhouses had been blown or washed from the dock and the decks of the docks over the bay were submerged by the storm surge and the boards on the docks began to pop loose. In some places whole sections of deck were pulled loose from the pilings and then floated west across the bay in the wind.

All the boats tied to the docks or pilings strained at their moorings and as the wind and waves rose in intensity the boats pulled loose and raced across the bay and rode the storm tide up into the mangrove forest along the western shore of the bay. Two deep sea fishing boats, 30 feet in length, broke away and both hit the M.V. Cap de l'Ile that was anchored in the center of the bay next to Anthony's dive boat. The dive boat remained untouched by other boats and was anchored with a single line.

When the fishing boats hit the M.V. Cap de l'Ile the collision snapped the freighter's large anchor line and the freighter floated into the mangroves and was lifted by the storm tide so that it became entangled in the trees and embedded on a sandbar. When the keel of the ship impacted the sandbar the keel snapped and water rushed into the hull of the ship and the ship began to roll back and forth further embedding the ship into the shore.

The people in the Ship's Store could not see the devastation occurring outside. The windows remained secure, covered with plywood shutters. The building remained essentially watertight; there were only a few areas of leaks in the roof. The sound of the wind was murderous. Some of the occupants sat on the floor and pulled their knees up to their chest and opened and closed their jaws to cause their ears to pop as the barometric pressure continued to drop.

***

Anthony had regained consciousness about 10 minutes after he had been elbowed, then trussed up and hooded. He understood what was being said in Spanish. He had been kidnapped by two men hired by a bounty hunter. The Bounty Hunter was hired by the insurance company that posted his bond when he was charged with stealing an airplane.

Anthony listened while the men said that they had been informed by the Bounty Hunter that Anthony would be at Punta Rosa. When Anthony heard that, he knew Jorge had probably ratted on him, because Jorge was the only member of the crew with access to the charts for the voyage.

The storm was much worse than the men had anticipated and they were cursing the Bounty Hunter for sending them out in this danger. Anthony realized he was cuffed at his wrists and ankles and the hood effectively rendered him blind and he could not speak because of the mouthpiece.

Anthony felt he had the best chance to survive if he remained quiet and did not fight. He let the man in the back seat know he was awake by slowly raising his hands in front of him but he did not resist.

"He is alive," said the man in the back seat. "More bad luck. It was only a matter of time before he woke up."

"Take his hood off and let him see the situation," said the driver.

When the hood was removed Anthony could see they were proceeding very slowly down the road and the sea was being pushed up the side of the road by the wind. The men each had masks over their heads with openings cut for their eyes, ears, noses and mouths. They smiled at Anthony. Anthony smiled back and shrugged his shoulders as if to say: "What can I do about it." The men began to laugh because they were all in the same predicament.

"We should unloosen his cuffs," said the driver. And the cuffs were removed.

The wrestlers began to speak loudly in Spanish and they all cursed the Bounty Hunter for causing them to be out on the road in this storm. They should have waited until the storm passed. They all agreed. None of them agreed more than Anthony. He knew he was caught and his fate was sealed. If he were to survive he would return to jail, or he would die on this road. If he died in the road it would be the Bounty Hunter's fault. If he was returned to jail it was probably Jorge's fault.

***

After the storm surge overtopped the beach at Punta Rosa, the sea began to eat at the beach and erode the sand from under the Ship's Store. The building held steady because it was supported by wooden piers that were deep in the sand and rock under the building. So the beach would have to erode 8 or 9 feet before the building would topple and break up.

The Airstream trailer, however, was not supported by pilings. It was only connected to the building by the copper tubing of the propane system and the wiring that connected the building's electric system to the trailer. The sea surged three times during the hurricane. When the second wall of water crested, the water flowed under the Ship's Store and struck the trailer. The copper tube and the wires snapped and the trailer was pushed into the bay. The Airstream floated for a while and then began to be pushed across the bay but it never sank. The trailer rolled over the water like a beach ball blown by the wind on a pond.

Once the trailer hit the mangroves across the bay it was blown up and over the top of the trees and was rolled inland, compressing and shredding its aluminum skin as it rolled along. A plane located the trailer after the storm. The bodies of Felix, his wife and three children were never found.

***

Anthony and the wrestlers were able to make it to Tulum by driving slowly, pushing through the water. They parked the Land Rover in the center of the Mayan ruin, pointed out to sea so the brunt of the wind hit the front of the vehicle. From this vantage they rode out the storm. Anthony had agreed that he would not attempt an escape. The wrestlers in turn agreed that they would not use any restraints until they turned Anthony over to the Bounty Hunter at the airport at Cancún. During the remainder of the storm, the men shared a bottle of peppermint schnapps that they found under the seat. As the storm abated the men fell asleep and awoke to a cold evening. The storm had sucked all the heat from the ocean and the land. It felt like winter. The eye of the storm did not hit Tulum but had made landfall south of Punta Rosa. Therefore, the worst of the storm hit the Ship's Store.

***

When the ocean was in the third surge, the waves were slapping against the side of the Ship's Store. The last of the three surges had gone under the building but the waves being pushed on top of the surges still randomly broke on the side of the building. The building began to rock as the pilings were lifted out of their bed. As a wave hit the building from the sea the building lifted up and then as the wave dissipated the building would re-seat. Once the building began to be slapped by the waves the occupants knew they were in real danger, but there was nothing they could do. They were quiet at first. But the waves increased and some of the occupants responded to an especially large wave that shook the building by yelling: "AIIEEEEEEE," and gritting their teeth. The other occupants joined in and when another wave shuddered the building then they would yell: "AIIEEEEEEEE," together, as one.

The native West Indians were familiar with these low pressure storms. If they went to school they were taught the word "hurricane" which is derived from the Indian word: "aracan" which was adopted by the early Europeans as: "huracán". Most of the native occupants of the Ship's Store had experienced a hurricane and they knew that there was a chance, based on the wind speed, the slope of the shore line and the distance the storm had come and the direction of the storm, that these storms could be deadly. The native people, Belizeans, Hondurans, Guatemalans and Mexicans were familiar with the fact that the wave of the storm could inundate a low coastal region and trap the inhabitants in their weak dwellings and kill them.

But the natives also knew there was little they could do. The occupants knew the building they were in was strong and preparations had been made when the building was constructed to strengthen it so it could ride out a storm. But the building could not survive the perfect storm—a storm that would hit the coast with such intensity that nothing would survive.

As the building was struck by the waves and rocked up on its pilings and held and did not rupture and the floor and the roof remained intact, the occupants began to gain confidence that they might survive. The confidence grew as the noise of the wind lessened. Finally, the sea must have subsided, they thought, because the waves no longer crashed against the walls of the building.

The building never broke and the building never rolled over. The goods inside on the floor of the building probably helped keep the building from rolling because the weight of the anchors, steel, rolls of rope, dry goods and bottles of liquids were so heavy that they retarded the building from being toppled.

When the wind subsided, and the occupants left the building, they were confronted by a scene of almost total loss. Some small shacks from the village were hung up in coconut trees. There were no piers or docks or outhouses. All of the boats that had been tied to the docks and piers were now across the bay lodged on top of the mangroves. The coastal freighter appeared to have settled on top of the sand bar, and the oyster bed on the far side was covered with sand and had disappeared. Only the dive boat Anthony built was afloat. It was still secured by the single anchor line in the center of the bay.

The occupants would need everything in the Ship's Store to rebuild their lives and to be fed and housed until they could rebuild. Felix and his family were gone. The logic was that anyone who survived owned that which was not destroyed. What was left was salvage and the salvage belonged to the survivors.

***

From Tulum, the driver of the Land Rover headed for the airport to meet the Bounty Hunter's plane. The wrestlers told Anthony they were sorry but they would have to re-cuff him and put the hood on his head. They promised to do those things at the last possible moment. They also agreed to tell the Bounty Hunter that they had lost the mouthpiece. The mouthpiece was the most annoying of the restraints and Anthony was pleased that he would not have to wear it again.

The wrestlers also explained that he would be secured in a large duffel bag once he was in the plane, but the hood would be removed once he was secured in the plane. The bag would allow them to place him in a seat and buckle him in. They promised him the time for privacy before he was re-cuffed to relieve himself and they also promised him a Valium so he could be more at ease. They assured him that they would cause him as little pain as possible so long as he did not resist.

Anthony told the men he would not resist. "We have become comrades by sharing the experience of surviving the storm."

The wrestlers kept their masks in place. One wrestler explained the Bounty Hunter would fly him in the plane to the USA. The wrestlers would fly with him as passengers. The plane would land at the airport at Key West. The wrestlers would remove him from the plane in the duffle bag and deposit him on the ground in front of the US Customs office. The wrestlers would have paper work to show which court had jurisdiction over him. They told him it was best if he did no more than identify himself to the custom's authorities and to ask that a lawyer be appointed for him.

Anthony asked if it would be possible to speak to the Bounty Hunter before they left Cancún. The wrestler said he would inquire.

***

At the airport the black Lear jet was parked in a hanger. They left the Land Rover at the hanger. Anthony was trussed up and put in a duffle bag and then seated and buckled in. The men put on the hood and told Anthony they would remove it once the Bounty Hunter spoke to him. Anthony was blinded by the hood and could not see the Bounty Hunter.

***

Anthony introduced himself to the Bounty Hunter politely and then explained that his capture was an error. He had paid the bondsman and the insurance company all of the money that they had posted to ensure his appearance in Court. Anthony claimed he had even paid extra money, a premium above the bond amount and the costs paid by the bondsman and the insurance company to the clerk. "Everyone was paid, plus a bonus."

Anthony wanted the Bounty Hunter to know that the bondsman and the insurance company had all been paid. Further, he had been told by the bondsman that he could flee and that, so far as the bondsman and the insurance company were concerned, he did not have to return to court.

"Understood," said the Bounty Hunter.

"Then, if you know the truth, will you release me?" asked Anthony.

"No."

"Why?"

"I have been given orders by the insurance company to return you to court for trial. I can't let you go. The decision has been made by a higher authority." Then the Bounty Hunter added: "It's political. The State Attorney wants to make an example of you."

"I thought I would ask," said Anthony. "It would only be fair." Anthony knew he was wasting his breath. He was fighting with a higher authority, whatever that meant.

"We are leaving. The flight should be smooth. My men will remove the hood once we reach cruising altitude." The Bounty

Hunter was very matter of fact. The Bounty Hunter moved forward into the enclosed cockpit so he could pilot the plane.

As the wrestlers took the hood off Anthony, he asked them to call his attorney, Thomas Night, Esquire, and tell him he was in jail and for him to come to see him as soon as possible.

The wrestlers said they would.

Anthony was quiet. He could not control the situation at this point in time. He took deep breaths. He did not become angry. He would not resist. He would solve the problem, just not now, in some other way. There was always a solution. You just had to recognize the solution when it presented itself. His capture may work out for the better. "I just need to get my boats to Belize," he thought. "I need to find the rat who turned me in."

Chapter 4

Jorge had seen Anthony leave the building before the winds of the storm had reached gale force. When his friend, Felix came in to check on things they spoke. Felix told Jorge that Anthony had been taken into custody by two Mexican wrestlers and they were driving Anthony to the airport at Cancún. The Bounty Hunter was going to fly Anthony to the USA. Felix guessed that if all went well Anthony would be back in jail by that night. Felix said he was going back to the Airstream trailer. He asked Jorge to watch things in the building. Jorge told Felix he was very relieved that this ordeal was over.

That was the last conversation Jorge had with Felix.

After the storm, when Jorge exited the building he could see the tail of the storm – a gray-black mist and low dark clouds heading inland to the west over the mangrove forest and the 450,000 acre preservation area beyond.

Jorge went to the side of the building to Felix's trailer. It was gone. Felix and Felix's wife and children were gone. When he saw the electric wires and the copper propane pipe sticking out of The Ship's Store and the raggedy ends of the pipe and wire he was convinced that he was looking in the right place, but the trailer was gone.

When he looked out in the bay to the west he was amazed that the dive boat was still anchored in the middle of the inlet but all the other boats had been destroyed.

The coastal freighter had been outfitted by Anthony to act as a warehouse. The hold of the ship had been fitted with racks that held motors and generators and steel and wood and saws – everything you would need to build a residence and a small factory. There were also duplicates of many items so that they could be used to barter or trade for food and other necessities once the freighter was tied up at its final port. Even before the voyage the M.V. Cap de l'Ile was on its last legs. It was intended that it would be dry docked and act as Anthony's warehouse for all his equipment, tools and materials.

The Hondurans approached Jorge.

"Where is Mr. Anthony?"

Jorge lied and said he did not know.

" When are we going to be paid?"

Jorge said he expected a call. He told them to wait by the ship to shore radio for a call from Anthony. They should come for him if he called. Meanwhile, Jorge was going to use the Zodiac boat to survey the M.V. Cap de l'Ile and the dive boat. The Hondurans would wait. They had no choice. They helped with the Zodiac (a rubber boat powered by a 25 HP engine). It was lightweight and they were able to get it down from its berth and float it easily. Then the Hondurans went to wait for the call.

The other survivors of the storm were in shock and intoxicated. They sat on the shore and watched Jorge and continued to drink beer. One of the men was very loud. He told Jorge that he was making a salvage claim on the coastal freighter and its cargo, together with the contents of the Ship's Store.

Jorge at first ignored the man but then said: "We represent the owner of the two boats and their contents. You and your friends can make a claim, but only on the building and its contents. We will move onto the dive boat as soon as I talk to the owner. For now, I represent the owner until he comes for his property. He will be here to take custody of his ships and cargo. You have no valid lien."

The man began to draw a crowd. The group began to argue. The locals wanted salvage rights. Jorge thought that he should have ignored the man. Now he had a mob to deal with. Jorge pushed the Zodiac from shore and got away from the crowd. He started the engine and went to the dive boat first. The only damage he found was a broken pillar. The damage occurred when the bow of the boat was hit by a wave. The deck flexed and a weld joint separated. Now, when a wave rolled past, the pillar hit the bow with a clank. This was an easy repair. (Simply re-weld the joint.)

The condition of the freighter was much worse. The ship was aground on shore. Jorge found the hull was split at a seam in the plate near the keel. With every wave, more sand accreted into the breach in the ship's skin and the ship sank deeper in the sand on shore. In Jorge's opinion, this damage was not repairable unless the ship could be put in dry dock. Further, the cargo was being impacted by the sea and sand that was entering the hold. The sea was beginning to cover the goods and equipment on board. Worse, the heaviest equipment that was the most valuable was stowed at the bottom of the hold to act as ballast, and these items, engines and generators and electrical equipment, had been inundated in salt water. The cargo of the coastal freighter could not be saved.

Jorge went back to shore. There he was confronted by an even angrier group of men. The leader of the mob yelled, "You cannot have the boats. You must have permission from the government to take them."

"I will tell the owner," Jorge assured the crowd. "We will do what is right … what is legal."

Jorge went to the building. The Hondurans had received a call. They would receive a call back in twenty minutes. They drank beer and waited. When the call came Jorge took the receiver and spoke in English. The Bounty Hunter recognized Jorge's voice. The Hondurans could hear the conversation.

"How did the ships fare in the storm?" asked the Bounty Hunter.

"The freighter has a broken keel and a split seam below the water line. The dive boat only needs a minor repair."

"Any other problems?" asked the Bounty Hunter.

"The locals want a government authorization before we can move the boats. They want to exercise salvage rights over the cargo and the ships if there is no government permit to remove the ships. They think that it is their property since Anthony, the owner, is gone."

"Can you stay in the dive boat for a couple of days?" asked the Bounty Hunter.

"Yes, but I don't think we can keep the locals away for long. The Hondurans will help but they want assurance they will be paid."

The Bounty Hunter then spoke in Spanish to the Hondurans and said: "If you men stay with the boat until it docks at San Pedro, Ambergris Caye, Belize, I will guarantee your pay plus a bonus of $1000 US. I will also send two men down to help with the locals and I will send another man, an abogado (a lawyer), who will have the paperwork necessary to let you leave with the dive boat." The Bounty Hunter paused. "Do you agree to stay with the ship?"

They had no choice except to hike 90 miles to Cancún. "We agree," said the Hondurans. The two men left the radio room and began reasoning with the locals and explaining they talked to the owner. "He will meet with the authorities and do what is legal." The mob cheered. They perceived they had won a victory.

Before signing off, the Bounty Hunter explained to Jorge in English that the men he was sending to rescue the dive ship were the same Mexican wrestlers who captured Anthony.

Jorge acknowledged that he understood. He felt secure that the wrestlers, men who had to answer to the Bounty Hunter, would be on board. They would not be Anthony's men. Anthony's men would put Jorge in fear because Jorge guessed Anthony knew Jorge had ratted him out.

***

The Bounty Hunter called the wrestlers over. They had just left Anthony on the tarmac in front of the US Customs office. The Customs officers were used to the drill. Fugitives were offloaded in this manner regularly for delivery to the court system. The officials checked the paperwork attached to the duffel bag in which Anthony was restrained. The wrestlers climbed back in the plane.

"When do you wrestle next?" asked the Bounty Hunter.

"We are on strike," said the wrestlers.

"I need you to return to Punta Rosa and salvage whatever is left of those ships. Take them to Belize. Somewhere in Mexican waters I want you to eliminate Jorge. He is not to make it to Belize. There are two Hondurans on board. Figure out a way to remove Jorge without having the Hondurans know what happened. Do it while the Hondurans sleep. If they find out you killed Jorge, they will have to die, too."

"We understand. What about dinner?"

"You can get a soda and some crackers. I need you back at the plane in 10 minutes. Did you tell Anthony what I told you to tell him about the procedure that he will go through in court regarding notifying his lawyer?"

"Yes."

"Did Anthony tell you who he wanted you to call?"

"He gave us this card. We got it from his top pocket. We didn't have to ask him. He told us."

"Give it to me. I will make the call."

The Bounty Hunter got out of the plane and went to a phone. He first reported to his boss at The Mutual Insurance Company. Then he dialed the number for Thomas Night, Esquire. It was after 10:00 p.m., but Tom answered the phone. He had a strong voice, but he had a persistent cough from an illness he had as a child that killed his parents and his twin brother. Never married, he was devoted to his work and a successful criminal lawyer. He was middle aged. He did not smoke or drink. He had abused those vices through his youth, but abandoned them some years back. He was middle aged, Caucasian, dark-haired, with brown eyes. He was about six foot in height, well built and, except for the nagging cough, healthy.

"Do you know Anthony Arnold?" asked the Bounty Hunter.

"Yes. He is my client. I am his lawyer," said Tom. "How can I help you?"

"He wants you to know he has been arrested and he is on his way to jail in Bushton, Florida."

"Why was he arrested?"

"He was in México. He skipped out on his bond and the insurance company hired me to find him. I arrested him and turned him in to Customs in Miami. Customs will have him back in your jail tomorrow."

"I did not know he was gone," said Tom.

"Listen, when you speak to Anthony tell him that his boats are in bad shape due to the storm. The big, old one is aground with a split hull. The other boat has a pillar support that is loose. Anthony is going to need some help or he will lose his investment. The natives will take everything if he does not act."

"What does he need?" asked Tom. He had pen and paper and took notes.

"He needs muscle, probably two good-sized men to bully the locals and get the boats out of México, if they can. He needs a lawyer to obtain a permit from the Admiral of the Navy in Cancún, México to move the boat out of México, to proceed south to Belize where they were headed."

"I guess you are offering to help?" asked Tom.

"Together we can salvage the ships. If you obtain the permit, I will provide the men. You can fly to Cancún on a commercial flight and my men will meet you and take you to the Admiral's office to obtain the permit and then you can take a pontoon plane with my men from Isla Mujeres to Punta Rosa where the ships are located. My men will get the boats out if they can and you will fly out of Punta Rosa in the pontoon plane back to the Isla and then fly commercial back to Miami."

"Why can't we drive to Punta Rosa?"

"The road has been destroyed by the hurricane."

"Why are you doing this?"

"It's business. I will charge a fair fee. Also my men think Anthony got a raw deal from the insurance company. You can tell him that."

"I will, if I see him. But why me? Why do you want me to get the permit? Don't you have a lawyer in Mexico?"

"Anthony owns the boats and you represent him. It would be a conflict for me to represent Anthony's interests. Also, I don't get along well with the Mexican Admiral. If this is what Anthony wants to do, have him wire $10,000 to my account number, which I will provide. You can reach me in Fort Lauderdale at 322-1612."

"I will tell him."

"I will wait for his call," said the Bounty Hunter.

"I will tell him," said Tom. "Thank you."

Chapter 5

Tom called the county jail in Bushton when he awoke at 6:00 am the morning after speaking to the Bounty Hunter. To his absolute surprise Anthony Arnold was re-incarcerated at that facility and Tom could visit him in the morning after breakfast at 8:00 a.m.

Tom grabbed a pen and the legal pad that contained the note of his conversation with the Bounty Hunter. One thing he noticed when he reviewed his notes was that he never identified the name of the Bounty Hunter, so in his notes he called him "B.H." Anthony would need Tom's help to contact the Bounty Hunter.

If a prisoner wanted to make a private phone call, the call had to be made collect from the public pay phone in the lobby of the jail. A guard was supposed to accompany the prisoner to the phone because the door to the street from the lobby was unlocked. It was the public entrance. The phone had been installed near the lobby door. It would be simple for a prisoner using the phone to escape. The prisoner would just walk out the lobby door. However, this had never happened. Security had become very lax regarding the use of the lobby phone by the inmates. Unless the prisoner was considered to be untrustworthy he was allowed to use the lobby phone on most every occasion, so long as the desk guard was on duty and he could watch the prisoner make the call from the guard's pos-ition at his desk in the lobby. Alternatively, the inmate's attorney could sit with the prisoner while his client made a private call.

Tom drove to the jail. It was actually a pleasant trip through farm land and forest and the drive would clear your head but it was a two hour drive.

Tom wanted to make sure he didn't get too involved in the rescue of Anthony's ships and property. He didn't want it to appear he was aiding his client except through the legitimate practice of the law. He could legally help his client by obtaining a permit from the Mexican government to allow the removal of Anthony's property from the Yucatán and he could go to Mexico and inspect the property as his client's representative. He could also make decisions regarding the disposition of the property so long as he had his client's permission.

At the jail, Tom and Anthony discussed the role Tom would play in any attempt that would be made to obtain the return of the property. Tom explained the proposal made by the Bounty Hunter. Tom was concerned about using the same person who engineered Anthony's capture to secure his property. Anthony felt the Bounty Hunter acted professionally. But Anthony wanted to speak to the Bounty Hunter personally and cut the deal regarding price for services.

Tom arranged for the call to the Bounty Hunter in Ft. Lauderdale, Florida, from the lobby phone at the jail, charging the call to Tom's office phone. The desk guard required Tom to sit in the lobby while Anthony spoke on the phone. Tom stayed back so Anthony had privacy and Tom did not hear the conversation.

***

"Can you hear me?" Anthony whispered.

"Yes. Is your attorney there?" asked the Bounty Hunter.

"Tom, get on the phone." Anthony handed the phone to Tom.

"Is this a secure line Mr. Night?" asked the Bounty Hunter.

"Yes, it is a public pay phone in the jail. It is not tapped." Tom gave the phone back to Anthony.

Anthony and the Bounty Hunter began to negotiate. They started with the cost.

"Ten thousand dollars is awfully expensive to retrieve these ships. Can you do better?" asked Anthony.

"To me it's a fair price. I have expenses too."

"Would you do it for $5,000?" asked Anthony.

"I will lose money at that price. I am operating a business, not a charity."

Anthony was in a weak bargaining position. The Bounty Hunter was his only option. He agreed that he would pay the $10,000. Anthony tried another tact. He wanted the Bounty Hunter to pay Tom's fee.

"You know I can't do that. Tom has to avoid any conflict when dealing with clients. He can't represent you and look to me for payment. If he would do that he would be acting unethically."

"Fine." Anthony became annoyed. He cut to the chase: "Look, what I really need to know is who gave you my location."

"I have a concern about giving you that information," said the Bounty Hunter.

"You can tell me. Or at least confirm my suspicion that it was Jorge Mendez," said Anthony.

"I have concerns with that."

"Do you have any responsibility to Jorge?" asked Anthony.

"No, I owe no duty to Jorge."

"He is certainly the obvious and the logical person who gave me up," said Anthony.

"I understand that you would want to eliminate the rats on the ship now if you had the opportunity? Is that what you are thinking?" asked the Bounty Hunter.

"He would be hard to find after he is off the ship and in Belize and then back in México," said Anthony. "He's trapped now on my ship."

"This would be the best time to eliminate him if he were the rat."

"Would you take care of that for me if he's the one?" asked Anthony.

"If he's the one, I will take care of him."

"What would that cost?"

"I would say another five."

"But you will already be there," said Anthony.

"There are other concerns. What about the Hondurans?" asked the Bounty Hunter.

"I hadn't thought of them. Would they be included?"

"Yes, but only if it cannot be avoided. I would try to avoid involving them. They are not necessarily part of the deal. They are not the reason you are in jail."

"I don't think the Hondurans were involved either. So then you're saying the other crewman was involved."

"You can say that with confidence."

"Then the total price is $15,000 – boats and people. I will pay that," said Anthony. "And I will pay my lawyer."

"I will send Tom Night the wire instructions for the money."

"Don't do that. I have another attorney for that. His name is H. Patel. He will call you for the wire instructions," said Anthony as he looked at Tom and smiled. "Tom is a good attorney but I can't trust him with this. He is too honest, a little arrogant, but what can you say, he's a lawyer. He thinks he knows what you are going to say before you say it."

"Yes, he's always finishing your sentences and putting words in your mouth," said the Bounty Hunter. "I know the type."

"You will be hearing from H. Patel before noon," said Anthony.

The Bounty Hunter then explained: "There is a plane from Tampa to Cancún this afternoon. Tell your lawyer to take that flight. He will be met by my wrestler friends and they will take him to the Mexican Admiral to get the permit to remove the ships. Tell him not to pay the Admiral more than $500 for the paperwork. Tell him to make sure he gets written authorization or your ships will be confiscated by the Mexican Navy."

"I will tell him."

"You have a 24 hour window to get the lawyer over to Cancún and then get south to Punta Rosa. I have the promise of the Honduran crew to stay with the dive boat, but only for a short time." The Bounty Hunter paused, then continued:

"Tom will need to rent a pontoon plane. The road south from Tulum is washed out. Tell H. Patel I will give him the information on the pontoon plane. The plane is on Isla Mujeres. The wrestlers will take the lawyer there."

"Ok," said Anthony. In this short conversation, Anthony put Tom's life in the hands of the Bounty Hunter.

"Does your lawyer speak Spanish?"

"I don't think so. Maybe he does just a little."

"Tell him to pretend he does but to be silent and let one of the wrestlers do the talking. The wrestlers will help him with the dealings with the Admiral and the pilot of the pontoon plane."

"Ok," said Anthony.

"I'll await the call from H. Patel," said the Bounty Hunter. "That will seal our deal."

***

Anthony spoke to Tom.

"Tom, I have a friend named H. Patel. He has all the title documents for the boats and some of my money. I need to send you to México. If you will go, you need to take the title documents that show ownership of the boats to the Admiral in the Yucatán so we can get permission to move the boats. Will you do that for me?"

"Yes. And of course I will be paid?"

"Of course. You will need to go now to make the flight from Tampa by noon today. You need to pack a pair of jeans. You will be riding in a sea plane from Cancún to the place where the boats are now located. I need you to act as my representative so I can get the boats back. You also need to place another call for me to Mr. H. Patel."

"No problem," said Tom. Actually, the logical way to schedule the trip would be to wait a couple of days because Tom was due to fly to Belize this same week. But if Anthony was willing to pay his fees and expenses, Tom was willing to make two trips to the Yucatan in the same week.

Besides, Anthony was insistent that Tom personally see what had become of his small ships. In particular, Anthony wanted to make sure the dive boat was safe and that it arrived in San Pedro, Belize. It was as though Anthony was desperate to protect that boat.

"I will be sunk if I loose that dive boat. It is my future."

"You can trust me to do what I agreed." said Tom.

Chapter 6

Since he had represented the Barnes Family in Central America over the last five years, Tom was used to traveling to the Yucatán Peninsula although he disliked flying commercial airplanes. He normally traveled in a private plane. The Barnes Family owned timber and lime rock and they had made Tom rich in legal fees.

Tom was always prepared for a work emergency. He had a Mercedes Benz 250 SL convertible/hardtop. In the trunk was a brief case with paper, pen, stapler, et cetera—like a desk set. He also had a small piece of luggage containing light sport wear (jeans and shorts and polo shirt with collar), and a suit and dress shirt. He figured he would already have shoes and a belt. He always took swim trunks and three pairs of socks and three pairs of underwear. He had one T-shirt to sleep in. Also in the suitcase was a travel kit and his passport was tucked below the personal equipment in the kit.

When Anthony asked him to go, Tom was ready. He had learned to travel light.

***

Tom arrived in Cancún on a TACA flight. No reservations were needed. A flyer could pay cash for his ticket. Airport security was non-existent. There had been hijacks to Cuba, but no one had been hurt, so no one checked the passengers. Mox. Nix.

The plane was a new Boeing 757. Boeing was shaking the kinks out of the plane and had leased a few planes to TACA. Boeing had sent along co-pilots to train TACA personnel and to take over if there was an emergency during flight. The co pilot announced these facts to the passengers over the intercom and asked if there were any objections. Hearing none, the pilot pulled the plane from the gate, taxied and made a successful take off. When the co-pilot announced that they were at cruising altitude of 31,000 feet everyone, including Tom, cheered and applauded.

***

The trip to Cancún was quick. About three hours, plus or minus a few minutes. Tom slept on the flight, which was unusual, because Tom hated to fly.

When he landed in México there were two men in sunglasses waiting for him. They were both big-chested, burly men who looked like they could be wrestlers. They held a sign with the name "Mr. Tom" written on it.

Tom introduced himself and the men quickly exited the airport after discovering he had not checked in any luggage and that he had everything in both hands.

Tom was directed to an old Land Rover. Tom walked around it and admired it. It was an antique. The men though, were obviously in a hurry. "Please get in." They pulled out into traffic, but their trip was immediately interrupted by a policeman driving a Toyota with a flashing light and siren blaring.

They stopped.

The policeman got out of the Toyota and he hiked up his trousers and walked to the Rover. The wrestler who was driving (Santos) showed the patrolman his license. It had an official red stripe printed on it. The officer apologized for stopping the car and went back to his car and drove away.

Tom asked to see the license, but couldn't read it. Spanish words were printed in the red strip over the top of the information contained on a normal license. Tom studied the words.

"It says I am an undercover detective," said Santos.

"And are you?" asked Tom as he returned the license to Santos.

"Yes, I am."

Tom was impressed.

The men drove to a large government building with the official seal of the Mexican Admiralty. The three men went to an office on the first floor.

Santos showed his license and the men were led into a small room with a desk and two chairs. Santos began to talk to the man behind the desk. The desk plate identified the man as an Admiral of the Mexican Navy. Tom was quiet as he had been advised. The men were negotiating the fee for the permit in Spanish. The man behind the desk did not have a hint of a tan. He couldn't be a seaman, thought Tom.

Santos turned to Tom and said: "He wants 700 US dollars."

"No," said Tom in English. "$500 US is all I will pay."

Santos explained.

The official held up four fingers and a thumb.

Tom looked to the ceiling then back at the man. "Si," Tom said as he mimicked the Admiral and held up four fingers and his thumb - $500 was the number accepted by both parties. Tom handed the man five one-hundred dollar bills.

***

The Land Rover was pointed to the sea port and docks and they were speeding. In order to get to the ferry to Isla Mujeres they had to run the gauntlet of the traffic police in their Toyotas. They passed the line of modern hotels on the main boulevard that México hoped would one day rival Miami Beach or Ft. Lauderdale or Daytona Beach in Florida. The hotels were built to accommodate sun seekers and indulgence. Locals avoided Cancún, and instead headed to the Isla to avoid the crowds. The Isla was a large island the size of Key West that had been occupied by the Spanish for hundreds of years and is shown on early European maps. The island had also been the home of Pre-Columbian native peoples, but they were long extinct.

They took the ferry to the Isla. The ferry carried the inhabitants of the island back and forth to the mainland. Many islanders worked in Cancún. The island also was home to a sizable group of American ex-pats who were involved in or supported by the drug trade. The smugglers posted informants on the ferry to eye the passengers, suspicious for police or competitors. Once the ferry landed, the informers for the American drug dealers followed the newcomers and reported their activities.

Tom and the Mexicans immediately piqued the attention of a little weasel of a man who followed them about once they got to the island. The rat watched them eat dinner and saw them tucked in at a small hotel. In the morning he was still there sitting in a chair in the lobby. Tom was going to say something but the wrestlers advised against it. It would only make them seem more suspicious. They had breakfast. Tom was going to avoid the melon but it was recommended by the wrestlers who chuckled as Tom scarfed down the fruit. (Tom was ill for two days.)

Chapter 7

The Caribbean coast from Cancún, to the Northern border of Belize was untamed. It was a nature preserve. There were no permanent local authorities in México or Belize along this stretch of coast. The government appeared at random and was mobile in the form of a military unit – either soldiers in full field gear on trucks or the Mexican Navy manning a PT-boat. There was no military base along the coast. The Army and Navy had no real interest in the coast south of Cancun. There was no government infrastructure – no City Hall and no city. There were people in the bush, some squatting and some poorly paid as overseers for copra plantation owners who lived in Merida, the capital of Quintana Ro state in the Northwest of the Yucatán.

It was expensive to patrol these areas and for a government that existed on graft, these rural areas offered poor pickings – no money, no drugs, and rough looking women. With no independent judicial authority the locals were left to dispense justice and sort out affairs and disputes on their own. Tom Night had learned that as an outsider, you avoided dealing with the locals in the bush because they were unpredictable. They were not driven by ethical considerations – by good or bad – but they tended to violent extremes based on need or mood. As a foreigner, you could only possibly read the mood. But since the locals were always in need, they were always unpredictable and therefore, dangerous.

The only way to safely navigate the coast south of Tulum after the recent hurricane was by boat or a pontoon plane. And so, Tom and the Mexican wrestlers, Santos and Diablo, were passengers in a Cessna plane outfitted with pontoons and they flew to Punta Rosa from Isla Mujeres. As with life in Middle and Central America, even the landing was eventful. The ocean was so clear that lime rock boulders on the sea bed beneath the waves appeared to be just under the water, and there was a fear the boulders would pierce or snag a pontoon. However, the boulders were at least ten feet below the surface and were no danger to the plane. Still the boulders gave the pilot quite a scare.

Once they deplaned, Tom, the pilot and the wrestlers were met by locals who were stripping Anthony's coastal freighter, the M.V. Cap de l'Ile, of all gear and stores.

After Anthony was captured the two Hondurans and one Mexican had remained on board the dive boat and they were trying to protect that vessel. They were armed with rifles and pistols. They also wanted to save the stores on the M.V. Cap de l'Ile. But the crew feared the locals on shore and during the night they bargained with them trading equipment to barter for time and their lives.

The pilot of the pontoon plane was known by the locals as were the two Mexican wrestlers who were on the pontoon plane with Tom. When the locals saw the pilot and his passengers they became upset. They could see they would lose their prize. The pilot calmed the locals. He spoke a Mayan dialect interspersed with Spanish. He called them honest men even as they stole another load of gear, including a valuable auxiliary motor. The pilot showed the locals the permit signed by the Mexican Admiral allowing the boats to leave. The locals accepted the signed official paper as fact. The dive boat would not be salvaged.

Greed had delayed the dismantling of the boats after the storm. The locals had been fighting over their share of the spoils through the night. Anthony's crew said they had listened to the intermittent bickering and fighting. In the morning one of the locals was observed badly injured, lying in a dinghy on the beach.

Tom knew he needed to save what he could and get Anthony's crew out of harm's way quickly. Other locals were now converging on the scene from the interior. They were concentrating on the ship that was aground. Tom consulted the crew and the Mexicans. They agreed the old ship could not be refloated. So, Tom ordered that ship to be abandoned. He would let the locals steal and kill each other over its gear while Tom, the wrestlers, the pilot and the crew escaped. Tom sent the Mexicans with the crew to move the dive boat with the tide to head out to sea to Ambergris Caye in Belize. Tom would feel more at ease once the dive boat was in Belize because the thieves in Belize spoke English. Tom was very familiar with Belize and had done business there for almost five years. The plan was for Tom to leave in the pontoon plane. Anthony Arnold wouldn't be happy because of the loss of the old ship and equipment, but what could his client do about it? He was in jail in Florida.

Before he flew back to Cancún, Tom spoke briefly to the crew. He asked Jorge and the Hondurans what happened when Anthony was arrested. They said they did not know who captured Anthony. They did not know the wrestlers took Anthony, and Tom did not educate them. They said that after the storm they were buzzed by a black Lear Jet that tipped its wings as it passed over. The crew felt that was a sign that Anthony was in the plane.

After Tom spoke to the Hondurans and Jorge he informed the wrestlers that the crewmen were unaware that they were the ones who had captured Anthony. He told the wrestlers to leave it like that. Then, Tom and the pilot were taken to the pontoon plane in the Zodiac. The plane was anchored about 200 yards off shore.

Tom and the pilot boarded the plane quickly and the pilot prepared for the take-off. The maneuver was a little tricky with the engine running and the propeller spinning. But the wind helped turn the plane and the pilot anticipated when the plane would swing into the wind and when the plane was in position he throttled up, the plane began to move and pick up speed, and the pontoons bumped over the water and they lifted off safely.

The pilot circled the bay once they were in the air. They could see the dive boat below. Jorge was at the helm on the flying bridge. The crew, now five men strong, was motoring out of the bay. They were not going to waste any time. They were scrambling about the deck lashing down all the loose objects and the boat was being pushed forward quickly by twin Volvo engines.

There was little wake created by the dive boat. The hull allowed the boat to operate in very shallow water.

The Bounty Hunter had not lied to Tom. Tom would be back to his office later that day. After the pontoon plane lifted off and dipped its wings to the men on the dive boat, the plane headed to Isla Mujeres; then a quick ferry ride; then a taxi ride across Cancún and then the flight to Tampa. Tom picked up his car in Tampa and he was on the bridge to St. Petersburg and home.

The police in Cancún did not disappoint. On the road from the pier where the ferry docked to the airport, the taxi driver suffered two traffic tickets. Tom told the driver he should apply for the license the wrestler, Santos, had. It would have saved him much money in fines. Tom wondered how you could do business successfully in a country so rife with corruption, particularly since graft had to be paid at such a low level in the operation of the government. Tom was familiar with pay offs, and quid pro quo in the USA but at a higher level. Tom had represented County Commissioners who were paid bribes to allow road building projects or to turn a blind eye to a company that wanted to avoid government regulation. But in México, you couldn't drive across town without paying two or three bribes.

It was very disruptive to business.

Chapter 8

The crewmen wanted to leave Punta Rosa as soon as possible after Tom left in the pontoon plane. Luckily, Anthony had insisted that the crew load up with supplies and fuel before the storm hit. Otherwise, they would have had to fight the locals for supplies after the storm.

The dive boat was fully supplied for the trip south to Belize and it took little work to cast off except to hoist the anchor and start the engines. This craft was almost new and except for the minor repair needed to re-weld the pillar, there was nothing required to make the craft operational and sea worthy.

***

The shore line in this area of the Yucatán was primarily mangrove swamp and lime rock bluffs. There were outcroppings of lime rock in the sea so they had to steer out from the coast about half a mile to avoid a chance of a collision. The helmsman steered from the flying bridge which was 35 feet above sea level and allowed him to observe the sea lane for reefs.

Because Jorge was the only person who had any familiarity with the coast, the crew decided to motor only during daylight hours. They felt two men had to be on duty at all times. The men communicated in Spanish as they all spoke that language. It was important that they remembered to communicate in the single language so that if there was an emergency they would understand each other's commands and words.

***

The first day of the trip was of no consequence except they were observed by a Mexican Navy PT Boat. It was outfitted with a .50 caliber machine gun and the sailors wore .44 caliber handguns on their belts. That was the only armament the crew could see as the PT boat cruised by slowly to observe the dive boat.

Jorge had the permit to travel for the boat in a plastic sleeve in a drawer on the upper deck prepared to prove ownership if they were boarded by the sailors. But the PT boat did not stop.

The authorities never ask for ownership documents if you have them.

The lieutenant in charge of the PT boat was aware of the possible presence of the dive boat by his superiors and was told to shadow it at a distance and to verify where it left Mexican waters. The lieutenant ordered the PT boat to come up close on the dive boat so he could recognize it and he counted five men on board. Then he waved his men to proceed east. They would come around so they would be about five miles behind the boat and follow it south.

***

The dive boat crew found a good harbor for the night and tied the bow off on the branches of a mangrove. They tried to reverse engines from the shore and fasten an anchor off the stern, but the water was so deep they did not have enough anchor rope to fix the anchor to the sea floor. So they let the boat come around in the current and the port side of the boat nestled into the limbs of the mangroves. After tying off they looked over the side into a clear sea. They observed many poisonous triggerfish below feeding on the rock and coral.

The wrestlers offered to stand watch overnight. Jorge agreed to dive for fish and cook it fresh for them for breakfast with grits with cheese and a tropical fruit bowl. His cooperative attitude put the crew at ease. Jorge was also relieved they had seen the Mexican Navy. He knew the navy would be out there, not far away. Jorge felt he was protected.

***

There was a bench seat at the helm of the flying bridge. The wrestlers moved up to the seat once the rest of the crew fell asleep. The night was clear and there were millions of stars. The seat on the bridge was out of listening range of the crew who were below decks in the passenger quarters. The only disadvantage was that they were seated 35 feet above a rolling sea and were treated to a ride like the weight on the stick of a metronome.

The wrestlers had very little room on the bench. They spoke in French and had waited until the Hondurans and Jorge had fallen asleep. They did not want anyone to know their plan.

Jorge would need to be dispatched quietly unless they also planned to kill the Hondurans. They would only kill the Hondurans if the Hondurans witnessed Jorge's death.

As they plotted, it became evident that they were taking a great risk. It would be difficult to kill Jorge without the Hondurans knowing. Whereas killing all three would be easy. They could round them up in the morning on the deck and shoot them and push their bodies into the sea.

But the Navy Lieutenant commanding the PT boat had seen that there were five crew members. So, their story would best be that something fatal occurred to Jorge in the morning while the Hondurans were still asleep. Jorge had gotten in the water, and suffered an accident of some kind and he was now gone, swept away in the strong current.

But how would that have happened without the wrestlers knowing? The wrestlers were supposed to be on watch. Suppose they said they were awake before he went in the water. So the wrestlers would be witnesses to the accident. Or they could say they helped Jorge get in the water and they then went to their cots and fell asleep and Jorge was injured. Or, when the wrestlers were awakened by the Hondurans, they could say they went to sleep after Jorge entered the water. They would say they did not know what happened.

Or they could say they fell asleep in the bench seat of the flying bridge and they didn't know what happened to Jorge. Their story would be that when they awoke, Jorge was gone. There was a small amount of blood on the step of the moon pool. He may have slipped and hit his head and then slid into the water and drowned. The current could have taken his body away. He was eaten by barracuda or a bull shark.

But that was enough thinking. Their heads were hurting.

They went to sleep. But neither was sure what would work and what would allow them to escape justice. They hoped for the best. Actually, they thought, the best would be if they had not taken this extra work. It's one thing to capture someone on the run from the law. It's another thing to commit murder. The wrestlers had killed in the past but they really weren't killers.

Chapter 9

The wrestlers were swinging back and forth sitting in the bench seat on the flying bridge in the calm morning sea being rocked by rolling waves. They were awakened by the Hondurans who appeared to be very concerned. The Hondurans said they had looked everywhere but they said they could not find Jorge on board the dive boat.

"Did you look in his berth?"

"Everywhere ... we looked everywhere," said the Hondurans in unison.

The wrestlers climbed down from the flying bridge. They moved down to the sleeping deck that contained five berths and a hallway down the center of the deck. The men looked in each berth.

Below there was a large room with a compressor and dive tanks and other sporting and fishing equipment. There was also a moon pool that allowed a diver to enter the sea from inside the boat. The moon pool had steel walls and a diver had to climb over a four foot high wall, and then down stairs inside the moon pool and open a hatch in the floor of the hull to enter the water. The water was the sea.

In front of the moon pool was the steel pillar that had been re-welded in Punta Rosa before they headed for Belize. There were boxes and crates on the floor containing rope, anchors and other necessities.

But there was no sign of Jorge. The men then looked outside all around the hull of the boat to see if he could have hung up on the bottom of the boat and they looked for his body to be floating on the surface. No luck. No Jorge.

They had to move the boat out from the mangroves because of the swells rolling in from offshore pushed by the wind. One man was stationed at the stern of the boat to see if Jorge's body had hung up in either of the two tunnel drive systems. Jorge was not ejected when the twin Volvo engines were started and put in gear.

Because of the wave action they had to move offshore about 200 yards and they motored parallel to the shore heading north with the current searching for the body. The Hondurans operated the boat and kept a lookout for Jorge. The wrestlers searched the boat one more time.

The wrestlers found blood on the inside step of the moon pool. Then they found a bloody rag and then a ballpeen hammer that looked like it had punctured flesh and bone and brain.

"Is this the murder weapon?" asked wrestler Diablo.

"Probably it is," said Santos as he inspected the steel hammer.

"Who did this?" said Diablo.

"There is only us and the Hondurans. It has to be the Hondurans."

"Who do you think the Hondurans are working for?"

"I have no idea."

"Could it be Anthony?"

"It could be."

"Could it be our boss?"

"Why would he hire them?"

"Maybe the boss doesn't trust us anymore."

"We need to clean up this mess."

The wrestlers wiped the step into the moon pool and tossed the ball peen hammer and rag into the sea through the hatch in the moon pool.

"We are both going to have to sleep with one eye open."

"Agreed," said Diablo.

The wrestlers went to the upper deck. One of the Hondurans was operating the boat from the wheel on that deck. They continued to motor north for about four miles. They saw nothing and so they turned around and headed the dive ship south.

The Hondurans asked the wrestlers if they found anything when they conducted the second search.

"Nothing," said Diablo.

"We need to stick together on this," said Santos pointing his finger at the Hondurans.

They all agreed. If they were to hang, they would hang together.

The wrestlers knew then that, for whatever reason, the Hondurans' had murdered Jorge.

Chapter 10

The four men who were now the crew of the dive boat landed at San Pedro. This was a small town on Ambergris Caye, a barrier island in the Caribbean Sea. This Caye is the northern-most island off the coast of Belize and its small town catered to tourists who came to fish, dive and visit natural wonders such as the Blue Hole and the largest coastal, coral reef in the Americas.

The crew docked the dive boat on the northernmost pier in the town. The pier contained no other boats and was isolated by a wild growth of mangrove trees. To land and tie up they needed a machete to cut back the mangrove trees. They also had to cut their way off the pier by cutting back the limbs of the mangroves that had grown over the walkway.

The harbor master made his way to the boat after the crew had finished the work trimming back the mangroves. After collecting the fee for dockage, one of the wrestlers told the harbor master they needed to report that a crew member was lost on the trip from Punta Rosa. The crew was told not to leave until they made an official report to the police. The harbor master told the men they could visit the establishments along the main street – a tourist trap of restaurants, hotels, dive shops and souvenir shops selling chunks of coral and shells. The harbor master said he would contact the police.

***

The first police officer who visited spoke limited Spanish and somehow misinterpreted the death of Jorge as being the report of a homicide (the unlawful killing of one human being by another), whereas, the crew was simply reporting Jorge to be a missing person.

The second policeman to speak to the crew was the head of the office in San Pedro. He spoke English, Spanish, Mayan and Creole. He took the men to a room in an abandoned building across the street from the docks. The building had once housed a restaurant. He righted a table and three chairs and the officer spoke to each of the crewmen privately and separately. The non-Spanish speaking officer stood guard over the boat.

Each man had a similar story on the issue of what might have happened to Jorge. They all said Jorge was going to dive for fish in the morning for breakfast. The four woke up and they looked for him and he was gone. They were not sure if he went free diving or took diving equipment from the boat. They saw no evidence he hurt himself. There was no blood or anything like that. They searched the ship thoroughly and they checked the water and the shore. They followed the current north for four miles and then backtracked south looking in the mangroves but they could not find his body. So they headed to San Pedro to report that he was missing.

The statements of each of the men was signed and witnessed by the two officers. The statements were flown back to the mainland by airplane from the airport on San Pedro to the International Airport where the report and statements were reviewed by a police lieutenant. The lieutenant was employed by the Belize Defense Force (BDF). He was well educated in criminal law and police theory. The lieutenant passed a message back to the island on the next tourist plane that the crewmen were not to leave the island until he spoke with them, and the crew was told they should expect to be in San Pedro for a week while the miss-ing person investigation was completed.

The lieutenant had been expecting the dive boat. Pablo Mendez, the Police Chief of Cancún, had called the lieutenant personally. Jorge was the Chief's brother, he explained. Jorge was married and had children. They were worried because the hurr-icane hit Punta Rosa and there had been no communication from Jorge since he had called ship to shore and reported he would be riding out the storm at he Ship's Store in Punta Rosa. Jorge's family had tried to take the coastal road south of town to Punta Rosa after the storm but the road had been overtopped and breached and was impassable. There had been no other communication but the family knew the dive boat would head to Belize after the storm had passed.

This report from the crew of the dive boat to the harbor master at San Pedro was the first communication received by the Belize Defense Force regarding the boat and it brought bad news. The lieutenant called the Police Chief of Cancún and told him the crew reported Jorge was missing and lost at sea.

"I will go tomorrow with the first tourist plane and speak to the crew. The first plane leaves about 8:00 a.m.," said the lieutenant of the Belize Defense Force.

"When can you get back to me, do you think?" asked the Chief of Police.

"Tomorrow by 4:00 p.m. if I have no problems."

"Can you give me the names of the crewmen? I can run a background check on them. Two of the men are Mexican and I should be able to have information on them for you before you interview them. I will also try a contact in Honduras to see what I can find out about the other men. I will teletype what I find to you tomorrow before 7:00 a.m.," said the Chief of Police.

"Thank you," said the lieutenant.

"I will tell my office to find me immediately when you call tomorrow afternoon so we can discuss your interviews with the crew," said the Police Chief of Cancún.

***

On the boat the crewmen went over their story. They reviewed what they had told the detective from the local police force. They knew that they would be interviewed by others over and over again and their statements would be reviewed for any inconsistency. The next person who interviews them would be more devious and perhaps violent. All four men agreed they had to remain stoic and stick to their guns. Their story was simple. They don't know what happened to Jorge. They looked for him. They could not find him. They came to the first port and reported him missing. End of story.

They agreed that they had to be truthful about their life. They must give their true names, their addresses, their family information and their employment. All of them had had a criminal past but the criminal convictions were minor and it did not prevent their respective home government from issuing a passport to each of them. But they had to be honest about their public past, marriages, divorces, the minor offenses, etc. The police will assume that if you lie about your family or your criminal record you are lying about what happened to Jorge.

***

When the detective from the local police force introduced the crew to the lieutenant the following morning there was a third man with them who was wearing loose fitting jeans and a T-shirt and flip flops. The man also had a dog.

"I'm going to have the local detective and the drug dog inspect the boat above the water line. The other man here is also a member of the Belize Defense Force. He is going to dive below the boat and take a look at the hull. Any problem?" asked the Lieutenant of the Belize Defense Force.

The crewmen did not answer.

"Do we have permission to search the boat and your possessions?" asked the lieutenant. "We intend to search for Jorge using the dog."

The crew each quietly said yes, the police had their permission.

"Is that correct?" asked the official loudly.

All of the crewmen agreed, but this time with more enthusiasm.

The detective had a printed form that was a written waiver of their rights to search the boat and their individual possessions by the police. Each of the crewmen signed the wavier of rights. The diver asked the men if they had been underwater since the incident. All of the men said they did not dive and had not looked under the boat. The diver began a series of dives. The lieutenant and the crew went to the abandoned restaurant for additional questioning. The local detective began to search the inside of the boat. The officer slowly led the dog through the boat, talking to the animal and encouraging him to find Jorge but the dog was only trained to follow a scent of drugs and it could find nothing.

Chapter 11

The Lieutenant of the BDF was calling from his office at the International Airport to the police headquarters in CanCun.

"Chief Mendez?" asked the lieutenant.

"Yes?" answered the chief of police.

They spoke in English. It was 8:00 p.m. and now dark.

"First, I want to thank you for the intelligence information you provided this morning. I had also reached out to the US Embassy here and received a report before I left for Ambergris Caye. The reports you telexed were very helpful," said the lieutenant.

"You are welcome," said the chief.

"Both reports show the boat is involved in the drug trade. The owner, Anthony Arnold, was on the run. He left the USA, skipping out on a court appearance. The Honduran crewmen, however, are not involved with the drug trade. The Hondurans are military. They work for the Honduran government and were assigned to the Special Forces tracking criminal activity from the US to the Honduras and Central America. They investigate trafficking – drugs, human beings, stolen property – anything that came their way. They say they were working their way back to Honduras and came upon the opportunity to travel as part of the crew on these two ships. They thought Anthony Arnold would be a source of information about the drug trade.

"The Hondurans were trapped by the hurricane and after the storm they feared they would be killed by the locals in Punta Rosa.

By the way," the Lieutenant added, "you need to get the military to the port as soon as you can. The locals are out of control and there is no communication out of there."

"We sent a PT Boat there yesterday after it made contact with the dive boat. They have a small war on their hands," said Chief Mendez.

"Anyway," the lieutenant continued, "one of Arnold's boats, a coastal freighter, was grounded, and the dive boat had some minor problems, but the locals were not going to let the crew leave with the boats or their cargo. The locals made a salvage claim. The owner of the boats or a friend hired the Mexicans and a lawyer to fly in on a pontoon plane with a permit allowing the dive boat to leave Mexico. The ship, the MV Cap de l'Ile, could not be floated so they abandoned the large ship."

"Did the dive boat have a ship to shore radio?"

"No, they had no communication except a walkie-talkie that the crews of the boats used to communicate as they crossed the Gulf of México."

"How did they communicate with the owner or his representative?"

"Jorge had arranged for the call—by ship to shore. Both the Hondurans and Jorge heard the call. The call was in Spanish and English. The Hondurans speak both languages fluently so they know what was said. The Hondurans said Jorge knew who he was talking to but it was not the owner. The Hondurans knew the owner's voice. The owner had been on board when they crossed the Gulf of México."

"Where was the owner of the boats, Mr. Arnold, after the storm?"

"The Hondurans think he was kidnapped by a bounty hunter. They think Jorge knew the bounty hunter and may have worked for him and helped him find Anthony Arnold. They never saw or heard from the owner after the storm hit.

The lieutenant paused and flipped through his notes and then began again. "The Mexicans, who admitted they were wrestlers, are twin brothers. They hire themselves out as muscle. They were sent to Punta Rosa in a pontoon plane to help protect the crew and the boats from the locals. There was also a lawyer who brought a permit from the Admiral of the Yucatán allowing the boats and crew to leave. It appears the Mexicans and the lawyer were acting legitimately on behalf of the owner."

"Who is the lawyer?"

"His name is Thomas Night, from St. Petersburg, Florida. We know him here in Belize. He is considered very ethical. Even the Solicitor General, who has been fighting with him since the new government took office, says that he is very honest."

"Where is the lawyer?"

"He flew back to Isla Mujeres on the pontoon plane and then back to the states. The pontoon plane is a legitimate enterprise. It flies in to Ambergris Caye bringing tourists to the Blue Hole. I have the phone numbers for the lawyer and the pilot. They are in my report."

"What else do you know from the crew?" asked the chief of police.

"The lawyer and the pilot talked the locals into letting the dive boat leave. Jorge and the wrestlers and the Hondurans motored south. They saw a Mexican naval vessel along the way. They were not stopped by the Navy but they were close enough that they thought the sailors would know how many people were on the dive boat. That night, the wrestlers took watch. Jorge had agreed to cook everyone breakfast in the morning but when they were all awake they couldn't find him. They said they looked for Jorge in the sea all day and then came here to San Pedro to report him missing. They all claim they do not know what happened to Jorge. It is a mystery."

"What about the boat? Did you inspect it?"

"There was nothing suspicious inside the boat. We have a canine trained to sniff out drugs. We had the dog search the vessel for drugs but the dog discovered nothing. We told the crew the dog could sniff out a corpse to try to rattle the crew but to no avail. There was a lot of electronics and boxes of equipment on board but it all looked to be in order. None of the containers were big enough to hold a body.

"The crew also allowed us to search their belongings. There was nothing illegal and no weapons in their belongings.

"I had a diver inspect the bottom of the boat. There is an interesting feature on the boat. It has a moon pool that allows a diver to enter the sea from inside the boat through a hatch. Once the diver goes through the hatch it closes mechanically. My diver noticed there was a yellow patch of cloth caught in the hinge of the hatch. You could only see the cloth from under the boat. According to the crewmen they did not look under the boat after Jorge went missing. The crew said they were not good swimmers," said the lieutenant.

"So Jorge could have been wearing a yellow T-shirt when he went through the hatch and as the hatch closed, it caught his shirt and he drowned." asked the chief. "So that is the theory?"

"That is a logical conclusion that could be made from the evidence. My diver said the moon pool was not manufactured by any company he is aware of. It's a one off."

"You mean the moon pool is handmade?"

"Yes. It was manufactured by Anthony Arnold."

"So what is your opinion?"

"I think Jorge went for a dive to catch fish for breakfast. He left through the moon pool and his T-shirt got caught on the latch of the moon pool. He was trapped underwater after the hatch closed and he drowned. He was probably floating underwater being dragged by the dive boat until the fabric of the shirt tore away or his body was ripped away by a shark or other animal."

"It seems logical. Did you tell the crew they are free to go?" asked the chief.

"They won't leave until they get paid, or so they say. I told them not to leave for at least 48 hours."

"Thank you. Please save any photographs you took and the piece of yellow fabric. We will conduct an investigation. My brother was a citizen of Mexico and I have a duty to investigate his disappearance."

"I will send my report and the copies of the photographs of the boat, the moon pool and the piece of fabric. I am sorry for your loss."

"Thank you."

The chief thought silently to himself. Jorge wasn't much, but he was his brother.

Chapter 12

The Chief of Police received a call from his sister-in-law almost as soon as he had finished talking to the lieutenant from the Belize Defense Force.

"If you are upset this would not be a good time to talk," said the chief.

"I will be quiet and listen." Jorge's wife whimpered as she spoke. "For the sake of my mind I must know what happened to Jorge."

"We still do not know. He is officially lost at sea."

"Will he be found, do you think, brother?"

"I hope so. He was lost in the early morning two days ago. I ordered the Navy to conduct a search along the shore. So far, there has been no report that he has been sighted."

"What is the best that we could expect?"

"That he swam to shore and could not alert the crew and they left him in the wilderness in the nature preserve south of Punta Rosa. The best would be that he stayed by the shore and our Navy boat has a chance to sight him."

"Jorge was a strong swimmer. But what do the police in Belize believe?"

"They believe it was an accident. The boat had an opening in the hull called a moon pool that allowed a diver to enter the ocean from the inside of the boat. The crew said Jorge was going diving in the morning but they were asleep. It seems there was a defect in the hatch of the moon pool. The police think Jorge's shirt was caught while he was underwater and he could not surface and he drowned."

"Do they have his body?"

"No, the only thing they found was a piece of fabric – probably material from a yellow T-shirt."

"Jorge did have a yellow T-shirt. Maybe he drowned. What do we do?"

"The moon pool looks like it is homemade. The person who manufactured it and installed it would be responsible for any damage, injury or death caused by the moon pool."

"Who made the moon pool?"

"The owner of the boat, probably. The owner built the boat and he probably built the moon pool. The owner of the boat would be liable for the death."

"Where is the owner?"

"In jail, in Florida."

"How will you contact him if he is in jail?"

"He has a lawyer. I will contact his lawyer."

"What about the boat. Where is it?"

"It is in San Pedro, Ambergris Caye. The police are watching it. They have ordered the crew to stay with the boat in San Pedro for at least one more day. After that we will have to impress a lien on the vessel so no one can remove it."

"Will you do that?"

"Yes, I will handle everything."

***

The crew was laughing as they debriefed each other after the interrogation by the lieutenant of the Belize Defense Force. They had purchased a half gallon of Botero Tequila to celebrate. The

Botero brand was noted for the fact that an earth worm was contained in each bottle. The tequila had loosened their tongues and they joked about the stupidity of the police. They believed their story, a mixture of truth and lie had put them in good stead. They felt they would go free. The possibility that Jorge was the victim of a manufacturing defect in the moon pool raised a serious doubt that they were guilty of killing him. It offered a good defense to the charge. Further, there was no known motive for them to kill Jorge. They had been thrown together by fate, by a hurricane.

The Mexican wrestlers were a bit edgy now knowing that the Hondurans were military undercover agents. They still did not know why the Hondurans had killed Jorge. The Mexican wrestlers knew that they had to stick with the story (that they knew nothing as to Jorge's fate other than he was lost at sea). Since they were conspirators to the crime, the Hondurans being the perpetrators of the actual murder and the wrestlers being conspirators in the cover up of the crime after the fact, they had a criminal bond that compelled them to protect each other.

Thus the men would wait the time that the lieutenant required before they would leave the dive boat and go their separate ways. They decided that they would each tell their employer that they actually committed the crime of murder and they would solicit the payment that had been offered by their employer to them if they committed the crime.

The reason the Mexican wrestlers' employer desired Jorge to be killed was a business arrangement, a killing for hire. But also, the Bounty Hunter did not have to pay Jorge's finder's fee if he was dead. The Mexicans were the tool used by the Bounty Hunter to accomplish the deed.

The Hondurans were working for a sovereign state that was eliminating Jorge because he had compromised one of their undercover operatives to the Prime Minister of Panama and the agent was killed. The motive for the Hondurans' action was political revenge. Since the death was ordered and condoned by the State (Honduras), the killers did not commit a homicide, at least so far as the country of Honduras was concerned.

Neither motivation for Jorge's death was a cause for the two teams of hit men to compromise the other. They were comrades, not enemies. They had an incentive to lie, cheat and steal for each other, and that evil bond would protect them from the authorities and each other.

During the next 48 hours they could sleep with both eyes closed.

Part II
Business in Belize

Chapters 13 through 18

Belize in the late 1960's ... Tom Night returns to the Yucatan in Rick Ibn's 1963 Aero Commander Model 500S ... Doing business in Central America ... A pig hunt ... George is injured.

Chapter 13

Another day. Another dollar.

Tom Night had been sitting up straight in the bench seat at the rear of the 1963 Aero Commander Model 500S. The plane is also known as an AC 500S. The plane had been skipping over the thermal up drafts 10,000 feet above the Caribbean Sea for hours.

The cabin of the plane hung below the wing. Tom always sat in the bench seat in the rear of the cabin where he had a view of the pilot, Rick Ibn. He could also see both engines, and on takeoff he could watch the plane's wheels retract backward and tuck into the bottom of the engine housing on the wing. The wing was positioned above Tom's head.

Tom was middle-aged and unmarried. He was early to bed and early to rise. He was hard working and a successful lawyer and business man and enjoyed a simple life and life's routine.

This was the second time within the week that Tom was in the Yucatán and he admitted he was tired. First he had traveled to Mexico for Anthony Arnold to attempt to save his ships in Punta Rosa and now he was making his regular bi-monthly visit to Belize for the Barnes Family interests. For the last year, since the election in Belize when the PUP political party had been voted out and the Barnes Family had lost their influence in the government, Tom had hired Rick and his plane service to ferry him to Belize to protect his client's interests.

The Aero Commander was said to be a sturdy plane but the reputation of the brand suffered due to cases of wing span fatigue and failure. Rick's plane was fully equipped and instrumented for a pilot and a co-pilot. Tom was invited to sit in the co-pilot seat but was not a pilot. He joked that he was really not well trained at anything in particular; except, he was licensed to practice law in the state of Florida. Tom had a mind for routine and he watched as the pilot went through his pre-flight at Albert Whitted Airport in St. Petersburg, Florida. Tom was familiar with what was required for a successful takeoff and landing and he had some idea how to fly the plane, however, Tom had doubts that he would take the yoke in an emergency.

Tom suffered from a fear of flying. He couldn't ride in the co-pilot's seat because of that fear.

In addition to the bench seat at the rear of the cabin and the pilot and co-pilot's seats there were two other passenger seats in the plane. One seat was behind the pilot's seat and another seat was behind the co-pilot's seat. These two seats faced the bench seat at the rear. Sitting in those seats was very disconcerting to Tom because you were flying looking back to where you had been, not where you were going. It was particularly disorienting to Tom to use one of these seats on takeoff. Tom couldn't fly backwards. Tom followed the routine of the flight from the bench seat where he would try to deal with his anxiety.

But Tom's aerophobia was a hard thing to control. The cabin of the Aero Commander hangs below the wing. Almost always before he flew in the AC-500S he had a peculiar dream. As he slept he had a vision that an osprey, a bird also known as a fish hawk, had captured a fish and was flying back to the nest with the fish dangling below in the bird's talons. The fish's head was pointed in the direction of flight. The osprey used the fish as a rudder to glide back to the nest. In the dream, Tom can see that the eyes of the fish are wide open and the fish opens and closes its mouth forming O's with its lips trying desperately to oxygenate to stay alive. The fish is totally out of its element. To Tom it was a terrifying dream and one which projected the queasiness he felt during flight.

Tom hated the dream and he hated flying, but he never admitted it. For Tom to fly from Florida to the Gulf of México and the Caribbean Sea to Central America took will and a good bladder. A large commercial plane offered Tom little less anxiety, but did offer a toilet. In the 1960's, the advantage of a commercial airline was that it got weather reports. For a small plane like the Aero Commander, there was little communication with the ground. You had very little warning of what was ahead. You could experience thunder storms that popped up with ferocious energy. There was wind shear in these storms that would tear at the plane and leak through the seals around the doors.

"Rick, Rick," Tom would plead, "Can you go higher or lower or somewhere and get out of this bad weather?"

Rick was African Dutch. He had very dark skin, and "Negroid" features. He was stout and strong. Tom never asked about his ethnicity, Tom figured he was born in South Africa or Rhodesia. Rick owned, flew, and maintained the Aero Commander. Rick had great confidence in his abilities and talent as a pilot and in the soundness of his plane. Rick knew about the possibility of wing span failure caused by metal fatigue and he checked the connections between the wing and the fuselage on his plane regularly. To Tom, Rick's ethnicity was irrelevant. The question was whether he was a safe pilot. Tom felt he was safe.

"Take a little nip," Rick would tell Tom if the weather was bad. Courage from the bottle. There was nothing you could do about the weather. You could not get above the weather in the AC-500S. The plane was not pressurized, 11,000 feet was about the limit or you would black out after time from lack of oxygen. You had to suffer through the clouds and the turbulence that existed below 11,000 feet. If the destination was Central America from Florida, the nature of the weather was always the same. There were always storms and clouds.

The flight path to Central America was south from the West Coast of Florida to Miami or Key West. You refueled and then flew West avoiding Cuban airspace then Southwest to the Yucatán, and then over Isla Mujeres, which lies off shore from Cancún, Mexico. Then you fly south over the Straight of Cozumel, past the Mayan ruins in Tulum, then South over Ambergris Caye in the country of Belize to Belize City. Belize City sticks out from the shoreline into the sea and from the air it looks like the teat on a breast. Belize

City was the first stop for commercial airplanes from Miami and from there you could make connections to any other major city in Central or Middle America.

Rick was not a legitimate businessman. He was not licensed to carry passengers for hire. Except for that fact, Rick operated an honest enterprise. But there was temptation and wealth from the drug trade for anyone who could fly these routes from Florida to Central America and back. Rick would have been a natural for the trade, but he refused to participate.

Tom's connection to Central America was the Barnes Family and their interests in natural resources in Belize. These licenses to harvest forest products and lime rock had been purchased by the family. Tom was their lawyer and he regularly flew to Belize on their account. Tom had no interest in the drug industry and he was engaged in a battle with the newly elected government of Belieze which had declared the Barnes Family had forfeited their rights to the resources held in the name of the company controlled by the family called Belize Resources, Limited.

In the 1960's many small airports and even paved roads on the coast of Central American were jumping off points for small airplanes conveying drugs to the Florida Coast. The small planes were like cannon fire, shot at Florida, regular and often. This method of delivery of contraband was, at the time, the most frustrating to law enforcement and provided the best economic model as a delivery system for the product. The 1000 Islands in South West Florida and the coast known as the "Big Bend" in North Florida offered remote locations to off load contraband on rural single lane roads or to make a drop from a small plane to a small vessel. Rick commented there were many runways in Florida – "roads to nowhere." These paved roads were built with public funds and were authorized by local governments that knew they were going to service drug trafficking, which was a cottage industry in these desolate and poor Florida communities.

A trip to Belize City was an expensive proposition and Rick tried to ferry at least two passengers to cover the costs and make a profit. Unless the person was a pilot, Rick generally allowed no one to sit in the co-pilot seat. That allowed two passengers on the bench seat and two other passengers in the seats flying backwards. Maximum, there were four passengers and two crew members.

The passengers on this flight were Tom Night and a newcomer – Jamie Sulby. Jamie intended to open a new market selling air conditioning and heating systems (HVAC) in Central America. The Aero Commander landed at Miami International Airport to take Jamie on board. He had no contacts in Belize; he was going in blind. Jamie figured there was a market for the A/C, as hot and humid as Belize was year round. Jamie also anticipated that with the money from the drug trade, the Belizeans would have plenty of cash for the expense of the system.

***

Flying South from Isla Mujeres over the Mayan ruins at Tulum, over Punta Rosa to México's border with Belize and South to Belize City, the occupants of the Aero Commander could view numerous crosses or "x" marks on the ground below. These "x" marks were the remains of planes that crash landed along the coast and buried their noses into wild mangrove swamps or copra plantations or pure white beach. Some pilots tried to land between the reef and the shore, and you could see the memorial cross below the clear water. All of these drug flights were solo flights. There was no room for a passenger; the cabin of the plane was stuffed with bales or packages of cargo and a fuel bladder was added for extra fuel and distance. Rick wondered what happened to the pilots, the crash victims.

"So Tom, what are these 'x' marks down there?" asked Jamie.

Tom explained they were failed drug flights.

"Oh," said Jamie, and he considered that fact. He was an honest business man and he was above the drug trade, but he should have realized that if there were no drugs, there would be no money to purchase air conditioning. It was axiomatic.

And really, Tom thought, what was Jamie thinking? He won't be able to sell air conditioners. There were no public utilities that operated electric power generators in the country of Belize except for one large generator in Belize City and another one in the capital, Belmopan. There was no true electrical grid for the country except for the small electric grid that served the airport and the largest buildings and the hotels and residents along the Caribbean, but there were well less than 1,000 homes and businesses on the grid to Tom's knowledge.

Tom felt Jamie had a bad business plan. Jamie said the key to his plan was to sell to the new middle class that had private generators.

Rick called out, "We are in the home stretch, there's Tulum." Below was the ruin. Tulum was the only Mayan structure for kilometers along the coast now. When the Spanish first saw these shorelines in the 1500's, there were many lime rock towers constructed by the Mayans along the shore of the Yucatan from the Campeche coast to Punta Rosa. The towers were thought to be akin to lighthouses for seafaring pre-Columbians who braved the Caribbean Sea to travel after dark.

This day, as the Aero Commander with Rick, Tom and Jamie aboard passed over Punta Rosa, Tom could see the ship he had traded out to the locals for Anthony's dive boat only a day ago. Tom asked Rick to circle around so he got a good look below. The M.V. Cap de l'Ile was now imbedded in the shore with its keel broken, rusting in the rolling waves – like it should be – another corpse along the coast. The men in the Aero Commander could not see the mayhem playing out below among the locals fighting over the cargo on the M.V. Cap de l'Ile and the goods and supplies that remained in the Ship's Store. These properties were treasures to the locals and they were at war over the spoils. The men in the plane continued their journey and flew south from Punta Rosa. The scene below of copra plantations and white sand beaches gave way to a tangle of mangrove and lime rock bluffs abutting the sea.

Tom thought about the dive boat. When he left on this trip to Belize City there had still been no word from Anthony Arnold's crew. Tom had done his job. He obtained the permit and got the dive boat out of Mexico for his client. Tom knew nothing about what happened to Jorge or the members of the crew, the Hondurans or the wrestlers. Out of sight. Out of mind.

Today is another day, thought Tom. Another day. Another dollar.

Chapter 14

Although Rick was Dutch his accent was British. Rick had a military bearing. His training was airborne. He claimed that the first one hundred or so times he took off in a plane; he jumped out of the plane and parachuted to the ground. He landed on his feet and not in the plane. Tom wasn't sure if he was joking, but thought that maybe Rick was a member of an airborne unit during the wars in Africa, Rhodesia or some such place.

Rick also claimed the first time he piloted a plane, he was a passenger and he intended to jump with a parachute but the pilot had a heart attack and Rick took control and landed the plane. He was so good at flying and landing the plane on the first occasion that his superiors promoted him to be a co-pilot and then a pilot. He mostly flew DC-3's in the military and he piloted DC-3's early on as a private pilot and then bought his own plane, first a Cessna and then the Aero Commander.

The AC-500S was very small compared to military and commercial planes. It was surreal to taxi in the Aero Commander between two commercial jets, then watch as those behemoths roared and ascended after taking the entire length of the runway for takeoff. The AC-500S then would have to wait for clearance after the commercial planes took off. The Aero Commander then rose from the ground and then had to veer off to avoid the jet wash of the commercial planes in the air ahead.

This trip Rick landed in Miami to pick up Jamie after first boarding Tom in St. Petersburg. But, there was a problem.

"Tom," Rick said, "This guy wants to pay his air fare with stock certificates. Would you talk to him?"

Tom got his story: Jamie owned common stock in a publicly traded company that manufactured heating and air conditioning units. The stock had value but was traded over the counter (OTC) and listed on the "pink sheets". Jamie was honest about the stock. He explained the stock was hard to sell but Jamie assured Tom and Rick, there was a market for the stock.

"Do you have the shares?" asked Tom. Jamie produced the most beautifully engraved shares Tom had ever seen. To Tom that was another problem, the shares were too pretty to have any value. Tom was not familiar with the company. Tom told Rick not to take the shares. Rick asked Jamie if he had a check he could negotiate in the bank at the airport to pay the fare. But Jamie had no checks.

The man had no hard currency or legal tender.

"Jamie, how do you expect to pay your bills once you get to Belize? We can't be expected to front your expedition. Can we?"

Jamie said they should wait and he went in the restroom and returned with three, one ounce gold coins, American Gold Eagles.

Tom told Rick to take one of them; they had a value that was over $1,800 per coin at the time and each coin was well worth the cost of the fare to Belize City and back to the States.

Rick was very thankful to Tom. Rick was embarrassed confronting Jamie, a white man.

Tom said: "No problem. You'll help me in the future, I'm sure."

Tom thought Rick drank, but he never appeared intoxicated and was always in control of himself and the plane. Rick was unemotional and reliable but he had an odd way of looking at things. For example, Rick described the plane as a mode of escape. Tom knew what Rick meant. Without a plane in Central America you could get away a short distance on the ground; you could delay your demise a little while, but capture would be inevitable because you were not a local and you couldn't blend in. To successfully get away, the escape had to be non-linear. You needed to avoid gravity and get up and away – high and fast in an airplane. You could only use a plane once, regardless. If you got away successfully the locals wouldn't forget the plane. If you were unsuccessful and didn't get the plane off the ground, the plane ended up being parted out at the end of the runway. Rick worried about his investment and he did not leave the plane when they traveled to Central America. He stayed in the hanger with the plane. He would do a little maintenance on the plane. He would even sleep in the plane. It was all he owned.

Tom did business alone. He had never married and was unattached except for his law partner, Roger Adams. Tom had been a carouser, but he no longer drank and he never took drugs. He had to be clear headed all the time to perform his duties for his clients. He trusted no one while on a trip except Rick. Though he only had Rick to watch his back, he was not paranoid. He felt confident in his ability. Further, the fact that Tom was an American gave him an edge. The locals did not want to explain a dead American on their streets. Besides, Tom tried to be honest in all his dealings. He wanted no trouble.

Tom knew he was always vulnerable to an arrest since he dealt with the authorities. He knew it was important to establish legitimacy for himself. He retained local counsel. He relied on people to perform tasks rather like relying on machines. They had a job and he expected them to be reliable. If they weren't reliable – did not perform as expected – he did not argue with them. He smiled, paid their bill, but he avoided their services in the future. He did not trust people when they were operating on a level involving emotion. Tom tried to gain the trust of the people he hired. Prompt payment for their services instilled their trust in him and in return, he expected reliable performance. Americans understood this concept. Locals most times expected pay and they would promise performance but they would not perform if it was inconvenient. Locals were therefore mostly avoided. However, a local who had been away to school understood the concept so Tom inquired of their education. University in Jamaica provided an adequate education of the concept of modern business practice. Over time Tom collected a group of locals who he could trust to perform to their best ability.

If Tom relied on someone such as he relied on Rick, he tried to avoid compromising the relationship. He did not micromanage. He did not request Rick to provide him with a parachute, life raft or life jacket. Tom knew he could probably trot eight miles to avoid danger, but he couldn't swim 150 miles after a crash at sea, so why compromise his reliance on the pilot. It was better to show Rick he trusted him; to show he had confidence in his pilot. Rick would do everything possible to save his own life and in the process he would save Tom. And so Rick had life jackets, parachutes and a life raft. Rick had talked Tom through a jump but Tom had never used a parachute. He figured if they had to jump he would hold onto Rick. Rick said he was ok with that.

The thing that gave Tom legitimacy was his client list. He represented many prominent Belizeans when they had problems in the courts in Florida and he was known as the attorney for the Barnes Family. That relationship gave him repute in Belize.

Regarding weapons, Tom carried no weapon. Having a weapon on his person complicated matters. First, with the exception of a shotgun, no firearm was legal in Belize. Second, Tom needed to remain above the fray. If he needed a weapon he brought someone along with him who he trusted who had a weapon. But he tried not to be in a situation where he needed someone who carried a weapon. From his experience he was as likely to get shot or stabbed by a person who had a weapon who was there to protect him as from the person who was trying to hurt him. It is hard to find someone who will stand and aim and fire a gun and not panic. Most people instead blasted away with multiple shots without looking. They are inefficient and miss the target. It was better to rely on someone who could help you avoid the fray and so he relied on Rick to get him high, fast, and away in the plane as a last resort; if his wits and his luck failed him.

Too few people could shoot straight.

Chapter 15

Rick asked, "Is this trip high or low profile? Business or pleasure?"

Tom replied, "High, I'm visiting officials for the Barnes Family."

Rick asked because he was wondering where to land. If the trip was high profile they landed at the International Airport. Customs clearance was simple. A customs official stamped your passport or any piece of paper you presented that contained your name and then the official charged a tariff to enter the country. The tariff was $20 American. The officials did not run a check on your paperwork; they only wanted your name. The name was not checked for any security reason such as criminal history or wants or warrants. Tom's guess was that when the country became independent the new officials, if they formed suspicions about an individual, made inquiries about them, but that became work and work was mañana. But they did collect and maintain files containing many names, creating the illusion of a security system. On one trip, Tom had his driver's license stamped. On another, he used an envelope that was addressed to him. All of these papers were properly stamped with Belize's triangle symbol and a date and an official initial was inscribed within the triangle. Later in the trip, if asked for identification, he would provide the item that had been stamped by Customs.

After you arrived, a visitor was allowed to stay in the country for ten days. No visa was required. If you were discovered to have been there longer, you would say upon inquiry, "Your country is so beautiful that time has eluded me." And then you'd say, "I am sorry, could we resolve the matter here without going back to the airport?" Then you hand the official $10, he initials the paperwork again, and you are good for another ten days. This tended to make the small police force vigilant to check identification. It was rewarding to the police, but a nuisance to the foreigner.

If you desired to avoid all of this, you could pay the government $10,000 US dollars for a permanent residency status. However, none but the Chinese felt this was worthwhile. The papers gave the Chinese, who were escaping the anticipated take-over of Hong Kong, a temporary way-station in Central America until they could establish their intended ultimate residency destination. For the Chinese, they desired to live in Canada or the United States. Belize was a protectorate of the United Kingdom. Hong Kong was still a colony. The rich Chinese in Hong Kong looked to Vancouver, British Columbia for a democratic sanctuary with a court system based on the rights that flowed from the Magna Carta – individual liberty and due process, a trial by your peers – your family was not made to pay for the single bullet used by the Communist State for your execution.

Chinese who were poorer had to look to a country like Belize to preserve their desire for individual civil rights, and protection from arbitrary government action as they waited to move to the USA or Canada. The simplest way to legally enter Belize per-manently was to pay $10,000 to the Belize Government. So the Chinese bought the residency status. They also needed an occupation to maintain residency status and so they bought retail shops from the locals to establish their bonafides and overcharged the consumer. The Chinese were hated by the locals. Tom knew of no one but the Chinese, or a criminal, who would pay $10,000 US for citizenship in Belize.

***

The landing path for the International Airport took you inland across the coastal plain. The land was low and saline. The bed rock was lime rock. The lime rock was close to the surface, and there was little topsoil. The land was able to support very little green vegetation. There were isolated, scraggly, thin pine trees. Most plants were low and brown. Interspersed in these flats, the grasses or sedges grew in large thick clumps. The soil was pebbly and must have contained iron that caused the rusty tinge to the landscape below. As the AC-500S came in over the coastal plain it then banked left at 1,500 feet and settled in to land to the east on the runway. The landing strip was a thread of smooth, level concrete, the longest concrete surface in the country.

Tom believed he needed to present himself in a particular way to successfully represent his clients. In Central America you needed to be perceived to not be a threat. You appeared serious and quiet, polite, but firm. You always told Customs the purpose of the visit was business. You ate local food – well cooked. In Belize fresh fruit was not a danger. The seafood was excellent. You avoided the tap water, even for brushing your teeth. It was safe to drink bottled seltzer water as it was pasteurized. You stayed out of the brush to avoid mosquitoes and diseases, such as dengue fever.

The British Army shared the International Airport with the commercial airlines. Defensive heavy weapon emplacements covered with camouflage netting were placed strategically to hide the guns at the facility from the air.

As poor as it was, it was difficult to comprehend who would want to take the country. Guatemalans openly desired Belize for access to ports on the Caribbean Sea. Guatemala claimed the country when Belize was known as British Honduras. Further, Guatemala refused to recognize Belize when it was granted independence by the British.

The British flight line at the airport contained a fighter group that included two Harrier jets, a transport helicopter, a Huey helicopter and four small Cessna class planes. The Harrier jets could take off vertically and were useful in the Caribbean where the runways were short and many times unpaved. The military activities at the airport in Belize City were not separate from, but were combined with, the civilian air transportation system. Belize was not able to support its own civilian airline. Air service to

Belize was provided by a Honduran company, TAN, and, by TACA, based in Costa Rica. The British controlled the operation of the airport, but its control was benign.

***

Rick landed the AC-500S safely.

Rick taxied to the terminal and the Customs house. Tom and Jamie exited the plane and Rick then taxied on to the central hanger. The Customs house was a white concrete block and plaster building. A covered walkway led from the pad to the building to shelter the uninitiated from the mid-day sun. The Customs building contained a large, single room with lanes leading to desks that were positioned so that an official could greet and inspect the visitors and their luggage. Only one desk was occupied. He was a native, a colored man wearing a guayabera and dark slacks. He wore glasses with gold wire rims.

"Identification?" he asked.

Tom complied, sliding his U.S. passport and a $20 bill across the table. The official looked up from the passport and asked, "Thomas Night? Is that correct?"

"It is."

The agent wrote his name on the list on the desk. "What is the purpose of the visit?"

"Business."

"Do you have anything to declare?"

"Yes, an answering machine. It is a gift for my solicitor, Herbert Johns." Tom had the receipt which he showed to the customs agent. The duty for electronics was 50% of the purchase price, so the duty on the $79.95 telephone was $38.88, U.S., which Tom paid. The duty on electronics was very high. As a consequence, Belize had a phone system that predated WWII. There was no incentive to upgrade the electronic infrastructure of the country. Tom's solicitor was one of the few attorneys in the country with phone service, but he never answered his phone.

Tom hoped that he might call back if Tom had the ability to leave a message on the machine. The solicitor still relied on a telex machine as it was cheaper than the use of the phone.

"Will anyone meet you at the airport?"

"No. My pilot will check in after he ties down the plane. He will stay with the plane if there is no problem. We have done that before?"

"No problem. I remember you, Mr. Night. Do you need a driver this trip?"

"No, but I will need a car."

"I know of a good sound car."

"I would wager it is your brother-in-law's car?" Tom smiled.

The Customs agent smiled. "Yes."

"Then it will do."

"It is a Chrysler. You will see it. We will bring it to the airport." The official said as he stamped the passport and initialed it with the date.

"Thank you," said Tom.

The official then made an inquiry of Jamie who was holding out his twenty dollar bill.

Tom said, "I will take him downtown to his Hotel. Where are you staying, Jamie?"

"The Fort George," said Jamie.

"Ok," the official was satisfied and Tom and Jamie were free to go after the official collected the twenty dollar bill from Jamie.

Tom and Jamie went outside to wait for the car. They stood under a Royal Poinciana tree that was in blossom and was flaming red-orange.

The Royal Poinciana tree provided good shade. There were bench seats available under the tree in the shade. The benches were made of rough mahogany timbers.

A local was cooking tamales on a grill on a bench. Tom and Jamie each ate tamale, hot and spicy, slathered in Melinda's hot sauce, the ketchup of Belize. If you ate a meal flavored with Melinda's hot sauce you had little fear of most stomach bugs and you had clean intestines.

As they waited for the Chrysler, Jamie quizzed Tom on what to expect on his first trip to Belize.

"You need to understand that the Belizean people are proud of their country," Tom said. "They passed power from their first government to the new regime about a year ago without a shot being fired. They have a parliament and the people believe in the election process. The government is under pressure from the turmoil in Central America. Honduras is fascist. El Salvador is communist/socialist. There is a proxy war in El Salvador between the Americans and the communists resulting in a flight of refugees from El Salvador into Belize that has doubled this nation's population. Guatemala is hedging its bets, but their government or the police 'disappear' citizens that they feel are trouble to the regime. Further, Guatemala doesn't recognize Belize as a country. Guatemala claims Belize is theirs. Really, you don't want to leave Belize. It is surrounded by uncertainty and danger to a businessman who is just trying to make a buck. However, México is good if you can afford the corruption. I was there earlier this week. Just a short trip ... in and out."

Tom continued, "To understand the outside foreign pressure, look at the airport. There are permanent gun emplacements and a British Air Force and Naval presence. If you travel in the bush up in the north to the Orange Walk district you will see the British military on foot patrol. The soldiers are well liked. Belize is a protectorate. It appears to have forfeited its military regime to the British. It also appears that the government has all but forfeited its foreign policy to the Americans. The American Embassy is out of size for a small, insignificant country like Belize. The Americans have a large contingent of marines on base. The Embassy compound is totally surrounded with a spiked steel fence that is topped with razor wire. The White House has a less secure fence. I think the CIA is trying to control El Salvador from here, but I don't know and do not want to know."

"What does it cost to do business here?" asked Jamie. The word "cost" was a euphemism for the word "bribe".

"Let the official set a price. They won't be shy asking a favor. It's not a bribe. And if the official can't deliver what you need, he'll tell you who can deliver. But you won't be able to steal from them. They just provide access; that is really all you get.

"Quid pro quo, I get it," said Jamie. "I worried about how I would get the gold coins in the country. I have a credit card for the hotel. I was afraid to bring a wad of cash. What is your connection here? You seem to be able to make this pay."

"A change of government can mean opportunity," said Tom. "I have a client from the States that lost big in the last election. He sent me down here a year ago to see if we could salvage the licenses that he owned for natural resources. They also wanted me to sell off his holdings if I couldn't get the government to reissue the licenses. I come down here once every month or so. I have also picked up other work from other foreigners who lost in the election. One client owns a newspaper. There is a banana plantation, turpentine still, a saw mill in Belize City, and a naval stores operation. There is also land in the Mountain Pine Ridge with a waterfall.

I'm also here to make sure the locals who owe my client, pay up. The judges here are honest - although sometimes easily confused. If worse comes to worse we file a lawsuit to have our demands met. I have met some of the new ministers. The Solicitor General had me thrown out of his office. Win some, lose some. Another minister is interested in an idea for small prefab houses to replace the wood homes set on concrete stilts that are common living space in the city. The wood homes have been invaded by New Orleans termites. A good storm and they will be dust in the wind."

"The car is here. That is a Chrysler, I guess?" said Jamie. Both Tom and Jamie were skeptical of the make of the vehicle under the rust, dents and scrapes.

"It'll do," said Tom. He thought Jamie wasn't all bad. They loaded their bags and were off to the Fort George Hotel.

The Fort George was constructed in stages over many years. It was the only facility that hosted the Queen of England when she visited. Queen Elizabeth didn't stay in the hotel but there was a plaque in the lobby that shows she was at the hotel to receive local officials. She stayed on the Royal Yacht Britannia. Tom thought it was odd that the plaque mentioned the fact she didn't sleep in the hotel. Maybe it was a comment by staff that she was too good for the place. Maybe the security was too lax. Tom understood her concern; he never stayed in the same hotel. He always moved around.

The Fort George had a pool, large rooms, dining facilities, grill and bar, and banquet facilities and international phone service. The halls were lined with mahogany that made the hotel cool, dark and secluded. The staff was pleasant. But Tom didn't stay there often. He went down by the sea and stayed in the rather ramshackle accommodations located there. Tom hated to be too predictable. He did not trust the police.

Jamie checked in and headed for the bar. Tom declined, "See you in a couple of days, maybe."

"Where you headed?" asked Jamie.

"To hunt wild pigs."

Jamie was skeptical that Tom intended to hunt pigs. "Spend the night. We can talk. You can hunt tomorrow." said Jamie. "I want to talk to you some more about Belize."

"I wrote a report for a client about Belize years ago. Nothing has changed. The report is still relevant. I will leave it for you."

Tom could tell Jamie was not satisfied with a written report. Since the television coverage of the Vietnam War, Americans expected historical accounts to be visual and distinct. For years an American would switch on the news and see the war up close and personal, albeit in black and white. The war was broadcast in color in some markets. Americans did not shy from the grotesque views shown in the color television reports. It was just that Americans did not have the money to pay for a color TV.

Chapter 16

Tom left a memorandum (see Appendix) at the Fort George Hotel for Jamie as Tom left Belize City for some entertainment in the bush chasing wild pigs. This report was written by Tom Night for the Barnes family following his first trip to Belize. During that first visit Tom was a serious drinker. He had an episode where he blacked out and he was hospitalized. Tom wrote the report to cover for the fact that he was drunk. He had also gone to a brothel and paid for a woman to stay with him in his hotel room. Having a woman other than your wife in your room for an assignation was a crime in Belize. Luckily, the woman had stolen his cash and absconded before the police raided his room. Tom suspected a man, Winston Grey, of having alerted the police to the possible crime committed in Tom's hotel room. The report contained Tom's opinions of Belize formed from that first visit and information from books and magazine articles he read. Tom wrote the report as he flew back to Miami from his first visit to Central America. Tom provided a copy of the report to his most important clients at the time (the Barnes Family) hoping they would not find out that he had spent the first trip to the country mostly incapacitated by drink, but rather that he spent the time educating himself about the country. The client discovered the truth and the lie cost Tom his client's trust. Tom kept the report to remind himself that drink made him a weak human being. Tom gave copies of the report to potential clients and used the report to show his knowledge and experience in the country. Jamie did not read the report.

Chapter 17

When Tom first came to Belize five years earlier he had been invited to the Caucasian country club. The members indulged in alcohol to excess. That was no problem for Tom because he was still drinking at that time. The whites amused themselves with drink and cards, a local pitch for soccer, a cricket field and a track for horse racing.

But after Tom quit drinking he had little interest sitting with the Brits at a venue which had as its reason for existence the inhaling of alcohol. Tom was impressed by the natural beauty of the country. He loved driving on the Hummingbird Highway where he encountered exotic wildlife. Once, he saw a jaguar sitting on the side of the road watching the few cars that took to the road pass by. Tom loved the birds. He particularly loved the macaws, red and blue yellow macaws.

Tom also developed a passion for wild pig hunting. It wasn't really a sport. It was extreme exercise that required a large pasture, 200 to 300 acres in size that had a herd of 20 or so cattle. It also required a flatbed truck to carry the men and at least 20 caged dogs.

Once it became dark, feral pigs would move into the pasture to feed with the cattle. Cattle and pigs abided the other and both had a common enemy – el tigre (the leopard). The cattle and the pigs grazed together in a silent scrum – the pigs on roots and the cattle on the grass. Into this mix you introduced a roaring truck that had no muffler, with men standing in the flatbed holding onto grips that were welded on the back of the roof of the cab of the truck. The men held torches (strong flashlights) in their free hand that they tried to shine into the pasture as the truck barreled along at speeds up to 40 mph. The truck hit depressions, some containing water and the men became soaked from the wet and sweat and they screamed and hollered and the dogs joined them, baying.

As soon as the driver saw a herd of animals in the torch light, he headed for them and the animals tended to stampede. The pigs were quicker than the cattle and bolted to the front of the herd. The driver, if he was good, would pull between the animals (behind the pigs and in front of the cattle). The cattle would stop and turn and the truck would continue to chase after the pigs and try to outrun and flank them. And as the driver pulled into the pack of pigs and stopped, the men on the flatbed of the truck reached into the dog pen on the back of the flatbed and began grabbing the dogs and flinging them into the racing pigs. The pigs squealed in fear. The dogs loved the hunt. Some dogs were more aggressive; they attacked the pigs and grabbed their ears. Their canine teeth punctured the tough flesh of the pig's ear and the dogs pulled the pig's heads down, stopping the pig. Once the pig was stopped, the pack of dogs piled on, grabbing anything that was loose on the pig.

The driver then stopped the truck completely and the men rushed into the pack of fur, flesh and muscle that whirled about on the ground-- a twister with snapping pig jaws and twisting tusks.

The point of this endeavor was to save the pig from the dogs so it could be captured and then returned to the farmhouse. The pig would be put in a pen and corn-fed and fattened and ultimately butchered for food.

The dogs had no fear and they would fight to the death. So the men had to save the dogs from themselves once the dogs latched on to a pig. The men began to snatch the dogs off of the prey and return the dogs to their pen. However, it was important to leave one dog on each ear of the pig to control the pig. Then, hard to believe, a man would grab the rear legs of the pig. By pulling the pig up from the ground by its rear legs, one man could control the pig, and then others could jump on the animal and tie its legs. Once on its side, the pig, if it was male, was castrated and released.

The purpose of the sport was birth control, to limit the population of the pigs and consequently, to save the grass in the pastures from rooting by ever more numerous, roving herds of pigs. Thus the boars were castrated. The gilts (female pigs without a litter) and sows (female pigs with their litter), and the litter if the baby pigs could be found, were caged to be fattened and slaughtered. In the case of the litter, they could be tamed if they were caged with tame litters, but you could not trust them to be left uncaged unless you fed them.

Once every four legged animal was in its pen or cage, the men jumped on the truck and they returned to the farmhouse. It was like a battle, and the men were exhilarated by a hunt in which they had the advantage and rarely suffered more than pulled muscles and cuts and scrapes. Tom thoroughly enjoyed these hunts and tried to participate each time he visited the country.

*****

After dropping Jamie at the Fort George Hotel, Tom drove the Chrysler 300 on the Western Highway toward Belmopan to join a hunt. The road was being widened and repaved with macadam and gravel. The road ran northwest then west to a wide spot in the road. There Tom stopped at the "D-8 Bar." The bar was owned by Sergeant Major James, a former British soldier who married a native named Marie, and they ran the bar and a station in the outback along the highway. The establishment consisted of the bar and the family home, a large utility shed, and a barn.

In front of the bar was a D-8 "Caterpillar" brand bulldozer. The machine had expired on the side of the road. It was worn out; it no longer ran and was useless and left to die. It was too expensive and heavy to move in one piece. However, parts could be salvaged from the earthmover. If you needed a CAT part for a dozer, the D-8 was available for salvage without cost. Sergeant Major and his wife, Marie, felt the D-8 would disappear eventually, one part at a time.

The D-8 Bar was headquarters for pig hunts. Cattlemen who wanted to sponsor a hunt to reestablish a swine yard, or fill a larder with pork, or reduce the damage from the pigs rooting through their pastures would meet at the D-8 Bar and enlist a crew. Everyone (except Tom) was provided with a pint at the bar for their pay and they were off.

Tom was greeted by Sergeant Major as he got out of the car. "So, you're back for more punishment."

The last hunt resulted in Tom receiving a cut on his right arm. It festered and Tom had to visit the clinic to see the new physician, Anna Hernando, in Belize City for stitches and penicillin.

"That bad experience was a year back. I've been on hunts since, with no consequences," said Tom.

"You're getting too old to run in the dark and wrestle with pigs. Go on the hunt but stay in the truck." advised Sergeant Major.

"Yes," added Marie, "They need someone who is sober to fire the shotgun if an animal gets the better of the men."

The men agreed not to carry handguns (furthermore handguns were illegal in Belize), but there was a shotgun in the cab of the truck behind the seat if an emergency arose. It was a fine old Beretta called a "thunder stick" because it made as much noise as a clap of thunder when it was fired.

"How was your flight to Belize?" asked Marie. She knew Tom hated to fly.

"It was quite a bad flight. We bounced all the way here," Tom lied. "Maybe I will stay in the truck."

The group that assembled, each with their pint, included Frederick, the landowner who would handle the dogs, and George the truck driver, who worked for Fredrick, the landowner.

Riding on back was an assortment of bar-flies and British military retires – four men in all, who would provide the muscle, dealing with the pigs. Plus Tom, who was to take it slow and easy.

George pulled the old Ford with the men and the dogs out of the parking lot of the D-8 Bar and headed up the road 5 kilometers (3 miles), then into a trail in the bush. This area of Belize had been jungle that was cleared by loggers 40 years ago. Then the cleared forest was burnt and Brahman cattle were put out to graze on the green shoots as it came up. Goats were also put in the pasture to control the growth and, as a last measure, a bush hog (a large mowing machine pulled by a tractor) was used annually to control growth so the jungle did not return. In place of the jungle there was a grassy pasture prized by the hogs.

Frederick and George worked a ranch. The land consisted of small rolling hills with streams, and there were flat areas – hundreds of acres each that were fenced – and these held the cattle, which were moved from pasture to pasture to feed, preventing the animals from overeating and destroying the grass.

The hogs were imported by the conquistadors. They became wild when they escaped. The hunts helped control them. The other predator was "el tigre". The jaguar had been mostly killed off in the area where the ranch land was maintained. At present the jaguar habitat was in the Coxcomb Basin, which could be reached off the Hummingbird Highway. The Coxcomb Basin was very wild and held the Mayan Mountains and Victoria Peak, the second highest peak in that range.

George drove to his ranch to pick up Winston Grey, another rancher, for the hunt.

Tom and Winston had known each other now for five years. They met when Tom first visited Belize.

George's ranch consisted of a main house, a barn and quarters for wranglers.

Winston was a strange duck. There were rumors that he had been evicted by the authorities from the Bahamas. His family, who were Caucasian, native Bahamians and had lived on the islands for centuries. He was a loner. He was short and squat. He spoke with a whiny feminine voice. He never looked you in the eye.

Winston claimed the passenger seat and said he didn't intend to wrestle with the pigs. So Tom was out of the truck cab and now Tom was holding a torch in his right hand and with his left hand he grasped one of the handles welded to the top of the cab as they drove out of the ranch to the pastures.

George took it along the dirt roads that were outside the barb wire fenced pastures. The men shined their torches into the pastures looking for cattle and hogs mingling and grazing together. At the second pasture they saw two or three litters of pigs with adults that were crossing the pasture heading for a patch of jungle. There were no cattle with the pigs. Winston jumped out of the front seat and ran for the gate. The gate was flung open. Winston got back in the truck and the hunt was on.

George maneuvered the truck behind the pigs that were now racing in front of the truck. The pigs, however, did not appear to be driven solely by the hollering of the men, the baying of the dogs and roar of the truck. George was a little confused by the actions of the pigs, but he followed and got among the swine herd.

Frederick opened the dog cage and the dogs needed no coaxing. They scrambled out of their cage on their own accord and jumped into the herd. They were grabbing for ears and hide. The men disembarked. Then (it was unusual) the pigs appeared to be desperate as they fought against capture. Most of the pigs were able to get away into the jungle. The men were left with two old sows and a few piglets. The men made quick work of the sows and threw them and their piglets into the pig pen. And then the men stood looking about. It was quiet. The dogs were cowed and whined lowly. Then from the jungle, they heard the sound of a large cat and saw the flash of yellow eyes. Two of the aggressive dogs bolted into the jungle.

Winston grabbed the Berretta and followed. "If the dogs can tree the cat, I can kill it," he yelled and ran into the trees.

The men followed at full stride running in the darkness. They tried to stay together, but two of the men were felled by a root as they entered the tree line.

"Enough for me" one said. It was George.

"Agreed," said the other and they went back to the truck rubbing their palms and elbows.

"I think I broke something" said George.

"This is dumb," said the other. "Running in the dark."

"Agreed," said George.

That left the dogs baying. They crashed through the jungle with four men trying to keep up. Winston was still in the lead. There was a snarl and a growl and the report of the Beretta ... once ... then again, the gun discharged. Then silence. The men surrounded the jaguar, now dead in the underbrush below a towering sapodilla tree.

Frederick leashed the most aggressive dogs to control them, and then he penned the others that were trying to dismember the cat. Frederick wanted to save the skin. Two of the barflies were told to return with Frederick to help cage the dogs. Winston and Tom shined their torches on the cat.

It was a jaguar. They trussed it up to carry it on a branch. "120 pounds, I'd say," said Winston as he hefted it up. Winston was in the front, Tom in the rear. They carried it out of the jungle in silence. Winston had never killed an animal like this one. Tom had never killed an animal, period.

Chapter 18

Back at the truck, the men shined a light on George's arm. It had been an hour since George fell and he was now in acute distress. He had vomited and he complained of throbbing pain. It was clear he had a displaced fracture of the tibia (a Coles' fracture). The bone had almost pierced the skin. Luckily, no vein or artery had been cut.

Shock was also a concern. Tom suggested to Frederick that George lie down and be covered with a blanket with his legs elevated. Frederick said the closest medical care available was at the Mennonite enclave at Spanish Lookout near the Guatemalan border.

When Belize was created there was always border conflict between the countries. Tom had been told this tension played out in the land called "Spanish Lookout." The Mennonites had cleared part of the jungle in the lookout area and had established a sawmill.

Fredrick and George did not believe the Mennonites would help them because they had taken advantage of the Mennonites. Frederick and George had ordered wood to build their barn from the Mennonite's sawmill. Then they refused to pay, figuring the Mennonites wouldn't sue them. They were right. The religious beliefs of the sect restricted them from using the courts to collect the debt. Frederick cheated the Mennonites. Of course, you could only do this once. The Mennonites were honest to their beliefs, but not stupid. Frederick was worried that if he asked the Mennonites for help for George that the medical care George needed would be denied because of their past dishonesty.

Tom knew about the dispute between Frederick and the Mennonites. But the situation with George's arm was bad. Tom offered to take George to Jacob's house to see if he would help George. Tom knew Jacob and his wife. They were respected Mennonites. Tom had sold them a large timber carriage for their sawmill at a very fair price. They owed Tom a favor.

Tom and the men put George in the back seat of the old Chrysler and had him stretch out with his feet elevated and he was covered with a blanket. He was given water and Tom told George to keep sipping the water so he was hydrated. Tom drove slowly trying to keep George from being jostled about. The enclave was about 15 miles away.

For an Amish sect, the Mennonites at Spanish Lookout were liberal in their beliefs. They were allowed the use of electricity and modern machines. They used cars and phones. The Lookout was like a small town. It even had street lights lit by a generator. The houses were laid out on a sensible grid-based road system. They produced chickens and had a grist mill to process wheat into flour. They had cows for milk and they produced other dairy products. Before the Mennonites emigrated, milk and flour were imported by Belizeans from México. The Mennonites also had truck farms and produced vegetables for the Belizeans. They made furniture that they sold at the Market in Belize City on Saturdays. Their sawmill produced construction and building materials. Last, they had a store where you could purchase cloth and general merchandise.

Tom had great respect for the Mennonites. The previous November, Tom had driven up to the Lookout to finalize the sale of the log carriage for the sawmill. As he drove into the property there were a group of 20 or so children playing in a field. The boys were dressed in white shirts and dark blue trousers and black shoes. The girls wore smocks with aprons and they each had a bonnet. It was a picture out of Lancaster County, Pennsylvania, but it was Belize, on land that had been carved by loggers and sawyers out of the jungle.

It took about an hour to travel to Jacob's house. The family was awake. Tom left George in the car and explained the situation. Jacob said he would help. George was seated in Jacob's living room and Tom and Jacob drove to Michael's house. Michael had the best medical training of any of the Mennonites. Michael and his wife followed Tom's car back to Jacob's house.

While Michael and his wife set the fractured bone, Tom and Jacob went outside to talk. The conversation came around to the debt for the lumber.

"Send your bill for the timber with me. I'll try to get Fredrick to pay you."

Jacob shrugged.

"I'm still going to mention the bill to Frederick. He needs to pay for this. He owes it to George. He's worked George to death for years for little or no pay."

"How was George injured?" Jacob changed the subject.

"We were pig hunting and were interrupted by a jaguar that was on its own pig hunt. Winston shot it," replied Tom.

"We have been bothered by a cat that had been up here after our chickens last week," said Jacob. "It must have been sick or hurt to attack the chickens. We were worried for the children. We didn't need to deal with a man eater."

"You don't have to worry for the children now."

Jacob then shared with Tom the fact that the Mennonites had a fear of Winston. "We have to watch the children if he's around. We told him to stay away. He would always follow a child into a room and we would find him alone with the child. We think he may be an abuser and we have agreed to shun him. He's not welcome here at the enclave and he has been told to stay away from the children."

"I know he's strange – his voice and affectation," said Tom.

"That is not it. Winston has a deaf and dumb boy he keeps at his ranch" said Jacob. "The boy is seven years old, that's all we could get Winston to volunteer except he calls the boy his cousin. We can't take a chance with Winston. Though I'm happy he killed the jaguar."

Tom knew Winston to be heterosexual. He was not a pedophile. On Tom's first trip to Belize Winston had taken Tom to a brothel.

"I think you are wrong about Winston," was all Tom had to say in Winston's defense.

Part III
The Escape

Chapters 19 through 27

Anthony Arnold escapes ... The Mountain Pine Ridge ... The Hummingbird Highway ... Dangriga and Big Creek ... The meeting with Solicitor General Andrew Prince ... The court in Florida.

Chapter 19

After returning George to Fredrick's ranch, Tom passed the international phone system located in the capital city, Belmopan. The facility was contained in a building about 30 feet long and 10 feet wide divided into 3 rooms. Each cubicle had a standard Bell System pay phone attached to the wall. There was a desk that was also attached to the wall below the phone. The phone was used to place international calls using a telephone credit card. There was no local operator. The phone connected you directly to an overseas operator. You told the operator the country code for the country you intended to call; the operator would connect you to the country, and then you would dial in the area code and the phone number. The phone was supposedly secure – but who knew. The unusual aspect of the facility was that behind the phone building there was an equipment shed and then a very high tower-maybe 150 – 200 feet high. Tom had no idea how it worked, but it did.

It was dawn now and Tom could call his office. There was an hour time difference between Belize and Florida so he would be able to talk to his partner, Roger, who was always in early.

After giving the operator the country code and the connection was made, Tom dialed his office in St. Petersburg. A male voice answered: "Roger, Roger."

"It's Tom, Roger." Tom hated it when Roger answered the phone greeting the caller with "Roger, Roger." It was a law office after all.

"Glad you called Tom, I have news. Anthony is on the loose."

"What do you mean? He was in jail."

"Anthony just walked out."

"What? That makes no sense."

"I guess Anthony didn't want to stay in that little jail in Bushton."

"Don't they lock the cells in the county Jail?" asked Tom.

"Doesn't appear they do. Anthony is a charmer. They made him a trustee. He was outside his cell, in the lobby. He was free to roam around the jail. He was even wearing his own clothes."

"How could the sheriff do that?"

"Our comment is: 'No comment.' Remember that Roger."

"Ok," agreed Roger, although Roger did like to see his name in print.

"How did Anthony get out?"

"He told the guard at the desk in the lobby he needed to make a phone call. The guard let him out of the lock up area into the lobby. The lobby door is unlocked and leads out to the parking lot. Anthony began to use the pay phone, the guard went back into the general lock up area due to a disturbance of some kind and Anthony walked out the door. Someone must have picked him up outside and drove him away. My bet is that the guard was in on it too."

"My guess is the inmate that caused the disturbance was the one that was in on it. The guards in Bushton are honest. The sheriff is too. The judge isn't going to be happy with the sheriff."

"Anthony will head for his boats is my guess," Roger said. "He called here three days ago before he escaped. He wanted to know if we heard anything about his boats. Did they arrive in Belize, is all he wanted to know."

"I saw the old boat broken up on shore in Punta Rosa when we flew down yesterday. The dive boat is on Ambergris Caye off the northern coast of Belize, if they made it there."

"It did. That was confirmed. Anthony's friends called but Anthony had escaped by then," said Roger. "Are you alright with Anthony? Is he going to be mad with you because the one boat was lost?"

"He's alright. I spoke to him when I got back and explained the situation on the ground there. He can talk to his crew. They agreed the old ship was run aground and couldn't be moved. He seemed to be more upset with his crew than with me. He felt like someone ratted him out. I was just the messenger. At least I got the one boat out of there. No one else helped him."

"He has a short memory," said Roger.

"If he's heading for his boat, it will take him awhile to get there. He won't be able to use commercial transportation. That will slow him down. I should be out of here pretty soon if I don't get eaten by a jaguar."

"Were you at the Belize Zoo again?"

"No, it was a pig hunt gone crazy. A jaguar was hunting the same pigs we were, and thought we were more appetizing than the pigs."

"You really shouldn't take these chances. I thought you were at the zoo talking to that pretty lady zookeeper."

"No, I haven't seen her. But the pig hunt was all billable hours."

"What? You can't bill for a pig hunt."

"Kidding, just kidding. I wish I could bill my clients for all of my time over here, portal to portal. Roger, I have to go."

"Stay safe," said Roger.

"Roger, Roger," said Tom.

"I wish you wouldn't say that," said Roger. "It's so undignified."

Chapter 20

Tom was looking for coffee now that he finished the international phone call with Roger. It was hard to find a good cup of coffee in Belize.

The streets of Belmopan were empty. Tom's lawyer in Belize, Herbert Johns, would not be in until 8:00 a.m. Nothing opened until 10. Belize deferred to Central Time. When it was 9:00 a.m. in Florida it was 8:00 a.m. in Belize.

Tom decided to visit James Shaheen, the Lebanese fellow who was interested in buying the turpentine still in the Mountain Pine Ridge. James was one of the few people who had their permanent residence in Belmopan, the capital of Belize. He lived in a small two bedroom house in a suburban community with his wife. They had two children who were in their late 20's. They all worked for the government. They had office skills that were vital to keep the county operating. Most government workers had homes in the capital and in Belize City.

Tom approached the door of James' house. James beat Tom to it and opened the door.

"James, do you want to look at the boiler at the turpentine still again?" asked Tom.

"Give me a moment. Come in and have a cup of coffee," said James.

Tom smiled as he poured a cup of coffee and added cane sugar and condensed milk. The family had a coffee percolator and a gas range and an electric refrigerator. They were a modern middle class family if it were 1940 in the USA.

Tom hoped James would buy the turpentine still and the equipment there at the facility. In turn, James would find buyers for the equipment and part it out, finding separate buyers for everything that was there at the still, the generators, the vats, etc. It would take patience and the knowledge of who would be able to adapt the equipment to their needs. The land was leased, Tom couldn't sell the land. He was looking for $20,000 US for the equipment.

The men got in the Chrysler and Tom let James drive. The streets were starting to fill with buses coming up the plateau from Belize City to their jobs in the capital and to visit the ministry buildings to conduct business and to deal with the legislature.

The buildings were spread out over an elevated plain. They were mostly constructed of concrete with filigree work that allowed the cool mountain breezes waft through the hallways. James maneuvered the Chrysler out of the city. They engaged in small talk and Tom sipped his coffee.

Two hours north and west of the capital they came to the water fall in the Mountain Pine Ridge. The water flowed down a steep rock covered hill. To Tom, the rock hill looked like there were steps carved into the slope.

"Do you think that was man made?" Tom asked. "It looks like the steps up a Mayan pyramid."

"Could be," said James. "You find small Mayan figures around this area if you dig. There are large stone pieces (stelae) that are found regularly, but no one has been able to interpret the hieroglyphic symbols on the stone slab yet. It's a good guess that there are steps cut in the rock in the falls and that they are man made, yes it is."

The pair collected water from the falls – it was cool and delicious. The Mountain Pine Ridge contained a pine forest that grew in a granite base and poor soil. The forest was over 100,000 acres. The granite was pushed up through the soil in some cataclysmic event millions of years ago and pine trees managed to take hold and grow on the granite. The type of pine that grew on the ridge was a variety of Honduran pine known as slash pine.

The trees were used for production of naval stores from pine sap. The resin or "tar" produced from the sap from the trees had been used in wooden ships to caulk and waterproof the seams between the wood planks in the ships' hulls. The use of pine resin in wooden ships ended by the 1920's but the pine resin was still collected from pine trees and converted to resin and turpentine. The resin was used as an adhesive and the turpentine was used in fragrances, flavors, cleaning products and medicine.

The method of collecting the pine sap or resin was very labor intensive. The face of the tree was slashed and the bark removed to the Cambrian layer and a strip of tin was placed in the slash. The tree would bleed sap into the tin strip; the sap would drip into a cup at the end of the metal strip, and then the sap that dripped into the cup was collected by the workers. This method of working in pine forests gashing the trees, and re-gashing them in subsequent years and hauling the resin out of the forest was difficult labor. The workers were low paid and by the 1960's the processing of resin to turpentine from the collection of pine sap was at an end in Belize and Tom had been hired to sell the equipment in the still.

James Shaheen re-inspected the equipment. It was no worse for wear since the last time they had visited. Shaheen felt he could make some money on the deal if he had a little more time to line up buyers.

"What do you think?" asked Tom. "Can you pay the $20,000 US?"

"I can pay ten now and ten thousand more in a month."

"That is fine," said Tom. "I'll have my lawyer, Herbert Johns, draw up the bill of sale and the promissory note." Tom laughed. "$10,000 is a perfect amount. I won't have to declare it at Customs in Miami after I pay the lawyer his fee. I'll return to the states with less than ten thousand dollars."

"Perfect all the way around," said James. As they drove back to Belmopan through the pine ridge, Tom could see that someone was removing the clay sap cups from the trees. You couldn't leave anything for a moment in Belize, even sap in a tree, or it would be borrowed by someone in need. Tom was glad to sell the equipment.

***

Tom delivered James to his job in the Department of Agriculture and he was off to the lawyer's office in Belmopan.

Herbert Johns received his undergraduate education at University in Jamaica and in Faculty of Law at University of Cambridge. The British government had provided him with a scholarship. Herbert had an office in the capital and another office in a building on stilts on the waterfront in Belize City he shared with large crabs with one red claw.

Herbert's office in Belize City was also his home. Herbert loved basketball – he called it "round ball." He was out at the hoop every evening making lay ups, hooks, and jump shots.

Lawyer Johns was a man in his seventies. He had been a member of parliament, had been a judge, and was now in private practice primarily providing services to business men. He was also a silent partner in Belize Reserves with the Barnes family.

Mr. Johns had the dustiest office Tom had ever seen. The dustiest article in the office was Herbert's wig. Tom was not sure if it was powder on the wig and not dust, but it affected his lungs and caused him to have coughing fits. Tom always invited Herbert to speak with him on the porch so he could avoid the dust.

"I need to see the Solicitor General and the Director of Housing tomorrow. Can you arrange it?"

"I'm sure I can. Anything else?" asked Herbert.

"I need some paperwork for the sale of the turpentine still equipment. I'm selling it to James Shaheen."

"I will handle it," said Herbert.

"I owe you for your fees. Prepare a billing that is current. James will bring you $10,000 US. Take your fee from the first payment. I will pick up the balance tomorrow at the Bull Frog Inn. I have to take the Hummingbird Highway to the coast to Dangriga."

"That road is very rough right now," warned Herbert.

"I have to see if there is a possible site for a harbor to ship gravel from Belize to the US. The last time I was there I took samples of the rock in the hills near the coast. I've been told the rock will make the best concrete gravel in the world," said Tom. "I have someone interested if they can build a pier out into the Caribbean Sea and transfer the gravel to a ship. I was asked to take photographs while I am here for that client."

Very industrious, thought Johns. "I will set the appointments."

"Thank you, Herbert, for all your help."

"Did Rick, the pilot, fly you this trip?"

"Yes."

"You don't fear flying with him in that plane?"

"No. Why?"

"He's a black African." Herbert smiled. He was always testing Tom for prejudice. Tom was prejudiced but he kept it to himself. Herbert Johns was "European," which meant he was Spanish, African, Mayan and Creole. Tom did not understand how that mixture was much superior to Rick if you were putting race to a scale.

"It's irrelevant. Rick is a good pilot. You are a good lawyer. I will see you tomorrow," said Tom. "I'll stay at the Bull Frog Inn tonight."

Tom's response was sharp and direct. He did not see his statement as hurtful, but it was. He did not understand the effect of his words when language was his stock in trade. Hubert Johns let the statement go by and ignored it. If he cared he would have said something, but he no longer cared.

"See you tomorrow if I can. I may have to go to the city," said Herbert. "I will deliver your money and the documents at the Bull Frog Inn in the morning."

"Remember that I need to see the ministers," said Tom. "That's the real reason for this visit."

"I remember," said Herbert. "You will see them in Belize City in their offices if that's all right."

"No problem," said Tom.

Tom was off to the coast via the Hummingbird Highway.

Chapter 21

Belmopan, the capital of Belize, had only one petrol station. It was an ESSO brand gas station with one electric pump for gasoline and other tanks that were operated with hand pumps. From those other tanks you could purchase kerosene for heating and cooking and bunker oil for a large electric generator to produce electricity for home or a private business. Small generators used gasoline and were very expensive to operate because gasoline was costly. There was no oil refinery in Belize.

Bunker oil was used to fuel the main generator that provided lights and electricity for the government buildings and street lights for Belmopan. The bunker oil was delivered by a coastal tanker from Vera Cruz, Mexico (PEMEX) to the port in the town of Dangriga (formerly, Stan Creek Town). Dangriga had a pier that extended into the sea. Tanker trucks would back down the pier and be loaded with fuel from the ship. Once loaded, the tanker truck would begin the trip from Dangriga to Belmopan across the Hummingbird Highway where it would unload the fuel at the electric plant in Belmopan.

When the tanker truck left Dangriga a twin tanker departed from the electric plant in Belmopan heading down the Hummingbird Highway to the dock to be filled at the ship. Thus the two tanker trucks had to meet in the middle of the highway and pass each other. The Hummingbird Highway was at best a lane and a half wide so there was an accommodation built in the road where the highway was about two lanes wide about halfway between the capital and the coastal city. Depending on the anticipated need for fuel these two trucks could operate 24/7. The highway was in very poor repair and curved through the Mayan

Mountains. As a result of the tanker trucks' operations any other traffic that intended to use the highway could expect many delays if one came up behind a tanker. The trucks traveled at about 20 miles an hour and took three to four hours to travel the distance required to deliver the fuel.

In addition to the oil transport there were orange groves in the valley between the mountains which generated truck and vehicle traffic. Further, if you wanted to travel south on the Southern Highway you first had to travel east toward Dangriga from Belmopan and then you turned south before reaching Dangriga to travel to the southern border or you had to hack your way through the jungle of the Coxcomb Basin.

Laughlin Powder Corporation had had a large black liquor operation on the Southern Highway where they accomplished the preliminary extraction of resin from virgin pine stumps. The resin was used in gunpowder and cosmetics as a binding agent or adhesive. Belize was an excellent source of virgin pine stumps because about every 20 years the southern end of the country was hit by a hurricane and the pine trees were killed by being blown over or having their needles and branches stripped from the tree. The pine sap in the dead tree collected through the effect of gravity into the stump and roots of a dead tree. The sap turned into gum and then into resin. Laughlin Powder collected the stumps; ground them into pulp; boiled the stumps and roots, and extracted black liquor that contained the resin. The black liquor was shipped to the US where it was refined into final end products. Because of this activity traffic on the Hummingbird could be heavy.

Tom had to leave Belmopan ahead of the tanker truck heading for the coast or it could take five hours to make a three hour trip.

Tom had spent the night at the Bull Frog Inn. He had arrived there late the night before after seeing Herbert Johns. The Inn's management left a few rooms open for visitors and they trusted the guests to pay in the morning. The Inn's staff left a light on outside a room if it was unoccupied. Tom was aware of this practice and he had taken a room with an outside light lit next to the door. The door was unlocked. The linens were clean and fresh. There was a pitcher of water and a basin. He washed and slept well though there was no air conditioning and his room was only cooled by a ceiling fan.

In the morning Tom went to the desk in the lobby and made a payment for the room and told the staff Herbert Johns would be dropping off cash and legal documents for him. Tom said he would pick them up after his trip to Dangriga and he would spend another night.

The clerk at the inn was pleasant. Tom had no misgivings leaving the money with the staff at the inn.

Before leaving Belmopan, Tom decided to phone the office. He would be out of touch until he returned to the capital in the evening, as there was no public international phone on the coast.

Tom went again to the international phone facility in the capital. He dialed his office.

"Roger, Roger," answered Roger.

"Roger, I just have a minute. Give me an update on Anthony."

"Well, the judge is really upset. He thinks the jailers and the sheriff were in on the escape."

"I'm glad I was out of town when he escaped. Being that I'm Anthony's attorney, the judge would have thought I was also involved in the escape if I was in town," said Tom sarcastically.

"The judge called for you and because you were out of the country he made me come to court on a hearing to determine the status of the case."

"Well, there is no status if Anthony is gone."

"The judge wanted to vent," said Roger. "He had me come to the hearing. He wanted me to tell him where Anthony was. He wanted to know if I had heard from him. I tried to be pleasant. I couldn't answer any of his questions. First, it would be unethical, and second, because I didn't know where Anthony was."

"I don't think Anthony will call you," said Tom. "If he does, you have to tell Anthony to turn himself in. You can make arrangements for his return to jail but you cannot give him any other advice."

"I understand." Tom had 15 years more experience practicing law than Roger and he always gave freely of his advice to his partner.

"Any news on where Anthony is located?" asked Tom.

"No idea. Where are you now?"

"I'm going to Dangriga to get photographs of the pier and dock and more photos of the lime rock hills near the pier and more lime rock samples to verify the quality of the rock near the pier for use as road gravel. Bob Barnes asked me to do it for him."

"Does Bob have a backhaul, a cargo for the ship that will bring the gravel to the states?" Roger was always trying to sound like an engineer, but he did not know what he was talking about usually.

You need a product that the ship can haul back to Belize after unloading the gravel in the USA.

"That will be the real issue. You need a backhaul to reduce the cost of transport of the gravel. Belize imports very little. It is a very small market. The backhaul would have to be something the whole Caribbean region needs. I was thinking maybe pre-fab housing. Pre-fabricated housing was an idea Bob and Albert were floating to replace the termite ridden housing in Belize City. I will try to talk to the housing minister while I am here to see if there is an interest."

"You know," said Roger, "some company in New Jersey is trying to dump barrels of toxic waste in Guyana. Maybe nuclear waste would be an option." Roger was laughing.

"I don't think toxic waste is a viable backhaul," said Tom. "I have to go and get on the road ahead of the tanker truck. I will try to call you in the morning."

"Be safe," said Roger.

Chapter 22

Tom filled up the tank of the Chrysler. He did not want to be stuck on the Hummingbird Highway without fuel. The rental car was a full size sedan with four doors. He had the attendant check the oil and the pressure of all tires, including the spare. It wasn't unusual to blow a tire on the Hummingbird because the road was in such bad shape due to the environment. In the mountains it rained most every day. The water infiltrated the asphalt and the asphalt deteriorated allowing the rainwater to dissolve the lime rock road base and a pothole formed. At first the holes were small and they caused the car to shudder from the impact of the tire with the hole. But then the pothole spread and an entire section of the road would lose its macadam shield and you could slide off the road surface and into real trouble because you were in the mountains.

From Belmopan to Dangriga you were heading east-southeast along the northern edge of the mountains. The Coxcomb basin is to your right and Victoria Peak is in the Coxcomb. Viewed from space the basin appeared to be formed by an asteroid. It was like a crater. Tom was aware that it was a haven for wildlife, and had the largest concentration of jaguar in Central and Middle America. Tom had never visited the Coxcomb, only driven by it. He would visit it one day.

All of Belize south of the Hummingbird Highway should, in Tom's opinion, be preserved. It was naturally wild and sparsely inhabited. The residents were used to the meager existence the jungle provided and the residents were not enemies of the jaguar.

"Damn," said Tom. Ahead on the road was a tanker truck heading to the coast. Tom was only 16 kilometers from the capital. It would take five hours to complete the trip.

"I might as well turn off and see the sights," Tom said out loud. He was talking to himself now. Tom was located near a large Blue Hole. He could take a swim. Since he was a kid Tom knew to pack a swimsuit. You never knew when you could take a swim. In the tropics it was the only way to cool off.

After staring at the rear bumper of the tanker truck for half an hour, Tom saw the marker on the road for the natural attraction and he pulled off the road.

Belize was blessed with two blue holes. One was in the coastal reef near San Pedro, offshore in the Caribbean Sea from Ambergris Caye. That hole is more famous than the one near the Hummingbird. The blue hole in the Caribbean Sea was formed in a prior Ice Age when lime rock dissolved and a hole formed containing fresh water. When the sea rose after the ice receded, the hole was left offshore and it contained fresh and saltwater. Blue holes in the sea are distinct for their deep blue color.

The other type of blue hole like the one on the Hummingbird was formed when a sinkhole was caused by the collapse of an underground river channel. This type of blue hole is turquoise in color. The site of the hole would strike the visitor as being primeval but for the concrete steps that carried you to the 100 meter wide pool. These concrete steps covered stone steps that were placed by the Mayans. The site of the blue hole also has a cave named after St. Herman. The blue hole was deserted. Tom changed into his swim suit and slipped into the water. Afterward Tom explored the cave to the point a half mile underground. There was a warning sign that one should not venture further. Tom walked back to the hole and took another swim. He then sat on the edge of the pool and observed the shrubs, bushes, vines, trees and flowers. The area was a bird habitat. Among other birds, he saw a pair of toucans out for their morning meal of seeds from a fig tree.

With nothing better to do, Tom began to consider the complications Anthony could make in Tom's life. Anthony had come to him to handle a problem registering his ships. Anthony's problem involving the two ships was a business matter. Tom was charging an hourly rate. But the core legal issue shifted when he was arrested for the theft of an airplane.

The facts:

A deputy sheriff in Bushton, a small city, the county seat of Summer County, Florida noticed a plane buzzing the private airport on the outskirts of the city and the deputy went to investigate. The deputy was suspicious because it was 2:00 a.m. and the tower at the airport was closed.

When he got to the flight deck there was an unmanned Cessna airplane parked with the door ajar. The engine cowling of the plane was warm. The deputy waited by the plane and then a man came out of the shadows. It was Anthony.

"This your plane?" asked the deputy.

"Sorry officer, I had to use the toilet." Anthony was tucking his shirt into his shorts.

The deputy could see inside the plane. There was a fuel bladder in place of the co-pilot seat. The bladder would allow the plane to hold additional fuel so it could fly further. The deputy felt this was probably a plane used to transport drugs. The deputy guessed cocaine. Anthony started to walk away.

"Stay here," said the deputy, "I need to talk to you."

Anthony stopped and said, "I know this seems odd, it being the middle of the night and all, but this is not my plane, I'm not the pilot and I don't have a license to fly a plane. I have a car over by the hanger and I want to leave."

"Well ... don't leave yet," said the deputy. "What's your name and address?"

"Tony," said Anthony.

"Are you from around here? Do you have ID?"

"No ... not on me."

There was a wallet on the dash of the plane. "This your wallet?"

"No," said Anthony.

The deputy reached for the wallet and inspected it. There was a license in the wallet for a man named Anthony Arnold. The man pictured on the license looked like Anthony except the man had a full beard. The deputy told Anthony he was under arrest for trespassing at the private airfield and he could post bond after he provided proof of his identity.

"I think you are violating my rights," said Anthony. "I don't even have a license to fly an airplane. I want to go home. I haven't done anything wrong."

"I'm arresting you for trespass. The Prosecutor can decide what to do with any charges involving the plane."

Of course, most everything Anthony said to the deputy was true except it was Anthony's wallet. He had gone in the bushes to relieve himself. His name was Tony, he was not the pilot, he didn't have a license in the US to fly and he didn't own the plane. But Anthony was not innocent. The plane was stolen. He was fixing the fuel bladder because it was leaking and the plane was going to fly to Belize once the bladder was repaired to transport cocaine back to the USA. The pilot ran from the scene when the police officer arrived and Anthony was left with the plane.

***

When Anthony spoke to Tom about the arrest he never deviated from the version of the story that Anthony thought would provide Tom with evidence there was a reasonable doubt that he did not steal the airplane. He denied knowing anything about the plane. Tom felt Anthony's story was weak. But, why should Tom, his attorney, know the truth? Tom knew most criminal clients lied to their attorney for fear if they told them they were guilty the attorney would not work as hard for the client. Most attorneys refuse to believe their clients. The worst strategy is to put your client on the stand to try to explain away their apparent guilt; ninety percent of the time the clients were tripped up by the prosecutor. A jury could see right through their lies.

In Tom's view, Anthony's best defense was that there was no probable cause for his arrest for trespass. Upon investigation, Tom's investigator discovered that though the tower was closed, the airport was open for air traffic if there was an emergency or the plane needed a place to land. The prosecutor realized he had problems with the case. Tom argued the theft charge should be dismissed because the arrest was illegal and all of the evidence collected as a result of the arrest (the wallet and the airplane and the statements made by Anthony to the deputy) was inadmissible.

John Hale, the prosecutor offered Anthony probation. Tom thought the offer was generous. Anthony had prior convictions for drug possession and if he was convicted he could be sentenced to 30 years in the state penitentiary.

But Anthony refused the offer of probation. He did not want any restrictions on his freedom to travel. If he was on probation he would have to obtain permission to leave the state..

Anthony had not told Tom he had no intention of resolving the charge for anything less than an acquittal by the jury or a nol pros by the prosecutor. Tom had cashed Anthony's retainer check and filed his notice of appearance with the clerk, Tom realized he had made a mistake taking Anthony's case, but there was nothing he could do about it then. Anthony had no intention to listen to Tom's sage advice that Anthony change his plea for probation.

Anthony also rejected Tom's advice that they file a motion to suppress the evidence and appeal the judge's ruling if the motion was denied. Anthony insisted he wanted a trial by jury and a chance to take the stand and convince the jury he was innocent. Tom was stuck with Anthony. He had no ability to force Anthony to enter a plea The judge would not let Tom withdraw as Anthony's lawyer simply because Anthony was insisting he would testify and convince the jury he had nothing to do with the stolen plane. Anthony's story was incomprehensible and unbelievable. But every defendant had a right to lie to their attorney and to lie in their defense to the jury.

***

After his swim, Tom headed back to the Chrysler. Two teenagers were at his car. It looked like they might be considering whether to steal the car. "Need a ride?" Tom offered.

"Please," they said.

Tom drove them to the next left turn on the road. There was a sign on the driveway giving directions to an orange grove. The Belize temple oranges were in season. They were specially bred for the climate and their juice. They were very sweet. The orange juice was processed into concentrate and shipped to Florida and the concentrate was mixed into juice from Florida oranges to sweeten the drink.

Tom spoke to the owner and bought two bushels of oranges.

The owner thanked Tom for bringing the kids back home. "They can get in trouble on the road." Parents everywhere worry for their children. Tom and the father shook hands. Tom found almost all Belizeans to be very friendly.

Back in the car, Tom motored out onto the Hummingbird Highway. He had traveled only 25 kilometers and four hours had elapsed. Tom had nothing scheduled, so what was the worry? Tom always felt relaxed in Belize. He was particularly at ease as a pair of Red Macaws flew above him chattering away as he took in the sound and color of the jungle.

Then Tom's pleasant thoughts were interrupted. This Anthony is a real problem, Tom thought. The last time they were in court, Anthony was studying a Spanish/American dictionary.

"What's the point of the dictionary?" asked Tom.

"Just brushing up on my Spanish," said Anthony with a smile on his face.

Tom should have known Anthony intended to skip bail. He as much as said so with the dictionary.

Anthony was mistaken if he thought he could just run away from the authorities. After his arrest, Anthony made his bail by paying a 10% premium of the amount of the bond to a bondsman.

The appearance bond was $100,000. It was a hefty amount of bond. But John Hale, the prosecutor, wasn't buying the story that Anthony had nothing to do with the plane – that he was just using the facilities. The prosecutor thought Anthony could be squeezed for information on the drug trade. Thus, they set a high bond. Prosecutor Hale had also charged Anthony with theft of personal property with a value over $250,000 (it was an expensive plane) which carried a penalty of 30 years' incarceration in the State Penitentiary. Because the possible sentence for the charge was so significant, the bondsman was concerned Anthony would run. If Anthony ran the bondsman would have to pay the court the full amount of the bond which was $100,000. The bondsman wanted to take no chances, so Anthony was required to pay the bond premium of $10,000 and collateral of $50,000 cash, and agree not to leave the State of Florida without the permission of the bondsman.

Anthony claimed he had to be able to leave Florida without notice for business. To obtain the bondsman's permission to travel, he gave $50,000 cash in additional collateral. In total he paid $100,000 to the bondsman, and he paid another $25,000 to the bond company.

Then once Anthony paid the $135,000 he took his boats out in the Gulf of México with the help of the Hondurans and Jorge Mendez, intending to escape.

The police were watching the boats. The US Coast Guard stopped the boats for an inspection, but they were trying to find Anthony on the boats. Anthony escaped the Coast Guard by jumping overboard in diving gear and hid under the diving chamber (the moon pool) he built into the hull of the vessel. The coast guardsmen couldn't find him anywhere on the boat and had to release the vessels because there was no maritime lien on the boats and the crew had proper paperwork for the vessels. After the US Coast Guard left, Anthony came out of hiding but stayed below decks until they made port at Key Largo, Florida. In Key Largo, Jorge contacted the Bounty Hunter and ratted on Anthony.

Then, they had bad luck. They ran into an intense low pressure storm, a hurricane that forced the vessels into port in the bay at Punta Rosa and they had to wait out the storm.

Bad news became worse when the Bounty Hunter's men showed up and arrested Anthony and took him to Cancún. Then the Bounty Hunter flew him to Miami in his black Lear Jet and Anthony was back in jail and $135,000 poorer and his ships were in Central America.

After Anthony had jumped bond the court had no sympathy. No bond was set on the theft charge.

When Anthony talked to Tom after he was returned to jail, Anthony told Tom he was convinced that someone on his crew "ratted him out" to the Bounty Hunter. Anthony was very upset. Tom had difficulty redirecting Anthony's thinking to the important issue. Anthony had no choice now. He had to contest the charges. Tom advised he would need money for a defense.

"I can get money if I can get the boats to Ambergris Caye," said Anthony.

Tom then told Anthony that he had spoken to the Bounty Hunter. He explained that only the dive boat was operational and the Bounty Hunter had offered his services to retrieve the boat.

The Bounty Hunter said he had the right men to move the boats if Anthony could get a permit to move the boats out of Mexican waters.

Anthony considered the offer then asked Tom: "You have legitimate connections in the Yucatán. I will pay you like it was business, on an hourly basis. You will have to get a permit from the Mexican Navy to move the boats. I'm desperate. Do you think you can do it?"

"I can do it. I can get the permit from the navy," said Tom. "But why do you care about the boat?"

"Everything I worked for my whole life is in that boat. I have to get it back."

Tom was off to México.

Tom couldn't really understand why the boat was so important to Anthony. The boat was built for diving and was unique for the diving chamber that allowed a diver to enter the water from inside the vessel. Tom thought this odd. Why not just jump overboard? But if you thought about it, the diving chamber would allow a diver to transfer contraband secretly from another ship to Anthony's vessel without anyone above water observing what was happening. You could move drugs or gold or whatever, secretly, under water.

Tom had obtained the permit. Anthony had gotten his one boat to San Pedro. Now Anthony had escaped.

As Tom drove down the Hummingbird Highway, Tom was convinced, particularly since Anthony had escaped again, that there was something of great value hidden in the dive boat that Anthony had built, and Anthony intended to retrieve it.

Tom thought like a lawyer. He was issue oriented. "If I stay away from Anthony's dive boat I will avoid Anthony. If I avoid Anthony, I will stay away from trouble."

The thought was logical. But was it realistic?

Chapter 23

The trip to Dangriga was uneventful. Tom passed by the intersection for the Southern Highway which allowed passage to the coastal plain and the sparse resources to the South. The Southern Highway deadended in the jungle about 100 kilometers south at the border with Guatemala. This area was swamp and jungle with no more development than skidder and logging trails. The Southern Highway was a test for your internal organs. Riding over the lime rock, washboard road was like enduring repeated kidney punches. Tom had been down the highway only once to see the virgin pine stump operation at the port of Big Creek. The port was nothing more than a wharf and dock where virgin pine stumps and roots were collected from the Stan Creek province and shipped to Brunswick, Georgia for processing. The black liquor facility was now closed. It had been the major source for employment in the South of Belize. the only other related industries involved logging Hondurean pine.

Tom was happy he didn't have to face that road. He thought that the port at Big Creek could offer a logical location to process lime rock into gravel and load a ship for passage to Houston, New Orleans, or Tampa, but he already knew what it looked like and he had taken plenty of photographs of the site. The problem again with the gravel was the lack of a backhaul from the richest country in the world to some of the poorest in Central America. Closer to Dangriga, Belize was constructing a road to the North along the coast to connect Belize City with Dangriga and the Southern Highway. But another highway seemed to be an empty enterprise because it would be a road to nowhere. The only asset between Dangriga and Belize City was the environment, the jungle and the animals and trees and plants. But this asset was just now being recognized for its importance. Tom's clients didn't see it yet. Tom felt saving the environment was the right thing to do, but the environment was not seen to be an asset. Like gold or silver, water and oxygen were assets. Trees equaled water and oxygen.

Dangriga was as Tom remembered. The Hummingbird dead-ended at the coast. He took his photos of the small pier. The coast was shallow. You would have to push rock out to sea 500 meters to get to a sufficient depth to land a ship with the necessary draft to carry the gravel to a cement plant in the states. It probably wouldn't work. It would be very expensive. Tom shrugged.

That's not my decision, thought Tom. It's a business decision for Barnes Lime Rock.

Walking back to his car Tom collected a group of children who were curious about the stranger and trailed behind him. The kids were walking carrying cheap, local, sugary soft drinks. They were like addicts with their bottles. Tom said "Hello." They took the bottles from their lips and smiled. No teeth, thought Tom. In place of their teeth were black buds. Their baby teeth were all rotted to a nub by the sugar in the soft drinks.

Tom went in a small general store and asked the time. Tom did not carry or wear a watch. No one in the store knew the exact time but they were sure it was after 2:00 p.m.

"You taking pictures of the dock and the hills and the rocks?" asked the owner of the store.

"Yes, I'm trying to get some information. They might build a mine down here."

"That true? We could use a little luck in the south of the country. There is not much business since the powder company closed up."

"Has anyone seen the tanker heading back to Belmopan?" asked Tom. He should not have said anything about the mine. It would probably just raise false hopes. Bob and Albert Barnes were having difficulty making a success out of Barnes Lime Rock in the state of Florida and were considering moving operations to Central America.

The men in the store all agreed the tanker had not left yet. Two of the men in the store wanted a ride to Belmopan. "Get in. I'm leaving now," said Tom. The men got their backpacks into the trunk of the car with the two bushel baskets of Temple oranges.

Tom invited the men to take an orange. They looked hungry. The men were happy to get a lift. They would go to Belmopan and look for work, they said.

***

Tom dropped the men off at the bus stop in Belmopan. Tom tried to engage the men, but they were very quiet during the trip. Tom ultimately decided they were from El Salvador. They were probably refugees from the war. They spoke little English and Tom spoke no Spanish. Tom had been coming to Central America for five years and he had not taken the time to learn even a few words.

The reason Tom felt the two men were Salvadorans was the interest the men showed in the refugees camped along the road as they got closer to Belmopan.

In the West of Belize, Salvadorans had built rough huts along the side of the road. Displaced families squatted there. They burned the hillsides and planted corn – subsistence farming. The immigrants had been camped along the road for two years, putting great stress on Belize's social system. The war in El Salvador left many dead. Tom didn't want to criticize the US government, but it seemed to him that most of the people who were killed were innocents who were caught up in the conflict.

Tom was surprised the Salvadorian men were on the coast. They were probably trying to get as far to the east as they could and become a member of a ship crew and head to the United States. They got to Dangriga and found no big ships in the south on the coast and they wanted to head north. But there was no road north from Dangriga. So they had to go back to Belmopan to find a road heading to Belize City.

It was 6:00 p.m. It was still light when Tom pulled into Belmopan. He dropped the men at the bus stop and gave them a bag of oranges and a few Belize Dollars he had in his pocket. The men gave Tom a big smile in return for the kindness. Tom would go to the Bull Frog Inn and use the communal shower and change for a meal and a good night's sleep.

Chapter 24

The Bull Frog Inn was a small hotel. It had ten rooms and primarily housed business people and foreign visitors who intended to visit members of the legislative and executive branches of government.

The Bull Frog served native food. Chicken dishes and fresh fish dinners. The dining area was simple. You sat on white wooden benches at white wooden tables. If the restaurant was busy you would be seated at a table with a stranger. No problem – you would make friends or eat in silence.

Tom checked in with the desk clerk while he waited to be seated for dinner. The clerk had his American funds, all in one hundred dollar bills. Herbert had taken $500 for his fee and provided an itemized bill accounting for his time. There was also a promissory note for $10,000 US and a copy of the bill of sale. Hubert would hold the original bill of sale until James Shaheen paid the balance of the sales price for the turpentine still and its equipment in the Mountain Pine Ridge.

Tom thanked the desk clerk and paid for another night's lodging and returned to the dining area. The tables were set in an area that had a sturdy roof and a concrete floor. The room had a partial wall that extended about two and one half feet from the floor and there was unscreened open space from the top of the wall to the ceiling (Tom's guess was that perhaps the owner ran out of money before he could purchase windows for the open area. But it would be impolite to ask.)

Since there were no screens there was the potential for mosquito attacks. The restaurant used citronella candles to keep the mosquitoes away. The smoke was very effective. It's scent was pushed around the room by ceiling fans that turned slowly. The interior of the room was decorated with blooming bromeliads and orchids that had been foraged by the staff from the wilds in the vicinity. Tom was unable to identify the individual plants except to know when they were bromeliads and when they were orchids. He could identify only two orchids. One orchid in Belize, the black orchid, was the official flower of the country. Florida had many wild orchids. Tom was only familiar with one, the Florida Ghost Orchid. One had been pointed out to him in a ditch near the Tamiami Trail through the Everglades. The Florida orchid was rare. The plant had no leaves and so it only became visible when it bloomed. It was fragile and did not live if you tried to transplant it, probably because it relied on the Giant Sphinx Moth with its six inch proboscis for propagation. You needed the two to tango, and both were rare.

The flowers in the room were exotic with vivid colors. The blooms were unrecognizable to even the eye of the native. The beauty of the plants and their blooms were taken for granted by the citizens. When Tom sat down he pulled the Black Orchid on his table over for a closer view. You never saw anything like this plant outside of the hotels in New York City or Chicago or Toronto.

Tom ordered fresh fish. The fish was marinated in salt, pepper, and sugar cane syrup and then smoked. It was coated in plantain chips and then roasted in an iron skillet before serving. The fish, a trout, was served with black beans and yellow rice. There was a fruit salad of slices of papaya and cantaloupe and various chunks of melon, and mango balls. Tom was offered a rum drink but he deferred, as he was not drinking alcohol, though he was tempted to drink the local beer whose brand name was Belican Beer. He settled for a seltzer water. He seasoned the fish and the rice and beans with Melinda's hot sauce. He ate slowly. There was no television and he had nothing to do before turning in except to make notes of his thoughts regarding the viability of a gravel and cement factory using the native lime rock in the vicinity of

Dangriga, or at the old Laughton Powder Company plant at Big Creek. In Big Creek a dock and wharf already existed that would accommodate a big ship.

In his notes to his client he suggested the client consider manufacturing the cement from the shell deposits near Big Creek and mixing in the gavel and bagging the products for sale in México and the United States, Tom was careful to give a disclaimer that this was merely a suggestion. The decision to build a factory was a business decision, not a legal decision, and Tom was a lawyer, not a business man.

Tom followed dinner with tea. He made small talk with the waitress. Tom found that as a foreigner he had little chance for conversation with a Belizean woman. The waitress was very pretty with light brown skin and black, wavy hair and black eyes. She wore ear rings that dangled in the lobes of her ears and they would bounce softly as she walked to the table carrying the meal.

Tom tried to interest the waitress. He suggested he would leave the light on for her. The woman gave him a look and said, "Don't be silly, you will be gone in the morning."

Tom nodded and said, "True, but we could have a wonderful time." He brushed her hand as she lifted a dish.

Tom was unattached. He still loved Marla, but he had not seen her in three years. She was in New York City now and married. Romance now came to Tom in brief interludes. The time between each contact had lengthened.

The woman said nothing more. They both knew that if Tom had an itch, there was a brothel in Belize City. Tom had been there. The front of the brothel was a bar. It was very raucous. The music was Mexican, plaintiff and loud. The prostitutes plied their trade in stalls which were divided in a large room behind the bar. The men paid for sex or to watch others have sex. It was not to Tom's taste. The girls were Guatemalan teenagers trying to earn passage to the US. The "johns" were old men and young boys.

Tom was not interested in sex under these circumstances or in voyeurism. Tom was interested in more than a roll in the hay.

Tom tipped the waitress at the Bull Frog and went to his room alone. It had been a long day and Tom was tired. He would leave early to meet the ministers in Belize City in the morning if they would see him. Tom hoped Hubert Johns would be able to intervene and set a meeting. Tom tried to set meetings but the ministers from the newly elected government would leave him sitting in the waiting room with a bunch of insurgents and Communists who were the government's new constituents and had voted the new party into office. The ministers would speak to everyone, including the maintenance workers, before seeing what he had to say. He had to rely on his attorney to obtain an appointment. Tom felt there was little chance that he would be given access to present his client's ideas for housing and a new lime rock mine in the south even though he believed that these projects would improve the lot of some of the poorest people in the world.

Instead, Tom would be ignored by the new government and he would be left to drum up some excuse for the trip to Belize. He would find Jamie to see if he had any success selling his air conditioners and see how Rick was doing with the maintenance of his plane.

After speaking with the waitress and being rebuffed, Tom was depressed and ready to go home. But just in case the waitress changed her mind, he left the light on outside his room at the Bullfrog Inn.

Chapter 25

Tom re-fueled his tank at the ESSO station before leaving for his meetings with the Solicitor General and the Public Works Administrator in Belize City. He checked the oil fluids and tires, again including the spare, and then left for the trip to Belize City. He was able to wrangle a thermos of coffee from the cook at the Bull Frog in trade for a bushel of oranges that Tom purchased at the grove on the Hummingbird near the Blue Hole.

It was 8:00 a.m. EST and 7:00 a.m. in Belize. The road to Belize City was being repaved and a driver had to take it slow. As Tom proceeded, the landscape began to change from forest to brush as the elevation dropped heading to the coastal plain. The plants took on a yellow orange twinge and there were more and more patches of dirt that were uncovered with no vegetation except for Spanish swords, a plant like the agave. There were homesteads where hearty souls were attempting to obtain a living from the ungiving soil. The homesteads were normally about 50 acres and owners primarily grew palms for copra and cooking oil.

A few of the farmers appeared to be successful. Their houses were made of concrete block covered with plaster and they had an automobile and trucks in the yard.

Probably because Tom was looking at the scenery and not the road, he misjudged a curve and the Chrysler left the road, the tires hit a muddy slope in the right of way and the car spun one full circle and impacted a pile of wet soil that had been scraped from the road by a grader during construction. Luckily, Tom was going slowly and the impact did not cause Tom an injury, and the car was still running.

Tom reversed gear and was able to get the car back on the road, but there was a terrible noise coming from the engine.

Tom got out of the car and raised the hood. He could see that the radiator fan was turning but it was hitting the cowling that had been bent when the front of the car hit the pile of dirt.

The car would overheat if the fan was not able to spin. So Tom turned off the engine and took time to look around. In the distance off the side of the road he saw a man standing beside a truck with a shotgun resting on his shoulder. As Tom walked toward the man he saw that there was a fence and a gate and about 300 meters from the gate there was an outcropping of lime rock and a grove of eucalyptus trees. Tucked into the trees and rock there was what appeared to be a secure government building. Tom thought maybe it was a small prison.

"You have some trouble?" asked the man with the "boom stick". Shotguns were legally carried and possessed by anyone in Belize. Handguns and rifles were illegal except in the possession of the Belize Defense Force or sworn police officers or the British Army.

"My car went off the road. I need to get into Belize City to meet with the Solicitor General. My car isn't drivable." Tom looked around. "What is this place?"

"The crazy house," said the guard. "This is the insane asylum at Ladyville. We have a phone to the city. You can call the minister's office from here."

Tom and the guard walked to the building. There was a large room at the front with metal bars in the large open windows to prevent the escape of the inmates. Inside the room were human beings that looked like escapees from an asylum in the 16th century.

"Stay away from the windows. They will spit on you."

Tom stayed back. The guard opened a door that led to the lobby. Tom was taken to a room. He took out the small directory he always carried and dialed the home number for the Solicitor

General. The minister personally answered the phone on the second ring. "Ola," said the minister.

"Minister, this is Tom Night. I have an appointment with you this morning at 11:00 a.m. but I had an accident with my car on the way."

"Where are you?"

"I'm at the insane asylum in Ladyville."

That's a good place for you, thought the minister. "Is anyone there from the hospital I can speak with?"

Tom handed the phone to the guard.

"Yes sir," the guard spoke into the phone and then hung up. "I'm to take you to the City so you can meet with him on time. Can your car be driven a short distance to this building?" he asked.

Tom nodded.

They left to move Tom's car and after it was secured at the building and the keys given to a nurse, the guard and Tom left in the guard's truck and drove to the city.

The ride was bumpy. The guard said very little. He did say that he had to get back to the hospital as soon as he could. Today was visitor's day. Tom misunderstood at first, thinking the visitors were friends and family of the inmates. But no, the visitors were members of the public who came to gawk at the patients. The visitors paid to see the inmates. The guard said it was quite a show.

Chapter 26

The guard from the asylum drove Tom to the Solicitor General's house in the city. The home was in a modest neighborhood. The Solicitor General's house was not large or ostentatious. None of the government cabinet members lived lavishly. The Prime Minister's house was a hovel built up on stilts. The only difference from the PM's house and his neighbors was that there was a guard box and sentry and a new government car at the home.

The guard left Tom at the minister's door. He knocked.

The door was answered by a white man in his 50's. He was fit, probably a retiree from the British forces. Tom knew the man. He was the one who threw Tom out at the request of the Solicitor General when Tom last visited. Tom had been ousted because he yelled at the minister. He could be passionate at times and he had begun to yell to make his point. The Solicitor General threw him out.

"I'm not going to have any trouble with you, am I?" asked the man, who was the minister's bodyguard.

"You will get none from me. If you want me to leave, just tell me. There was no reason to throw me out bodily the last time I saw the minister."

"You were raising your voice and I was told to remove you." Tom had been physically manhandled by the security officer and pushed out the door.

The bodyguard patted Tom down for a weapon.

"That is not necessary. I do not have a weapon."

The guard completed the search and then led Tom into a back room that contained a large desk and two chairs. The minister stood up and motioned for Tom to have a seat.

The Solicitor General was short, overweight and his features were European – Spanish, but a dark complexion.

"What do you want to see me about?" asked the minister in a most officious tone. He was ready for an argument.

"I intend to file suit in the World Court against Belize regarding the licenses that have been appropriated from my clients. As you know, we have lost the ability to harvest timber, naval stores, chicle, and turpentine. My clients also hold long term leases on over 600,000 acres of land, and we are unable to sublet the leases because the Government has filed liens and claims against our rights in the land."

"The Government had every right to take this action. Your clients have failed to live up to the terms of the lease and the licenses. You don't pay the rent, Mr. Night."

"I agree, Minister, that my clients have failed to make payment for the leases and license, but your Government transferred my clients' rights to the resources to Belize citizens. According to the official property records we no longer own the licenses and the leases. In fact, the property cards show that you, personally, were the government agent who signed the documents transferring the rights away from my client."

"Your clients have failed to fund the operations here. You have not paid your employees their wages and they have not paid the Treasury for the resources that were shipped out of the country."

"We can't make payment for resources or for salaries if we do not have a right to export the resources. Be reasonable, Minister."

"The Government feels your clients were given the right to the resources at too cheap a price by the last administration. The Country has expenses that have to be paid. There was no provision for inflation in the agreements."

This was the real bone of contention. The government wanted more money.

"How much more are you looking for?" Tom expected this. The world had experienced a bout of inflation.

"A 25% increase in the price your clients pay for rents and residuals would be fair."

"We can't do that," said Tom "That is too much. My clients could not make a profit."

"What are you going to spend suing us? If you go to court, you will have an expense. And your clients may lose. They would have more expense. And your clients' equipment will not be protected by our police while you wait for a decision in the court system. Delay, it is yet another expense," said the minister.

"We expect to win the suit and when we do the Country will pay our fees and costs." Tom paused. "I have some authority to negotiate. We can pay an across the board increase of rents and residuals of 5%. But the contracts need to be rewritten so the next administration does not ask for an increase just because there has been a change in the Government. We would agree to an inflation index that would allow an increase for inflation, capped at 3% a year."

"We will agree to a one-time increase of 15%. We will take nothing less. You will also have to pay the expense of the lawyers."

"Ten percent and we split the fees," said Tom.

"We will agree to 10% but your clients pay all expenses of the transaction and a 2% cap for inflation annually," said the minister.

"Done," said Tom.

The minister said, "We will seal the deal with a Belican Beer."

"I agree. However I am not sure about the beer. It will be the first drink of alcohol I have had in over a year."

"You do not drink alcohol?" The minister understood Tom was an alcoholic when he admitted he should not drink the beer. "You like coffee?"

"Yes."

"Then I will make it. Come with me," said the minister.

They went to a back room which served as a kitchen. The minister took a handful of the dark beans and filled the top of a hand grinder. He turned the crank, then loaded the percolator with the ground coffee. The two men stood and spoke while the coffee brewed.

"You know that diving ship you have at San Pedro has some problems," said the minister. "It's not here legally. It will have to be moved or it will be confiscated."

"I was unaware of that." Tom did not want to get into a conversation about the dive boat. "It's not my ship; my only involvement with the ship was to obtain the permit that allowed the ship out of Mexican waters."

"Why is the dive boat here in Belize?" The minister saw Tom was uncomfortable speaking about the subject so the minister pressed on.

"The ship needs repairs. It came to San Pedro because that is the closest port to make the repairs. It is being refitted at the marina. Is there no exception that will allow the vessel to stay while it is being repaired?"

"Probably ... if that was the only problem." The minister paused. "The Mexican police believe one of the crewmen on the ship was murdered.

"Really."

"They say it was a Mexican crewman – that he was drowned intentionally as the ship came out of México. We are trying to determine who has jurisdiction over the case, México or Belize."

"Well ...," This was the first Tom heard about a murder investigation and Tom was shaken by the news.

The minister interrupted, seeing Tom's concern and said: "You are not a suspect. All the witnesses say you obtained the permit from the Admiral in Cancún and then you went to Punta Rosa. Then you returned to Cancún in the pontoon plane and returned to the US. I was actually hoping we could establish probable cause to arrest you." There was a big smile on the minister's face.

"Thanks," said Tom.

"It would have been great fun to arrest you. There would have been much publicity." The minister set out cups and crème and sugar for the coffee.

"It would not be appropriate to prosecute an innocent man," said Tom with a half of a smile on his face. Tom had visited the jail in Belize. It too, like the mental hospital, was a throw-back to the 1600s. It had no roof above the cells and there were shards of glass imbedded in the top of the walls so a prisoner who tried to escape would be severely cut trying to overtop the walls. Tom did not want to wait for his trial in the prison should he be arrested.

"Do you know that I am acquainted with Anthony Arnold?" The minister sat down. "I represented him before I was appointed solicitor. He is a superior mechanic. I think he learned how to fix and construct machines in prison. The prison system in your country is very harsh. He was incarcerated at hard labor when he was 18 and was paroled when he was 30. It was for a minor offence involving the marijuana trade." As the minister spoke he motioned vigorously with his hands to make a point that he had sympathy for drug smugglers. On the walls of the kitchen Tom noticed numerous certificates showing that the minister had been granted reciprocal rights to practice law in US District court in the federal courts in Florida. Tom realized the minister was 'for real'. He knew his way around a courtroom.

Tom sat down, more relaxed. The minister's bodyguard was dismissed. "Anthony and I met after he was arrested for the theft of a plane," said Tom. "I got him out of jail on bond. I guess he didn't trust the system and he took matters into his own hands and ran."

"Or maybe he was guilty." The minister poured the coffee. "Anthony is a great diver. He spent a couple of years diving for Mayan treasure near Punta Rosa."

"I was unaware of that," said Tom.

"He was diving there in the Cozumel Channel searching for treasure from the Grijalva Expedition. "

"I am not familiar with the expedition." Tom was interested. This was the first time he had any hint that his client was something more than a common thief.

"Grijalva was a conquistador who commanded four vessels in 1518 and sailed from Cuba to the Yucatán and then the Bay of Campeche where his men were in a battle with the Indians at the Isla de Sacrificios.

"Then they sailed back to the Yucatán and south to Punta Rosa. It is believed that the Grijalva expedition was very successful and that the Spanish obtained gold bars and many items made of gold. There were masks, fish hooks, earrings, suits of armor, necklaces, a jaguar head and many stones and cloaks and shields made of feathers. There were secret records kept of the discovery by the crew that were found by researchers in Spain about ten years ago. Anthony paid the researcher for the translation of the records.

"The reason the records were kept secret was that the expedition was paid for by the Governor of Cuba, Diego Velasquez, who would share in the find. The men on the expedition would also owe a share of their treasure to the King and Queen of Spain. According to legend, Grijalva and his men left a cache of gold buried in Punta Rosa and cheated the Governor and the King out of their share. Anthony told me that he had a map to help locate the treasure."

The minister continued, "It was thought that Anthony discovered the treasure at Punta Rosa. Anthony left Punta Rosa quietly and moved to Belize City. I had represented him here in Belize. He fixed a number of planes that were later confiscated because they were transporting drugs. He claimed he was owed a fee for repair work on the planes. The police always objected to his claims. The police were trying to obtain the planes at forfeiture hearings. I represented him and we split the recovery if we won. Our partnership was quite lucrative."

"Do you know if Anthony is back in Belize?" asked Tom. "I was told on the phone yesterday that he escaped from jail in Florida."

"I think he may be in Belize," said the minister. "You should know that he is not wanted by my office if the only charge he faces is the charge that he escaped from a jail in Florida. He hasn't been convicted of that charge in Florida and we would not recognize the foreign warrant. Extradition from here to Florida would fail. That is why the Bounty Hunter in the black Lear jet is making so much money. None of the governments here in Central America will arrest the defendants that run before trial in the courts in Florida. The governments refuse to return the drug traffickers that escape from the US to Central America. So the bondsmen have to pay the Bounty Hunter to kidnap the wanted men and to return them to the States."

"But Anthony escaped from jail. Isn't escape an extraditable offence?" asked Tom.

"No. To extradite there has to be a conviction, or the sheriff from Florida would have to bring witnesses to the court in Belize to prove the charge beyond a reasonable doubt. We will not accept an affidavit or an arrest warrant. We would require live testimony. Also there is the matter of the body ..." The minister's voice trailed off as though he had said too much. Then he continued. "So if you see Anthony, give him this card." The minister took a business card, from his pocket and gave it to Tom. "Mr. H. Patel is an excellent attorney, particularly in matters involving extradition cases. He is well liked in the courts and by my office. He will provide Mr. Arnold with good representation."

"I know Mr. Patel by name only. I will give the card to Anthony, but I do not expect to see him," said Tom. "I will no longer represent him since he escaped."

"You will see him here in Belize. I feel sure of it. Give him the card. The murder charge will complicate matters. The police in

México are taking heat from the dead man's family. The poor fellow's brother is an important man in Quintana Roo. The brother is the Chief of Police of Cancún."

"Do they have the body of the victim?" asked Tom.

"Not yet."

"Is the body required to establish the corpus delecti in México?"

"Yes," said the Solicitor General.

"So Anthony may be free if the authorities do not find the body. They need a dead body to prove the crime occurred."

"Yes." The minister agreed.

Tom took a gulp of coffee. He felt like he was being tricked into making incriminating statements by the minister. He needed to change the subject. "Minister, I have two other matters. First I need to know if the country would be open to granting a license to mine gravel from the Stan Creek District either at Big Creek or Dangriga. I have a meeting with the Minister of the Interior after this regarding that matter."

"We had heard of that proposal before we had these difficulties with the Barnes family. I will call the minister for you. There will be no problem with the gravel so long as we have no difficulty with the documents increasing the price of these other resources." The minister paused. "And I have a favor to ask. My son is a law clerk. Would you think your attorney, Herbert Johns, would hire him to work with him on these documents?"

"I see no problem," said Tom. "You realize that my client would be paying your son. The government would need to waive any conflict that might result."

The Solicitor shrugged. "What else do you need?" asked the Solicitor.

"This fellow, Winston Grey?"

"The white Bahamian? What about him? He is a great supporter of our political party. When we won the election he provided us with cars for our newly elected officers to ride in for the inaugural parade."

"The Mennonites believe he is abusing the boy Winston calls his cousin."

"There is nothing I can do about it. It's a political problem. He may be an abuser but we are stuck with him. I cannot have him arrested. But if he is an abuser he is a nasty sot and he will be taken care of." The Solicitor made a motion with his finger slicing his neck. "We will investigate and take the appropriate action."

"Tell whoever is going to take care of him, that Winston is an awfully good shot."

"Whatever," said the minister. "I have another meeting. I will have my bodyguard take you wherever you need to go in the City."

"I need to see Herbert Johns to see what he will need to prepare the paperwork for the leases and licenses."

"My bodyguard will take you to his office," said the minister.

Chapter 27

Attorney Herbert Johns had international telephone service at his office. That was probably the primary reason for the large number of business clients he attracted. That and his government connections.

After his meeting with the Solicitor General, Tom went to Herbert's office to call the United States and speak to Roger to have him begin work on the documents necessary to reinstate the leases and licenses from their clients' side of the transaction. Roger would work in St. Petersburg and Tom would work in Belize City.

Mr. Johns had a clerk and a secretary. Tom was dropped off at the law office by the minister's bodyguard. As usual he was left to sit on the porch with the secretary. She said nothing, but communicated with a smile and dialed in on the intercom to the clerk, who Tom guessed would alert Herbert to Tom's presence. The secretary spent all her time, it seemed, filing papers in files using ACCO clips to secure the paperwork. She occasionally looked at Tom, who was seated on a stained and raggedy rattan couch, but she said nothing and only looked at the papers as she entered them in the files.

The clerk came out to greet Tom.

"Do you have an appointment, Mr. Night?"

"No, but I need to see Herbert if possible and use the phone to call my office."

"Let me take you to an extension, you can make the call."

Tom would now enter the inner sanctum of the offices. This was the area that appeared to have never been dusted or cleaned.

Tom always sneezed after he spent a few moments in this part of the office. Tom kept his fingers beneath his nose.

The clerk went to the desk. He motioned to Tom to sit in the chair behind the desk. Then the clerk checked the line for a dial tone and Tom dialed the local operator. Herbert did not have a touch tone phone and Tom had to have the local operator connect him to an overseas operator who would then dial back to Belize with the call to Tom's office once a connection had been made to his office.

Tom asked the clerk if they had connected the answering machine Tom brought to Herbert when they met in Belmopan.

"Not yet, but we have it here." The clerk pointed to the box that sat unopened in the corner of the office.

The clerk left to give Tom privacy. The operator was having some difficulty and said she would call back.

Tom sat there. Then Herbert came in. "How did it go with your meeting?" he asked.

"Very well," said Tom. "We will have work to do this afternoon. The government has agreed to reinstate the leases and licenses. Can you help us?"

"Certainly, "said Herbert.

"There are changes from the original agreements. Essentially, the government receives a onetime increase in rents and residuals and then annual increases for inflation of the value of the resources over time, and my client is guaranteed a long term contractual right to the leases and licenses. We won't have to renegotiate every time there is an election and change in the government."

"We will be happy to assist you," said Herbert.

The phone rang. It was the operator. She had successfully placed the call.

"Hello, Roger."

"Good news, I hope," said Roger.

"Very good news. We resolved all issues with the new government. We also have an agreement that will bind future governments to our rights to the resources. It seems to be fair to both sides," said Tom.

"Congratulations."

"Do you have any more information about Anthony's whereabouts?"

"Nothing from here."

"The minister told me that he knows Anthony. He was his attorney at one time here in Belize."

"Small world," said Roger.

"The minister said Anthony would contact me. I have a feeling Anthony is in Belize."

"Well, our law firm doesn't represent him anymore so far as his criminal case is concerned in Bushton. I made a motion to withdraw at the court's invitation and the court granted the motion this morning," said Roger.

"That was probably best for us." Tom was relieved they no longer represented Anthony.

Roger continued, "It seemed like the judge was trying to cut our firm out of the loop as much as anything. They don't want us to have any information that we might pass on to Anthony. I was in court on another case and the judge called me and the State Attorney and the court reporter to the bench and told me it was his suggestion that I make a motion to withdraw from Anthony's case. The prosecutor said nothing. It was like he was in on the arrangement. I said we agreed to make the motion and the judge granted the motion," said Roger.

"This isn't good. They must think we were in on the escape somehow. I will need to spend some time with the judge when I get back."

"I think you're right."

"If the court doesn't think we did something criminal aiding the escape, the court thinks we did something unethical." Tom began to hurry along the conversation. "I need you to call Bob Barnes and tell him that we have an agreement and that the terms are all within the parameters of the authority I was given for my negotiations with the government. Tell Bob I will stay here at least another day to make sure Herbert has no problem with the documents and I will telex copies as soon as the paperwork is acceptable to me."

"I will do that. Do you think I did anything wrong by failing to object to the court having us withdraw?"

"We won't know until we know. We are being left out in the dark by everyone, so far as Anthony is concerned. The Solicitor General here in Belize had a lot of information about where I had been and what I had done involving Anthony's ships. He knew I went to the admiralty in Cancún, México for a permit to move Anthony's diving vessel to San Pedro, Belize. Apparently one of the crew members drowned as the boat was being motored south. They think the crewman was murdered."

"But you were on a plane returning to the States then, weren't you?" asked Roger.

"Yes, I was on the plane. The minister acknowledged that fact and said the police chief in Cancún had investigated my movements and the course of travel of the two men Anthony sent down here to help his crew remove the ships to Belize. I am really glad I had nothing to do with hiring those men. They looked rough. Apparently the police chief told the Solicitor General that he agreed I had nothing more to do with the matter other than obtaining the permit and then hiring the pontoon plane and taking the two men to Punta Rosa in the plane that I rented."

"I guess we will just have to wait," said Roger.

"Roger, Roger," Tom said as he hung up.

Part IV
The Assault

Chapters 28 through 37

Anthony Arnold surfaces in Belize ... Winston and his cousin ... Rick Ibn is attacked ... The AC-500S is stolen ... Tracking the stolen plane ... Rick Ibn's convalescence with Anna Hernando, M.D. ... The Belize Defense Force (BDF) locates the AC-500S ... Judge Barrow and Judge Lucius

Chapter 28

After he hung up the telephone, Tom sat there at the desk in the dust of Attorney Herbert Johns anteroom for a while trying to figure out just what was going on. Finally, he decided he couldn't understand it because he wasn't part of the conspiracy. He knew he was vulnerable. The best thing to do was be truthful if he had to say anything. But if possible it was best to just keep his mouth shut.

The law clerk came in. Herbert followed the clerk. It was getting dark and Herbert and the clerk were in their shorts ready for a game of round ball (basketball).

"You are going to have to make room for another player." said Tom.

"Are you going to play basketball with us?" asked Herbert.

"No," said Tom. "The Solicitor General is going to make you hire his son as a clerk for the work on the revised licenses."

"I guess you will be paying his salary, Mr. Night," said Herbert.

"Yes, I guess I will. I'm going to dinner at the Fort George. I'll see you in the morning and we can work on the documents. You will need a retainer. How much?" asked Tom.

"$2,000 in US Dollars," said Herbert. "It will be very much work."

"Ok." You always have to resolve the money issues first, Tom thought.

***

It was 8:00 p.m. in Belize, 9:00 p.m. back home. Tom took a cab to the Fort George Hotel and checked in. He then called the International Airport and asked for Customs and spoke to the agent and got the local number for the man who rented him the Chrysler. Tom called and gave the man the bad news about the accident and the damage to the car and gave the location of the car at the asylum in Ladyville. Tom asked for another rental and was offered a Ford pickup truck. Tom made arrangements to pay for the rental to date and for the expense of the repair. He was told Three Hundred US Dollars would cover the cost. Tom thought it was a ridiculously exorbitant amount. The Chrysler wasn't worth One Hundred Belize dollars to begin with. Tom began to be angry that he was being taken advantage of. But what could he say? Tom agreed to leave the money with the desk clerk. Then Tom used the house phone to call the central hanger at the airport.

Tom asked for Rick.

"Can you be ready to leave tomorrow evening or early the next day?"

"Sure," said Rick. "I'm not rebuilding the engines or anything major."

"Be serious now. I may need to get out of here on short notice. Finish your repairs."

"No problem," said Rick.

Tom hung up the phone and walked down the hall to his room at the hotel. The door was made of mahogany and had toucans and tree branches carved in high relief in the wood. The door to his room at the hotel was unlocked.

"That's odd," thought Tom. He pushed the door open slowly. There was a light on in the bathroom. That room was to Tom's left. He could hear the shower. To his right an older man was sitting in a low-backed upholstered chair. The room was dark. On the end table next to the chair there was an ice bucket and a bottle of expensive whiskey. There were two glasses on the table that contained ice and scotch.

"I must have the wrong room," said Tom.

"I'm David, Tom. This is your room."

The man was a stranger to Tom, but he thought he recognized him from a photograph.

"Anthony is in the bathroom," said the man. "We flew in from San Pedro today. We came to the hotel and Anthony asked one of the doormen if you were staying here. The doorman said you had a room and he let us in."

So much for hotel security and confidentiality, thought Tom.

"Anthony said it was alright." said David. "You are his attorney and all."

"You don't intend to stay here with me do you?" asked Tom.

"No, no. We just came in to clean up. We'll get a place down on the beach." David took a sip of his drink. David was intoxicated. Tom turned on the light and sat down in another chair at a game table just as Anthony came into the room in his underwear and made himself at home.

"How you doing?" said Anthony.

"I'm not really sure. Aren't you supposed to be in jail?" asked Tom.

"Maybe I got a reprieve."

"I got a call from Roger; it's in the newspapers that you escaped. The judge was very angry with Roger and me. The judge is acting like we had something to do with your escape. You being here in the room won't help much quelling that suspicion."

"Well, you cannot control where I go," said Anthony.

"Particularly if you don't ask my permission to be invited into my room."

"That was selfish and unthinking on our part," Anthony said sarcastically. "Aren't you my lawyer? I have paid your retainer."

"We were removed from your case by the court."

"Who's the judge?" asked David.

"Raymond Barrow," said Tom.

"I know Ray," said David, "I can talk to him and smooth this over. Ray had a problem I fixed a short time back."

Now Tom recognized David. He was an appellate court judge in the Northern District of Florida. Tom had never argued before him so he had never seen him in the flesh. Tom now felt really ill. Tom had seen David's picture in the Florida Bar News when it was announced that he had been suspended and no longer heard cases.

"I need to clear you two out of my room. You can get cleaned up and then meet me in the bar," Tom took his key and left. Tom walked down the hall to the bar. Before he left, Tom felt in his breast pocket and fingered the business card for H. Patel, Esquire, the lawyer Solicitor General Andrew Prince had insisted Anthony speak with. Tom decided not to give Anthony the card at that time.

Chapter 29

Tom slid into a seat at a table in the darkest corner of the bar at the Fort George that he could find. He had had nothing to eat since a bag of crackers for lunch and he was starved. He ordered a bowl of boiled shrimp with a side of chips and Melinda's sauce and cold vegetables – onions, carrots and celery. There were few people in the bar. The staff was quick and Tom had his food in about 5 minutes.

Judge David Lucius was a member of the district court and only handled appeals. Tom and Roger rarely filed appeals on behalf of their clients. There was no reason for Tom to know Judge Lucius. But the members of the Bar were a close knit society and you had an idea if a member, particularly a judge, had a problem with the Florida Bar Association. Tom knew there were some ethics issues that Judge Lucius had hanging over his head. The judge's picture and his story was in the Florida Bar newsletter but Tom remembered the judge's problem was a technical rather than substantive lapse. Tom thought it involved an interaction with an attorney who represented a judge who had a matter before the appeals court. It was Tom's guess that Judge Lucius had a drinking problem and he made poor decisions choosing his friends.

Anthony led the way into the bar with the judge following. The judge had a glass and his bottle of scotch. Anthony had a rucksack with his belongings that he threw on a chair at the table. Both men sat down. Anthony reached over and took the plate of Tom's shrimp, fries and vegetables and pulled it into the center of the table and Anthony and the judge devoured the food.

After they finished, Anthony sat back and smiled. He was fit, trim and tan from a lifetime of physical labor. Anthony's hair was blond with tight curls. He laughed with his eyes. His cheeks were scarred from acne when he was young.

"I am really happy to be out of that jail." Anthony breathed loudly.

"I would like to set some ground rules for this conversation," said Tom. "First, I do not represent either of you so anything you say to me is not privileged. I can be compelled to testify about anything you say to me. Any statement you make regarding your escape could be presented to the court as an admission. And really, I don't want to know anything about the particulars of your crimes or how you got here to Belize."

Tom did not want to know because he did not want to be eliminated, killed, because he had information about the men and could relate it to law enforcement.

"Second, Anthony, I have an obligation to tell you that I am aware there is a warrant out for your arrest and that you should turn yourself in to the authorities."

Anthony and the judge looked at each other and burst out laughing. "Look Tom, you don't get it. I am free. Florida has no jurisdiction over me here. I paid my $20 entrance fee to the Custom's official at the border and I can stay here as long as the Belize officials say I can," said Anthony.

"Tom, we are not asking for your help. This was a friendly visit to have a chat," said the judge. "Anthony is here to collect his property and we are moving on south to Bogota, Columbia."

"Too much information ... " Anthony frowned at the judge. "Tom, the judge is right. I appreciate all you did for me and the help you gave me getting the permits to move my boat out of Punta Rosa to San Pedro. I had thought you made a mistake not taking the coastal freighter too, but the crew on the dive boat confirmed that the M.V. Cap de l'Ile was a derelict and grounded on shore. You did right. You saved what you could. I will have to hire a lawyer here in Belize. I can't use you as my attorney. I understand you are compromised and cannot represent me."

"Which reminds me ... " Tom pulled the card from his pocket. "The Solicitor General, Andrew Prince, wanted me to give you this business card. This fellow is a lawyer who Mr. Prince thinks can help you. Isn't Patel the person you talked to about paying the Bounty Hunter's men to move the boats from Punta Rosa to San Pedro?"

"H. Patel is my personal lawyer. Thank you for the card," said Anthony. "How long are you going to be here in Belize?"

"Just long enough to prepare some documents for a client," said Tom.

"Are you flying out then?"

"Yes."

"I doubt we will see you again. Good luck to you."

"And the two of you," said Tom.

Anthony retrieved his rucksack and the judge retrieved his bottle of scotch, which was now only half full, and the two men left the table.

That was too easy, thought Tom as he watched the two men walk out the door.

Chapter 30

Tom could not sleep anymore. It was Saturday morning, and he usually got an extra hour's sleep on the weekend, but not today. He had to go to Herbert's office to work on the documents to present to the government and he hoped he would be able to leave Belize and arrive home sometime on Sunday. So Tom rolled out of bed, showered and dressed casually in a knit shirt, tan pants and penny loafers (no socks).

As he walked down the hall he could see that the vendors were setting up the Saturday market on Cork Street in front of the Fort George Hotel. The street was about two and one half lanes wide and it had sidewalks. The vendors set up their displays on the sidewalks and the customers took over the street. The market lasted about four hours, so the street reopened at about noon when the market closed.

Tom walked down the street looking at displays. There were fruits and vegetables. There were also items that were hand worked – carvings in mahogany, and also in hard stone like flint called "Chert" that could be found in local lime rock outcroppings. Other groups had brought items to sell. The Mennonites were there with dairy products and eggs and freshly killed and dressed chickens. The group also built furniture from the wood they cut in their sawmill. A specialty was tables with tops constructed of a single slab of wood. The tops were a full inch thick and were cut to show the grain of the wood. Three years back Tom had bought one of the tables to use in the conference room of his office.

Tom saw Michael and his wife. They were the couple who had treated and set the break in George's wrist. Michael told Tom that

Jacob was in the hotel talking to the manager about replacing some mahogany chairs that were old and broken. Tom left the street, walked into the circular driveway and then entered the front door of the hotel and walked into the dining room. He saw Jacob with the manager at a table. Also present were Fredrick and George and Winston, who was seated next to a young boy, 8 or so years old. The boy was devouring a stack of pancakes that were covered in syrup.

The group made introductions. The boy did not acknowledge the group until Winston touched his shoulder and got the boy's attention and then had the boy speak to each of the people at the table. The boy spoke in a hum and added a "ma" sound after the hum. "Hum, ma" the boy would say. The boy then went back to his meal.

The manager was called away. But before he left, he took Tom's breakfast order for bread, tropical fruit and coffee.

"Well George, did you come to town to see the doctor?" asked Tom.

"I think he needs a cast," said Frederick. "Tom, I want you to know we made arrangements to pay for the wood Jacob and the Mennonites supplied us for my barn."

Frederick turned to Jacob and said, "I'm sorry I failed to pay you. I had no excuse."

"There is no problem."

"You helped my friend George. I am truly grateful," said Frederick, who was becoming sniffy and his eyes were red. He blew his nose in his napkin.

"How is the leopard skin?" asked Tom.

"Beautiful," said George and Frederick as one. Then they said goodbye and went to the cashier and then headed out for the medical clinic.

The boy wanted more syrup. It was contained in a plastic squeeze bottle shaped like a bear. The boy pulled on Winston's shirt to get his attention and made the same "hum ma" sound. The sound though was made in a pleading way. Winston passed the boy the syrup.

"Winston, you know the Mennonites have a school for the deaf and dumb in the Spanish Lookout. They could help the boy." Tom had been observing the child and recognized he could not hear or speak.

"We don't need any help," said Winston.

"Maybe not now, but you will in the future when the boy is 18 or so. He needs special skills to get along in the world. You won't be there for him forever."

"We would be happy to take the boy into our care," said Jacob. "We have five other children, all less than 10 years of age, who we work with at the Lookout. He could learn to sign and he could communicate with you and with other children. If a child needs special medical care we send them to Texas or Florida where we have larger communities that are near medical centers that offer specialized care."

"No, not now," said Winston. His answer was final.

Jacob left to help at the market.

Tom leaned close to Winston and said, "People misunderstand your relationship with the boy. I give you the benefit of the doubt. But others are not so kind," said Tom, "People here think you are abusing the boy."

"No one can touch me here in Belize."

"You are not immune from action by the community. I am not talking about you being arrested. I am talking about citizens taking action themselves," said Tom. "You could be killed."

"They don't have the spunk to take me on," said Winston. His face turned red.

"You are making a big mistake not taking my advice and giving the boy to the care of the Mennonites."

Tom's meal was served. He took a couple of sips of the coffee and a bite of fruit. It was good but he had lost his appetite. He pushed the plate over to the boy who began to eat the fruit with vigor. He was all smiles and totally ignorant. He was happy in the moment. He slathered the bread with the sweet syrup.

Tom thought the Mennonites were mistaken. The boy loved Winston and did not appear to be abused.

Tom said goodbye and headed for Herbert's office. It looked like it would be a beautiful day. The sky was blue and clear. He could relax. He forgot about Winston and the boy.

Chapter 31

The tide was in and the large fiddler crabs with the single red claw were on the move. The crabs had to retreat to high ground. Tom stepped over and around the crabs as he crossed the yard to Herbert's law office in Belize City. He managed to arrive at the door without being pinched.

"Hello," said Tom as he was let in the door. Herbert had his clerk, Henry, and his secretary, Laura, available to work on the documents. Of course Herbert was not available. He was "otherwise occupied," Laura said.

Also present was Minister Prince's son, Andrew Junior. Tom knew that Andrew was a shill for his father. He would go home after they were finished and tell his father what the group had done and what they had discussed so that the minister would know how and where to attack the paperwork if the country was at a disadvantage. Tom had no intention of making any changes to the documents other than the ones he and the minister had agreed to. Therefore Tom gave Andrew a list of proposed changes that Tom believed accurately represented the agreement that Tom and the minister had arrived at during their meeting. Tom's client would be assured the right to natural resources and the right to do business in the country so long as his client made the agreed upon payments. Otherwise, any dispute would be subject to arbitration. The government would have no right to unilaterally cancel the licenses and leases.

Tom had the clerk draft the changes and the secretary began to type. Typing was the most rigorous and time consuming task.

Accuracy was the most important attribute of the typist. If she made a mistake that could not be erased and retyped then the typist had to retype the page. So it was a slog.

The clerks drafted the new changes into a copy of the old agreements and then the changes were approved or amended by Tom. Once Tom approved a final draft, Laura began to type.

Unfortunately, the original agreements were produced by an attorney who was apparently paid by the word and thus the original documents were verbose. Tom tried to remove as much of the verbiage as he could, but maintain the intent of the parties.

Tom saved all the pages that were corrected and told Andrew that he should take the pages with the corrections to his father so that the minister could understand the way the final documents had been constructed and created.

Tom felt that the agreements needed to be accurate and honest so that the parties could get back to a position where they trusted one another.

As the process moved forward and Tom became confident that Laura, Andrew, and Henry were following his instructions, Tom called the central hangar and left a message for Rick that he should be finished with the documents in the evening. The messenger was also asked to tell Rick to prepare the plane for the flight back as they could head back tonight or in the morning. It would be Rick's decision. Tom asked Rick to pick up some snacks and drinks at the Fort George and charge them to his account.

Tom also asked Rick to find Jamie. Tom had asked for him with the doorman at the Fort George when he left in the morning and the doorman said he had seen him going in and out of the hotel and that he spent much time in the bar with local businessmen and that he had had a number of women in his room, "entertaining them". The doorman went on and on.

Too much information, thought Tom. Tom gave the doorman $5 BZ and also asked him to find Jamie and have him call Rick at the Central Hangar for some important information. Tom thought he could rely on the doorman to give Jamie the message.

Tom went back to his work. Herbert made an appearance and he was assured everything was going along well. They should be through at dinner time. Herbert pulled Tom aside and asked if they could obtain the retainer for the work. Tom had withdrawn $2,000 US from the safe at the hotel. Tom counted out $2,000 and paid Herbert. He received a receipt for the retainer and for the $500 US that Tom previously paid to Herbert for the work on the documents for the sale of the boiler at the turpentine still.

Tom also made arrangements for Hubert to hold the FOB (freight on board) payment Tom expected for the mahogany cants that were being delivered from the Belize City sawmill to the ship in the harbor. Herbert agreed his law firm would hold the funds for the Barnes Family account. The payment should be in an amount in excess of $100,000 US. Then Herbert left. His work collecting the retainer was done.

Tom got a call from Rick. The doorman had called him to report that Jamie was in Orange Walk and would be not be back until later tonight. There was no way to contact Jamie.

"We can't leave until morning," said Rick. "Anyway, I'm checking for cracks where the wing attaches to the fuselage."

"That makes me nervous." said Tom.

"It is just routine maintenance. I received a notice from the manufacturer. That will take a couple more hours. I had rented a car to pick up parts and I will need to return the rental and I can best do that in the morning. So I say we leave in the morning. I will meet you and Jamie at 9 a.m. in the lobby and I can return the car, pick up the food and drinks, and we are off for Miami."

Tom was alright with the arrangement. He should be home before 9 p.m. on Sunday Eastern Standard Time. Tom went back to the grind of the paperwork.

***

The documents were finished at 8 p.m. They never saw Hubert Johns after he collected the attorney fee.

Andrew drove Tom to the hotel and thanked him for the experience he gained working with him.

The doorman greeted Tom. "Your friend, Jamie, called in and we told him you were leaving in the morning."

"Ok," said Tom as he got out of the car. Tom had a light dinner in his room, packed his suitcase for the trip in the morning, and fell off to sleep.

Chapter 32

Rick purchased his Aero Commander model 500S used from an airline in Australia that ferried commuter passengers from the outback to the continent's main cities. Rick was sold on the testimonials that the AC-500S was big for its job. "Big", in other words, the plane was oversized for the work it was designed to do and heavier and stronger than comparable makes.

Of course it was not expected that a plane that was built for strength would have a flaw that allowed the wings to fall off in flight, but it did.

Wing spar failures were reported in 59 of the 2,000 Aero Commanders that were manufactured. The defect was determined to have caused 24 wing separations while the plane was in flight and another 35 planes were found to have a crack in a spar that could have separated in flight had the defect not have been discovered and refitted. Further, the point at which the wing attached to the fuselage was susceptible to corrosion and upon inspection hundreds of other spars had to be replaced due to defects caused by fatigue, corrosion, stress, and static overload.

Aero Commander attempted to make fixes for the problem and it designed and sold an external reinforcing strap for planes that were in operation and constructed before the wing was re-designed to strengthen the seam where the wing attached to the body of the plane. The manufacturer issued service bulletins advising the operators of the plane to inspect for cracks, particularly at WS24 (wing station 24) for short wings and at point WS39 for planes that were built with long wings.

After the external wing straps were designed, Aero Commander added a wider and longer internal stainless steel strap that was installed at the time of manufacture. However cracks and corrosion continued to be found. At one point Aero Commander offered to provide external spar caps for free.

Rick was aware of the problems with the wings of the plane when he purchased the plane. Rick had read all the material he could find on the issue. The best general information was published by S. J. Swift in the "Aero Commander Chronical."

Rick felt, however, that by doing careful inspections of the locations where critical loads were placed on the wing/fuselage connections, and by avoiding stressors on the wings such as severe low level terrain flying (strafing maneuvers), the potential defect would not occur. Rick even added a magnetic inspection of the stainless steel spar as part of his pre-flight and he had a radiographic examination completed every year of the end of the internal strap to inspect for cracks. Rick felt that the plane was sound for the use to which he put the plane, which was charter flights.

Rick compensated for any wing weakness by flying like an old lady and he took advantage of any fix that came from the manu-facturer for the defect.

So it was not unusual for Rick to take the time to replace the spar caps and reinforcement on the wings while he was out of service waiting for his charter at the Central Hanger at the Belize International Airport. The spar caps had been provided to him free of charge by the manufacturer. Rick understood that the cost of the kit with spar replacements, instructions, reinforcement and tools was $10,000.

Rick had hired a local machinist at the airport in Belize City to give him an extra pair of hands handing the parts as Rick read the instructions and he replaced the caps. Rick looked for any sign of corrosion on the underside of the caps as he replaced them but he could find none. This fact made him feel that he had not sacrificed safety when he bought this plane at a bargain price from the airline in Australia.

When Tom called to tell him the plans for leaving Sunday morning, Rick had finished the repair and had showered and changed for the evening. He intended to stroll to the front of the airport and order a couple of tamales and a Mexican beer and sit under the Royal Poinciana tree on the mahogany bench and let the evening breeze cool him off.

When he arrived under the tree, two older men had the same idea. They were cutting up, joking with the vendor. Others joined in the conversation. Then Rick began to speak with the group. Except for the vendor, everyone under the flowering tree seemed to be connected to the airline industry. It was a fine Saturday night. Everyone was blowing off a little steam and drinking a little beer. But after an hour the group dispersed and left the vendor to his chores cleaning the area under the tree so he would be ready for the next day's business.

Rick was last to leave. He finished his beer and intended to return to the plane and settle in, stretching out on the floor in the passenger area of the plane's cabin. But, as he walked behind the airport terminal he heard a noise and he turned and he was hit in the face with a hard object and he went down to his hands and knees. He was then hit again on the back of his head and he went down to the ground, out for the count. He felt someone in his pockets. They had his keys. Then he was hit again and he was unconscious.

***

"God, you hit him awful hard," said one of the men as they entered the plane.

"He'll be fine. Buckle up." The three men were in Rick's plane.

The Aero Commander taxied with no lights to the end of the runway and the pilot throttled up, increased the RPMs and eased off the brakes and the plane coursed down the runway, lifted off smoothly and headed NNE.

A member of the British Army unit on the ground shined his spotlight on the side of the plane on takeoff and the sentry was able to identify the "N" number that was inscribed on the side of the plane: N500PT. The sentry wrote down the number.

"These idiots close the airport but leave the landing lights on. The plane is probably full of pot. It's heading in the direction of Cozumel," said the sentry to his mates. "If they don't care about security, we're in real trouble. Make sure this is reported."

***

The plane turned more to the east. It was only a 15 minute flight to the airport in San Pedro, on Ambergris Caye. They circled the landing strip once. There were no planes at the airport. There was only a lime rock runway and a shack. The planes to San Pedro ferried tourists who would fish and skin dive. There were a few night spots and private hotels that could only accommodate small numbers. The island air facilities were used primarily for day trippers.

There was no one at the airport when the AC-500S landed. The pilot pulled onto the grass to prepare for a take-off to the SSE, ostensibly to fly south to ultimately reach Cartagena, Columbia, or so people were led to believe.

The pilot flipped on the interior lights and he admired the interior of the plane. It was spotless. Between Rick and the local mechanic cleaning for three days there wasn't a speck of dust or dirt or grime anywhere. "This plane is a marvel," said the pilot. "Sorry I will have to sell it."

Two of the men walked to the shack at the airport. The third man stayed with the plane. There was an old station wagon parked at the shack. It was used to ferry passengers to the docks on the east side of the Caye. The vehicle's keys were in the visor above the driver's seat. The men drove to the wharf area on the northeast of the Caye. There, tied to a pier, was a small ship with a flying bridge that was customized for diving. It was Anthony's dive boat. The two men went to the ship, boarded it and went directly to the wheel.

The short stubby man reached under the wheel housing and felt for the box. To loosen the straps holding the box, the two men had to lie on their backs with one man unscrewing the straps and the other man supporting the weight of the box. The box was three feet long and a foot and a half high and a foot deep. The box was heavy, loaded and locked. It appeared to be an old Craftsman brand tool box.

Once the men got the box loose and on the deck they opened it and they could see it was full of treasure. There was silver and gold in the bottom section of the box. Very little bullion but works of art in gold and jewels, crosses and fish hooks and masks and animal figures, most Pre-Columbian and some manufactured by the Spanish. In the tray inside the box on top of the precious metal there were stones, primarily emeralds and jade.

"My God! We are rich."

"Let's get this out of here and back to the plane."

"What are you doing with this ship?"

"I'll sell it here to an operator of one of the dive shops."

"We need to get in the air. We need to be in San Pedro Sula, Honduras to refuel and then on to Bocas del Toro, Panama and then on to Cartagena, Columbia and to Bogotá," said the pilot loudly so he could be heard by anyone listening.

The short stubby man giggled. "How's your Spanish?"

"I kept in practice."

"Good, good," said the short man as they struggled down the pier to the station wagon with the weight of the box. At the airport, the third man met them and they dragged the box to the plane and then set it in the middle of the rear bench seat and buckled it in so it wouldn't roll off the seat.

"If that thing falls off the seat it will punch a hole all the way through the bottom of the cabin and the fuselage. Make it secure. I will leave the box in Bocas Del Toro with a friend." Again they laughed. "I sure hope they follow us to Cartagena."

There was no better information for your enemy than disinformation.

Chapter 33

Tom was antsy; he always was when he was going to fly. But this was different. Tom knew there had to be a problem. First, Tom had to wake up Jamie. Jamie insisted he had not been told by the doorman to be ready to leave in the morning. Tom confronted the doorman. The doorman said he did not talk to Jamie; it was Anthony that he talked to. And the doorman went on, "Wasn't Anthony your friend?"

"No," said Tom, "Anthony is not my friend. What did you tell him?"

"I told him you were out with another attorney, but that you were leaving in the morning and that you had an airplane and a pilot at the International Airport. I think I told him it was an Aero Commander and the pilots name was Rick."

The doorman kept speaking and Tom interrupted, "What time is it?"

"9:15 a.m."

"What? We are late. Where is Rick?" Tom left the lobby and went to move Jamie along. After he spoke to him in his room while he showered, Tom used his room phone to call the main hanger at the airport to talk to the receptionist.

She told him Rick had been found injured and they had taken him to the doctor in town. He was unconscious. "And his airplane, the Aero Commander, is missing."

Tom yelled the information he had received from the airport about Rick to Jamie and told Jamie he was going to the medical clinic and he added, "Don't get drunk. I may need your help."

"Hair of the dog?" asked Jamie.

"No," insisted Tom. "I want you sober. How much money do you have in cash, US dollars?"

"I have $26,000 in checks. "He bragged. "I sold a ton of A/Cs. I have six gold pieces left and about $700 US in cash. How much do you have?"

Tom ignored Jamie and went out to the front of the lobby and hailed a cab. Tom hoped the funds paid FOB for the mahogany lumber had been deposited in Herbert's escrow account. They may need the money, he thought.

***

Tom's cab pulled up in front of the combination funeral home ("Rest in Peace," the sign said) and medical office ("Dr. Hernando's Clinic"). Tom told the driver to wait and he hurried upstairs. There was a lady with Rick, attending to his head. He had cuts and lumps but he was awake and speaking to the lady medical worker.

Tom identified himself and told the lady doctor (Anna Hernando, M.D.) that Rick was a pilot and he had flown a charter flight from the USA to Belize and that he was supposed to take Tom and another passenger back to Miami today.

"No, no, no," said the Doctor. Whether the word "no "was Spanish or English Tom knew what she meant.

"When?" asked Tom, "When will we know if he can leave?"

"Tomorrow," said the Doctor. "He needs to stay quiet today and he will know if he can fly a plane depending on how feels tomorrow morning." Her English was perfect. She was very nice but a little condescending. But Tom had also been curt. He was anxious.

"Can I take him to the Fort George and let him rest up there? I will make sure he stays quiet. The room would be cool."

"I think that would be good but we would not be responsible if something happened." said Dr. Hernando. "I can give you the same medicine that I would provide him if he were here in the clinic. In addition you will need to wake him every two hours and talk to him. Make him sit up. If he does not wake up, you must call me and I will come to see him. If he wakes up but you can't make any sense of what he is saying you should call me also. Understand?"

"Yes." Tom paid the doctor's bill and he helped Rick down the stairs to the street. The cab was waiting. They went back to the hotel.

***

Tom put Rick in his room. Rick went to sleep immediately. Tom went to Jamie's room. He wasn't there. Tom went to the bar. Jamie was showing a man and his wife a brochure for an A/C system and the ductwork necessary for their house. Tom stood back and watched Jamie's sales technique.

"... And if you bring me any new customers I will take $100 US dollars off the price of your system."

The woman looked at her husband with an evil eye when the husband tried to hedge on the purchase of the A/C system. Jamie smiled. The woman was not going to be denied the luxury of a cool home.

He's made the sale, thought Tom.

The couple left. The woman was obviously happy. The man ... not so much.

"Did you find Rick?" asked Jamie.

"He's in my room. He was beaten really bad. It looks to me like someone intended to kill him. It's a good thing he was as strong as he is."

Chapter 34

Rick hurt terribly from his toes to the top of his head. The only question was where he hurt worse. But that seemed irrelevant. He was unable to function other than to throw his feet over the side of the bed, sit up and hold his head in his hands.

And whose bed was he in? How did he get to where he was? He couldn't answer any questions. He recognized Tom's voice. He had talked to him but it didn't make any sense. He was told that his plane was gone. Had it crashed? How was it gone? How could it be gone?

There was a mirror across the wall from the bed. Rick saw his image in the mirror but failed to recognize how he had obtained the lumps, cuts and bruises.

Dr. Hernando was there. Rick called her "Anna." Tom had called the medical clinic. Tom was concerned Rick had gotten worse after they returned to his room and he tried to wake Rick up in the afternoon. She had examined Rick and they got him up and to the bathroom. They talked to Rick for a while. Rick knew who he was, and where he was and was oriented as to time and date. Then he was back sitting on the edge of the bed. He was given something to drink and he fell back to sleep.

"I think he'll recover," said Dr. Hernando. "He may be like this a day or two. Call me again if you think he has a setback."

Rick was now snoring.

Tom went to the table. He took a yellow legal pad and made a list of things to do. He needed to call the airport security office or some official and make sure the plane had been reported stolen.

He needed to call Roger and update him regarding Anthony's appearance at the hotel and that he was with the judge. (What is up with that? thought Tom. I guess its ok for a judge to be drunk on vacation. But drunk on vacation with a fugitive saying he's going to Cartagena, Columbia?) Tom needed to call the office and have Roger report Anthony's sighting to the sheriff and tell the judge in Bushton and report the sighting of the judge to the Chief Judge of the Appellate Court.

"The Chief Judge will love to hear this," thought Tom out loud. Tom also needed to contact the Solicitor General's office in Belize City, so Mr. Prince doesn't think he was hiding anything. Mr. Prince was very interested in Anthony's well-being, asking Tom to give Anthony the card for the attorney and all. Everyone had an angle. Anthony probably owes the Solicitor General some money.

Tom went to Jamie's room. "You go over to my room and stay with Rick. I have to make some calls. Do you need me to call anyone for you?"

Jamie said he was good with that. It was still the weekend. He wasn't due back until sometime on Monday at the earliest. Jamie left and Tom got out his small address book.

"Minister Prince's residence." It was Andrew Prince Junior speaking.

"Andrew, this is Tom Night. Is your father available?"

"Just a moment," said Andrew.

"Tom, how can I help you?"

"Minister, I saw Anthony Friday evening at the Fort George. I gave him the card for Attorney Patel.

"I also wanted you to be aware that the plane I flew down in, an Aero Commander AC-500S is missing and the pilot, Rick Ibn was assaulted and he is in my room at the Fort George recuperating from his injuries."

"Any idea who did it?"

"Not yet, but I have a few ideas," said Tom, who then quickly got to his point. "You have a small military air force here, don't you?"

"Yes, but it is very small. We have a Cessna 182 Skylane."

"I don't know if airport security is aware of the theft of the AC-500S. The plane's identification number is N500PT. Could you make a report to the Belize Air Force that the plane was possibly stolen? Also it may help if you called airport security personally, so they know this is a matter of importance."

"Yes, yes, I will be happy to do that for you."

"Thank you, Minister." They hung up.

"Operator, I need to be connected to an overseas operator." Tom figured he would try Roger at the office first and then his home. There is something wrong with younger lawyers as far as their work habits are concerned. They were always at work.

"Roger, Roger."

"This is Tom ... we have a problem."

"Yeah?" There was static on the line. Roger pushed the phone tightly to his ear.

"We got up to fly back this morning and we received a call from the airport that Rick was badly injured and his plane was gone. I need you to make some calls for me, please."

"Right."

"Call the sheriff in Bushnell and tell him that Anthony and an older man who identified himself as David Lucius approached me at the Fort George Hotel last night. You can tell the sheriff I will come in to see him as soon as I get back there to tell him what I know." Tom felt he needed to get ahead of whatever was happening. This has to be Anthony Arnold's doing, he thought.

"Don't we have a David Lucius who is an appellate judge in North Florida?" said Roger.

"I think he is one and the same, which is why I want you to contact the Chief Judge for the District Courts, North Florida Division and report to the Court that the judge was sighted in Belize and that I will give further information on my return."

"Anyone else?"

"Contact Judge Raymond Barrow and the State Attorney, John Hale, and tell them I reported to you a sighting of Anthony in Belize City last night. We do not have any obligation of confidentiality of communications to Anthony as far as I know. He's not our client anymore and he is a fugitive. I am sure some smart lawyer can split hairs over this issue but we will wait to see what happens once we can get into the books and look at the case law."

"I will start the research if you want me to," said Roger. "What are you going to do next?"

"I'm going to San Pedro and look at Anthony's dive boat. I will call you tomorrow. We will be delayed here. I don't know for how long. I don't want to leave Rick here until he's ok to travel or we know why he was attacked, so this will not happen again."

"Ok."

Tom hung up, went back to his room and told Jamie what he was doing. Tom grabbed a few things, his I.D. and cash and a canteen of water, and headed out.

Chapter 35

As Tom entered the lobby the desk clerk got his attention and passed him a note from Minister Prince asking him to call. That was quick, thought Tom. It only took the minister ten minutes before he called Tom back.

The clerk took Tom to a small room behind the reception desk. The area was private and had a phone. The clerk dialed the minister's number, then handed Tom the receiver and left the room closing the door.

"Minister?"

"Tom, I was able to contact the captain of our air force. He had a report this morning from the British Forces at the International Airport that a plane with the identification number N500PT took off at 9:07 p.m. Central Time last night. The plane flew to the north and then NNE at low altitude. They could not obtain a good radar track because it stayed at low altitude but they believed it was heading to the Straight of Cozumel or San Pedro. There were no reports of the plane landing on the mainland or back-tracking but it was flying very low and could have returned to Belize and be hiding in plain sight under a tarp or in a shed outside the city or in Belmopan or Orange Walk. It could be the plane is being refueled today and will take off this afternoon. We will keep a lookout."

"I am going to fly to San Pedro to see if I can find Anthony," said Tom.

"I think it's more likely Anthony is with your plane than with his dive boat, but it is possible he's on Ambergris Caye. Have the hotel order you a cab to take you to San Pedro Tours. Ask for Darryl. He is a reliable pilot. He will fly you to San Pedro."

"Thank you," said Tom.

The cab driver took Tom to the airport. He went to a tiki hut occupied by San Pedro Tours. He was directed to a small plane described as a push/pull plane. The plane had an engine and propeller in the front that pulled the plane through the air and at the rear of the cabin there was another engine and propeller that pushed the plane forward. Either engine was powerful enough to keep the plane in the air. It was considered very safe.

Darryl immediately taxied the plane once Tom was settled in. They were in the air and had landed in about 20 minutes.

They went to the shack at the airport. Darryl had called the caretaker before he took off. He wanted to show Tom the rear seat of the station wagon. The seat had a large rectangular dent and the springs of the seat were sprung. The caretaker said the gas tank of the station wagon also was low on fuel. Their conclusion was that someone used the car without permission and the vehicle was used to carry something heavy. Darryl offered to drive Tom to the dive boat. It was getting dark and Tom was happy for the company. Barrier Reef Drive was the only street in San Pedro with lights. Heading north on the street you passed bars and dining spots. Fresh seafood and rum were always on the menu. Tom promised Daryl a meal after they looked in on the boat.

They drove to the last pier on the road. There were no street lights now and it was dark, but there was a full moon. There were mangroves that had rooted below the pier and the dock was overgrown with the vegetation. Someone had used a machete to clear a path to the side of the boat. Darryl brought a flashlight from the station wagon and he shined it into the top deck. There was a wheel to the right and a stairwell that led below decks. Darryl rapped on the steel bulkhead with the flashlight. They waited for an answer, but no one replied. They went on deck and tried to find the lights but the light switch did not work. The batteries were dead.

Tom asked Darryl to shine the flash light on the wheel. It seemed to have been disturbed. There was an area where there were metal straps laying loose on the deck. Tom noticed a small green stone and he showed it to Darryl. In the light it appeared to be an emerald. "The minister said we might find a treasure on the boat." said Darryl.

"There isn't much treasure left," said Tom as he fingered the small stone. The men searched the boat but found nothing else of value or interest.

"I will contact the minister from the radio on the plane. I will tell him what we found, but let's eat first," said Darryl.

They drove back down to the restaurants and parked on the street. Darryl saw a friend there who worked part time with the police. Darryl asked him what he knew about the dive boat.

"Yesterday, two men showed up. They paid off the crew and the crew left. I thought I saw someone there last night but never could take time to go and have a look," said the officer.

Tom wished the man had intervened, but then the policeman would have been assaulted.

Tom and Darryl offered a meal to the patrolman. He declined. He said he would watch for activity on the boat and he left, walking up the street.

"This looks like the typical dead end."

"What do you mean?" asked Tom.

"No one will follow up on this and it will be forgotten," said Darryl.

The meal was good and fresh. They went back to the plane. Darryl was confident enough to take off in the night sky, lit by a low full moon. Twenty minutes and they would be back in Belize City.

***

Once back at the Fort George, Tom went to his room. No Jamie and no Rick.

Tom went to the dining room. Rick was sitting in the corner of a booth with his feet propped up. He was drinking a mango/ orange juice drink. Jamie was talking to a group of men and women at another table. He had his brochures out and he was drawing diagrams of the homes of the potential customers and also drawing ductwork for the A/C systems. The man definitely was a salesman.

Rick said he was alright sitting where he was in the dining room and he didn't want to sleep now. He felt better in the dining room where the lights were low and he could sip his drink. He also had an ice bag that he moved from his neck to his head to his face. He said he felt much better. His bruises were less swollen.

Tom went back to his room. He showered. Afterward he received another page from the front desk that the minister had called.

Minister Prince shared with him that he had spoken with the Mexican Air Force. They had not seen Rick's plane visually or on radar heading north over the Straight of Cozumel, which confirmed the plane was probably still somewhere in Belize. The minister had also spoken to the Belize National Police, a quasi-military unit, to make them aware of the situation. That unit also had volunteers who provided information to the police. There was some information that the Aero Commander could be in Orange Walk. This was an area that had been heavily logged and now had cattle ranches and a few distilleries and tourist attractions.

Because of the logging, many roads were cut through the area to remove the logs and bring them downriver to the mills. There were many air drying sheds that were now empty. The lumber had been cut, stacked, dried and shipped. From the air Orange Walk was a maze of timber roads and drying sheds. The sheds could hide the shape of a plane and the road system was dry and level and would be adequate to act as a runway for the operation of a small plane transporting drugs. A few of the police volunteers lived in Orange Walk and they kept an eye on their neighbor's activities and shared the information with the police. The ranches belonging to Winston Grey and George Frederick were in the Orange Walk District. Frederick and his foreman George operated a distillery that made a kind of peppermint schnapps that tasted like liquid fruit cake and was served at Christmas time.

Winston Gray was another story. Most people were appalled by his reputation as an abuser. They shunned him and everyone talked behind his back. Some talked to him to his face, cursing him and his alleged activities. But no one took him to be in the narcotics trade, although all the signs were there. He had a 2,500 foot road on his property that was graded regularly by one of his neighbors who was a known trafficker. There were nights when trucks were seen carrying baled items covered in white plastic to and from his ranch. The trucks were recognized as belonging to drug traders.

So if one thought about it, Winston may have been covering his criminal drug activities by pretending to be a pervert.

In any event, the Orange Walk district had a reputation for being involved in the drug trade. But there were pockets of activity throughout the country, so Orange Walk was just a place where a plane could be hidden waiting for a load of pot to transport to the west coast of Florida or to backhaul money and treasure to Columbia. The Aero Commander was bigger than most drug planes and the dealers in Belize would have to collect product from two or three other small planes if the AC-500S was headed to the States. If the plane was heading south to Columbia with treasure it could leave as soon as it was considered safe.

***

The Cessna 182 Skylane has a single engine and has four seats. The model 182J was powered by a 230 HP piston engine. Its "never exceed speed" was 201 MPH. Its maximum speed was 173 MPH. The plane that was owned by the Belize Air Force was donated to the Belize military by the USA. The plane was used for surveillance and rarely was flown more than 167 MPH.

The Cessna was perfect for surveillance because with a pilot and one passenger it could fly about 500 miles and cover areas of the country that were the most obvious locations where the AC-500S would be kept. And so, the Cessna was ordered to fly from the International Airport, over Belize City then south to Punta Gorda and then north to Dangriga then northwest to Belmopan, avoiding the Mayan Mountains. Then the plane flew a north south pattern from the west to the east over Orange Walk District to the Corozol District, then back to the west over Orange Walk to Belmopan.

The plane flew at an altitude of 5,000 feet over the route and then once it was back to Punta Gorda, the pilot of the Cessna repeated the route but now at 2,500 feet and then at 1,500 feet. At that point the pilot landed and he would start again in the morning.

The pilot reported to his Captain and the Captain called Minister Prince and then Mr. Prince called Tom and reported that they had no success finding Rick's plane, but they would go up again in the morning.

Tom asked if there was any report about the thieves who stole the plane. The minister said he knew nothing on his end and wondered if Rick had any memory of the assault or if he could describe the persons who assaulted him. Rick said he had no memory. Rick was not familiar with the possible suspects, so at best he would only be able to provide a general description.

"Let's hope we have better luck tomorrow with the aerial search."

***

Dr. Hernando made another visit to the hotel at 9:00 p.m. on Sunday. Rick was better. He passed a neurological exam and his eyes and hearing were normal. He had a slight headache. The pain was dull and not sharp like yesterday. Exposure to full light did not bother him. The doctor felt he was much improved and would be able to work some in the morning but he could not fly a plane. That made Rick very depressed.

Tom again spoke to him about the assailants. "I don't know who hit me."

"Did you see anyone at the airport who seemed out of place?"

"There were two men ..." and he went on to describe the impromptu party under the Royal Poinciana tree. "The men were white and older than me. One was short and stout and about 50. The other was older, maybe 60. He appeared to be intoxicated. He was carrying a bottle of expensive scotch whiskey."

That description, of course, fit the appellate judge and the other man could be Winston. But to Tom, it seemed improbable that these two men knew each other. Tom described Anthony to Rick. Rick said there was no one there under the tree that met Anthony's description – no one with the blond hair in ringlets and the scarred face.

***

To not miss a clue, Tom called the minister and passed on Rick's descriptions of the two men. The minister said he would pass it on.

"By the way, do you want to go up with our pilot in the Cessna Skylane?"

"No" said Tom. "I'm actually afraid of flying." It was the first time he admitted the fact.

"I fear heights also" said the minister. "I think it's a lack of control over the plane."

"Not with me. I have no desire to fly the plane," said Tom. "It's not a control issue with me. I think it's more basic. It's fear of dying."

They both laughed.

***

Tom called Roger. Roger relayed the follow-up information he learned from the calls he made:

1. "The circuit judge cussed me out for bothering him on the weekend" and

2."The chief judge cussed me out for calling him on the weekend" and

3."The State Attorney cussed me out for calling him on the weekend."

Tom's response: "You need to stop working on the weekend."

"You know Tom, all of those people seemed to know what I told them before I told them. The news about Anthony and Judge Lucius and the theft of the plane was old news to them."

"Did they actually say they already knew?" asked Tom.

"They didn't say it but they acted like you were just telling them to keep yourself out of trouble. Like the little kid who tells his mom on his older brother for something they both did, thinking it would keep the little brother out of trouble. But the little brother gets in worse trouble because he was a snitch," said Roger.

"Well, I did the right thing. If I get in trouble for making a record of this situation our justice system is in a bad way."

"I think you need to be very careful," said Roger. "I don't know where this is going to end up."

"Amen," said Tom. "You are wiser than your years."

***

Tom went back to the bar. Jamie was finishing up with his last customer.

"How did you do?"

"About $70,000 total."

"That's amazing. How are you planning on getting all these A/C units down here?" asked Tom.

"I may need a ship; there is a hell of a market here. I am going to have to rent a warehouse and hire installers. I think there will be a good market within 100 miles of any electric generation plant. You would sell to the homes that are on the grid that receive service from the plant and to homeowners who are off the grid but have private generators."

"I'm glad this has worked out for you. I didn't think it would, actually," said Tom.

"I thought you had that feeling," said Jamie.

"Listen, I am going to be here awhile longer. I want to see if I can help Rick and at least make sure he gets back to Florida."

"Does he have insurance?" asked Jamie.

"You know, I should have thought of that."

"Yeah, I know what you mean. Sometimes it's best to get some sleep and start over in the morning."

Tom walked back to his room and sat in the large lounge chair and put his feet up on the ottoman and fell asleep immediately. He was not disturbed at all by Rick's snoring.

Chapter 36

The Cessna Skylane was cruising at 160 MPH at 5,000 feet and was about to finish the north/south flight pattern over the Orange Walk District attempting to find Rick's Aero Commander.

It was Monday morning. The pilot, a lieutenant in the Belize Military Force, was assigned to the Air Force division. He loved his job and flying was like being in church to some degree, particularly when he was up in the clouds in the plane alone. His flight mate had begged out of duty this morning, saying he was sick. He said that staring at the ground yesterday had soured his stomach and he couldn't fly again today.

The pilot had the radio and could communicate with the ground for companionship. But he didn't have anyone to sit to his right side and concentrate on the ground below. The pilot felt that if he found the plane it would be pure luck. But he enjoyed the flight. It was clear and there was little turbulence.

As the pilot was about 20 miles from the Grey Ranch he began to look for the 2,500 feet of road on Winston Grey's property that was suspicious for being a runway. He saw the runway/road in the distance and he saw a glint of light reflecting from metal on the surface. As he passed over he was able to see a plane on the road. He could not tell if the plane had two engines and he decided he would take another look. He reported what he saw to his superior: that he was reducing altitude to 2,000 feet to surveil a suspicious airplane that was located on the road on the Grey Ranch.

The communication was acknowledged. The pilot turned to the west and traveled about ten miles and then banked to the right and made a slow circle at about 120 MPH. The Cessna decreased altitude as the plane came around and headed south. The pilot continued to circle and the Skylane was now heading south at 100 MPH and at 2,000 feet about three miles from the runway on the Grey Ranch and he continued to decrease altitude, but held his speed.

"This is Belize Military Force Skylane 182. Over. I am now at 2,000 feet above the Grey Ranch and can observe a light colored, two engine aircraft believed to be an Aero Commander model 500S. Over." The pilot continued to report that the plane appeared to be in operation on the road and was taxiing to the north end of the runway with apparent intent to take off to the south. The dispatcher patched the Captain of the Air Force into the conversation.

"Lieutenant, you are not to in any way engage the suspect plane. Follow the plane but if the plane crosses the Belize border you are to return to base. You are not to pursue the plane."

"Roger," said the lieutenant. "Out".

The lieutenant closed on the twin engine plane as the AC-500S was climbing from takeoff and they met side to side, both heading south at about 1,000 feet. The lieutenant could clearly see the "N" number, "N500PT", painted on the side of the plane. He was also able to see at least two occupants in the plane, a pilot in the left front seat and a passenger sitting behind the pilot in a seat facing backwards. The lieutenant reported what he saw as he saw it and a record of his observations was made by the dispatcher at the air base at the Belize International Airport.

The lieutenant was unable to recognize the occupants of the Aero Commander or to even tell their gender. Both planes increased altitude.

The Aero Commander was flying at 1,500 feet and at 180 MPH and it began to pull away from the Cessna which continued to climb to 5,000 feet and it was now at 160 MPH. The Aero Commander rose to 2,500 feet and this still allowed the larger two engine plane to slowly pull ahead. From the Grey Ranch the planes headed south, then southwest over the capital, Belmopan. The Aero Commander then turned and flew southeast over the Hummingbird Highway. The Aero Commander was flying along the edge of the Mayan Mountains. The mountains were low as mountains go. The best known peak was Victoria Peak, height 3,675 feet. At Mount Margret (approximately 3,600 feet) the Aero Commander turned south. Victoria Peak would be coming up on the right.

The last two officially recognized airports in the country were on the coast at Big Creek and at Punta Gorda. If he is going to land in Belize, those are his last chances to fuel up, thought the lieutenant.

Once out of the mountains, the Aero Commander flew low, at only 400 to 500 feet above the coastal terrain below the plane. The plane passed over a large swamp. The plane then passed Big Creek, 20 miles to the southeast. Next up was Monkey River Town.

He isn't going to land, thought the lieutenant. He'll be over the ocean soon and out of the country. The Aero Commander must have increased speed because the plane was out of sight or lost to the vision of the lieutenant in the haze over the Caribbean Sea. The BAF pilot reported that the last sighting was west of Monkey River Town, heading southeast toward the Gulf of Honduras.

The lieutenant was told to return to base.

The Captain reported to Minister Prince and the minister called Tom Night and relayed the information. Tom told the minister that Anthony and the judge said they were heading for Cartagena, Columbia.

The minister relayed that information to the Captain and he alerted the authorities in Guatemala, Honduras, Panama and Columbia.

The minister told Tom they had reported the missing plane to the surrounding authorities. Tom thanked the minister for their efforts.

Fat chance they will find the plane, thought Tom.

***

The D-8 Bar was located on the western highway. Beside the fact that the Sergeant Major was the most congenial barkeep in the country, his establishment had phone service because the phone line from Belize City to Belmopan ran by the D-8 Bar along the Western highway. Even if you didn't drink alcohol you sometimes needed to make a phone call.

Sergeant Major charged $5 US to make a station to station call anywhere in the country that could be reached by the line. Frederick and George went to the bar with a five dollar bill and said they needed to call Belize City.

It was 10:00 a.m. Monday. Frederick was on the line to the hotel asking for Tom. The caller said he wanted to speak to Tom privately. Tom was in his room where he was talking to Jamie and Rick about the report on the Aero Commander last being seen over Monkey River Town. The desk clerk came to Tom's room. Tom was ushered into the private room behind the desk in the lobby by the desk clerk.

Frederick was on the line but Tom could hear George in the background.

"Winston came to our house last night. He dropped off his cousin and said he would be away for a while. He gave us $10,000 US for his cousin's care and wanted me and George to make arrangements with the Mennonites to take the boy and try to rehabilitate him from his disabilities. Tom, we want you to talk to the Mennonites for us."

"I will do that for you. Where was Winston going?"

"He was with three men and he said he was going to Columbia, South America. He had a chance to make big money, he said."

"Can you describe the men?"

"They were older than Winston. They were in a truck and it was dark. I was looking through the windshield. I think one had blond hair, but that is all I remember. Winston also wanted you to know he was not a sissy."

"What prompted him to say that?"

"He said you called him queer."

"He misunderstood me. I will send someone to pick up the boy at your ranch today. Give the money to the person who comes for the child. It will probably be Jacob and his wife who will come to your house."

Tom retrieved an envelope and hotel stationary from the clerk. Tom wrote a message with the particulars about the boy for Jacob and he sealed the envelope. Tom went out of the lobby and got the attention of a cab driver and gave the cabbie the letter and told him to deliver the letter unopened to Jacob at Spanish Lookout. Tom gave directions to Jacob's house on the hill. He paid the driver $35 US.

Tom called the minister and told him what he just learned from Frederick and George.

The minister said he would personally call the Attorney General in Columbia. "I must admit though that it will probably do little good."

Tom thanked the minister and they talked about the agreement involving the licenses and leases. The minister had only minor objections. He would forward the paperwork with his son to Herbert's office so that a final draft could be completed.

Tom said it looked like he would return to the States the next day by a commercial flight. He would bring the documents to Florida for his clients to sign and then they would be returned to the minister within a day or two after that.

Tom returned to his room to discuss what he knew and talk with Jamie and Rick about leaving Belize the next day.

Chapter 37

When Winston, Anthony, the judge and H. Patel drove back from Frederick's ranch after meeting with Frederick and George and dropping off the boy with a suitcase with his belongings and the cash for the Mennonites, they were quiet.

Finally Winston spoke, "The boy will be better with the Mennonites. I couldn't teach him anything anymore. He was very frustrated."

"You did the right thing," said Anthony.

"I agree," said the judge.

"I don't know what to think," said H. Patel. "I didn't expect we would be in this position – that we would have to leave Belize."

The others remained quiet. The original plan had been that Winton's and Anthony's clout with the politicians would allow the men to stay in Belize, but Tom Night unintentionally interfered with their plans.

***

On the way back to Winston's Ranch the four men stopped at the overseas telephone facility near Belmopan and the judge made a collect call to Judge Raymond Barrow's private line in Bushton, Florida.

Judge Barrow was curt answering the phone on the first ring. "Who is this?"

"It's David Lucius."

"Are you calling collect?" said Barrow.

"Yes."

"I don't want a record of this call on my phone bill," said Judge Barrow.

"I called on your private line for God's sake. How is anyone going to get a record of this call? Don't be so paranoid."

"Ok," said Barrow. "Just be quick."

"Look, we are going to have a problem with this attorney, Tom Night. He will not play ball with us. He won't help us down here," said Judge Lucius. "We will have to leave Belize. We are trying to figure out where to go."

Judge Barrow was angry. "I knew this would happen. Once Tom Night comes back to Florida I can take care of him. I need Anthony to contact the Solicitor General, Andrew Prince. We need a witness from Belize to testify against Tom in Florida," said Judge Barrow.

"Let's not go overboard" said Judge Lucius. "We are just looking for someone to slow Tom down so we can sell the gold and jade. He's going to figure out we stole his plane and injured his pilot and be upset and maybe do something rash."

"I will take care of it," said Judge Barrow.

"We are all in this to make a lot of money," said Judge Lucius, "We have the treasure with us now and it's just a matter of selling it and turning it into dollars. I promised you a share of my take and you know I am a man of my word. But I am out on a limb, too. This is the last chance I have to make some big money – a stake that will keep me going for the rest of my life."

"If Tom gets in the way I may have to crush him. I want the money but I want to keep my job," said Judge Barrow. "I don't intend to retire."

"We'll get you a witness," said Judge Lucius.

***

The four men had gone back to Orange Walk. They covered Rick's plane with camouflage netting and went around the perimeter of the plane to make sure the netting was secure.

Winston made sandwiches and took bottles of juice for the trip. Winston also hid the rum from the judge. He had brought the rum with him when he left the Bahamas. "Home Brew," he called it. His family had had a distillery before he was run out of the country. He had sold all his family's hard assets at a discount, but he kept up a good front in Belize, appearing to be a wealthy ex-pat from the Bahamas. When he came to Belize, he spent money on Belize politicians knowing that the lack of political contributions and clout had lost him his family estate in the Bahamas. He wouldn't make that mistake again.

Since arriving in Orange Walk he had made his donations regularly to the ADP Party and he was lucky when the party won the election two years ago. The party ran everyone in the Liberal Party out of office and appointed their own family and friends to government service. The ADP had also suspended all licenses and leases. Tom's clients had been hurt by the policies of the ADP.

Because of his donations, Winston was among the businessmen who benefited from the party's protection. Winston had fashioned a portion of his road into a runway and he ran a way station for aircraft flying drugs from South America to the USA. Winston was paid a fee every time a plane landed or took off from his property. And he offered the service of a mechanic and laborers to repair or to load or unload the planes. Winston was paid separately for each and every service he provided, and Winston paid part of what he received to the authorities.

Winston also paid the Captain of the Belize Defense Force to direct air force surveillance flights away from his property when there would be activity on his runway.

This enterprise had worked well and Winston had stashed $500,000 US in cash in a safe at his ranch. But Winston began to have an uneasy feeling in the last six months. It was over. He felt that he was vulnerable and that it was only a matter of time before his illegal activity would be exposed by someone. He worried most about the DEA or the CIA at the US Embassy. The ADP could not protect Winston from the US authorities. He would be jailed forever if the US drug enforcement agency arrested him. Winston realized he had to move on.

Anthony had offered a similar service to the drug traders in Florida that Winston offered in Belize at his ranch. Anthony rented land by a small airstrip in the middle of the most densely populated county in Florida. Planes carrying drugs were primarily looking for fuel. Anthony ran a fuel service for small planes at the airport. He would deliver the fuel to the planes, which would park on the taxiway. Anthony did not discriminate. He serviced legitimate private planes or drug dealer's planes. The fuel delivery was made with a fuel truck that was also outfitted with tools and parts to repair the plane if needed. Drug dealers relied on Anthony for repairs. Anthony had seen most every type of mechanical problem and he had successfully made the repair. It got to the point that he would be advised of a problem while a plane was still in the air, and he would meet the plane at a deserted or little used airstrip if the plane was crippled and couldn't make it to his airstrip. Sometimes the repair took hours, but Anthony had been successful and had not been caught until he was called to meet the plane in Bushton to fix the plane's fuel bladder. He was arrested for trespass and his troubles began.

But it was a mistake. He should not have been arrested.

Anthony had paid off the police to ignore any activity at the airport in Bushton, but the fix didn't take and he was caught by an officer who wasn't advised to ignore activity at the airport. The officer saw the plane land on a strip with no lights and taxi and park. It was bad luck. It was all bad luck.

***

Anthony liked Tom but he was too honest. Anthony couldn't trust Tom. So Anthony hired another lawyer, H. Patel, who knew Judge Lucius. The judge sat around bars talking up his talents as a fixer and after listening to his spiel, Anthony decided to hire him and H. Patel to fix his case.

The judge and the new lawyer advised Anthony to give them $100,000 and they would pay off the bondsman. Then once he was paid off, Judge Lucius reasoned, Anthony could take his boats and head back to Belize. Anthony was convinced he would be convicted on the theft charge if he relied on Tom to defend his case at trial. But regardless, he could accept the fact he would be a fugitive and on the run. But the judge's strategy was expensive. Anthony paid $135,000 and then the insurance company reneged and had him arrested by the Bounty Hunter.

A bondsman didn't want his clients to run because he would get a bad reputation and his other clients would think the bondsman was soft and his other clients would run, too. It was a bad business model.

Tom was unaware of these complexities and conspiracies – that the bondsman and the insurance company had been paid off. Tom was only hired to attempt to obtain the permit to move the boats from México to Ambergris Caye (San Pedro, Belize). Tom did his job. As a result the boat with the treasure hidden in the bulkhead made it safely to Belize.

But Winston, the judge, and H. Patel were in a desperate situation. They were all out fees and cash and Anthony was still in jail and the treasure was somewhere on the dive boat. Anthony would not tell the men where the treasure was so long as he was in jail in Bushton.

So Anthony charmed the jailer to let Anthony out of his cell to make a phone call.

And when Anthony was let out of his cell to make a phone call in the lobby of the Bushton County Jail and the guard was distracted, Anthony walked out the door. Winston was there in the parking lot. Winston and Anthony drove to Tarpon Springs to the harbor to an ocean tugboat and were taken on board as members of the crew. They motored in the small ocean going tug pushing a barge full of 55 gallon barrels to be filled with orange juice concentrate to Dangriga, Belize. Once in Dangriga, they were met by Judge Lucius and H. Patel.

Since then, the group had committed an assault on Rick and stolen his plane and retrieved the tool box full of treasure. This was not what they had planned, but these events were what "luck" provided. The men went to sleep that night after giving the child to George hoping there would be better days again, and three of the four of the men, Anthony, Winston and the judge, felt safe and free for the moment.

H. Patel was not so sure.

Part V
Criminal Contempt

Chapters 38 through 46

The BDF chases the AC-500S ... Airplane defect ... The C-47 ... México City ... Tom Night returns to Florida ... Darlene Street represents Tom Night ... The hearing before Judge Barrow ... Tom Night is sentenced to jail ... The prosecutor and the newspaper ... The Police Chief's investigation ...

Chapter 38

The men at Winston Grey's ranch had seen and heard the Cessna flying a pattern over the ranch the afternoon before. Winston knew the plane was owned by the Belize Defense Forces (BDF). Rick's Aero Commander was under camouflage netting and they thought it was safe from view from the air, particularly if the surveillance plane was flying at 5,000 feet or higher. They could hear the plane again in the morning and the engine noise was closer to the ground. They felt they had to get out now or they would lose their best chance of escape.

Anthony would fly the plane. Winston was co-pilot and the Judge and H. Patel would fly backward. The bench seat held the Craftsman tool chest which contained the gold and jade.

The men quickly removed the camouflage netting. Anthony stowed it in the plane. The plane had been loaded the night before after they returned from Frederick's ranch. They waited for the Cessna to fly to the north over the ranch and they took off to the south. Anthony felt he would be away and out of sight of the Cessna by the time the Cessna had made its turn and was heading back to the south, but the pilot of the Cessna must have seen them earlier then they thought.

As the AC-500S reached 500 feet, the judge alerted Anthony. "Look to your left ... look to your left."

There was the Cessna at their side, no more than 200 feet from the Aero Commander.

"Damn," said Winston. For sure he was now identified as a member of the group that had stolen the plane and assaulted Rick. To date no one had been able to identify him as part of the gang but now the plane had left his ranch and he was discovered. The only member of the group who had not been identified as a participant in the conspiracy was H. Patel. From now on H. Patel would have to speak with the authorities.

Winston would not return to his ranch again. But he had relocated before and he had more of a stake than he had the last time when he left the Bahamas. Now he had almost $500,000 US in cash and he owned a third of the value of the contents of the tool chest. He would be OK. But he was thinking like a drunk. He had forgotten all the mental and emotional and physical pain he had suffered accumulating his assets, the ranch in Belize and his position and clout with the politicians in the country.

All of the men had lost a great deal by conspiring together. They were identified as thieves. If they considered it logically it would be best to turn themselves in and hire a good lawyer. But they had tricked themselves into believing that they could still overcome all obstacles and prevail. They were all in denial.

Anthony could see the face of the pilot of the surveillance plane. Anthony knew that the Aero Commander was more powerful than the Cessna and that he could outrun the other plane. Anthony also had the advantage because he knew where he was going. So Anthony followed his flight plan with confidence. He flew to Belmopan from Orange Walk. Then he flew low over the Hummingbird Highway so that he was just above the altitude of the Mayan Mountains. Then he turned south at Mount Margaret and Victoria Peak and flew over the coastal plain past Big Creek and Monkey River Town. Then he flew out over the Gulf of Honduras.

***

When Anthony lost sight of the Cessna he changed direction. He flew southwest toward Guatemala. When they again reached the coast they saw a large river flowing into the Atlantic. This was the Motagua River, which flowed northeast through the Motagua Valley. This valley formed the boundary between Honduras and Guatemala. This is a dry region that exists between two mountain ranges in the north and the south. The mountains deny the valley any precipitation. The Motagua Valley lies on the fault line between the North American and Caribbean continental plates. The valley is hot and has a long dry season but there are many streams that flow from the mountains to the North and South into the Motagua River. The valley has many farms that are irrigated by the river and its tributaries. Agricultural uses include subsistence and commercial farming and cattle grazing up the steep slopes of the mountains. The river is the longest in Guatemala, about 300 miles, and extends inland to a point where the pollution from Guatemala City (industrial waste, sewage and black water) affects the cleanliness of the water.

***

Anthony had held the plane steady at 7,500 feet and they were now half way up the Motagua River. He asked if everyone wanted a smoke. None of the men smoked, and they looked at each other quizzically. "Cigars. I mean a cigar. We are coming to Zacapa. The best cigars outside of Havana," said Anthony.

"Great, we want out of these seats," said Winston.

The airport for Zacapa, Guatemala was in the Town of Chiquimula.

As they landed, the men felt a rush of air into the cabin. This had not happened on the few occasions that they flew the plane. They could see that the door seal had bent and allowed air to rush into the cabin and there was a bulge in the upholstery above the pilot's seat. Anthony feathered the engines slowly letting the plane glide in. He had to counter a drift of the plane to port side.

Anthony did not have time to declare an emergency to the tower. The AC-500S was almost on the ground when the incident occurred. The sky was clear and there was no turbulence and he was able to land safely. The men did not have time to be scared. Rather, they were confused.

"Damn, what happened?" the passengers asked together.

"We'll see. We had a major failure. It was like the plane bent in half. I am going to taxi to the flight pad for an inspection."

When the plane stopped, members of the ground crew immediately came to the plane and began to look at the forward side of the wing. The ground crew knew something was wrong. There was a distortion in the skin of the plane where the wing and fuselage met.

The wing was constructed to sweep forward five degrees. This was accomplished by bending the main spar of the wing forward when the spar was manufactured. The location of the distortion was at wing station 24. This was the location where wing failure had occurred on the wing of other Aero Commanders. Luckily for the men there had not been a total wing separation while the plane was inflight. That would have been fatal. The plane would have fallen from the sky. Instead, there had been a crack or partial separation of the wing and fuselage which held during the landing. Fortunately, this plane had also had an after-market patch or fix for the defect that prevented total separation. The fix was the stainless steel strap that Rick had fitted between the main spar and the fuselage. The strap strengthened the joint in the spar which was bent to allow the sweep of the wing. That piece of steel had saved the men's lives.

Harish Patel, now acting on behalf of the men, spoke to the ground crew and ordered an inspection. Everyone knew the wing had to be reattached so Patel also requested an estimate for the cost and time for repairs of the plane.

Before leaving Belize, Winston had had a forged bill of sale prepared transferring ownership of the plane from Rick Ibn to himself. For a fee the papers were signed and notarized by the Interior Minister in Belize. There was also an inventory, a history of the owners and lessees of the plane that was also forged. According to the paperwork, the last lessee was H. Patel, Attorney at Law from Tampa, Florida. H. Patel was in possession of the ownership papers when he spoke with the ground crew.

When he was asked, Attorney Patel advised the ground crew that the purpose of the visit to Zacapa was business and that they had landed to purchase cigars and at that time they discovered there was a problem with the plane.

Winston and Anthony stayed with the plane and watched as the skin was removed from the wing by the mechanics. The workers discovered the main spar which sweeps forward five degrees and is bent up five degrees was cracked at the dihedral angle. The dihedral angle is the upward angle of the wing from the fuselage to the wing tip. The crack could not be welded. They needed a new wing which would cost $15,000 for the part plus the cost of labor for the repair, assuming they could find a replacement wing that was sound.

***

Anthony made sure the lock was fastened on the tool chest and he and Winston went to the coffee shop at the hanger and sat down to figure out what to do.

If they stole a plane, they were in the middle of Guatemala, about 70 miles from Guatemala City. This wasn't Belize. Guatemala had an air force with jets that would chase them down, catch them and shoot them out of the sky.

They couldn't wait for the repair of the plane. Someone would become suspicious and they would be found out and arrested. Anthony had been in jail in Guatemala City once for having too much fun, and he was starved and beaten. He didn't want to repeat that experience. Anthony had a license to fly a plane that was issued in Columbia, South America, and he had ID under the name Anthony George from the same country. As of this day Anthony Arnold was Anthony George.

"We need to buy a plane," Anthony decided. Winston agreed.

The judge and H. Patel were brought into the conversation. "What about a rental?"

Anthony and Winston laughed, "These people are not stupid. They know if we rented the plane we would never bring it back."

Winston went to speak to someone about the C-47 (DC 3) that had a "for sale" sign in the window. The plane appeared to be in good shape, both engines were rebuilt. It was forfeited to the airport after it was repaired and the owner ran out of funds. It could be bought for $55,000 US, which was the cost of the repairs. The owner of the airport was anxious to sell the plane to recoup his expense in fixing the engines. For his profit, he would take the Aero Commander in trade.

"No problem," the group decided. Winston went back and counted out the cash. He marked across the title that the Aero Commander was sold "for salvage only". The purchaser did not object. He wouldn't sell the plane as sound for flight. Since the plane was sold for parts it would not be as easily traced as in the case where a plane is sold as a used plane to be operated privately or commercially.

Anthony had a quick lesson in what was where in the C-47 (DC-3). He was qualified in any prop driven twin engine airplane and he caught on quickly. The plane had a pilot and co-pilot seat. There was a bench seat behind the pilot that would hold three men. "This is perfect," thought Anthony. A Douglas C-47 is the version of the DC-3 that was used to haul cargo and troops during World War II. It was extremely durable and all the bugs had been shaken out of the plane during the war. This plane was outfitted for cargo only.

The men had dinner. Chicken with rice and beans. They were also served fresh tomatoes and fresh cantaloupe which were locally grown. They finished the meal with a cigar rolled in Zacapa. The tobacco was aromatic and mild.

They went outside and watched the porters move all of their belongings from one plane to another. They could see the tool chest. Their property was placed in cargo bins attached to the floor on the inside of the plane.

After the plane was loaded, Anthony entered the plane, closed the door and unlocked the tool chest. He went through the contents. Everything was there. He looked at the Mayan jade. Anthony was aware that this jade probably had been mined here in Guatemala 600 years before. The Motagua Valley near Quirigua was the only known source of jade in Mesoamerica. Jade from mines located in El Parton in the Motagua Valley had been traded by the Mayans and was found throughout the Yucatán and in the islands in the Caribbean Sea. The jade trade was an important factor in establishing this valley as a Pre-Columbian commerce route.

"These rocks saved us when the wing separated," Anthony said to Winston. "I think they gave us luck and the time we needed to land." Anthony claimed the jade felt hot to the touch.

When Anthony jumped down from the plane after his inspection he asked a mechanic if there were any jade mines in the area. He was told that in Zacapa there were marble mines and "maybe some jade is found there."

As he walked back to the men there was a large cry. It was the noise of a million insects. Anthony was startled by the sound. It was the "chic arras" said the mechanic. They chirped in the field in the late afternoon in the dry season.

"It's time to go. We are all fueled, I see," said Anthony, referring to the judge who was holding a bottle of Zacapa Rum which was distilled locally. Anthony felt the judge would not last the trip.

They settled in their seats, took a deep breath and Anthony taxied to the runway. He braked fully and then revved the engines until the plane shuttered and bounced off the tarmac. "Better to blow an engine on the ground than in the air," thought Winston. The engines held.

It was 3:00 p.m. CT. Anthony wanted to make Santa Ana, El Salvador before dark. He would not fly at night because he had to rely on sight to determine his position.

Anthony felt Winston should also learn to fly the C-47, so as they flew, Anthony checked him out in the plane.

***

Anthony flew with Winston as co-pilot past Zacapa through the valley through the mountains. They reached Santa Ana, El

Salvador without incident. They landed and spoke to the ground crew. For a few dollars they were allowed to park the plane on the taxi way and they slept soundly inside their new plane.

Anthony was relived they had rid themselves of the Aero Commander. It was like a sore thumb and it would have been identified as being stolen at some point. Now they were in a plane that was "clean." They had purchased it in a legitimate commercial transaction and they had good paperwork for the plane, not the forgeries Winston had had produced by his political cronies in Belize for the AC-500S.

Chapter 39

Anthony intended to sell the pre-Columbian gold and the Mayan Jade pieces in the capital of México. Anthony researched and knew México City would offer the best price for the objects because the dealers in antiquities in México City would be familiar with the authenticity and provenance of Anthony's treasure. The worry for the dealer is that he buys a piece of treasure that he does not recognize as stolen or fake. The dealer only wants items that are legally salvaged with the permission of the government. The dealer makes his money by underpaying the seller and over charging the buyer.

Everything that was in Anthony's tool chest was legitimate. Over the years, as Anthony found the pieces treasure hunting in the waters off Punta Rosa, he would take the pieces to the Minister of Antiquities in Merida in Quintana Roo, Yucatán, México. There the piece was recorded, a tax was paid, and a certificate of authenticity was issued for the find. Thus, these objects became legitimized and they were merchantable.

The only issue was the value. The dealers only allowed a small number of pieces to come on the market each year. To protect the pricing the dealers were sometimes forced to purchase legitimate, authentic pieces at a handsome price when they came to their attention. The dealers acted like a cartel. By purchasing all legitimate art works that came to their attention, they controlled the number of pieces that ultimately went to market. The dealers were able to inflate the price because they had created a market for a rare item.

When the four men arose in the morning in Santa Ana they loaded up and took off and they flew back north through the mountains and retraced their steps past Zacapa and then northwest to the western border of Belize across low, 3,000 foot mountains.

Winston was flying now and he was pleased with the control and response of the plane. The Aero Commander would not have felt as solid as the C-47 going over the mountains, even though the mountains were low and in some places more like the hills in the Carolinas in the States. There was much turbulence as they crossed the mountains.

After the mountains, they headed north and west to the coast to the city of Ciudad del Carmen on the Bay of Campeche in the Gulf of México. They landed and refueled. The C-47 could go 1,600 miles with its tanks full. Anthony wanted to be sure they had enough gas. No telling what could happen on the trip. Even though there was little he could control, he at least could control the amount of gas they had in their tanks. If they were chased out over the Gulf of México with full tanks they could fly across the Gulf to Florida and then to the Bahamas before they ran out of fuel.

Winston took control of the plane and now they flew over the Bay of Campeche to Veracruz. Anthony took the yoke and they headed due west to México City, following the trail the Spanish Conquistadors took on their way to conquer the Aztecs.

Anthony did most of the flying and even when Winston was in control, Anthony remained in the co-pilot seat in case there was an emergency. There was none. Winston flew into México City and landed uneventfully. They made arrangements to keep the plane at the airport and rented a room at a small airport hotel. They were only a block from the plane.

Now that they were in México City, they would again be lost in plain sight. The city had a population of five million people. Because of the possible notoriety of Winston and Anthony they decided that H. Patel and the judge would meet with the antiquities dealers and sell the treasure. Neither the judge nor the attorney, H. Patel, were wanted in the courts in the States or

Central America, and they had no family who would have issued a missing persons alert and they had no warrants in Belize for the theft of Rick's plane. Therefore they would handle the sale of the gold and jade.

***

Back in Belize City, Tom and Jamie prepared to fly back to the States on a commercial passenger plane operated by TACA. The flight was only three hours to Miami. Jamie would be home and they would know if there was an arrest warrant for Tom when he passed through US Customs. If nothing happened at Customs, Tom would go on to Tampa. He would have a tough conversation with Roger Adams, his partner. Tom felt Roger would agree they needed to split up the partnership. There would be a negative publicity onslaught coming.

Rick stayed in Belize City waiting for word on his plane. He really wasn't feeling that well and the doctor was kind. They met for lunch and dinner each day. Rick found out she was not married.

***

On the plane back to Miami, Tom and Jamie got seats side by side.

"This isn't anything like the ride in the Aero Commander," said Jamie.

"Why did you take Rick's plane to Belize?" asked Tom. "You could have flown commercial."

"I didn't know what to expect and I thought you or Rick would give me some advice; like a travel consultant. When I called Rick to make a reservation he said you were going too and that you had experience with the people and the government. I thought you could keep me out of trouble."

"Well, you certainly did well with your sales."

"It was a lot better than I ever thought." said Jamie. "There is a market and money to pay a fair price for the product. I couldn't ask for anything more. I just hope I can get a foothold before someone else finds out. What I really see is a market for electric appliances. There is no store or outlet that provides installation, warranty and repair of electric products. It's like I fell into a time warp and I'm back in the 1940's in the Deep South."

"If you need help in Belize with the government, give me a call. It's kind of hit or miss, but I may be able to help. You have to remember to be patient," said Tom.

Jamie fell off to sleep. It was a smooth flight to Miami. Tom had no problems going through U.S. Customs.

Chapter 40

Tom came to the office early after his return from Belize. As he expected, Roger was already there with coffee brewing and donuts. Tom had coffee but abstained from the sweets.

"I have to call the court as soon as you are back in the country. The State Attorney and the judge want to speak to you under oath," said Roger. "I promised I would call."

"Ok, well, welcome home," said Tom sarcastically.

"Yeah, I know," said Roger, "What can I say? They are really upset. I took it upon myself to call Darlene Street to act as your attorney."

"God, I didn't think about Darlene. She's perfect. Judge Raymond Barrow and the little snake of a prosecutor, John Hale, both hate her. She will aggravate them to death."

"I know," said Roger laughing. "She said we should not talk to one another about any of this. Darlene said we do not have an attorney/client privilege. We are just two business partners. We are not each other's lawyers. We can be compelled to tell anything we talk about between ourselves that was not a communication from or about another client."

"I understand. Darlene will be my attorney. Are you hiring an attorney, Roger?"

"Let's see how it goes."

"Don't you expect negative publicity for the firm from this?" asked Tom.

"I don't know yet. Darlene said she got Judge Barrow and Hale to agree to meet with you and Darlene in chambers. There will be no hearing on the court's calendar so there should be no press unless Hale lied and he intends to call the newspaper," said Roger.

"If there is no press, Darlene has already earned her pay," said Tom.

"You have a meeting with her at 9:00 a.m. at her office, so you better get moving."

Tom unloaded his briefcase. In it he was carrying all of the documents to reestablish the rights between the country of Belize and Barnes Lime Rock Company.

"Roger, could you please get these documents over to Bob and Frank Barnes and have their in-house attorney read them? I am hoping to return to Belize with the documents signed by our client in the next couple of days," said Tom. "I also have the documents and cash for the sale of the equipment at the turpentine still. The costs were $500. Net to client is $9,500. Bob Barnes told me to get what I could. I think he will be pleased with the result. There will also be about $100,000 paid into Herbert Johns' escrow account representing the money owed for the mahogany cants that are being shipped to England. Ask them for instructions on the use of that money."

"I will pass on the information to Frank Barnes. I guess you will be flying commercial now. How is Rick?" asked Roger.

"From what I could see he should fully recover," said Tom, "He and his doctor have hit it off. He may have lost a plane and gained a wife. If we need anything down there he will have time on his hands. He can help us close out the transaction with the government." Tom got serious and looked directly in Roger's eyes and asked, "What about you and I? Are we good? You can fire me if you want."

"No, I fully trust that you are honest and you won't intentionally hurt me or the firm. You need to go and see Darlene. Hurry."

***

Tom left and drove across town to the Imperial Tower in downtown St. Petersburg. Darlene practiced law out of her penthouse condo. She had an office with a secretary and a law clerk. She also had two old cats who held reign in her office and who determined if a person would become a client of the practice. One cat was missing an eye and the other was almost hairless. To pass the test to become Darlene's client you had to fawn over the cats and scratch their chins. After greeting the secretary, Tom followed the protocol and sat at a couch and petted the animals.

Darlene appeared shortly after her secretary paged her. She was dressed in a tailored navy blue suit. She was trim, well-groomed, with greying black hair. In her forties, she was petite until she spoke and then she blasted away at the listener with her words. She smoked too much and had a raspy voice.

"Tom, how did you let this low life drug dealer hang you out to dry like this? I talked to John Hale and he says he has a witness who will testify that you and Anthony Arnold and that crooked judge were conspiring in a bar in Belize City."

"Well, we did have a conversation but we didn't conspire to do anything." Tom let the hairless cat sit next to him and the other cat sat in his lap and stared at him with his one eye. It was an intense feline cross-examination.

"Was Anthony Arnold your client at the time you spoke with him in the bar?" asked Darlene.

"I was terminating the relationship, so to some degree, yes, he was still my client. But there was a third party to the conversation, the judge, so I don't know if the privilege was waived or not."

"As far as we are concerned the conversation was privileged." Darlene pointed her finger and cigarette and flicked an ash into a large tray on the desk to emphasize the fact. "If Anthony was present and talking to you, even if he was at a microphone announcing the arrivals and departures at Grand Central Station, then you were his attorney and the communication was privileged. Even if Anthony is dead, any conversation you had with him is privileged. The privilege belongs to Anthony and only he can waive the privilege.

"In my opinion," Darlene continued, "Anthony has to give up the privilege in court on the record before the court, or he has to give up the privilege in a writing that is witnessed and notarized, or if the facts of the conversation are such that the court on appeal finds there was a waiver, then, and only then, will you be advised by me to tell anyone what Anthony told to you. It doesn't matter to me if Anthony was in the presence of this half-baked judge from the Appeals Division of the State of Florida. Ok?"

"Ok. What do you want me to say at the hearing?" asked Tom.

Darlene's eyes blinked and she yelled. "Weren't you listening? You are saying nothing, unless I tell you to."

With that the cats jumped to the floor. Darlene handed Tom a questionnaire that Darlene made all her clients complete. The questionnaire asked a client's vital statistics, history of their life, that type of thing. Then Tom was to write out what Tom thought the case was all about and what it was that the client, in his opinion, did that was wrong or illegal. In effect, Darlene wanted a confession. Tom did the best he could. One thing that Tom was concerned about was the conversation he had with Solicitor General Prince about Anthony and the fact he was given H. Patel's card by the minister to give to Anthony and the fact he did give the card to Anthony.

Maybe I did something wrong, thought Tom.

Chapter 41

The trip from St. Petersburg to the courthouse in Bushton took about two hours and Darlene and Tom rode together. Most of the trip was through a pine forest planted by the DuPont's. Tom drove his car, a Mercedes SL series convertible. During the trip, Darlene went over the questionnaire Tom had filled out and Tom's statement of the facts.

This was an odd case because Tom had been summoned by the court to give testimony under oath about Anthony Arnold, a criminal defendant who Tom had represented. The law is divided into two processes, civil and criminal cases. In a criminal case, there is a charge that in Florida is called an "information" issued by the State Attorney or an "indictment" if a grand jury makes the charge. In civil court the case is brought by a "complaint" or a "petition". In either case – civil or criminal – there is a piece of paper that explains to the defendant in writing why he has to go before the judge and the consequence (jail or money judgment) that he faces if he loses.

In this case Tom was not named as the defendant in an information or an indictment, or a complaint; he was coming before the court as an officer of the court to answer questions about a former client who had escaped the jurisdiction of the court. Because Tom had represented Anthony the attorney/client privilege came into play. If Tom exercised the privilege on behalf of his client and refused to answer the court's questions he could be held in contempt of court and jailed until he answered the court's questions, but he could only be jailed if he exercised the privilege improperly.

"This is all screwed up," said Darlene. "I don't see how they are going to prove anything. And I don't know what you are supposed to have done. You were in Belize at the time Anthony escaped. There is no allegation you aided his escape."

"Correct, I didn't know about the escape until Roger told me by overseas phone call. We would have a record of that call at the office. That would be easy enough to prove with our phone records."

"And you didn't meet with Anthony or talk to him until Friday when you saw him in your hotel room and then later that same night when you talked to him in the bar at the Fort George Hotel?" asked Darlene.

"That's right. The only thing I did for him was give him the business card for attorney H. Patel that was given to me by the Solicitor General of Belize," said Tom.

"I don't understand that part. Why would the Solicitor General give you the card and how would he know that Anthony would see you in Belize?" asked Darlene.

"I don't know. I didn't think about it at the time. I took the card and when I saw Anthony I gave him the card. It seemed innocent enough," said Tom.

"I don't know." Darlene pondered the legal ramifications of the facts.

"Besides," said Tom as they pulled into the courthouse, "how would anyone know I gave Anthony the card other than the people who were present? I don't think Anthony or Judge Lucius will be at the hearing today."

Tom let Darlene out of his car near the entrance. "Meet me in the courtroom. We are late," said Darlene.

Darlene ran in and went to the judge's suite of rooms. His secretary, Jane, was there at her desk in the waiting room in front of the judge's chamber. She and Darlene were friends. They had gone to high school together. Jane had married a farmer in

Bushton and she had worked for Raymond Barrow when he was an attorney in private practice and she had been hired as a county employee as his secretary after he was elected judge.

A little history: Darlene's first husband had worked to put her through college and law school, then they divorced and she married the top civil lawyer in the county. He was so arrogant he didn't require Darlene to sign a pre-nuptial agreement. The second husband felt he could control Darlene. As a result of the fact there was no prenuptial, all of his assets were at risk. When they divorced Darlene was given half of everything. She bought the condo and she took long vacations and chose her clients carefully. She became rich beyond her dreams through the divorce.

"How are you doing, Jane?"

Jane smiled, "I am doing real well. I retire in two weeks. I've worked as the judge's secretary for twenty years."

"Well, lucky you." Darlene was not being catty, she was serious. Jane and her husband had worked hard and raised three children. They were out of school now. "Are the kids good?"

"Yes."

"You are very lucky."

Jane beamed. She liked Darlene. They were still good friends. Jane could never have done what Darlene did. Darlene had married well and stuck up for her rights. Jane did not like controversy. Jane did not like to deal with the conflict in the courts and was happy her duty as the judge's secretary would soon be over. She wanted a quiet retirement. She loved her husband and children.

"You need to get in there." Jane motioned to the door to chambers. "John Hale has been filling the Judge full of lies about Tom." Jane liked Tom. He was one of her favorites. Jane did not care for John Hale.

Darlene entered the room. There was a long table that was pushed up to a large desk to form the shape of a "T". Judge Barrow sat in a chair with a high back behind the large mahogany desk. The table in front of his desk was surrounded by chairs. Each side took a seat in the chairs opposite each other. If testimony was to be taken the witness would sit in the large chair that was placed at the opposite end of the table so the witness faced the judge. The judge's chamber was big enough for a banquet. The courthouse was old, constructed of coquina rock. There was a fireplace in the judge's hearing room and the chamber was decorated with antique furnishings. There were many plaques on the wall. There was a calendar on a tripod showing the schedule the court had set for its business for the next month.

The hearing was open to the public but there was no one in the room except Judge Barrow and Hale, the prosecutor. When Darlene entered, she looked around the room.

"I guess we will need a court reporter," said Darlene.

"Jane, get a court reporter over here quick, I want to start," the judge yelled out the door. "Where is Tom?" the judge was jumpy. "I want him in here now."

Darlene went to get Tom and brought him before the court.

"Tom," said the judge curtly.

"Yes, your Honor."

"Tom, it saddens me to bring you in here," said the judge.

Darlene immediately piped up and said: "Judge, I insist you not address my client unless we have a court reporter so we have a record and can make a transcript if we need to appeal. No record, no appeal. You know that. It's elementary."

"I don't need you to instruct me on the law or to tell me what to do, Darlene." The judge made notes as he spoke. He was impeccably dressed in a brown Wolf Brothers three piece suit. He was sixty and wore his hair in a crew-cut. He wore thick, gold-rimmed glasses.

Darlene smiled to herself and thought, I don't know how Jane put up with this man for so many years.

The court reporter came in and set her machine in front of her after she noted who was present and she began to strike the keys on the machine to make a record of what was said in the room.

"Now, Tom as I was saying, it saddens me to have to bring you in here, but it seems you have aided the escape, or at least allowed a prisoner to evade the authorities and the Order of my court after his escape."

"Your Honor," Tom began to speak.

Darlene cut him off. "Judge, I am here representing Mr. Night. We do not know what Tom is charged with. Can we start with that?"

Hale injected, "He has counseled Anthony Arnold to evade the jurisdiction of the court and avoid justice. He is in contempt of court."

"Mr. Hale, is this a criminal contempt?" Darlene stayed on the point of her argument.

"Of course, it is criminal." The judge's voice rose. "Anthony Arnold had a warrant issued for his arrest the day he escaped and Tom here was speaking to him in a bar in Belize City a few days later telling him what to do to avoid my order. This is a criminal contempt."

"A criminal contempt has to be charged formally in writing. Where is the written charge?" demanded Darlene.

"Don't tell me what I need to do in this matter," said the judge. "Darlene and Tom, you two sit down. Mr. Hale, call your witness."

"We have a right to depose the witness to know what he has to say before he testifies at this hearing," said Darlene.

"I will give you a copy of the witness's sworn statement after he testifies and before you question the witness," said Hale.

"That is improper, we object," said Darlene. "We have the right to take the statement of the witness before he testifies."

"This process is good enough for Federal Court," said Hale.

"I agree," said the judge. "I have a right to discipline the attorneys who practice before me. Tom cannot avoid that oversight by asserting mere technicalities. Mr. Hale, call the witness."

"Please rule on my objection, Judge."

"Objection denied," said Judge Barrow.

Hale went to a door that led from the hearing room to the witness room and opened it. A man walked out of the room, looked around and took the witness chair.

Tom wrote a note on the pad of legal paper in front of him that said, "He's the doorman at the Fort George Hotel." Tom showed the note to Darlene. She considered what Tom had written.

"I wish to speak to my client and I ask for a short recess." Darlene stood up.

"Overruled," said the judge. "Sit down and be quiet, Darlene. Listen to the testimony, you may learn something important."

"Please state your name," said Hale.

"John Joseph Henry," said the witness.

"How are you employed?"

"I am a doorman and police officer assigned as the house detective at the Fort George Hotel in Belize City, Belize in Central America."

"Are you a sworn law enforcement officer?"

"Yes, I am licensed by the Office of the Solicitor General of the country of Belize."

"I direct your attention to last Friday. Were you present at the hotel where you work undercover as the doorman?"

"Yes."

"Are you familiar with a man named Anthony Arnold and a man named Tom Night?"

"Yes, I know both men. Mr. Night is seated here to my right," and he pointed to Tom.

"The record should reflect the witness pointed to Mr. Night," said the judge. The court reporter nodded to the judge.

"Did you have any involvement with the two men while you were at work that night?"

"I was on duty in my undercover capacity as a doorman last Friday, and Anthony Arnold and another man came in and asked for Mr. Night. Anthony Arnold said Tom Night was his attorney and so I let the men in Mr. Night's room."

"Objection, hearsay." Darlene stood when she objected.

"Denied," said the judge. "Quit interrupting, Darlene. And please sit down."

Hale continued his direct examination. "Did you see Mr. Night later with these men?"

"Yes, Mr. Night came to me when he was on his way to the dining room. Mr. Night asked me to make a copy of a business card. Mr. Night was upset that I let the men in his room. I didn't see the harm."

"Did you copy the card?"

"Yes, I made two copies, one for Mr. Night and one that I folded up and put in my pocket."

"Do you still have the copy of the card?"

"Yes, I have it here." The witness handed Mr. Hale the copy of H. Patel's business card.

"Did you have any more contact with Mr. Arnold and Mr. Night?"

"I saw Mr. Arnold and an older gentleman sitting and dining with Mr. Night. When Anthony and his friend left the hotel I followed them out to speak to them."

"Objection. Testimony regarding what those three men said would be hearsay," said Darlene.

"Overruled, it's not being offered for the truth of the statements. It's part of this officer's investigation," said Judge Barrow. "Proceed, Mr. Hale."

"What did they have to say?" asked Hale.

"Objection. Hearsay."

"You are being obstructive Ms. Street. I have already ruled. Mr. Hale, just ask him what was said and let it go at that. We will be here all night."

"Tell the judge what was said."

"I told the two men I was a police officer. Anthony said he knew that. He said he had been to Belize before. He had been a client of my boss, the Solicitor General, before Minister Prince took office. I knew Anthony was a treasure hunter and he had a good reputation as a businessman in Belize. I also knew Anthony faced charges in the U.S.A. I asked Arnold about the warrant from Florida. I did not want any trouble in the hotel. Anthony said the charges were a mistake. Anthony said Tom was his attorney and Tom was helping them correct the mistake."

"Objection, hearsay."

"Denied."

"Had Mr. Night admitted to you that Anthony Arnold was his client?" asked Hale.

"Well, when Mr. Night asked me why I let the men in his room, I told him that Anthony said Tom was their attorney. Tom never denied the fact."

"Objection, improper conclusion. Mr. Night's silence cannot be introduced as an admission," said Darlene.

"Overruled. Tom can straighten all this out when he testifies," said the judge.

"This is a criminal hearing. Mr. Night cannot be compelled to testify," countered Darlene.

"Overruled," said the judge. "Do you have any more questions for the witness, Mr. Hale?"

"No."

"The judge turned to Tom and said, "If you testify, you may or may not go to jail. If you don't testify, based on the testimony presented to me, you go to jail. Which is it?"

Tom looked at Darlene.

"We have a right to cross examine the witness, your Honor," said Darlene.

The judge ignored Darlene and looked directly at Tom. "Mr. Night, I have heard sufficient testimony from Mr. Henry. I'm waiting for your decision. Do you want to testify and explain yourself?" said the judge.

"I rely on the advice of counsel and assert the attorney/client privilege as the basis for refusing to testify," said Tom.

"Further, your Honor, Mr. Night has the right to assert his Fifth Amendment right to remain silent," said Darlene.

The Judge looked at the note pad in front of him and then he read the following statement into the record:

"This matter coming to be heard before the Court on a charge of Criminal Contempt, and the court having heard testimony of the witness John Joseph Henry, it is Ordered and Adjudged that the crime has been proven and it is the sentence of the court that you, Thomas Night, be incarcerated for a term of six months in the county jail in Bushton, Florida."

"Thank you, your Honor," said Hale as he collected his papers and he and his witness left the room quickly.

Darlene went to the court reporter and ordered a copy of the transcript of the hearing.

The judge smiled and said, "Darlene, my bailiff is gone. Will you take Mr. Night over to the jail? Tell the sheriff I will have the order of commitment delivered to him first thing in the morning."

Chapter 42

Even when Anthony was diving and treasure hunting and he was out of pocket for months at a time, he had a stock broker who was trading on his account in the equity and bond markets. The broker bragged he was successful because he followed the movement and anticipated trends in the markets. There had been two recessions that were close together and as a result the market had stagnated for about ten years. The broker had hedged the market and he avoided the recession.

Now there was inflation and turmoil as the government raised rates to arrest inflationary trends. Anthony had cash and his broker invested in US bonds and notes. Anthony's investments were beating inflation. The times were also good for hard assets, gold, art and precious stones and ancient artifacts. Mayan Jade and Pre-Columbian art works fashioned from gold by the Incas, Aztecs and Mayans were rising in value.

Anthony entrusted his broker with some gold pieces and gave him the authority to sell to raise cash for purchases of stocks and bonds. The broker had made contacts with antiquities dealers in México City and he would photograph pieces Anthony delivered and then send the photographs by courier to at least three dealers and then take bids on the items. The dealers knew they were in competition for the pieces and this made the process reasonably fair. The dealer would make a bid and if he was the winner he would receive the original piece and would make payment by wire transfer to the broker's bank for Anthony's account in a Netherlands Antilles bank. The money wire would be made after the dealer had inspected the artifact. This procedure had worked well.

Now, however, Anthony wanted to cash out. Anthony had paid the stock broker 20% of the sale price for handling the transactions. Winston objected to paying the broker. They agreed to sell the treasure themselves and cut out the broker. The original plan was to have Winston and Anthony sell the artifacts to the dealers, but because Anthony and Winston were seen flying Rick's plane, H. Patel and the judge would have to sell the pieces in person to the various dealers that Anthony's broker had identified over the last five years.

Anthony was concerned about the arrangement because the judge was a drunk and H. Patel was too nervous. Patel looked guilty. Winston calmed Anthony down and the four worked out a plan. H. Patel or the judge would call a dealer first and advise that they had a certain piece, describe it and explain the provenance of the piece to prove it was authentic and that they had rightful possession. If the dealer was interested they would set an appointment for a viewing. It was expected that payment would be made at the time of the appointment if the dealer made a purchase. The idea was to sell only one or two pieces to each broker so as not to exhaust the cash the dealer would have available, and there would not be a delay in the purchase. It also prevented the judge and H. Patel from stealing the proceeds of any more than a single sale, or of them being robbed with all the pieces in their possession, resulting in a total loss. The men knew that they would not be able to report a theft of the art works to the police so they had to reduce the risk of the loss of their property by allowing Patel and the judge to only have possession of a limited number of the artifacts.

In addition, the men had worked out a division of the spoils that allowed Winston to be paid back the $135,000 that he paid to the bondsman and the insurance company to obtain Anthony's release from jail. In addition, they owed Winston $55,000 for the DC-3 airplane. After paying Winston back, the balance would be divided equally.

The men sold the gold items first. Anthony picked the piece to be sold and provided the judge with an address and phone number of the dealer. The judge called from the phone in their hotel room and set the appointment and then he and Patel went to the appointment and made the sale. Anthony required the pair to come back after each sale with the money. The payment was in US Dollars. The money was placed in the tool chest.

After seven successful sales and deliveries on the first day of trading, the men agreed to stop. They were being delayed by the traffic in the city and the taxi drivers were making the route as long as possible to increase the fare. They also used a different cab each time, so this would be a long process if the gold was sold one piece at a time. So Anthony agreed to increase the number of pieces of gold that would be shopped to each dealer to reduce the time needed to complete all the sales. The way it looked it would take about a week to sell the gold and another three days to sell the Mayan jade.

But they were ecstatic. After the first day, Winston was shy only $10,000 from being paid back. Also Anthony had been able to slow down the judge's consumption of alcohol by giving him only one ounce of rum each time he delivered cash from a sale.

By the fourth day the proceeds of the sales were such that Winston had been paid back and they had almost a half million dollars besides. Then on the fifth day after the third sale of the day, H. Patel said he felt like they were being watched in the jewelry store when they were in the back room while the dealer was inspecting the gold pieces. They were also asked a number of questions about the signature of the official in the Interior Department of the Mexican government who verified the tax on the piece had been paid.

At that time, H. Patel did what Anthony had told him to do and he showed a letter of introduction signed by Solicitor General Prince that attested to the bona-fides of the bearer of the letter and relayed the message that the Country of Belize was a participant in the proceeds that would be generated from the sale of the treasure.

"I didn't think it would be necessary to use the letter from the minister until we were selling the jade. Do you still have the letter?" asked Anthony.

"I did as we agreed. I held the letter while they read it and I refused to allow them to keep the original or make copies."

"Good, good. We need to stash this cash and move to a new location tonight. We should move now. We will keep the room in this hotel and keep some of our clothing here so the room looks lived in, but we need to move. It's a good thing I paid for the room for this hotel two weeks in advance," said Anthony.

The men agreed to suspend their plan for a week or so and see what activity occurred at the hotel room at the airport. Anthony would keep an eye on the room. He and Winston would do routine maintenance on the C-47 and see what gossip there was at the airport about the stolen AC-500S. Anthony felt he could find a place in the hotel in a closet or airshaft where he could hide the cash. Winston was paid his money for his advance and the men each took $1,000 US in pocket money. It was agreed that Anthony would be the only one who knew the location of the cash and where the tool chest with the jade and the balance of the gold was located. After five days of sales there was very little gold left, so the tool chest did not weigh that much and could be handled by Anthony alone.

***

Rick Ibn had a routine every day. He called the Belize Defense Forces (BDF) to see if there had been any report in Honduras, Panama or Columbia about his plane. There would be no such report because his plane had never been in Honduras, Panama or Columbia, but Rick did not know that.

After the call to BDF he went to the airport to see if anyone needed his services to fly or fix their plane. He spoke to the manager for the airline, TACA and he made an application to work as a mechanic or flight engineer, but he had no luck. One bright spot, the mechanic he had hired to help him replace the spar caps on the Aero Commander did get him some work, and so Rick had extended his stay and was granted a 30 day work permit to do maintenance on an old DC- 3 that was being refitted to fly tourists to Pre-Columbian sights – the ruins at Tikal, Copan and Palenque. A model DC-3 is the same as a C-47 except a DC-3 is fitted with seats to carry civilian commercial passengers.

Belize had the right to a narrative of Pre-Columbian peoples because historically the Fort George Hotel was built on the original sight of Fort George, which was constructed by the British to defend their rights to British Honduras. In 1839 the Walker-Caddy Expedition proceeded up the Belize River to Lake Itza and then over land to Palenque where John H. Caddy, a British Lieutenant, sketched and painted the Mayan city and Patrick Walker wrote the account of the expedition.

***

Dr. Anna Hernando, M.D., and Rick Ibn, had fallen in love. They spent evenings walking through Belize City before the drug addicts got on the street. They walked in the plaza with the clock tower, over the swing bridge past the fish market, to the Fort George, to the Lighthouse, to the Courthouse, and they purchased exotic postage stamps at the Post Office. They also visited the Belize Zoo a number of times.

If there was a patient in the clinic, Rick would sit up with the doctor and help her if he could. They became a good team which would make for a good marriage. Rick inquired of the Belize authorities what he would need to do to remain in the country. He was told if he married a citizen of Belize he could obtain residency status for the term of the marriage. Anna Hernando was a citizen of Belize.

Chapter 43

As Tom and Darlene walked to the Bushton County Jail after the hearing before Judge Barrow, it was a beautiful evening, cool and dry, not a cloud in the sky.

"Sorry," said Tom.

"That's my line," Darlene corrected Tom. "I'm supposed to say 'sorry', not you."

"We were blindsided. We didn't have enough time to prepare."

"Our next shot to get you out is to have an appeal bond set."

"You think they would grant bond on a Writ of Habeas Corpus?"

"Yes, and I think we also have to file a direct appeal on errors that Judge Barrow made on the record. We may have to file both the writ and the appeal at the same time. I will sort that out tonight," said Darlene.

Next came the question that was of most concern to Darlene. "Was the witness telling the truth?" was her question.

"The witness implied that I knew things based on what Anthony told him when I was not present. I don't know what Anthony told him. I told Anthony that I no longer represented him. The witness wasn't present when I told Anthony that. I don't know what Anthony told the witness when they were outside because I wasn't there. But I never told Anthony or the judge that I was still representing Anthony or that I was going to help Anthony out of his troubles in the States. Anthony and Judge

Lucius told me they didn't need my help. Judge Lucius said he knew Judge Barrow and he was going to call him to set aside the warrant for Anthony's arrest."

"How could he do that?" asked Darlene.

"I don't know, but could you check with the sheriff to see if there actually was a warrant issued for Anthony for the escape charge? Also, see if there is a record of a call from the Fort George to Judge Barrow."

As they entered the lobby of the jail and walked to the guard's desk past the pay phone, Tom whispered, "This is the scene of the crime. There's the phone Anthony used before he walked out the door." Darlene looked at the door as Tom presented himself to the guard for lock-up.

"You going to be alright in there?" asked Darlene.

"I'll be fine. Give me your smokes."

"I don't smoke," Darlene lied.

Tom held out his hand. Tom did not believe her. Women always had cigarettes. "I may need the cigarettes to make friends," said Tom. "I might as well start smoking again. Everyone, prisoners and guards, smokes back there."

"Good luck, Tom." Darlene gave Tom her pack of cigarettes. Tom gave Darlene the keys to his car.

Darlene called her secretary using the pay phone in the lobby of the jail and told her to go in and open the office. Her secretary was to make the inquires Tom suggested regarding the records of any phone call to or from Belize and for a copy of the warrant as soon as the Sheriff and Clerk's offices open. She was to have her law clerk come into the office immediately. "Now, tonight, to begin research on the legal issues that would need to be addressed for the appeal, the writ and the bond hearing." Darlene hoped the bond hearing would be before the court of appeals so Darlene would have an opportunity to get the facts before a new and hopefully a more sympathetic judge.

The Writ of Habeas Corpus required the appeals court to review the record of the hearing and decide quickly if a new hearing should be held on the ruling on the petition.

The appeals court could also take the case away from the trial court and issue an order that Tom was not guilty of the contempt charge. The record on appeal (the transcript) had to be produced by the court reporter. Darlene could not file the appeal until she had the transcript of the record of the hearing before Judge Barrow. So, Darlene gave the court reporter's number to her secretary and told her to try to encourage the court reporter to hurry.

Darlene asked the jailer behind the desk in the lobby where she could get cigarettes at this time of night. There was nothing open in Bushton. Police officers generally were heavy smokers, so there would be a cigarette machine somewhere nearby in the jail. The jailer asked for fifty cents and the brand she wanted, he went under the desk and retrieved a pack of filtered menthol cigarettes.

Darlene sat at a chair in the lobby of the jail and made notes of what she felt were the issues that would be successful on the appeal and the writ. She needed to concentrate on one or two of the most important issues on the petition for the writ. The writ is issued if a prisoner can show that he is being illegally held by government authority. The basis of the writ is English Common Law that was adopted in the courts in the Colonies, and thereafter in the State and Federal Courts in the US.

Darlene felt there was an important procedural issue which was the lack of proper notice that Tom's hearing was a criminal hearing. There was no information or indictment filed and served on Tom and there wasn't even a notice of hearing that said what the hearing was to be about. But the State had a counter argument, called a "waiver", because Tom had said he would come in voluntarily to speak to the court and the prosecutor. Darlene felt she could counter that Tom's cordial nature was not a substitute for a formal charge and written Notice of Hearing.

The substantive issues involved whether an attorney/client privilege allowed Tom to testify about what Anthony had told him and whether the court could imply as fact the tacit admission which allegedly occurred when Tom did not deny to the doorman, John Joseph Henry, that he was Anthony's attorney. Another issue involved the admission in evidence of the out of court statements allegedly made by Anthony to the doorman that Tom was helping Anthony defend against the escape charge and that the charge was a mistake.

Darlene closed her pen and put her notes in her purse. She took another cigarette and lit it and walked out of the jail, got in Tom's Mercedes convertible and drove it to the office to begin a new day.

The sun was rising.

Chapter 44

Judge Raymond Barrow was also working the phone after the hearing.

"Hale?" said Judge Barrow into the phone.

"Yes, Judge, what can I do for you?"

"Does your daughter, Lucy, still work for the newspaper?" (He knew she did.)

"Yes."

"I want her to write a story about how Tom interfered with the judicial process and was giving advice to Anthony Arnold to assist his escape."

"It's going to look bad if I am known to be the source of the story." said Hale.

"The source could be anonymous. You don't have to be quoted. You can just tell your daughter to search the criminal court files and look for a contempt order in the Anthony Arnold court file. Your daughter will take it from there. She's tenacious. Make sure she talks to Tom's partner, Roger. That will upset their office," said the judge.

Hale began to laugh. "Ok, I'll do it. But remember, it was you who sicked Lucy Hale on these people. She can be mean as a snake."

"I know. That's what I want. I don't want Tom to survive this," Judge Barrow admitted out loud.

***

Lucy Hale had worked for the hometown newspaper for two years. She rarely was given a good lead and she was hungry to advance in her career.

She was excited when her father gave her the tip regarding Tom's incarceration and she agreed to treat her father as a confidential source. The lead was given "off the record."

Lucy went to the Clerk's Office and found the Order holding Tom Night in contempt of court. She obtained a certified copy and took it to the City Editor who would assign the reporter to the story if a story would be written. Because there was a final order and a county jail sentence had been imposed and Tom was in jail, the editor would not be afraid of a libel suit from Tom. Both shoes had dropped. He was guilty and jailed.

Tom was a respected lawyer. The fact he was respected and was in jail made the story significant and something the public needed to know. The newspaper would be doing a public service plastering the story on the front page of the papers, or at least that was the theory.

Lucy's editor knew Lucy really wanted the assignment and he felt she was ready professionally and he would give her the story, but he had a condition. She had to give Tom Night or his attorney a chance to read the story and comment on it.

"Agreed," said Lucy.

"You are not to show the story to anyone once it includes the comment or the lack of a comment from Mr. Night or his attorney. In particular, you cannot show the story to your father. The story comes to me for final editing."

"Agreed," said Lucy.

***

Lucy went to her desk and wrote the story using the court's order as the factual basis for what she hoped would be front page news. Lucy then called Tom's office. She spoke to Roger, but she could get no comment except Roger told her it was best if she contacted Darlene Street, Tom's lawyer.

Lucy called Ms. Street and was put on hold. She was expecting to wait on hold for a long time but the phone was answered quickly by Darlene.

"How can I help you?" asked Darlene.

"I am doing follow up on a story I am writing about the conviction of Thomas Night for contempt. I have written the story and I need your comment after you review the story. When can I come over?"

"I normally do not make a comment, but I may in this case. What time is your deadline?"

"Tomorrow at nine p.m.," said Lucy.

"Come by my office at eight p.m. I'll read your story and I'll see what we have to say, if anything." Darlene hung up.

I do not have any idea what I am going to say, Darlene muttered to herself as she continued to review case law for Tom's appeal.

***

Darlene continued to review the legal research her law clerk had prepared for the petition and appeal they would file in the appellate court. The research showed that they would have to go back before Judge Barrow to attempt to set an appeal bond. Fat chance, thought Darlene. Judge Barrow is not going to set a bond for Tom. Still, she had her secretary set time on the Judge's calendar to hear the motion.

***

Darlene was paged again. Roger, Tom's partner was on the line.

"Look Darlene, I just got a call from Lucy Hale, the writer at the newspaper. I referred her to you. Did she call?"

"Yes."

"Do you think there will be a story?"

"Well yes. That's why she called us. She wants a comment."

"What are we going to say?"

"I hope we don't have to say anything."

"Do you have any good news?" asked Roger.

"No," Darlene admitted. "Nothing specific."

"Look Darlene, you need to tell Tom that we ... our partnership, cannot continue with this hanging over our heads here at the office. We have had calls from our clients this morning and they want answers. They have heard gossip that Tom is in jail. Bob and Frank Barnes are concerned. We will have real trouble if there's a newspaper story."

"I don't have any idea what I can do about that, Roger."

"Well, this can't continue. We need to dissolve the partnership," said Roger.

"Tom said you were comfortable with this and you would hang in there with him."

"That was before he was convicted of contempt and sentenced to six months in jail."

"Ok." Darlene knew there was more bad news coming. (Spit it out Roger). "What else?" asked Darlene.

"The Bar Association has called," said Roger. "They are asking if Tom will voluntarily resign his license to practice law. They want to interview me and see what I knew, when I knew it and what I did to help Tom aid Anthony Arnold."

"That's not good," Darlene commiserated.

"I am being a realist," said Roger. "We will lose all our clients and both of us will be disbarred and lose our licenses unless we dissolve our partnership."

"Ok, I will talk to Tom today."

"Tell him I'm sorry." Roger was actually crying.

"I will explain your position. Get a grip Roger. This will work out." Darlene was lying.

***

Darlene went to her car, a Ford Thunderbird convertible. She put the top down and sped up the road toward the jail two hours away. She had to make stops at the office of the Clerk of the Court to obtain a copy of the Order of Contempt and a copy of the audit conducted by the Clerk of the expenses expended by the County Commissioners for the judiciary. She was hoping the audit would show that Judge Barrow had made or accepted calls from Central America and that the County had paid the long distance charges.

She also had to stop at the court reporter's office to obtain a copy of the transcript of the hearing. And she had to obtain a certified copy of the Arrest Warrant naming Anthony Arnold for the offense of escape.

Last she had to see Tom. She had to tell him his law partner wanted a divorce; that Judge Barrow retains jurisdiction to decide whether he would be granted an appeal bond (so he won't be out of jail any time soon); that there was a newspaper reporter who was looking for a comment on a story that would destroy his reputation, and that the Bar Association wanted to know if he would voluntarily give up his license to practice law.

Darlene knew the Captain at the sheriff's office who was in charge of the guards at the jail. She considered telling him Tom might be a suicide risk after she finished giving Tom all the bad news. She really had nothing good to say to Tom. So she did what was best in the situation. She went to a café and ordered a cup of coffee and smoked one cigarette after another.

After she got herself together she decided to run errands. That would give her something to pass the time and she might be able to figure out something good to say to Tom.

But it didn't look promising. The court reporter was still working on the transcript and Darlene would have to come back for it the next morning. She was able to obtain the Order of Contempt and the Audit from the Clerk. When she reviewed the Audit there were no records of any phone billing made by Judge Barrow to Central America. To be certain she even spoke to the Clerk's accountant who assured Darlene that the records were complete and contained every phone call the County Commission paid. Next Darlene spoke to the captain of the guards. He kept the records of all warrants and there was a warrant that had been issued for the arrest of Anthony Arnold for the crime of escape. The captain made a copy of the warrant for her to take with her. And the captain showed her the communication he sent to the Solicitor General of Belize telling his office to be on the lookout for the escapee and that he was in the company of Judge Lucius.

The captain also told Darlene that he thought Tom was treated unfairly. He said that was the consensus of the court personnel. They all liked Tom. An attorney can make the job very difficult for the bailiffs and the clerks and the secretaries. But Tom did not do that. He was always congenial.

The captain said he asked the guards how Tom was being treated by his fellow prisoners. It was reported that he was doing fine. He was sharing his smokes with the other inmates. As Darlene went to leave, the captain gave her an envelope that was sealed. He said Jane, Judge Barrow's secretary, had given it to him to give to her.

"It's probably the invitation to her retirement party," said Darlene.

"Yes, probably," said the captain.

"She said she was about to retire," said Darlene.

Chapter 45

It took Pablo Mendez, the Police Chief of Cancún, only a few hours to locate the Mexican wrestlers after the police in San Pedro, Belize let the wrestlers and the Hondurans leave the dive boat. The wrestlers, Santo and Diablo, were celebrities in the Yucatán, and they had a manager. The manager's office told the chief that the men were scheduled to wrestle in an auditorium in Playa del Carmen, México, the next evening. Playa Del Carmen was a city within the chief's jurisdiction located south of Cancun.

The Chief sent eight men to make an arrest of the two wrestlers. The squad included two uniformed officers and six men dressed in civilian clothing. The undercover officers' job was to disperse into the crowd and when the uniformed officers approached the wrestlers to make the arrest they would see the crowd's reaction and act appropriately. The chief worried he might have a riot on his hands during the arrest because the twin brothers were very popular.

***

When the wrestlers entered the arena, but before they could enter the ring and remove their capes and prepare with their final stretching and warm-up for the match, the officers approached and told the wrestlers they were wanted for questioning in Cancún and they were under arrest.

When the police took out their handcuffs the fans became particularly upset, however, the wrestlers did not want to destroy their image and Diablo asked the Master of Ceremonies for the microphone and announced that they were being arrested but it was a misunderstanding, and they were going to go with the officers and resolve the matter. The management got the next match into the ring quickly and the officers, and the two wrestlers left the arena peacefully.

Once outside the arena, the group was met by the chief.

The chief wanted to see the men before they were transported to the station. The chief told the men they were going to be questioned about Jorge's murder. The wrestlers were then put in separate cars and driven to the station.

Let them think about that as they ride to my office, thought the chief.

When they arrivad, the wrestlers were cuffed to chairs in the back of a large room full of people sitting in rows of hard chairs. There was an officer who sat between the men. In front of the room there was a large desk. Seated behind the desk was the chief. Next to the chief there was a woman, a clerk, who was seated with a stack of files in front of her. As the proceeding began, the clerk would call a name and hand the chief a file. An officer would bring forward a prisoner. The officer would explain the factual basis for the charge against the prisoner and the chief would read the file that contained statements and review any photographs and reports relating to the alleged crime. The chief then questioned the prisoner. If the prisoner offered a defense, the victim was brought forward from the audience and the chief asked questions of the prisoner and the victim and then decided the verdict and handed down a sentence. The prisoner could accept the sentence or he could hire a lawyer and appeal.

Many of the cases went quickly. When the chief recognized the inmate from a past offense the chief did not review the file, he simply told the prisoner what sentence he would impose. The prisoner knew this disposition was as good as it was going to get and he accepted the verdict and sentence. Thus as the audience watched, a wife beater with a history of assaults on his wife was given a one month sentence (the wife wanted him back home). The habitual small time thief was sentenced to six months. Since the sentences were accepted and the matter took only a few minutes, the chief gave the inmate a break for their honesty in accepting their guilt and not wasting the chief's time.

Some cases took longer. The audience sat through a long hearing where a woman who alleged she previously was a virgin accused a man of rape. The man alleged the act was consensual. After listening to the woman's father complain that the prisoner and the victim had been dating for over a year but they had not announced a wedding date, the chief recessed the hearing for two weeks. The chief instructed the detective in charge of the case to obtain additional statements regarding the background and credibility of the witnesses. During the two week continuance the man was to remain in jail but he could communicate with the victim during regular visitation. The chief hoped the two could work the matter out on their own and set a date for their wedding and he would not have to make a decision in the case.

***

After many hours the wrestlers were called forward. They were the last case and there were few people left in the room. The men said they wanted to speak to an abrogado (a lawyer) before going forward with a hearing before the Chief of Police.

The chief ignored their request for counsel and began questioning the wrestlers.

"Did you know the lawyer, Tom Night, prior to flying into Punta Rosa with him in the pontoon plane?" asked the chief.

"No, he just handled the permit to allow us to take the dive boat from México to Belize. He did nothing wrong," said the wrestlers.

"Where was the dive boat when Jorge drowned?" asked the Chief. "Mexico or Belize?"

"We do not know. Jorge was at the helm before he was lost. He knew where we were when we tied up for the night. We were unaware of our location," said Santo.

The chief began reading the file that was handed to him by the clerk seated next to him.

As the chief read, Diablo interrupted and said, "We do not think it is right for you to hear this matter. We know you are Jorge's brother."

The chief ignored Diablo, although the crowd in the room tittered with that news.

The wrestlers became agitated as the chief continued to read the file. But the prisoners settled down as the chief shared the file with them. The chief gave them copies of all the statements taken by the police in San Pedro. The chief also laid out photographs on the desk for the wrestlers to view. First there were photographs of the dive boat and of the crewmen taken by the San Pedro Police.

The wrestlers were very interested in the evidence and the chief invited them to come closer and participate in the review of the file.

The chief opened another manila envelope that contained more photos. The photos showed the underside of the dive boat and there were numerous shots of the moon pool that were taken inside the boat.

"Had you seen a moon pool or dive port before?" the chief asked.

"No," they each said. They offered that the police in San Pedro had found a piece of yellow fabric caught on the hatch of the moon pool. "They told us the edge of the hatch caught Jorge's T-shirt and trapped Jorge underwater and he drowned," added Santo.

"Did you ever see Jorge's body after he drowned?" asked the chief.

"No," they each said. "We looked for him but couldn't find him," said Diablo.

"Did you find any blood in the moon pool to indicate Jorge had hit his head before he opened the hatch and went into the water?"

"No," they each lied.

"Did you find a bloody weapon of any kind?"

"No," they lied.

"Did you find a bloody rag?"

The wrestlers did not answer. They both knew the rag was destroyed and the murder weapon, the ball peen hammer, had been thrown into the water. Only the Hondurans would know this evidence was destroyed.

The wrestlers were concerned and asked if they could talk to each other in private.

"Of course," said the chief. "Go over in the corner."

"How did the chief know there was a bloody rag?" said Santo. "Maybe the Hondurans told the police about the rag."

The wrestlers only looked in each other's eyes. If that were true, they knew they were defeated. If the chief had talked to the Hondurans and the Hondurans revealed facts about the hammer and the rag, they knew the Hondurans had blamed them for Jorge's death. "We have to tell the chief what we know," they said to each other in a panic.

When they came back to the desk after their conference the chief had laid five photos face down on the desk. The chief turned over the first photo. It was a photo of a mangrove swamp with a red flag tied high in a branch of a tree.

The men looked at the photo. Mangrove trees, as was their nature, grow out into the sea. The wrestlers did not see the relevance of the photograph of the mangrove tree with the red flag.

"We believe the Hondurans killed your brother," Diablo offered in his most sincere voice.

"The Hondurans killed Jorge while we were asleep," said Santos. "We would have stopped them if we knew beforehand what they were going to do to your brother."

The chief ignored the men and turned over the next photo. It showed a border marker that had been driven into the shore. There was a wooden plaque on the marker. There was a capital "B" on one side of the plaque and a capital "M" on the other side of the plaque.

"The 'B' means Belize and the 'M' means México. This marker identifies the border between the two countries," explained the chief to the wrestlers.

The wrestlers ignored the chief and continued to try to exculpate themselves. "We found a ball peen hammer that was covered with blood and brain matter. We think that was the weapon. We also found a bloody rag, but the Hondurans burned the rag," they lied.

The chief turned over the next photo. The picture showed a long distance shot of the border marker. To the left of the frame of the photo and to the far right of the photo you could see the red flag in the mangrove.

"The Hondurans did it. They admitted to us that they killed Jorge." The wrestlers were lying.

The chief turned over the next photo. It was another long distance shot. It showed the upper part of a body lying tangled in the limbs of a mangrove tree. It must have been low tide when the picture was taken because the body was not submerged in the water but caught and tangled in a limb. The limb was out of the water because it was low tide. The limb would have been submerged at high tide.

The wrestlers looked more closely at the photos and Diablo asked, "So when we drove the dive boat north in search of Jorge's body it must have been high tide and Jorge's body was caught in the tree limb and he was submerged and we couldn't see Jorge's body. Is that correct?"

The chief explained, "You are correct. At low tide when the PT boat searched, they could see the top part of Jorge's body in the tree limb."

"What was he wearing?" asked Diablo.

"He was wearing a swim suit. He had no other clothing," said the Chief.

"Who took the picture?" asked Santo.

"The Navy," said the chief. "I asked them to search the coast and they found the body."

The chief turned over the last photograph. The picture was gruesome. The picture showed the top of a human head. The top of the skull showed a round hole where an object the size of the head of a ball peen hammer had entered the skull. It was easy to see the top of the skull because the crabs and fishes had nibbled away Jorge's hair and picked at his skin and eyes.

"Do you want me to read the autopsy report?" asked the chief.

"No," said the wrestlers.

"Why did you kill Jorge?" asked the chief.

"We didn't kill him," they pleaded. "It was the Hondurans."

"Please be honest with me. I know the Honduran's killed my brother. I need to know who else was involved. I need to know who sent you to kill Jorge. It will help you with your sentence. Was the lawyer, Tom Night involved in anyway?"

"No, he had nothing to do with it. He only helped obtain the permit so we could take the boats out of México," said Santo.

Diablo nodded in agreement.

"Was anyone else involved?" asked the chief.

"Our boss, the Bounty Hunter, paid us to kill Jorge. But we did not kill him," they insisted.

"Again, I need to know all who paid you to kill Jorge?" asked the chief.

"Anthony Arnold paid the Bounty Hunter to contract with us to kill Jorge."

"Why did Anthony Arnold want Jorge killed?"

"Jorge told the Bounty Hunter where we could locate and arrest Anthony Arnold. Mr. Anthony was upset with Jorge because he was a snitch. He ratted on Anthony."

"Was there any other reason the Bounty Hunter was involved?"

"The Bounty Hunter owed Jorge a fee for telling us where to locate Mr. Anthony. If Jorge was killed the Bounty Hunter did not have to pay the fee."

"Thank you for your honesty," said the chief.

The chief looked to the rear of the room. In the corner was a woman. The chief nodded to the woman who was crying and wiping her tears with a handkerchief.

The woman was Jorge's wife.

Chapter 46

Following the hearing the Chief ordered his staff to issue warrants for the arrest of the Bounty Hunter and Anthony Arnold for solicitation of the murder of Jorge Mendez. The warrant for the Bounty Hunter was to be kept sealed but the warrant for Anthony Arnold would be circulated among all law enforcement agencies in México. The chief had no jurisdiction over the Hondurans. The Hondurans were military and a political problem for the Mexican government. They would have to be dealt with by the federal authorities.

The chief was very dedicated to his job and he kept attuned to what was happening in his jurisdiction, which included the International Airport in Cancún. He was aware of the activities of the Bounty Hunter in México. Many fugitives from Florida settled in the eastern part of the Yucatán. He was aware that the Bounty Hunter was feared by these fugitives and their fear was justified. The Bounty Hunter captured many persons wanted by the authorities in the States, primarily in Florida, and returned them to face justice.

The Chief knew that the Bounty Hunter owned a black Lear jet that he parked in a hangar at the International Airport. The Bounty Hunter leased the hanger to house the jet when he was not conducting his business in the Yucatán. The chief knew that the Bounty Hunter paid for information and that he probably knew that the wrestlers were being held in his jail following the hearing, and that the Bounty Hunter had been implicated in the death of Jorge Mendez. The chief explained to his employees and staff that it was important that no one reveal the fact that the chief issued a warrant for the arrest of the Bounty Hunter.

The chief felt it was worthwhile to stake out the hanger at the International Airport on the chance the Bounty Hunter did not know of the warrant. He hoped the Bounty Hunter would not learn that he was in jeopardy and he would fly into Cancún one more time. If he did, the policemen the chief sent to the airport would be waiting for him. If he could capture him, the chief would also confiscate the plane and the Land Rover and any other property that was in the hanger. He was also aware the Bounty Hunter had an office in the hanger and a ship to shore radio. He hoped there would be evidence in the office in the form of accounts and bills and records of the criminal activities of the Bounty Hunter, particularly kidnappings in the state of Quintana Roo, México.

Bounty hunting was not a romantic occupation in México as it is in the United States. It was unlawful to take someone against their will and assault and sometimes kill them, even if there was a warrant for the person's arrest in the United States. These activities of the Bounty Hunter were crimes in México. The chief intended to arrest the Bounty Hunter and to prosecute him to the full extent of the laws of México.

***

In México City, the four men, Judge David Lucius, Anthony Arnold, H. Patel and Winston Grey, were not getting along. The primary problem was that they were incompatible and they got on each other's nerves.

The judge was a drunk and sloppy. All he wanted to do was drink. If he were denied alcohol without the care of a physician he would be raving, then sick, then dangerous, and then comatose.

H. Patel was nervous with the company he was keeping. He was a second generation American from an East Indian family. (He was an Indian from India.) His family had sacrificed for him to complete law school. The family had set up his law practice. But he couldn't find a client until he hooked up with Judge Lucius, who fed him clients in return for referral fees. This, of course, was totally illegal and unethical. H. Patel was nervous dealing with

Anthony and Winston because they were criminals. They were amoral. Anthony and Winston did not limit themselves in their criminality. No crime was too heinous so long as their needs were satisfied. H. Patel felt they would turn on him in a minute and he was right.

Winston Grey intended to live the rest of his life in Thailand. But it was taking too long to get there. He was used to getting his way and that was not happening. He intended to have a face lift at a clinic in the Bahamas as soon as he had his money from the sale of the treasure. When he recuperated and the scars healed and could be covered with makeup he would fly out of the clinic in the Bahamas to his new home in Thailand. He even considered having his vocal cords modified to change the timbre of his voice so he didn't sound so girlish.

Anthony was selfish, hardheaded and cruel. He learned these attributes in order to survive in prison. No matter what Anthony said to his partners in crime, he did not care a wit for their well-being and he did not feel that he owed them any share of the treasure or the cash derived from selling the treasure. The cash and the treasure was all his and he would end up with all of it, eventually. Prison had taught him patience.

Part VI
Exculpatory Evidence

Chapters 47 through 52

The phone bills ... John Hale's investigation ... Florida Statewide Grand Jury ... The Police Chief makes arrests ... Tom Night is released on bond

Chapter 47

Tom had faced few predicaments involving his legal career, primarily because he was honest and tried to do right by his clients. The one time he had been dishonest by trying to trick the Barnes family with the report about Belize, he had been found out and embarrassed. He learned a lesson and lost millions of dollars.

There were plenty of temptations in the practice of law; theft of client's funds, taking advantage of a client's weak position, having sex with a client, et cetera. And though Tom had been honest and not mixed with clients socially and avoided temptation, here he was, incarcerated in the Bushton County Jail. He had been tricked by someone much smarter and very devious. But, though a number of people contributed to his incarceration, he did not know who the primary culprit was. There were a number of suspects, but as he considered each suspect, it appeared that that individual was not the evil genius, but only a participant in his demise. All of the suspects – Anthony Arnold, Judge Lucius, Judge Barrow, Winston Grey, H. Patel, State Attorney Hale, and John Joseph Henry, were participants to some degree, but the person who appeared to have trapped him was himself, Thomas Night, Esquire. He had not anticipated that someone would set a simple trap that employed the true facts (that he had been in Belize, and that he had met with an old client when he knew the client was on the lamb), to concoct a lie – that Tom was aiding in the escape of his old client. Tom did not consider the trap to be believable because it was not true.

Had Tom followed the simple ethics rule, to avoid even the appearance of impropriety, and if he had refused to talk to Anthony, he would have avoided his incarceration. He had always been on guard against the appearance of impropriety. Here he thought that since he had withdrawn from representation of Anthony and since he was no longer his attorney he could commit no evil. But add a few facts, the conversation between Anthony and John Joseph Henry and the fact that Tom was silent when John Joseph Henry confronted him with the statement that he still represented Anthony ... and it appeared that Tom continued to be representing and helping Anthony when he was a fugitive. Obviously Anthony and Judge Lucius were in on it. And Solicitor General Prince was involved, or how did John Joseph Henry get to court in Florida to testify against him? But these facts all just rattled around in his brain. Tom knew he was at great risk, but he could not figure out how he could get out of this unscathed.

What Tom decided was that he had to put his fate and faith in Darlene Street's hands. He had to do what most clients refuse to do and that is trust the system and his attorney and the truth. And the truth was that he was innocent and he did not aid Anthony in his escape or violate any of the rules of conduct or canons of ethics as an attorney in his dealings with his clients.

Tom became very calm. During the night in jail lying on the thin mattress on his cot he slept as well as he ever had. He and the other inmates were congenial. The inmates and the guards could have been mean and confronted Tom as a person who had fallen from grace. But they seemed to know that he should not be behind bars, and they left him alone.

After the great sleep, Tom spent the day in jail making notes for Darlene. He was trying to educate her about the characters involved in the case. He had managed to write a novel, it seemed. He had compiled about 100 pages of notes written on a couple of legal pads so that when Darlene came in to see him he could help her.

***

It was about 10:00 at night when Darlene arrived at the jail. As she was let into the cage, she thought the only advantage was, if your client is in jail you at least knew where he is. The other advantage is that if you were friends with the captain of the guards you could be allowed entrance to the jail late at night after regular visiting hours.

The captain had given Darlene such a pass. The guard put her in a room with a glass window facing the guard at the desk in the lobby so the guard could watch her and Tom as they met to discuss the case.

Tom knew he was in trouble when he was led into the conference room. As soon as the guard left the room, Tom could see tears welling up in Darlene's eyes. Tom let her cry. He understood. She was deeply frustrated. She wanted to make things right but she couldn't. She wanted to tell him something good but there was nothing good to say. In two days Tom had lost his practice, his profession, his reputation and his liberty.

Finally, Darlene pulled herself together. She sat up straight. She took a tissue and blew her nose and wiped the tears away.

She took out a fresh pack of cigarettes, opened the pack and offered one to Tom. Tom remained silent. He took a smoke. He wished she was not smoking filtered, menthol cigarettes. He had quit smoking 15 years before and when he quit he smoked regular unfiltered cigarettes. Since he came to jail it had only taken one or two cigarettes to become hooked on nicotine again. He loved the sensation tobacco and it's by-products gave him. To quit smoking 15 years ago he had to quit five minutes at a time. He would abstain for five minutes and then had to talk himself into abstaining for another five minutes. He knew he would have to quit again the same way. He had already smoked a couple of packs the first day of his return to the drug. Tobacco was deep in his lungs again.

"So, it's pretty bad," said Tom.

"Terrible," said Darlene and she let go with a flow of words replete with expletives explaining that in 24 hours it appeared that Tom's work for his life to date was at risk. "Nothing has come out the way we thought it would. I'm almost to the point that I suggest I go and talk to Hale about some plea arrangement that trades your license for restoration of your freedom."

"It can't be that bad," said Tom.

"The only thing positive is this invitation that Jane gave me to her retirement party," said Darlene as she fingered the sealed envelope. And then she slit open the envelope with her fingernail. The envelope contained a note from Jane and a copy of a phone bill.

The note said:

"Darlene, ever since I have worked for Judge Barrow I have kept his checkbook and paid his bills while I was being paid by the county taxpayers. I knew that it was wrong to do private work for the judge on county time. Anyway, I keep the records in the bottom drawer of the file cabinet in my office behind my desk. The judge also keeps a drawer of personal papers in the drawer above the one that contains the bills and accounting work I do for him. I do not know what is in that drawer because it has a lock on it and Judge Barrow is the only one with a key. I do know that Judge Barrow knows Judge Lucius and that they speak over the phone at times. The calls are made to or from Judge Barrow's private phone line. I know that he got a call last week from Judge Lucius from Central America. Since that call the judge removed all of his paperwork that was in the bottom drawer from the office. I know that he received a call last week from Judge Lucius because it was placed by an overseas operator and I answered the phone and spoke to the operator before giving the phone to the judge. Since that time the judge has asked me every day if we have gotten the bill from the phone company. The bill came in today and I opened it. It shows that there was a call from Belize, Central America that was made last week from 0-0-1-202-97506. I called the phone company to get an explanation for the charge and the billing office said that the call was made from a room in the Fort George Hotel in Belize City, Belize, Central America. I called the hotel and they identified the room as room 506 and that the room was rented last week by Tom Night. I made a copy of the phone bill and put the original bill back in the envelope and put it with the rest of the judge's mail. I felt guilty about doing this and talked to Captain Frank, (the head of the guards) after the contempt hearing and Tom was put in jail yesterday. Captain Frank said I should put a copy of the phone bill along with a note explaining what I knew in a sealed envelope. He said I should give the envelope to him and he said he would give the envelope to you. He said I could trust you and Tom to figure out a way to use the bill. Hopefully you can use the bill without identifying that you got it from me. /S/ Jane McCormick."

Tom looked at Darlene. "You know you can't hide anything from your secretary."

"You're right. You shouldn't even try," said Darlene.

Chapter 48

Darlene and Tom met again late the next morning after taking some time at night to try to determine the best way to use the information and Judge Barrow's phone bill provided by Judge Barrow's secretary, Jane McCormick.

"I don't know why we don't put Jane under subpoena and take her testimony. That would be the quickest way to get the heat off you and put the judge under scrutiny," said Darlene.

"I would like to figure out a way to use the evidence but not involve Jane," said Tom.

"The only people who have power over Judge Barrow are the Supreme Court and the State Attorney. We have to prove he violated a canon of ethics or a Supreme Court Rule or we have to convince the State Attorney the judge violated a law such as conspiracy, accepting a bribe or some such. I do not believe John Hale, the State Attorney, will file a charge against the judge, and I don't think we will get very far with the Supreme Court," said Darlene. "The only other thing to do is to forget about trying to prove you are innocent and instead defend the Contempt verdict on appeal."

"If I wait for the appeal to run its course, I will not be able to act quick enough to save my license. I will be disbarred. I believe I have already lost my law practice. Roger is on his way to Belize today to meet all my contacts over there and to return the documents signed by Frank and Bob Barnes for Barnes Lime Rock Company relating to the renewal of the leases and licenses with the government."

"You are going to suffer losses if you rely on the appeal as your only remedy, but you will win the appeal." Darlene was very confident.

"My thought is that we do both," said Tom. "We proceed with the appeal and we put pressure on the State Attorney to do a complete investigation of Judge Barrow."

"How can you pressure the State Attorney?" asked Darlene.

"Do you still have a meeting with Lucy Hale, the newspaper reporter?"

"The State Attorney's daughter? She hasn't canceled. I think her boss wanted to give us a chance to respond to the allegations before he will print the story about your conviction. Her boss is trying to play by the rules, fair and honest reporting and all that."

"What do you think Lucy and her editor would do if I told them the whole story and showed them the phone bill without involving Jane or her note?" asked Tom.

"If they are going to print anything they will have to confront Judge Barrow and the State Attorney," said Darlene.

"Other good things might happen. Particularly if the daughter confronts her father and he fails to take any action to investigate the allegations against Judge Barrow. If John Hale doesn't investigate and the judge is charged later, Hale will be thought to have been part of the conspiracy," said Tom.

"I don't think it will work. You are still going to expose Jane. The State Attorney will probably ask the judge for an explanation of the phone bill and Judge Barrow will know there is only one person who knows about his private line and that is Jane, because she was his bookkeeper and paid his bills. He would know she had access to the bill and made a copy," said Darlene.

"I don't think it will get that far. I think John Hale will figure it out once he sees the bill. Once he knows what my testimony would be regarding Judge Lucius being with Anthony, an escapee from Judge Barrow's court, and the fact Judge Barrow called Judge

Lucius the same day, Hale will have to think something is wrong. I will testify to the truth, that Judge Lucius said he was owed a favor from Judge Barrow. I think this will explode in Judge Barrow's face," said Tom.

"I don't know, but we'll try it."

***

Darlene was back in her office. Her secretary paged her. "That newspaper reporter is here."

"We can meet in the library," said Darlene.

The women sat across from one another. Darlene didn't feel comfortable with the 'tell only part of the story' strategy.

"I want to ask you if your newspaper takes a position on keeping a source of information confidential," said Darlene.

"I need to make a call," said Lucy Hale.

Darlene left the room to give Lucy privacy.

In a minute Lucy came out and got Darlene and asked her to come in the library and speak to her editor. Darlene picked up the receiver and began to listen.

"Who are you trying to protect?" asked the editor.

"The source and content of a writing that was given to me. The letter is relevant to the comment we want to make to the story regarding the charges brought against Tom."

"Why can't you just provide the information?" asked the editor.

"My client is trying to protect the source of the relevant document. The document is a piece of evidence the source provided to my client that shows he is the victim of a criminal conspiracy," said Darlene.

"I will call you back. Tell Lucy to stay there and wait for me to call back."

They hung up. Darlene went back to work. Lucy read magazines.

***

"Well," said the editor, "my lawyer thinks we can claim in good faith that the source should be protected as a confidential source. So, the short answer is we will protect the source."

"Will Lucy Hale still be the reporter on the story?"

"Yes," said the editor. "She has agreed."

"Is she aware that if a subpoena is issued by the State Attorney for her source for the story that she will be the one who will be subpoenaed? And she will be the one who could go to jail during an appeal?" asked Darlene.

"Yes, I am aware of that," Lucy Hale piped up. "My father got me into this. He will be the one who has to face my mother if I go to jail."

The editor hung up and Lucy and Darlene both got coffee and then the interview began.

"So who knows what?" asked Lucy.

"We believe there are five conspirators who helped Anthony Arnold escape from prison so he could retrieve Mayan treasure that was hidden on his dive boat. The conspirators are Mr. Arnold, Judge Lucius, Judge Barrow, H. Patel, a lawyer, and Winston Grey, a Belize citizen. These men have been involved in the drug trade in Belize and Florida. Arnold and Grey operated way stations for traffickers flying drugs from South America to Belize and Florida. If the planes needed to be refueled or needed repairs they would be serviced by Arnold and Grey. Patel represented or found lawyers for traffickers who were arrested and Judge Barrow helped with plea deals and bonds at the trial level, and Judge Lucius helped if there was an appeal," said Darlene.

"So let me get the details," said Lucy, rubbing her hands together.

"You'll be here awhile and you may want to speak to Tom and John Hale."

"I definitely want to speak to my father and also to Judge Barrow," said Lucy.

Chapter 49

John Hale did not have to wait for his daughter to call him. He received a tip. He received a copy of Judge Raymond Barrow's telephone bill for the judge's private phone in his mail at his river cabin. Few people knew Mr. Hale's address in the country on the river. Being the State Attorney he made enemies, and he didn't publish his address. The only people who knew this address were in his office and the Sheriff's Office. Captain Frank, chief of the guards, knew the address.

There was no note or letter with the phone bill. The bill looked innocent but Hale was suspicious. The bill was two months old. It was not the same bill that Darlene received from Jane. Hale noted that the bill was addressed to Judge Barrow at the courthouse, which was odd. The county was strict about mixing personal affairs or outside business with the official affairs and duties of County employees. Judge Barrow was a County employee and he was subject to that rule.

John Hale looked through the accounting and the phone numbers. Again, it was odd that there were so many calls to and from foreign countries. Mr. Hale opened the white pages of his phone directory and studied the country codes listed in the phone book. He identified the foreign telephone numbers on Judge Barrow's bill as coming to and from Columbia, Belize, México and Honduras. To Hale these countries were suspicious for criminal activity involving drug trafficking.

John Hale turned the pages over, looking for the name or address or any identification of the person who sent the bill to his cabin. Nothing was on the bill or the envelope. There was no return address on the envelope. The postage cancellation on the envelope was St. Petersburg, Florida and it was mailed the day before. He did notice a mail code that was printed on the front left corner of the envelope.

Hale called his office and asked the front desk for the mail room and he asked the mail clerk who in St. Petersburg used mail codes to separate the mail that they were sending from their office. He was told that a code was only used by the local newspaper, The Times. The newspaper separated their outgoing mail by codes because they mailed newspapers all over the country and the state.

"Why would the code be stamped on regular mail, on a regular envelope?" asked Hale.

"I'm no expert, I don't know."

"You sure the newspaper in St. Petersburg is the only entity that uses a mail code in St. Petersburg?" asked Hale.

"Positive."

Mr. Hale didn't have any friends at the newspaper. The newspaper endorsed his opponent in the last election. John thought perhaps the letter and the phone bill came from his daughter. Then he thought that had to be wrong. She wouldn't compromise her position at the paper. Hale considered why the paper had the judge's bill. If this came from the newspaper it was going to be used in a story and the story was going to be about the Judge.

Or, maybe it's going to be about me, thought Hale, mumbling, "That would be bad." Whatever, Hale realized he had been given a tip and he needed to be in the office and start work on this.

As he drove in, John turned the facts over in his mind. This phone bill has to involve Tom Night. "This is a trap." He was suspicious that Tom was involved in helping a client by doing something illegal, especially a person like Anthony Arnold. It wasn't like Tom to act illegally.

Paranoia then set in. How was Hale going to take action without getting into trouble? The judge was going to be shown to be using his secretary and his office in the courthouse to conduct private business. That's enough for the judge to be scolded by the Supreme Court. Hale figured he probably wouldn't file a criminal charge for something like that. He would wait to see what action the Supreme Court took and then decide. Most of the time the public will forget a newspaper story after a few days. It could all just blow over. But if these international phone calls prove to be made by the judge to criminals, Hale would have to act and act with all the power of his office or he would need to find another job.

Hale's mind continued to wander. He needed to get the judge's phone record for the last year and have the phone company identify the owner of every phone number that was called by or to the judge. Then he could decide what to do.

***

The phone company was a good citizen. Phone companies would volunteer information to the police if requested. Hale would explain to the manager at the phone company that this was an emergency. He might have to finesse it a bit since the records were for Judge Barrow.

The manager was a man he knew from church and someone he felt he could trust. The manager set a time later that day for Hale to come and talk about the information requested. The manager said he didn't think he would have a problem disclosing the information to Hale.

***

"There are six calls here that I am concerned with," said John Hale. "Tell me about these." John pushed the billing in front of the manager.

"These are all foreign calls. The calls were made two months ago. One is to Columbia, two are to México, one is to Honduras and two are to Belize. The calls were all made in the early evening from a private phone in the courthouse. The phone is leased by the phone company to Judge Raymond Barrow. The calls to México and Columbia are to prominent criminal defense attorneys in those countries. The two calls to Belize are to the private line of Andrew Prince, the Solicitor General of Belize. The phone call to Honduras is to a private line. It is a residence line. It is very unusual for a private home to have a private line. The person who rents the phone would have to have great wealth. I have written the names and address of the owners of the phone numbers.

"I can also tell you that there is other government interest in these phone numbers."

"What do you mean?" asked Hale.

"I can tell you that other law enforcement agencies have inquired about the ownership of the phone numbers. These are phone numbers that could be involved in criminal activity."

"What kind of criminal activity?"

"All of these foreign phone numbers on this phone bill are being investigated for drug trafficking activity."

"Who is investigating?"

"Subpoenas were issued by the Florida Statewide Grand Jury and the US Justice Department. That's why I wasn't too concerned talking to you about this account. There is already an investigation."

"Are the investigations still active?"

"Yes."

"Is one of the phone numbers under investigation Judge Barrow's private phone line at the courthouse?"

"Yes," said the manager.

Hale looked through his notes to see if he had any questions he had failed to ask. "I meant to ask, are there any taps or interception devices on the lines?"

"The local line for Judge Barrow's phone at the courthouse is tapped," said the manager.

"Who is conducting the surveillance?"

"The Florida Statewide Grand Jury."

"Have all of the phone calls on Judge Barrow's private line been recorded by the Grand Jury?"

"Yes, it appears they have been recorded."

"Thank you, that's all the questions that I have."

"See you in church," said the manager.

Chapter 50

The Police Chief of Cancún received the call very early in the morning from his detective bureau. The only matter they would call him about was the stakeout of the Bounty Hunter's hanger at the International Airport.

His Lieutenant of Detectives had been monitoring aircraft communications between the controllers and air traffic. There was communication between the black Lear jet and the Cancún tower announcing the intention of the pilot of the black Lear jet to land in 30 minutes.

The chief dressed quickly. He should be at the airport before the plane landed. His men were to wait until he arrived before they took any action. The chief wanted to take the Bounty Hunter alive so he could question him.

When the chief arrived at the surveillance post he could see that the hanger doors were open and there were two men inside. One was in the office in a corner of the hanger. The chief was worried that the men could destroy potential evidence, but the man in the office was communicating on the ship to shore radio (perhaps with the Lear jet) and the chief was afraid that if he arrested the men while they were talking the Bounty Hunter might become aware the police were at the hanger and the Bounty Hunter would not land after he was warned.

"The plane should have landed by now," said the chief.

"The air traffic controller is hailing the plane now," said the Lieutenant of Detectives who was monitoring the conversation.

"Apparently they lost the plane on their screen over Cozumel, about 90 miles out. They think it may have crashed."

The men in the hanger were now taking files containing papers from the file cabinets in the office and putting them on a long table in the office. Then one man in the hanger was carrying a canister marked "fuel" to the office.

The chief ordered his men to arrest the men to prevent the destruction of the evidence. There was no resistance from the two men. They were arrested for attempted arson.

The men were American citizens. That was all they would tell the police.

The chief told his men to secure the hanger. The alleged arsonists were taken to the station and put in lockup.

*****

The chief went to the control tower. He was well known there. He wanted to speak to the air traffic controller who had responsibility for landing the Lear jet.

"What happened to the plane?"

"We don't know. It disappeared from radar east of Isla Mujeres. My first thought was that it crashed."

"Has there been a report of a crash?"

"No."

"Was the plane in its landing pattern?"

"Yes, it was on approach."

"Was there other traffic behind it?"

"Yes, but that aircraft was 30 miles behind."

"Talk to the pilot of that plane. What did he see?"

The controller communicated with the pilot and reported, "He saw a flash of light. It could have been an explosion but he doesn't know for sure."

The chief went to a phone and called his office. "Are there any reports of an explosion in the air coming from residents of the Isla?"

"Yes, our office is reporting a plane crash out to sea. We will probably get more calls once the fishermen come in at the end of the night."

"Collect all the reports of sightings. Make sure you obtain all the names and addresses of the witnesses."

"Yes sir."

"I'm going back to the hanger. Send a truck. I want to collect all of the paperwork in the hanger and store it securely at the station. Tell the Lieutenant of Detectives that he is to personally photograph the scene and he is to catalogue the papers that he finds in the office."

Chapter 51

"Ms. Jones, I'm calling because I think I may have stumbled into one of your investigations," said John Hale.

"How so?" asked the Advisor to the Statewide Grand Jury.

Judy Jones was an attorney in the office of the Florida Attorney General. Her job was to provide legal advice to a panel of citizens drawn from around the State of Florida to investigate criminal activity in the state. The panel usually involved the investigation of a conspiracy to commit a criminal enterprise or a particular criminal subject matter like drug trafficking or organized crime.

The reason a statewide grand jury is impaneled is to investigate criminal activity that was occurring in more than one county of the state. The State Attorney for each county could empanel a grand jury to investigate crime, but the grand jury was restricted to criminal activity within the boundary of its county. The legislature passed a bill creating the Statewide Grand Jury which was not restricted by any boundary except the boundary of Florida.

"I am the State Attorney in Bushton, Summer County, Florida."

"I'm aware of that Mr. Hale."

"I began an investigation of a Judge based on evidence that was mailed to me. The evidence was a copy of a phone bill for the judge's private phone. The phone bill contained listings of calls to Central and South America for individuals who were known as sources of drug trafficking activity. When I investigated I learned that the Statewide Grand Jury had issued a subpoena for the judge's phone number, and I was told the subpoena was active."

"Who does the phone number belong to?" asked the advisor.

"Circuit Judge Raymond Barrow," said Hale.

"And what do you think you have found?" asked the advisor.

"Well, I have to take you back a bit."

"No problem, I have the time."

"This started when a local attorney, Tom Night, called my office and the judge's office to report that he had seen a fugitive who was also his client named Anthony Arnold in Belize. Tom felt he should call because Anthony Arnold had escaped from the jail here in Summer County."

"Did Tom represent Anthony?" asked the prosecutor.

"That was unclear."

"Did Tom speak to Anthony when he saw him in Belize?" asked the prosecutor.

"Yes, and that raised a number of legal questions about what Tom could report about what Anthony had said to him. But Tom felt that the fact that Anthony was a fugitive and the fact that Tom knew where he was because he actually saw him, was not a communication. Anthony did not tell Tom where he was, Tom saw Anthony with his own eyes and that was not a communication. Therefore, Tom felt he had a duty as an Officer of the Court to tell us where he was."

"Sounds correct," said Ms. Jones.

"Tom also said he would come to court and be available for questioning but we knew he would assert the attorney/client privilege and then let an appeal court tell him what, if any, of the conversations that he had with Anthony that could be revealed under subpoena."

"Was there a hearing?"

"You need to know a couple more things. First, I received a communication from the Solicitor General in Belize telling me that one of their officers who was operating as an undercover officer at the hotel where Anthony met Tom was a witness to conversations between Tom and the undercover officer and a separate conversation between Anthony and the officer."

"I am confused. Did you call the Solicitor General or did the Solicitor General call you?"

"Out of the blue, the Solicitor General called me."

"Did you know the Solicitor General?"

"No."

"What did the Solicitor General tell you his office knew?"

"The import of the two conversations was that Tom admitted he still represented Anthony and that he was aiding Anthony in avoiding arrest on the escape charge."

"Did those allegations seem credible to you?"

"Frankly no, but when I told Judge Barrow, he became irate and seemed to believe Tom was aiding Anthony in his escape."

"The second thing you need to know is that Tom told us that Anthony was in the company of Judge David Lucius, an appeal court judge."

"I am aware he has a drinking problem," said the prosecutor.

"Whatever, the question is why was he with Anthony Arnold in Belize?"

"Correct, that would be relevant," said the prosecutor.

"So we had the hearing. In my opinion Judge Barrow was arbitrary and he ruled constantly against objections raised by Tom's attorney. The objections were valid, and would have been made by a first year law student. The objections should have been granted. For example, the judge would not let Tom's attorney cross examine the police officer from Belize, which was fundamental error. The way the hearing was handled was an embarrassment. Judge Barrow was openly antagonistic to Mr. Night."

"Was Tom sentenced after the hearing?"

"Yes, to six months in the County Jail. No one thinks this is right, even the Captain at the Jail complained to me that I should release Tom."

"Have you considered doing that?"

"Yes, actually I had considered a release without the requirement of bail even before I got Judge Barrow's phone bill. Since I have received the bill, I am convinced Tom is just a scapegoat. Judge Barrow's phone bill shows he has been in contact with the Solicitor General from Belize, the same man who provided the witness against Tom. The Solicitor General paid for his plane ticket to Florida. The phone records show the judge also spoke to a couple of powerful law firms in Central and South America who handle drug defendants, and the judge also called the richest man in Honduras, who is a drug trafficker."

"So it seems suspicious," said the Statewide Prosecutor.

"Anthony was involved in drugs, we know that," continued Hale. "And what about Judge Lucius? This man, a sitting appellate judge, is running around Central America with an escaped plane thief/drug trafficker. And Tom Night is the one who is in jail. Doesn't that seem ironic?"

"You are a prosecutor, Mr. Hale. You know the proceedings before the Statewide Grand Jury are secret. So I cannot tell you what our investigation has revealed or what the report of the jury panel might be. I can tell you that the panel has authorized a press release and that it will issue a report within the next two weeks."

"Can you give me a direction to go here?" asked Hale.

"The only thing I can say is that you should follow your gut. You told me your gut says to release Tom on his own recognizance. Is that what your gut still says?"

"That's what my gut says," said Hale.

"I personally think that is a good choice."

"And that is what I will do," said Hale.

Chapter 52

Darlene Street waited in the lobby of the jail for Tom to be released. Earlier in the day she had received a call from John Hale's office. Hale's assistant had told her that Mr. Hale had signed a stipulation to allow a release on recognizance, meaning Tom Night would be free without having to post a bond.

John Hale's office was across the street from the jail. Darlene went to Hale's office to retrieve a true copy of the stipulation before going to the jail to get Tom and take him to his home. She asked to see Hale. She wanted to know why he had agreed to Tom's release. Hale had told his aide to tell her he was unavailable. Hale had never taken action like this on his own without a prior request from a defense attorney. He did not want to appear soft. Darlene had a tendency to go on and on. He really did not like her. He thought he might change his mind about the release if he had to speak to her.

After his release, Tom asked Darlene to drive home the long way on a back road so they could talk. But Tom just wanted to look at the trees in the forest that they had to pass through on the route back to the city. As they drove, Tom remembered a little backwoods bar and bar-b-que stand along the way and he asked Darlene if she had time to stop. He would buy her a pulled pork sandwich with coleslaw and a side of baked beans.

The place was called Whities Bar, (yes "Whities" was misspelled, but that was its name). The food was good. You could smell the aroma of the smoke house from the road. The bar was open from 5:00 a.m. to 12:00 midnight. Early every morning, workmen came by and purchased a bag lunch that included a sandwich and a half pint of whiskey. There was a lunch trade and dinner seven days a week. After 7:00 p.m. there was music until midnight.

Inside, there was a long bar made of a single slab of cypress. All of the large cypress had been cut out of the woods along the Withlacoochee River more than 60 years before and the lumber in the bar top was a slab harvested back then. The bar top was 30 feet long and three feet wide and three inches thick. The bar had been worn in spots along its surface from men leaning against it rubbing their hands and elbows into the wood. The wood had been sanded and finished only one time and thereafter over the last 60 years it had gained a dark brown patina from sweat and grease and booze.

"You bring me to the best places," said Darlene as she took it all in.

"I thought you probably missed Whities Bar in your travels. You'd be at a loss to miss it before you die," said Tom.

They were seated in one of the wooden booths that lined the wall opposite the bar. On each booth there was a kitchen knife that was attached to a chain that was fastened to the table. The knife was there if you ran into a tough piece of meat. The chain prevented the knife from being used in a fight.

Down the center of the room that was Whities Bar there was an old shuffleboard game. The participants tried to amass points by sliding a heavy round chrome metal disk over a slick wooden surface covered in sawdust. The participant tried to land the chrome disk within a triangle painted on the slick board. If the player was successful, landing a disc in the triangle, the opponent would try to slide his disk down the board and knock the opponent's discs out of the triangle.

As they sat in the booth waiting for their sandwich and drinking sweet iced tea, a man came in the back door of the bar from the direction of the "facilities." Behind the man toddled a medium sized dog. The man was skinny with a big beer belly. The dog's body matched the owner's physique. The bartender greeted the man and handed him a pillow. The man pulled a stool up to the bar and placed the pillow on the seat of the stool. The man looked down at the dog. The dog twisted his head and the man pulled the stool away from the bar just a scooch and then looked at the dog. The dog twisted his head as if to say "no." This went on for a while. The man would position and reposition the stool and the dog would twist its head. Finally, the man positioned the stool to the dog's satisfaction and the dog jumped up and landed directly on the pillow. The dog turned to the people in the bar and looked at them with a smile on his face.

Everyone laughed and applauded. The dog looked up at his owner and his owner motioned to the bartender who put a dish in front of the dog and then opened a long neck bottle of beer and handed it to the owner. The dog's owner filled the dish with beer and then said "Ok, you can drink." And the dog began to suck up the brew. There was more laughter and another round of applause.

That was as much excitement as occurred in the bar or that any of these customers could stand. Everyone went back to talking and leaning over their drinks.

"So did you find out why Hale let you out?" asked Darlene.

"No."

"Do you have a guess?"

"Yes," said Tom.

"Well, what is it?"

"I think a little bird told him I was innocent."

"That can't be it, you idiot," said Darlene. "John Hale has never cared a wit if someone was innocent."

"I don't know about that," said Tom. "One thing though, since he released me we won't have a bond hearing, so no one is going to know about the phone bill and the fact Judge Barrow is a crook."

"Do you think Hale knows about the phone bill? The only place he would get that phone bill is from his daughter."

"Maybe, maybe not. I doubt if Jane only copied one of the judge's bills. She may have had even more incriminating evidence that she gave to Hale. Or maybe she gave other evidence to the Captain. He's the one who gave you Jane's note and the phone bill."

"You don't think Lucy Hale showed her dad the phone bill to give him a warning so her dad could protect himself?"

"No, she said her father got her into this. That means Hale alerted her to the possibility that my conviction for contempt may be news. Remember, she said, 'My dad got me into this. He put me at risk.' That's why she agreed to take the chance of being subpoenaed and going to jail to protect the source."

"I guess," said Darlene. But she was not sure.

"We do not need to worry about why Hale released me. What we need to do is to fight back. We need to prepare the best appeal in the world so I can get out of this mess. You also need to contact the Bar Association and tell them I am contesting the ethics charges. You can start by telling them I have no intention of forfeiting my license. You can also call Roger and tell him not to count me out of my share of the partnership profits. Then I will call Bob and Frank Barnes and tell them they need to have more faith in their attorney."

"We will defend the case," said Darlene.

"Yes, we will offer a vigorous defense," said Tom.

Part VII
Mexico City

Chapters 53 through 59

The sale of the treasure ... Oro de México ... The FBI ... A new business ...The midwest insurance company ... Judge Lucius ... H. Patel

Chapter 53

H. Patel and the Judge were selling artifacts again. They had been very successful. They had sold all but one last piece of treasure, a gold mask with jade inlay. The piece was unique and priceless.

Anthony intended to sell this work to a high end dealer in downtown México City where he was likely to get the best price. Anthony was hoping this mask would bring them close to a million US dollars.

The gallery he chose was named "Oro de México." It was known for the high prices paid to it for exquisite works of Mayan gold and jade. The gallery had recently sold a gold mask for $2.5 million US Dollars. The gallery had a reputation for paying large amounts to sellers of genuine Mayan works.

Over the last couple of weeks, the judge and H. Patel had become practiced in the way they approached the galleries. The judge was allowed a drink before he entered the shop. The alcohol would cause the cheeks of his face to flush. Red and blue blood vessels would highlight his nose. The judge would bumble about and he appeared to be drunk. H. Patel appeared to be trying to help his companion obtain a good price for the gold mask.

The men appeared vulnerable and the vulnerability was what gave them success in selling all the treasure to this point in time. The buyers in the galleries felt they could get treasure at a discount. The sellers appeared to know what they had was genuine but were unsure of the value of the mask and so the dealers felt they could take advantage of the men on the price.

Once the last piece was sold, the men intended to split the pot and move on separately. Anthony had advised H. Patel and the judge that they should be prepared to produce the documents of authenticity from the Minister of the Interior in Mérida, México and the letter from the Solicitor General of Belize if there was any question about the provenance (ownership) of the piece. Any expert at the gallery would know the piece was genuine, and they should make their sale if the gallery agreed the mask was not stolen and that the judge had good title.

Upon arrival, the judge and H. Patel had to show the guard at the front door the gold mask before they were let in to see the owner. The galley owner at "Oro de México" was polite. He looked over the mask, first with a jeweler's loop in the showroom and then the sellers were invited to a private viewing room in the back of the store. The men would not leave the piece in the hands of the experts. They insisted they were to accompany the artifact through any process of inspection the gallery intended to conduct on the work. The gallery did not object. It was the gallery's protocol to lock customers in the viewing room with any valuable. The customer could not get out.

***

The men produced the ownership papers.

The owner of the gallery asked to make copies of the documents showing how the mask was found in Mexico and that the country of Belize had partial ownership of the gold mask. H. Patel did not object to the owner making a copy of the letter.

The men sat for half an hour waiting for the owner. H. Patel felt the gallery was taking a long time to copy the papers attesting to ownership. He asked if there was any problem and was assured there was none. The men were told that the gallery was very interested in a purchase but they had to complete their due diligence according to their protocol. The gallery owner reminded the men that they were asking a great deal of money for the piece, over a million dollars US, and they had to be patient. And so the men were patient. H. Patel accepted a glass of wine and he allowed the judge a small glass also. The men watched as the team of experts conducted their examination and they tried to read the face of the gallery's scientist and archeologist for a clue as to whether these experts felt the mask was "right."

Meanwhile the owner of the gallery was in his office working the phone. He called Mérida, México and spoke to the person in charge at the Department of the Interior and verified that the letter from the department was genuine and that the mask had been found in México in the Yucatán in the area below Tulum. The tax had been paid and the piece was legitimately in private hands. Good news.

The owner was having more trouble locating the Solicitor General in Belize however. No one could find him and the store owner was told to leave his number and they would look for him and have him ring back. This made the owner of "Oro de Mexico" suspicious that the letter from the Solicitor was not genuine.

H. Patel was starting to fidget and the judge was withdrawing from the alcohol. H. Patel gave the judge a second, larger glass of wine. They had arrived at the gallery at 10 a.m. and it was now 4 p.m. The experts had finished their examination, but the judge and H. Patel were told they had to wait for the offer, that there was one more matter that needed to be resolved.

The men asked what that was and were told the gallery owner wanted to speak to the Solicitor General of Belize. H. Patel said, "That should be no problem."

H. Patel had questioned Anthony about his relationship with the Solicitor General. H. Patel knew the story of how Anthony found a wreck of one ship of the expedition of Juan de Grijalva and the Solicitor General had represented Anthony before the government of México Antiquities Department to establish Anthony's right to salvage the wreck site.

The Solicitor General had residuals that were owed to him personally upon sale of all or a part of the treasure discovered at the wreck site. H. Patel had even reviewed the paperwork attesting to the rights Anthony had as a salvager of the site and the rights the Solicitor General had in the proceeds once the property was sold. The Solicitor's residual totaled 5% of the net after expenses. Based on the sales to date and the anticipated sale price of this last piece for near a million dollars, the Solicitor General had every reason to verify the contents of his letter. Solicitor Prince should speak highly of Anthony and his partners once the gallery owner was able to locate him. H. Patel just had to get the judge through the ordeal of being denied his favorite high octane whiskey.

***

An hour later, the gallery owner came in with another man who was identified as a person who would partner with the gallery owner if there was a purchase of the piece. The gallery owner explained the sale price was more than he wished to take on at present. He was stretched thin by the cost of other recent purchases.

The gallery owner apologized and then asked H. Patel to again explain how he came to own the mask. H. Patel said it was no problem and he explained how he was an attorney from Florida, and the judge was his partner in business dealings. That the judge introduced him to Anthony Arnold, who was looking for partners who would help him sell treasure he had salvaged in México at a wreck site recognized as an official site for the collection of Mayan antiquities. And further, that the Country of Belize had an interest in the treasure.

Three times during the presentation, H. Patel was asked Anthony's full name and each time H. Patel spelled out the name. He was also asked about other matters concerning Anthony including his present whereabouts.

The owner and the other man began speaking in Spanish in the presence of the judge and H. Patel. "They both seem to believe their story. They are very convincing," said the gallery owner to the detective.

"Yes, they both seem to be honest, but when we spoke to the Solicitor General he denies that he knows them or that Belize is in any way involved with this treasure." The owner of Oro de Mexico had called the Mexican police as soon as he had spoken to Solicitor Prince and Prince denied knowledge of the sellers.

The owner and the Detective continued to speak in Spanish. "It doesn't seem they are aware Anthony Arnold is wanted in Cancún for soliciting a murder. These men seem to have valid identification and they are who they say they are. Our investigation shows there are no warrants for their arrest. Do you think they are simply dupes?"

"It appears the mask is genuine. There is no report it is stolen, is there?" asked the gallery owner.

"No, you could purchase the mask if you wish and you will have good title, if that is what you are asking."

"Yes, that was my concern," said the gallery owner. "If I make a deal, what are you going to do with the Americans?"

"I will arrest them. I will try to find out where Anthony Arnold is located," said the detective. "When I find out where Mr. Arnold is located, I will go and arrest him too."

"Probably, if you asked them they would tell you. They appear to be very dense."

"I don't want to ask them anymore questions about Anthony Arnold until after I arrest them."

"That is your business. I guess you are going to stay here while I talk to them about a sale of the mask?"

"Yes, I will wait out front in the showroom. Make sure you let them out through the showroom so I will see them and I can arrest them," said the detective.

"Please arrest them outside the store. I do not want my other customers to see the arrest."

At that point the detective, who had been playing the role of potential buyer, walked over to Patel and said he was not interested in participating in the purchase of the mask and he left the room.

H. Patel and the judge became ashen faced. This turn of events was unexpected.

The gallery owner waited for the detective to leave. He motioned for the pair to come close and then he whispered to the two men that the Solicitor General from Belize denied he had written the letter that H. Patel had been given by Anthony. The gallery owner also shared that the man that left was a police detective and he was going to arrest them as soon as they walked out of the showroom. The gallery owner also told them that Anthony Arnold was wanted by the police for solicitation to commit murder.

The faces of the two men became pasty and pale.

The gallery owner continued. "If you want to sell the mask I will pay you $50,000 dollars US and I will assist you to escape. I will let you leave from the rear door and I will drive you wherever you want me to take you."

"Can we have a minute together?" said H. Patel.

"Certainly."

With that the galley owner left the room, locked the door, and went in his office and prepared a bill of sale for the mask with a sale price of $50,000 and waited to be called back to the private viewing room. The gallery owner was convinced the men had no choice but to sell him the mask for the ridiculously low price of $50,000. Greed had gotten the better of the gallery owner.

"We can't sell the mask for $50,000. Anthony will kill us," said H. Patel.

"I have a number for the desk at the hotel. I will try to see if someone will bring Anthony to the phone," said the judge who was now sobered by these unanticipated events.

The phone at the hotel was answered after many rings. The judge asked for Anthony. The desk personnel said they would get him. They waited. Finally, Anthony picked up the receiver.

"Anthony, we have bad news." The judge explained what had occurred.

Anthony said nothing.

The judge then repeated, "The owner also says the police are going to arrest us if we try to leave, but if we agree to the sale of the mask for $50,000 US he will help us escape to the hotel."

"Stall them. Just keep talking," shouted Anthony. "Winston and I will be there shortly."

***

Winston quickly stuffed four .44 caliber handguns between the side dividers in a brief case. In the center compartment he tossed in four boxes of .44 caliber ammunition for the weapons. They hailed a cab.

As they rode to the Oro de México Gallery, a plan evolved. Winston would get out of the cab in front of the gallery. Winston would go in the front door unarmed, pretending to be a customer. He would be checked. He had $25,000 cash in his front pocket in rolls of $100 bills. He would flash the money to the security guard. The guard would take him to a sales lady who would try to charm him into a sale.

Meanwhile Anthony would circle the building in the cab and look for a delivery door. Once at the delivery door, Anthony would get out with the briefcase with the four weapons. He would tell the taxi driver to go back to the front and wait. Meanwhile, Winston would begin to raise a ruckus and distract the guards. After the guard at the rear left his post Anthony would enter at the rear and together he and Winston would free their co-conspirators.

"How do you know there will be a delivery door?" asked Winston.

"We will have to take that chance. It's a gallery; they have to have a separate door for deliveries. They don't take the deliveries through the front door," Anthony assumed.

***

And so Winston was dropped off in front of the gallery. He was allowed in by the guard and taken to a salesperson. As soon as Winston began to talk in his female voice the sales lady began to laugh and Winston began to yell and scream, claiming the woman was making fun of him. Winston's outrage and display was so flamboyant that the Mexican police detective intervened and he and one of the security guards dragged Winston into the back. Winston continued to scream with such volume that when Anthony went to the back delivery door, the guard had already abandoned his post to find the cause of the disturbance. Anthony also followed Winston's shrieks and came upon a brawl involving Winston, two security guards, the gallery owner, H. Patel, the Mexican detective and the judge.

Anthony opened the briefcase and pulled out a gun. He fired the weapon into the ceiling to make the security guards aware he was armed, and they surrendered. These three men were then pushed into the viewing room, the phone was pulled out of the wall and destroyed, and the gallery owner was told to lock the men inside.

The gallery owner was then taken to his office and told he was going with the four men. He would be released once they believed they were free. They told him that they would all be riding in a cab and they would all speak English.

"Agreed?" asked Anthony. "If you say anything to the driver in Spanish you are dead. Also give me the $50,000 cash."

The galley owner retrieved $50,000 from the desk drawer and gave it to Anthony.

The five men left the gallery and stuffed themselves into the small Toyota cab that was waiting out front.

Four blocks later the gallery owner was let out of the cab.

The cab continued on. Then the four men got out. They split into pairs and caught two separate cabs and then rode back to the hotel. They grabbed what was left of their possessions and Anthony retrieved the tool box from its hiding spot in the bathroom and they took a taxi to the airport.

Winston went to the office in the hanger and he paid all the airport fees and fuel charges and said that the plane was going south to Honduras. Once Anthony was in the plane, he quickly checked the tool box for the cash. Everything was in order. He added the $50,000 he stole from the Oro de México Gallery. He put the gold Mayan mask in with the cash and put the tool box in the cargo bin on the floor of the plane behind the bench seat and the three men waited for Winston.

Ten minutes later Winston returned with a cardboard box full of prepared food. They all thanked him as they flew away from Mexico City.

"Where are we going?" Anthony asked Winston.

"Let's try for Texas. It seems like we have worn out our welcome in México."

As the plane began to ascend about a quarter of the way down the runway, the judge whispered to H. Patel, "I left my whiskey at the hotel. I will die if I keep drinking. I need your help."

"I will do what I can," said H. Patel. "But I think you have to do this yourself."

The judge curled up on the bench seat and fell asleep.

Chapter 54

Rick Ibn had faithfully paid his insurance premium to insure against the loss or destruction of his Aero Commander.

Every day since his plane had been stolen, Rick called Miami to speak to his insurance adjuster. "When will my claim be processed? When will I be paid? I need to be paid to be able to buy another plane to get back to work."

The insurance adjuster was aware of Rick's need and he would use that need against him. First the adjuster would delay him with endless requests for information. They had him fill out forms describing his loss even though the plane had been fully described when the policy was purchased. They wanted him to establish the value of the loss, which was unnecessary. The insurance company had appraised the plane yearly and inspected the plane biannually. Further, Rick was required to provide his maintenance logs (which, luckily, were not in the plane when it was stolen) to prove that the plane had been maintained according to factory specifications. The logs were sent from Belize City to the insurance company in Miami by messenger.

The insurance company insisted they were conducting an investigation but no investigator had contacted Rick to ask him to describe how the loss occurred. Rick would be just as happy to get his plane back as he would to be paid by the insurance company for the loss of the plane. But it was obvious that the insurance company was not looking for the plane and they were not going to pay for his plane quickly so he could continue to operate his business. He had already called friends in the States who had private plane services and he had provided his customers with pilots who would fly them to their destinations as scheduled. He felt he could get his business back if he got his plane back, but soon he would lose his customer base.

Eventually, Rick would be forced to take whatever settlement the insurance company offered. Luckily, Rick owned the plane outright. He did not continue to owe payments to a bank while the insurance adjuster strung Rick along. He was very careful with his money. He saved religiously. He paid for capital expenditures for his company with cash. He had no worries about interest payments to a banker.

Rick was being taken for a ride by the insurance company. He had paid $10,000 US a year in insurance premiums for the last five years. If the insurance company had invested his money it had probably doubled it. So the insurance company would probably make money on his policy even if they reimbursed Rick for his loss. The next time he started a business he would self-insure, thought Rick.

***

Rick decided that what he needed to do was to take a few days and try to find the plane himself. He was working now pretty much full time for TACA. During the last week one of their planes, a Boeing 757, had sucked a flock of wood storks into one engine on take-off and the bodies of the birds destroyed a number of fan blades in the plane's port side engine. Rick had worked 45 hours straight and he and a mechanic the company flew in from Miami successfully completed the repair and the plane was back in the air. TACA was impressed with Rick's work. The company put Rick on full time and he obtained a work permit.

Rick considered moving to Belize. He and Dr. Anna Hernando were very compatible and Rick thought about settling down and asking her to marry him.

But first Rick wanted to find his plane or settle the matter with the insurance company. He decided he would rent a plane, a puddle jumper, and fly around the area and see if he could find the plane. The Aero Commander had not been found in Columbia or in Ecuador or Peru. If the plane was going to be converted to a drug mule there would have been some word on the plane in those countries because that's where a load of dope would originate. Rick's thought was that perhaps the plane was still in Central America.

And so Rick rented a small plane and flew into the panhandle of Guatemala, then southwest toward the mountains along the coast. Then he flew east, passed Guatemala City and into Honduras. In Honduras he got a tip that there was an AC-500S that was for sale for parts near Zacapa, Guatemala. Rick fueled up and flew there directly. Once he landed, he taxied to the hanger. There was his plane, in parts laying on the floor in a corner of the hanger.

Rick spoke to the new owner of his plane and was told how the plane was in the process of landing and suffered a total stress fracture of a part of the wing located above the pilot's seat. There were four men in the plane at the time of the wing failure. No one was hurt and the plane did not crash, but the wing and fuselage were twisted and could not be repaired so that the plane could operate safely.

Rick looked over what was left of the plane. The aluminum skin had been removed from the wing. The cabin was intact with the exception that all the instrumentation and the radio were gone. Both of the engines were removed as was the fuel tank bladder in the wing. The three landing gear and the tires had been sold. Rick asked how the plane had been dismantled so quickly. The owner of the plane said the AC-500S was a work horse for the drug industry and was very popular and parts for the AC-500S were in demand.

Rick took many pictures of his plane. In particular he searched for any identification numbers on the parts. The "N" number was still stenciled on the sides of the fuselage. Rick left the new owner of his plane with the information he had for the insurance adjuster and the insurance company and the claim number together with Rick's address and phone number at work with TACA. Rick told the new owner he would contact the insurance company.

Rick flew back to Belize City. He had been gone two days. He concluded the plane was going to be a total loss to him so far as collecting from his insurance. Even though the plane was stolen and now destroyed, the insurance company would probably claim they owed nothing because the plane had a defect that caused irreparable damage to the plane when it landed. The insurance company would say Rick's remedy was with the plane manufacturer for the defect, not with the insurance company. The argument that the thieves may have stolen the plane but the damage was caused by the defect was technical, but the policy Rick bought from the insurance company excluded losses caused by manufacturer's defects.

When he landed in Belize City, Rick went to the TACA office and used their international telephone to call Tom to help with the insurance company. Rick didn't know the troubles Tom had faced since his return to St. Petersburg. Tom was out of jail and the Bar Association had not suspended his license. The State Attorney, John Hale, had called the Bar Association and told them the charge of Contempt would be dismissed. But Tom's reputation was tarnished.

Tom was in his office working when he took Rick's call.

Tom listened to Rick's story and said he would be happy to represent him. Tom's fee would be one third of the amount recovered. It was music to Rick's ears. He would owe Tom nothing unless Tom recovered damages for Rick. The way it was going the insurance company wasn't going to pay him unless they were forced to.

Tom asked Rick for the news in Belize. Rick said he was going to ask Dr. Hernando to marry him, but maybe not right that minute. But it was going to happen. Rick said Tom would be invited to the wedding.

Rick did share with Tom the gossip about his partner, Roger.

Roger visited Belize City when Tom was in the county jail. It seems that Roger stayed at a hotel near the lighthouse when he traveled there to deliver the paperwork for the licenses and leases to the Belize government. Apparently he celebrated too much in the bar after his meeting with the Solicitor General. He was bragging to everyone about how great an international lawyer he was and then to cap off his night he invited two women to his room. They made so much noise the police were called. Roger wasn't arrested but the next morning he was so sick on the rum he drank that he ended up at the Hernando Clinic.

After he gave his history, Dr. Hernando gave him a prescription for periwinkle clam soup for the hangover and a shot of 500 cc's of penicillin to ward off the potential effects of disease he might have contacted after his night of romance.

Until he heard the news of these events, Tom had wondered why Roger had been so gracious when Darlene told Roger that Tom would be coming back to the office. Roger had no objection to Tom returning to work. The only thing Roger said was that Tom would have to do all the traveling from now on. Roger said, "I'm not built for it."

Chapter 55

A short man, early 60's, meticulously groomed, in an expensive tailored suit entered the office of the US Marshal in Fort Lauderdale, Florida, through the front door. He strode over to and entered a booth that allowed him to view a secretary sitting at a desk. She was located behind a clear Plexiglas shield that was one and a half inches thick and bullet proof. The glass stretched from the floor to ceiling. There was a speaker box in the booth at chest height. The man went to the speaker, bent down and announced his name: "Raymond Barrow is here for his appointment."

Judge Barrow looked petite and helpless without his robe.

There were no seats in the room on the visitor side of the glass. He stood for a moment and then a door opened that seemed to be invisible in a grey colored wall to his right. He entered the door and was greeted by a Negro male in uniform. He was taken to a dressing room. He knew the routine. He leaned against the wall with the palms of his hands and he was thoroughly frisked by the uniformed guard. He had to remove his shoes. Each shoe was inspected. The guard pulled at the soles and heels of his shoes. He was required to remove his suit coat and his pants. He was allowed to wear his shirt, underwear and socks but only after the guard felt the seams of these items for anything such as a thick wire hidden in his shirt collar that could be used as a blade in a shiv. The guard went through his pockets and then rolled up the coat and pants and tie and went over each section of the clothes. The guard found a book of matches, a wallet, a pack of cigarettes, a pair of dark glasses and a case, a handkerchief, a comb, a pen and a packet containing personal care items (nail file, clippers, etc.). He found no keys. "I took a cab," he explained. The guard put all these articles in a metal box that was then locked.

The guard then told the judge he could wear his shirt and underwear and socks and pants. After redressing and donning slippers, the judge smirked at the guard. The guard ignored him.

The guard directed Judge Barrow into a small room painted the lightest shade of rose or pink. There was a table with a thick glass top in the room and two men in black suits sat at one side of the table. There was an empty seat on the opposite side of the table. Barrow was directed by the guard to have a seat. The men could see their legs and feet and hands through the clear glass table top. The guard stood behind the judge as the men began to talk.

"As you remember from our prior conversation, my name and my partner's correct names shall not be given to you and we shall remain anonymous. We know you as Raymond Barrow, however, you will be given another identity after you have been processed.

"First, we will review the documentation of the re-settlement agreement between yourself and the Government of the United States of America. Before you on the table is the original agreement. No copies will be made. The original document shall remain in the possession of the Office of the US Marshal, an agency of the United States of America. The existence of the document shall be denied by the government. At this time you are to read the document in our presence and we will witness your signature if you decide to sign it. You are to make no additions, corrections or any other mark on the document except to sign your name and enter your social security number on the line below your signature, if you agree to the contents of the agreement.

"We are employees of the government," the agent continued, "and we cannot give you advice or any explanation of the contents of the document. If you sign the document, you will go with the guard who will take you for processing which will include education of your new background and identity. Part of your agreement is to give testimony before a federal grand jury and to later testify truthfully at any subsequent trial that results from any indictment returned by the Grand Jury. The document also states that part of your agreement requires you to serve a sentence of one year in prison. That sentence will be served in a Federal Prison. The Federal Government will have a duty to protect you from harm from the criminals you testify against. Although the government has a duty to protect you, the duty is one that only requires us to act in good faith. It is not an absolute guarantee of your safety.

"With those preliminaries being stated, please advise us if you wish to continue with the process."

"I wish to continue," said Barrow.

"Please read the document," said the agent.

Barrow carefully read each page. It took an hour.

"Do you have a pen?" asked Barrow.

He was given a pen. He signed his name and inscribed his Social Security number.

Barrow stood up. He was handcuffed by the guard and he was taken through a door behind the agents for processing and placement in the Federal witness protection program.

***

John Hale received a call from his assistant. His assistant was in court but Judge Barrow was absent with no explanation for his whereabouts. Hale called the Chief Judge who told Hale that a substitute judge was on route.

"What cases will the substitute judge hear?" asked Hale.

"I received a call from the Chief Judge of the Florida Supreme Court," said the Chief Judge of the Circuit Court. "Judge Barrow has resigned. The substitute judge will hear anything that is scheduled on the calendar," said the Chief Circuit Judge.

"I want to dismiss all charges against Tom Night, is the reason I asked," said Hale.

"I will personally sign the order of dismissal. You and Darlene Street put a stipulation together with an order dismissing all charges against Mr. Night and have it delivered to my office today. I will sign the Order and have it filed with the Clerk of Court immediately. I know you spoke to the Bar Association. I will contact the association and tell them the Order has been signed and that the contempt charges brought by Judge Barrow were not well founded. What about the newspaper?" asked the Chief Judge.

"I will call the editor myself. I will tell him the charges have been dismissed. I won't be able to control what he does, but I doubt he will print a story that hurts Tom. He may want to know what happened to Judge Barrow. What am I supposed to say?"

"The Supreme Court is issuing a press release that Barrow resigned. The release will refer all questions to his home address and home phone number. I tried to call him this morning at home and his phone is out of order. I guess you can just refer the editor to the Supreme Court or to my office. No one in the court system knows where he is at this time."

Chapter 56

When Jamie returned to Miami and contacted his A/C suppliers with the contracts he had entered into with customers in Belize City, they were amazed. The suppliers had no idea there was a market for air conditioning systems in Central America. The suppliers were unaware that the population could afford the systems.

Jamie had hit a sweet spot in the market and the suppliers were happy to fill it with product.

Jamie needed a representative in Central America. He contacted Tom Night. Tom explained that he needed to find a representative who was a citizen or a resident of the country of Belize. He suggested he talk to Rick and his fiancé, Dr. Hernando. She was a citizen and Rick had a work permit and resident status. Tom also felt Belize was a stable country so far as Central America was concerned. The main problem was the tax system. They would need to carve out an exception for the taxation of Jamie's product so that the A/C imports were not oppressively taxed as electronic devices.

Tom felt that Attorney Hubert Johns would be able to call upon the Solicitor General for an interpretation of the tax law to exclude appliances and electric systems from the 50% tax that was imposed on electronics. Since the Solicitor General's son, Andrew Prince Jr., now worked for Attorney Johns, he would present the government with the proposal. Tom felt Jamie would receive prompt attention for his request for an interpretation of the tax code. Further, all of the persons on Jamie's customer list were prominent citizens and they would lobby for the lower sales tax rate, which was four percent (4%) of the sale price of the appliance rather than 50% of the sale price if the A/C was considered to be electronics.

Tom also suggested that Jamie enlist the help of Jacob and Michael from the Mennonite community. The Mennonites had been able to crack the retail market in Belize, first selling agricultural products and then wood products, boards and then furniture, and they would be a source for advice. Tom would be happy to send Jamie a letter of introduction.

Tom also told Jamie that his law firm would be able to represent his legal interests in the State of Florida and he could provide consultation services for international business dealings in Central America through the law firm in Belize City.

Tom said the first thing Jamie should do would be to return to Belize City and talk to Rick, Herbert and Jacob from the Mennonite Community.

***

Jamie booked a flight for the next day. He contacted Rick through his job at TACA. Rick would round up the people he needed to see. They would meet at Herbert John's law office in Belize City.

And so the four men met the next afternoon. Also present were Dr. Hernando and the Solicitor General's son, Andrew Prince, Jr.

The six decided to form a Belize Corporation. Rick and the doctor, (a resident and a citizen) together would be owners of 51% of the shares of the company and Jamie would be owner of the last 49% of the shares.

The Mennonite Community had a warehouse in Belize City near the International Airport and they would share space to store the appliances and equipment after Hubert obtained a favorable ruling on the tax rate for the product.

Jamie intended to purchase a new plane which would be used to transport systems and appliances from the warehouse in Belize

City to other countries in Central America. Rick would also work with the installers. He had a good handle on anything mechanical and electrical. They were all getting ahead of themselves but the excitement of the prospective business venture was contagious.

After the meeting, Rick called Tom on Hubert's international phone line and outlined the proposal. Rick and Jamie wanted Tom to draw up the agreement between the parties. Hubert would handle the corporate work in Belize and the lobbying effort with the government. Rick also wanted Tom to attempt to attach a maritime lien against Anthony Arnold's dive boat and obtain a judgment to cover the deficiency between the value of the AC-500S and the amount the insurance company would finally pay. Rick also wanted to be compensated for the personal injury he suffered when he was attacked the night his plane was stolen.

"Just a last bit of information," said Tom. "I spoke to the insurance adjuster regarding the AC-500S. He tells me that when they talked to the man who bought the salvage rights to your AC-500S, he said he sold Winston Grey a plane. It's a C-47. The owner of the hanger at the airport in Zacapa, Guatemala is sending a copy of the paperwork from the sale of the salvage rights and the sale of the C-47 to your insurance company. The insurance company will forward the documents to me. If I can find the C-47 in the States I may be able to get a judge to attach the plane so we can obtain title and procession of the plane to partially satisfy any judgment."

"If I get the C-47 we could use it in the air conditioning business we are starting. We could make deliveries with the plane. It's perfect for cargo," said Rick.

"I'll keep you informed," said Tom.

***

Within a week, the Solicitor General, the Chief legal officer of the Country of Belize, met with his son, Andrew Prince Jr., and his boss Herbert Johns.

Solicitor General Prince agreed the tax on electronics should not apply to air conditioning systems. In any event, the tax on the system was too high at 50%. Mr. Prince did not have an A/C system in his own house because of the cost. However, the Solicitor wanted to make sure there was no issue of conflict of interest involving his son presenting the request to lower the tax to the government and so he assigned the matter for an opinion to one of the assistants in his office and he made sure he did not influence the assistant's decision.

The Solicitor General was attempting to keep a low profile. Luckily, he had not become the subject of any investigation into the drug trade or theft of Rick's plane or any murder or the sale of Anthony's Mayan gold and jade, and he wanted to keep it that way.

Tom felt the Solicitor General would not be immune from charges resulting from the theft, murder, and corruption. The question was, when would the shoe drop?

Chapter 57

The Cancún Police Department needed an entire room to store the evidence collected from the hanger owned by the Bounty Hunter at the International Airport. The paperwork consisted of financial documents: canceled checks, check stubs, accountings, receipts, billings, reports and journals.

The first thing that the detective found of particular interest was that the owner of the Bounty Hunter's business was a large mutual insurance company from the midwest of the United States. The company had a reputation as being honest and law abiding. It was known for sponsoring a popular television show that aired on Sunday nights in the States.

In spite of its stellar reputation, the company appeared to have endorsed contract killings among other crimes. The most frequent miscreant activity was bribery of judges and public officials in order to recoup the bond money that was escheated to the Clerk of the Court if a defendant charged with a crime failed to appear in court to answer the charges leveled against him. Legislatures in all states had enacted laws that allowed the insurance company to recover the amount of the bond it paid if the defendant was returned to the court within a certain period of time after the non- appearance occurred. In addition, a judge could make certain findings that allowed the insurance company the return of money it forfeited to the Clerk even if the deadline expired. The discretion allowed to the judge encouraged the insurance company to make pay offs in return for findings by the Court that allowed the insurance company to recover its money.

There in the paperwork collected from the hanger at the International Airport in Cancun were the names of judges who accepted bribes.

Judges were not the only officials who were illegally compensated. The records showed prosecutors and clerks failed to pursue the collection of forfeitures from the insurance company in return for bribes.

There were also accounts that showed that defendants (Anthony Arnold, for one) had paid the insurance company to look the other way and fail to pursue the defendant. The records showed the cost paid by the insurance company to the jurisdiction from which the defendant failed to appear. There was even a study produced by an insurance industry consultant that concluded that it was more cost efficient to employ their own in-house bounty hunter than to pay an independent bounty hunter a premium of 10% of the amount of the bond.

However, by allowing the Bounty Hunter to be an employee of the insurance company, the insurance company exercised control over the Bounty Hunter and thus the insurance company necessarily conspired with its employee when the Bounty Hunter committed a crime such as kidnapping or bribery to affect the return of the defendant to court or to obtain the return of a bond by paying off a judge. In short, the insurance company was liable for the actions of the Bounty Hunter if the Bounty Hunter was an employee.

The records in the office in the hanger showed that the Bounty Hunter with the black Lear jet was a vice president of the insurance company. His name was Joseph McDugal. Thus the insurancy company was liable for his actions.

The Cancún Police were astounded that the insurance company had allowed these papers showing evidence of crime to leave corporate headquarters in the United States. It was just an oversight, they guessed. Or maybe the paperwork was being hidden in México, far from the eyes of corporate counsel back in Omaha, Nebraska. Further, the two American men they captured attempting to burn the evidence were mid-level managers of the company in a division called "Security Compliance." When they were arrested, the men had standard identification – driver's license, voter registration, etc. on their person. They did not have false ID. The insurance men refused to speak with the police.

***

The chief received a visit from a local lawyer at his office early on the morning after the arrest of the insurance executives and seizure of the evidence. The lawyer wanted to know "what it would take" to release the men from prison and allow them to return home. The lawyer also asked for the return of the insurance company's documents and argued they did not belong to the men who were arrested but to the company, and since the local lawyer represented the company, the chief should give him the documents. The chief ignored the lawyer.

The chief asked the lawyer the location of the Lear jet, if it had crashed, and who owned it. The attorney said he was sure he could provide the Cancún Police force with a Lear jet if that's what it would take to allow his clients and the paperwork to return to The States.

But, the contact with the local lawyer went cold.

The chief knew he would have to wait. The insurance company needed a meeting to determine the course of action.

Then, two days later, after the two Americans had spent the night in the darkest, nastiest, most crowded cell in the prison, and after they had been allowed to speak to their lawyer in the hallway of the jail, the chief began to receive communications from people of importance in the government, the financial community and the Church concerning the release of the insurance executives and the evidence.

The chief knew what the government official and the bankers would say but he was intrigued that the Archbishop wanted to speak to him on behalf of the prisoners. Therefore he invited the holy man to his office.

The Archbishop humbly asked the chief to release the insurance men. The chief asked the archbishop if he would go to hell if he did not release the men.

"No," replied the churchman, "but you may get to the afterlife much sooner if you do not release the men and their documents."

"I will consider your words. Tell me, is this conversation that we are having like one that I would have if I were making a confession? Is the communication confidential?"

"Yes, it could be confidential, my son," said the archbishop. "Is that your wish?"

"Yes. I wish to confess my sins confidentially. Bless me Father for I have sinned, it has been five years since my last confession."

"Tell me your sins, my son."

"I consider my family more than myself or my office. My sister-in-law, who has five children, lost her husband, Jorge Mendez. He was murdered on the order of the insurance company for whom you are soliciting. She has no ability to care for her children. I think evil thoughts about the insurance company that employed the Bounty Hunter who did this to my brother, my sister-in-law and my family. I also feel the insurance company should pay our city for their criminal acts."

"I can absolve you of the sin of these evil thoughts. Is there anything else that you wish to confess?"

"That is all I wish to confess at this time," said the chief.

"Are you sure? This could be your last chance to confess."

"Is there more that I need to know about my fate if I do not release the men and release the paperwork to the lawyer for the insurance company?"

"You are a wise man. I do not have to tell you your fate. You know your fate if you do not accommodate these devils. It will be slow and painful and they will still get what they want in the end, no matter what."

"I have decided that I will hold a bond hearing this afternoon for these men."

"I understand," said the archbishop. "Setting a bond would be good. The insurance company understands bonds. That is its business."

"I will set a bond to allow the men to leave México with the business papers. It will not be a cheap bond. It will be many millions of US Dollars for the devil to get what he wants. Tell them that."

"I will," said the Archbishop.

"Also tell them I need good legal reasoning for the return of their men and their business documents. I do not want to look like a fool when I let these men and the paperwork go. I want there to be a solid legal reason."

"I understand, is that all?"

"Yes, Father."

"Make a good act of contrition, say a rosary for each year you have failed to confess your sins."

"Yes, Father," said the chief.

***

The penance that would be ordered for the two Honduran undercover officers who caused Jorge Mendez's death would be much more severe than the recitation of five rosaries. The Hondurans were doomed to suffer on this earth and burn in Hell on their death.

There was no legal action he could take against the Hondurans. They would be protected by their government.

The chief did make an exhibit of all of the evidence, including the recorded transcript of the wrestlers incriminating the Hondurans for Jorge's death. That information was delivered to all the security forces in Central America so that the Hondurans were marked as assassins. They could not hide and soon they too would die.

It was less difficult for the chief to fashion a penalty for the wrestlers that was not revengeful but rather rehabilitative. They were under the chief's jurisdiction. The chief had five years to decide the punishment.

Chapter 58

The good vibrations felt by the four men in the C-47 when it took off from the airport in México City only lasted as long as it took for the plane to experience extreme turbulence an hour out from México City. The men began to argue about where they should land and split up and go their separate ways.

After they were four hours out, Judge Lucius became ill and vomited into his hands and lap. The C-47 was not a commercial passenger plane and no one had provided air sickness bags to the passengers. In fact, Judge Lucius had no problems with turbulence and air sickness until he quit drinking. Anthony asked H. Patel what was wrong.

"He said he was going to quit drinking. I know he had stopped since before we ate lunch. He told me he left his case of rum in the hotel before we left."

"You need to clean him up and get him intoxicated again or he will die on us," said Winston. "My father died of alcohol withdrawal. Plus, he is going to shake and he will be a mental wreck. He will start seeing things. It's the DTs. We need to tie him to the seat so he can't move around. He will start fighting with us and he could cause us to crash."

"This isn't a car. We can't just pull over to the side of the road," said H. Patel.

"Well, you better find a place to land so we can stabilize him," said Winston.

Anthony had charts for Middle America, but they had been in the air for four hours and they were over the Mexican Plateau that stretches between the foothills of the Sierra Madre Oriental to the foothills of the Sierra Madre Occidental. He had no charts for northern México and southwest Texas, where they were heading. Anthony figured they were near Gomez Placio.

Winston said, "He needs to be in the hospital. Why didn't you tell us he quit drinking?"

"I didn't know this could happen," said H. Patel.

"Look for a road or someplace we can put down," said Winston to Anthony.

The three men began to search and then they all pointed at once to a long straight road. Anthony took the yoke and brought the plane around in a series of wide circles, so he could decrease altitude and get a better look at the road. Once the plane was at 250 feet they could see that the road was badly rutted. Anthony was afraid the ruts would destabilize the plane on landing and the plane would run off the road and into the brush and they would never be able to take off again.

"Did anyone see an airport since México City where we took off?" asked Anthony.

No one remembered anything.

"Great." Anthony increased altitude to 5,000 feet.

***

Anthony continued to fly at 5,000 feet. In the distance, he saw a white, level area that was miles wide and miles long. He went to explore and realized it was a salt flat. He could land and take off there, he thought.

"Everyone buckle up, I am going to land just up here." Anthony pointed.

Anthony extended the flaps and the plane slowly descended until the wheels were barely skipping on the surface of the salt flat and then he set the plane down slowly increasing the weight of the plane on its wheels. The salt flat felt like concrete. It was smooth and hard. The plane sat on the surface after coming to a halt. It would be easy to take off, thought Anthony.

They got the judge out and laid him on a tarp they placed under the wing of the plane in the shade. The judge was shaking and unresponsive but mumbling to himself. Anthony dug around in the cockpit for a first aid kit, or whatever he could find that he thought might help. He told H. Patel to look for a bottle of anything alcoholic. Patel again said the judge said he left the booze in México City.

"Don't believe that. The reason he's a drunk is he doesn't have confidence that he can quit, so he will have stashed a bottle somewhere," said Anthony.

H. Patel started looking for a bottle.

Anthony went outside the plane and looked at the judge. He appeared to be having seizures that caused him to stiffen and shake. He stared blankly. This wasn't good, Anthony thought. Even if the judge lives he will need medical attention or he will have mush for brains. They needed to find ground transportation but there did not appear to be any help for miles.

H. Patel came out with a bottle of rum.

As H. Patel handed the bottle to Anthony, the judge suffered a severe seizure that caused him to shudder, and then stiffen. His breathing became shallow and finally he exhaled tensely and then the judge just stared, dead eyes. Anthony told Winston to see if he could find a shovel. The rum could not save the judge.

Chapter 59

The three men could not find anything to dig with and so they wrapped Judge Lucius' body tightly in the tarp. Anthony doubted the tarp would stop the coyotes from finding the body and chewing on the corpse.

The three men sat on the salt flat under the wing of the C-47 and discussed their plans now that the judge was dead. Where to go was the question. They felt their chances of capture were higher if they went into The States. They could stay in the mountains of México, but they would not fit in unless they played the role of tourists. The plane was also a problem. The authorities had to know about the plane by now. They needed to dump the plane but do it near a city so they could be near a place to buy a car.

"If there is a road near the salt flat I can land near the road about a mile away and we can walk to the road and hitch a ride. If we see a vehicle on the road I can fly us far enough ahead of the car that we can land and walk to the road before the car travels to where we landed. If the plane is a mile off the road it won't be visible from the highway," said Anthony.

They agreed to the plan.

The men went into the plane and located two backpacks in the cargo bin and stuffed them with the cash and the last gold Mayan mask.

They had four guns with ammo belts. They put these items along with three canteens of water into a duffle bag. There was some water left over. Each of them had something to carry. They ate a last meal by the plane and the judge's body and drank as much of the excess water that their bellies could hold and they got back in the plane.

Anthony flew to the west anticipating a highway within 50 miles in that direction. It was evening but still light. They found a highway – a two lane blacktop road. There was much traffic. The road ran through the salt flats so they had a hard surface to land on.

They didn't have to time the landing because there were numerous cars on the road. They would have sufficient time to walk across the flats to head off a single car on the road. Anthony took his time landing and the men walked to the road at a slow pace, conserving their energy. They got to the edge of the road and waited. Anthony spoke some Spanish, so he approached a vehicle that had stopped voluntarily to help the men.

Anthony explained they needed a ride to town so they could buy a car. They had cash. The driver said he could help and so the men all piled in with their backpacks and the duffel bag and rode the 35 miles into a medium sized town that had numerous car lots. The driver took them to a friend and the men purchased a Ford sedan. They paid $750 cash and gave the driver a $20 bill. He was happy.

The three men drove northwest toward New México. They were numbed by events of the day. It was too much, too quickly.

"Let's stay in the mountains for a few days and heal up. What do you say?" asked Anthony. "I need to call Belize and see what our status is there. Maybe we could return to Belize."

They all agreed to delay return to the USA.

Part VIII
The Wrap

Chapters 60 through 65

Resolution ... The Copper Canyon ... The Tarahumara ... The caracara and the snake ... Fire ...

Chapter 60

The Chief of Police of Cancún, México was at his desk in his hearing room. Before him today were the usual squabbles, fights, disputes and thefts. The last matter on the docket was a request for release of the two men charged with attempted arson of the airplane hangar located at the International Airport owned by the Bounty Hunter.

There was no indication who would represent the men. The chief would wait and see, bide his time.

The woman handling the paperwork finally came to the last matter on the docket. The two men were brought before him. They were handcuffed.

The chief directed that the restraints be removed.

The chief had run a background check on the men. The men were in their mid-40s. They were married, with children. They owned houses in Omaha, Nebraska, USA, and worked as security officers for the midwest insurance company. A division of that company employed the Bounty Hunter. Neither man had a criminal record.

The chief asked, "Who of you wishes to speak first?"

The shorter of the two Americans stepped forward, "I do."

"How do you explain your actions at the airport?" asked the chief.

"Respectfully, we are guilty of attempting to burn our employer's documents. We did this with the permission of our employer. We did not believe we were committing a crime."

"Wasn't that the defense the Nazi generals used? They said they were ordered to commit crimes by their superiors. Just because you were ordered to commit an illegal act does not make the act legitimate," said the chief.

"We are saying we had permission to destroy the documents. We were doing it in a safe manner and only intended to burn the documents and nothing else. Not the hangar or anything else in the hangar. We were protecting our employer's confidential documents by burning them."

"Were you involved in any of the activities described in the documents? The documents describe criminal acts that were committed in México ... in my jurisdiction."

"Those acts were committed by the Bounty Hunter. He operated without any oversight from us. We did not control him," said the American.

"What is his name?"

"Joseph McDugal," said the American.

"As a representative of the insurance company, do you admit that your employer failed to properly supervise Mr. McDugal?"

"We work for Security Compliance, a division within the insurance company, and we were trying to close McDugal's operation because our investigation determined it to be illegal. We were sent here to close the operation and destroy the documents and nothing else. McDugal was fired by the company."

"So, you are saying you are innocent but your company is guilty?" asked the chief.

"We did what we did. If what we did was wrong, our company will pay the fine or penalty."

"You destroyed evidence," the chief said.

"Yes, but we did not know it was evidence," admitted the man.

"Of course it is a crime in México."

"If we committed an illegal act you should fine us and let us go," suggested the man.

"You will not go free unless your employer pays a penalty for these illegal actions."

"We agree to stand in place of the company in your prison until a fine is paid. Our employer will pay the penalty."

The chief stood and told the insurance executives to stand.

"I have considered the penalty to be assessed for your release. $25,000,000 is both reasonable and appropriate. If your employer desires to obtain your release, your employer shall pay that amount. It will be paid to the City of Cancún. Do you disagree that the amount is reasonable?"

"We do not disagree," said the men.

"That is all," said the chief.

The men were cuffed and removed from the hearing room and taken back to prison.

***

In the early afternoon, the Controller of the City of Cancún received a wire transfer from the Federal Depository Bank in Omaha, Nebraska, payable to the "fine and forfeiture fund, City of Cancún, México" in the amount of $25,000,000 US. The controller contacted the chief to verify the payment of the fine had been made. The two Americans were released and all charges dismissed.

Later, the chief's sister-in-law called and said she received an annuity contract payable to her and her children in the amount of $5,000 US Dollars per year for 45 years.

***

The chief noticed when he went to the cathedral to say one of the rosaries he owed to God as his penance that there was a notice posted on the door that the roof of the church would be replaced.

The notice said it was a miracle. There had been an anonymous donation made to the church.

Chapter 61

The three men became more relaxed the farther they drove. They were in Durango Province and then Chihuahua Province, which was very mountainous. Anthony was looking for two things as they passed through small towns. He wanted to find a store that sold camping gear – probably a hardware store would do. And he was looking for a transmission tower that would broadcast an international phone signal. He needed to make a call to the Solicitor General in Belize City.

Finally in a town named Cuauhtémoc, which was near the top of a mountain, he found the transmission tower with the same type communication system with three phone booths that were connected by wire to a metal tower that extended into the clouds that he had used before in Belmopan.

* * *

Anthony self-dialed the number. Belize. Belize City. Office of the Solicitor General, the Chief legal officer of the Country of Belize. He could hear the system mechanically allowing the line to switch from Country code to City code and then connect at the home of the Solicitor General.

"Andrew, it's me, Anthony."

"I can't speak to you," said the Solicitor.

"Is it safe in Belize?"

"For you, no, it is not safe."

"Do I owe you anything?"

"You owe me nothing."

"Then, I will see you in the hereafter," said Anthony.

"Good-bye," said the Solicitor General.

When Anthony returned to the car he told Winston and H. Patel they could not return to Belize. They would not be protected by the Solicitor General if they returned. Anthony pulled the car back onto the road.

"Let's look for that store."

The men drove away; their options were limited with the loss of protection from Andrew Prince, the Solicitor General of Belize. With the death of Judge Lucius they had decided to cut out Judge Raymond Barrow too. The math was easy – they only had to divide the cash by three now.

In the City of Chihuahua they found a store. They purchased blankets and mess kits and a hand ax, a knife and a can opener. They bought a five gallon water jug to refill their canteens. They bought cans of beans and peaches and beef jerky in case they could not find a restaurant. They each bought hiking boots and wool socks, shorts and flannel shirts and a denim coat lined with wool. They bought a first aid kit and mole skin for blisters and each got a poncho that would double as a tent. And they bought matches in waterproof boxes and they purchased three extra-large back packs with a rack that would allow them to attach extra gear to the rack.

Most people only spoke Spanish in Chihuahua. Anthony was able to converse in Spanish if the conversation was slow and steady.

Anthony wanted to know where they could camp and hike legally. The clerk gave him a map of hiking trails in the area and for other trails on toward Sonora Province. The trails were through government lands. The clerk enjoyed camping and hiking and he suggested they go to Ciudad Guerrero. The area also had a river that flowed out of the Sierra Madre Occidental Mountains. The water was cold and clean, said the clerk.

In the car, the men discussed the suggestions of the clerk. Anthony had a road map that showed a feature called the Copper Canyon (Barranca del Cobre) and a small town called Creel that had a river and he suggested that they go camping near that city.

They all agreed.

***

The land around Creel had pine forested mountains that had been harvested many years ago. The forests had not been clear cut and the trees left by the loggers were now very tall. There were two roads into town. Creel was in the valley of two mountains. The roads were gravel and lime rock. The town had a railroad. There was a hotel between a restaurant and a bar. These buildings were on the main road which was covered in gravel. Most of the buildings were constructed of logs or rough cut pine.

The local natives were called Tarahumaras. They were Indians who sported multi-colored dress; sometimes the men marked their legs and arms with white dots. The decorations were in their tradition and also for the benefit of tourists.

There was a general store. The men refilled their water supply and received directions to a trail they could hike up toward the impressive but unnamed mountain that immediately caught the men's attention as they drove into town.

The attendant was accustomed to tourists. Most visitors were young and they hiked into the area and then they were on to the Copper Canyon to sightsee. After loading up with fresh supplies at the store, the clerk explained the best place for the men to start their trip was located behind the store.

He showed them where they could park. They agreed to leave the car in the lot. However, they intended to take their treasure with them. The attendant explained that it was a 30 mile hike up the trail and back. They would probably see other people hiking along the trail which was well marked with red blaze marks painted on trees along the way. The trip would take three days, more or less. The attendant had the men show him their jackets. He said it would be cool at night. The attendant felt their coats would be warm enough for this time of year. In the winter it could be snowy and very cold.

Once the attendant left them, the men re-packed their packs, and stuffed the small back packs containing the cash and the duffel bag in the bottom of the new backpacks they had purchased in Chihuahua. Then they attached the food and other camping articles, the ax, etc., to the rack on the outside of the new packs. They were carrying about 55 pounds each. They left the five gallon jug at the car. The water in the jug weighed 40 pounds (5 gallons x 8 lbs. per gallon) and they did not want to carry the jug. They were assured there was water along the trail that was very good to drink and the location of the water was well marked.

The attendant also told them there were tour guides that would accompany them if they wished.

The men declined the guides. They did purchase fresh fruit and potatoes to add to their larder.

***

The men began the trek from behind the store. As they had been told, the trail was well marked. They rested about every two miles but did not drink any water until they reached the first stream. The water was very clear and cold. They found the source of the stream. At the source, the water burst up from the ground into a pool before rushing down the slope through the rocks. They refilled their canteens after drinking their fill. They ate some fruit – pieces of pears and apricots. They sat and rested and closed their eyes and lay down and they were asleep in the afternoon sun.

***

When they awoke there were other hikers nearby. They heard the voices of the group. They were a family from California. The family explained that they tried to get far away from society when they vacationed and so this year they came to the town of Creel.

They said they had completed the hike and had gotten into the high country where the trees were sparser and the pines were smaller and scraggly with imperfect crowns full of small needles.

The family said there were caves that they saw that would offer shelter if it rained, but for them, the weather had been perfect. The three men had extra fruit and they shared the apricots and pears. The family gave them apples in return. The family told them they were about four miles from where they last saw a nice campsite. The site also had water and a pool large enough for bathing. They had seen no animals. Bears were a worry, particularly now that the animals would be fattening themselves for the winter. But they saw no signs of bear. Anthony was more worried about other hikers. The family had come upon them without notice. They needed to hide the cash and the gold mask at night when they slept, he decided.

The men and the family parted ways and the men headed toward the camp site the family had described. They had been told the site would be an hour away and they would have time to cook a meal and relax by a fire. Once they arrived and settled in, they relaxed as the pine scent mixed with the cool mountain air. Anthony pulled the backpacks into the crook of two branches of a tree high above the trail for the night. They were exhausted. They slept as soon as their heads hit their blankets.

***

In the morning, H. Patel stoked the hot coals and breathed on the coals and ignited a handful of pine needles below the twigs and the layers of successively larger pieces of wood that formed a tee-pee of fuel about a foot and a half high. The fire started quickly. There was a breeze blowing up the side of the mountain that stirred the fuel with a hefty supply of oxygen.

H. Patel made coffee in a percolator type pot that he sat directly on a bed of coals.

"Coffee smells great," said Anthony. "I forgot to buy any."

"I found a package of beans in the duffle bag. I had to crush the beans with the hammer end of the ax. We will have to brew it awhile. It will be a weak brew. Right now I am going to wash up. I also found soap in the duffle and a razor for you and Winston." (H. Patel had no facial hair.)

"I hope there were cups in the duffle because I forgot to buy any."

"We have one cup to share," said H. Patel, as he stripped to his shorts and walked into the cold pool.

***

The men talked.

"What do you plan to do once we split up? I do not think the USA is a safe place for us. We will be caught there as sure as can be," said H. Patel.

"For me and Winston, yes that's true. But you have a chance in the States. You have money now and you can hide in your Asian community in the States or you can move to India," said Anthony.

"I am not an East Indian. I am an American," said H. Patel.

"You will have to adopt another personality or you will be caught. You could live in México, or in Panama or in Honduras. Learn the language fluently and mingle. You will find a woman and make a family and you will become anonymous. You have the physical disguise. You were born with it. You are short and dark. With the right clothes you would fit in, Or not, maybe being an Indian ex-pat would work better for you."

"I have to think about it. What are you going to do?"

"If I had the guts I would sell beer in a palm roofed bar in Tulum."

"What?"

"When the Mexican wrestlers kidnapped me we had to stop in Tulum and wait out the storm on the temple grounds. Its 40 feet above sea level and we were safe from the storm surge. Tulum also has a beach that has pure white sand and when the weather is favorable there are visitors every day. Some enterprising person built a bar with a thatched roof there between the Caribbean Sea and the ruins. When the Mexicans and I left Tulum after the storm the bar had been washed away. I would go there and open a bar … that is what I would do, if I had guts."

H. Patel was fully in the water now. The water felt comfortable. He dog paddled around and thought about running a bar.

"What about Winston? Where will he go?" asked H. Patel.

"He will go back to the Bahamas, is my guess. I really don't know."

At the mention of his name, Winston stumbled out of his blanket in time for his turn with the coffee cup. The color of the coffee was dark green and had a weak taste and aroma.

"Mmmmm, good!" said Winston as he threw the liquid on the ground without taking even a sip. "Let's get on the road."

The men packed up, put out the fire and headed up the trail after a careful inspection of their feet for red areas where a blister might be forming. They used the mole skin to cover the red areas leaving a hole over the red spots to allow the skin to breathe. Their boots were new and still needed to be broken in. They were in shorts and flannel shirts. Each one wished they had bought a hat. They were beginning to burn on their cheeks and noses and ears because they were exposed to the sun in a blue, cloudless sky.

Chapter 62

Early on the second afternoon of the hike, the three men were surprised by young men and teens running up the trail. The youths looked to the men like native Indians, but they were of a tribe they had never seen before. They wore sandals and white diaper-like shorts. They had brightly colored bands around their waists and kerchiefs and bands on their foreheads. Their hair was long and stuck out like a bad case of bedhead. And, most unusual, they had spots or dots of white paint on their arms, legs and faces.

The young men were swift and ran striking the ground with their toes and pushing off so that each pace was like the lunge of an animal – a large cat, perhaps.

The three men got off the trail and out of the way of the runners. These Indians were Tarahumara. They were an ancient indigenous people who had once inhabited all of the land encompassed in the Chihuahua and Senora Provinces. They were known for their running prowess and athletic ability. They had fought the Aztecs, and the Spanish, and were never conquered. However, their world shrank over the years due to economic pressure. They lost their land to the loggers and the miners. Now their villages primarily lined the route of the train tracks that brought tourists to the area. They made handcrafts and clothing that they sold to the visitors who departed the train and entered their villages to see the sights and purchase their crafts.

Traditionally, they had lived in family units that were distant from each other. They did not live in towns. Some families continued to live in natural shelters like caves. They farmed and grew staple crops including maize, beans, green squash, corn and tobacco. They also grew apples, apricots, figs and oranges. They constructed and played violins and drums and three holed flutes. Their lives were greatly affected by music.

The Tarahumara were affected by the cultivation of illegal drugs for trade in the United States. The drug lords stole the natives' land and enslaved the men and women to cultivate the drugs. The people did not use the cocaine or the morphine or the cannabis. Nor did the Indians benefit from the trade in these drugs. Their only vice was to imbibe in an alcoholic brew made of corn, but only on celebratory and religious occasions.

The three men watched as the runners flew by. They had no understanding that these people were victims of the men's trade in drugs.

***

Later on the afternoon of the second day of the hike the men came to the official end of the trail. They could go further, but the trail map informed the men that there would be no blazes painted on the trees ahead that would mark the trail. They did not want to become lost and they did not intend to be on the mountain for more than three or four days. According to the map it looked like it would now take two days to follow the trail back to the town of Creel. The map of the trail showed that there were a series of switchbacks that would lead them back down the mountain. They would actually travel a further distance going down than it took to go up because rather than hiking in a straight line, the trail would zigzag down the side of the mountain.

Anthony found a water source on the map just a short distance away down the first switchback and he asked if his mates wanted to stop there or go on. The consensus was to stop at the small pond shown on the trail map about a half-mile down.

Anthony wanted to make sure they had a secure spot for the cash and the gold mask that night. There had been too many people on the trail for his comfort. He didn't want to be robbed.

As they continued down the trail they could see that what was described on the map as a pond was actually a substantial body of water created when streams emptied into a trough which was about a half mile long and 400 yards wide. After forming the lake, the streams continued to flow down into a tunnel in the rock to a small water fall and then the water sped down the mountain. Anthony guessed that the lake and this stream were the source of the ponds and streams that they had encountered as they hiked up the mountain.

The men climbed down to the lake. The rim of the lake consisted of large boulders that had been placed with such precision that they were water tight. They looked to have been constructed by modern engineers or by Incans or Aztecs or by God.

The men filled their canteens and washed their clothes; hung the clothes to dry on tree branches, and swam in the cold lake water.

It was getting late. Their clothes were still wet. They put on their boots without socks and they climbed the boulders nude holding their clothes that were still dripping.

Anthony passed three large pine trees whose roots had broken through seams in the boulder to establish themselves. The trees obscured the front of a cave. There was a rock that jutted overhead above the entrance to the cave to shelter the cave from the rain. The floor of the forest was covered with pine straw and tree limbs that had blown off the trees in storms racing up the mountain.

The men gathered pine straw for their beds to be located inside the cave and Winston built a large fire at the mouth of the cave. The heat radiated into the cave. The men hung their clothes to dry on sticks placed near the heat of the fire. There was a chill in the air. It was almost cold in the wind.

Anthony broke out rations, fruit and jerky. Each man had wrapped themselves in their blanket. It appeared the cave had been popular with campers as it was full of pine straw that was used as a mattress to soften the rock floor of the cave. The men ate. The men were tired. They wanted to rest. They wore their jackets and underwear to bed. Their shorts and shirts and socks were left hung by the fire and they hoped they would be dry in the morning.

Anthony took all of the back packs to the rear of the cave and covered them with straw and wood. He couldn't see the backpacks from the front of the cave. A thief would have to get by Winston and Anthony who were lying inside the cave to get to the backpacks with the gold mask and the cash.

The men slept, exhausted.

Chapter 63

Andrew Prince, the Solicitor General of Belize, knew this day might come. He knew that if he dabbled in corruption and was caught he would lose his office. If it was corruption he would be out, at least until the next election cycle. He would have to lay low for a couple of years after resigning. If he did not fight the charge the matter would be ambiguous. So it was important to resign and not be impeached, tried by the legislators and removed from office.

The Prime Minister had called, greatly agitated. This call came soon after the Solicitor received the call from Anthony Arnold from Chihuahua. Mr. Prince knew that what he had expected all along was true. His phone was tapped and his conversations were being intercepted. Mr. Prince wondered exactly what he said to Anthony that was incriminating. But he knew from experience that words written on a page can be misinterpreted because the inflection in a person's voice is lost on the transcript. Maybe they would provide a copy of the tape so he could understand. Mr. Prince didn't think anything he said was so bad, merely telling an old client that if he came to Belize he would be arrested; that it was not safe for him and his friends to return to Belize.

In any event, Mr. Prince wrote a letter of resignation to the Prime Minister stating that his wife was ill and he needed to spend more time with her. That was the truth. His wife was ill and he should attend to her more.

And so the Solicitor General resigned. It would save his party the necessity of holding hearings and voting him out of office. Actually, this might be for the best. In each of the election cycles so far after independence the voters had forced the incumbents out of office. So if he was not an incumbent chances were he would be a political star next election. Maybe he would create a new political party. Maybe ... Maybe ... In any event, Andrew Prince resigned his post as Solicitor General of Belize. The Prime Minister promised him there would be no other retribution for him for warning his former client, Anthony Arnold not to return.

Solicitor Prince knew he could not rely on the Prime Minister, although he considered the PM to be his best friend. As a friend the PM would try to fulfill the promise that the government would not retaliate against him if he resigned. He thought that the Prime Minister would at least try to protect him. Andrew Prince and the officers who comprised the leadership of the government all knew each other; had gone to school together; became political partners, and were elected together.

Andrew Prince hoped he would not lose the relationships with the fellow members of his political party. But he knew that it was very possible that he would never hold elective office again. The party would do what was best for the party so that the party could survive. Minister Prince knew that the most effective political model was a food chain in which the weak were eaten by the strong. Rarely were members of the party equally strong because that caused division and weakness of the entire party. There had to be a pecking order or the party would not function.

***

Many years ago when Andrew Prince took his son to the Mayan ruins at Palenque, Chiapas Province, México, they walked the grounds and came upon the earliest known example of a pitch, or ball field where Mayan warriors played a game of life and death. Two teams attempted to score a goal by striking a rubber ball with their hips attempting to send the ball through a ring of stone that extended out from the wall. The goal was like a sideways hoop. The warriors who prevailed had the honor of slaying the warriors who lost.

Andrew and his son wandered onto the field. The boy was young, six years old. The boy pointed to a snake. It was venomous and dangerous. It was known to attack. It did not shrink away, even from man. It spent its day not only looking for food but for its enemies, to fight and kill them.

Andrew Prince, who at the time of the visit to the ruin was at the beginning of his career, was a Member of Parliament in the opposition party. He cautioned his son to come away from the snake and they went into the stone grandstands and sat and watched the snake. It was swift and could coil and change directions with ease.

From the sky a caracara, a bird of prey, a raptor larger than a hawk appeared. The bird had a strange hooked beak and odd head feathers that lay on its head like a cheap toupee. The bird dived into the field of play and grabbed the snake by its tail. The bird and the reptile were enemies. The snake invaded the bird's nest and devoured the caracara's fledglings and the bird's eggs. The bird was always on the lookout for the snake to eliminate the threat from the bird's territory.

And so the two sworn enemies met on the pitch, the battlefield. They were equally dangerous. The bird entered the battle to protect its progeny and the snake out of hate and animosity for any animal who would dare to mount an attack on the snake.

When the snake was lifted into the air it was confused. What had caused this imbalance in the natural order to occur? The snake was the Supreme Being occupying the floor of the earth. The snake coiled, lifting its head so it could see the cause of the pressure on his tail and he saw he was in the grasp of a bird. From the coiling position, the snake straightened out in a flash forming into the shape of a rod and the jerking motion caused the bird to release the grip of its beak and the snake fell out of the air to the grass and then slithered toward the wall that defined the edge of the ball field. Once on the ground the snake had the advantage. The bird could not hop and dart as quickly as the snake could alter its direction and strike. The bird was mature and knew it was at a disadvantage and that it should retreat, but it was urged on by the thought of the hatchlings that it had cared for this season that were still in the nest and vulnerable to this reptile. So the bird hopped forward and it parried with its hooked beak aiming to the neck of the snake with the goal to encircle the neck with the hooked beak and snap off the snake's head.

The bird lunged and the snake coiled around the body of the bird and the animals rolled over the grass on the pitch. The snake had been able to wound the bird by scratching the leather like covering of its leg and shooting venom from its fang into the wound. The bird felt the poison immediately but held a death grip on the upper body of the snake. And the bird continued to squeeze until its beak invaded the protection of the snake's scales and into the skin and the body and the organ cavity and there the bird's beak froze inside the body of the snake. The snake was still alive but the snake was doomed. It would have to wait for someone to kill it or it died desiccated by the sun in the grasp of its enemy. The snake was resigned to its fate and waited for death.

This memory came to the Solicitor General as he signed the letter of resignation and he handed the letter to his best friend, the Prime Minister.

"For the good of the party," said the Solicitor General.

"And for the good of the Solicitor General," the Prime Minister replied.

Chapter 64

The floor of the forest in front of the cave entrance was covered in pine straw. When the heat of the fire from the pine logs that Winston had stacked reached their zenith, the pine straw closest to the fire reached its flash point and the straw caught fire.

And unfortunately, the wind blowing up the mountain pushed the flame over the straw toward the mouth of the cave where H. Patel was sleeping in the cool wind blowing into the cave.

H. Patel's body, which was covered with the blanket, was not immediately affected by the flame which jumped over him and the fire raced into the cave in the wind.

When the fire reached the exposed areas of his skin H. Patel awoke in pain. Parts of his hands and scalp which were not covered by the wool blanket were exposed to the flame that engulfed the cave. He was on fire. He screamed in pain, jumped up and ran out of the mouth of the cave.

In a while he remembered that Winston and Anthony were farther in the cave. Yet he heard nothing from them. They must have gotten out already, he thought.

The cave was now a furnace, boiling pine resin gasses exploded into flame. The fuel was the accumulation of straw lugged into the cave for use as a mattress, and sticks, branches and logs kept dry in the cave for future fires. Now all that fuel was sufficient to cause a conflagration that melted flesh and burnt bone into powder so there was no trace of the two men who were first rendered unconscious from smoke and who were then obliterated by the fire.

***

H. Patel had blisters on his hands. He went down to the lake and put his hands in the cold lake water.

In the moon light, his face reflecting into the lake, he could see he no longer had hair on the top of his head where his hair had not been covered by the blanket. Am I in shock, he asked?

He inspected his entire body. Other than the blisters which were mostly on his fingers and his hair that was singed to the root, he was not injured. But now he felt a horrific pain in his scalp and hands and he dove into the cold lake to numb the pain. In a while the pain abated.

He went back to the cave. Some of the clothes hanging in the bushes around the fire were untouched by the flames. The fire in the cave was mostly out. He could see into the cave from the light of the flames that remained burning. He could not see any trace of Anthony or Winston. And so he dressed and sat on a large rock and waited for the two men to return.

He stared into the cave while he waited. With the last light of the fire in the cave he could see an ash line where the residue of the fuel consumed in the fire had adhered to the wall of the cave.

He remained by the cave except when he went back for water at the lake. During one trip to the lake he found soap by the shore and washed his hand, fingers and head gingerly. With each hour that elapsed he knew the two men were gone. Probably he had been deserted. They had stolen his share of the money. He had been cheated.

Then when the cave had cooled, he took a stick and went into the cave and began to poke in the ash on the rock floor of the cave.

In the spot where he remembered Winston was sleeping he found the steel buttons from his coat. The buttons were singed gray. He found the same buttons where Anthony had last been seen. In addition, he found the ignition and trunk keys for the

Ford sedan. In the back of the cave there was nothing – no backpacks, no cash. He continued to look and as the last of the sun shone into the cave he saw a glint of light from something. He traced around the object with the stick. It was a piece of metal that had melted and then solidified in a hole in the floor of the cave. It was a glob of gold. He dug it out and hefted the weight in his hands. "Probably five pounds, is my guess." But you could not tell what it had been … once an antiquity, now it was a warm black blob.

He went outside and re-started the fire and dressed for warmth. It was cold.

By the light of the fire, he inventoried his wealth. He had three pair of socks and three pairs of shoes. He had one pair of shorts, and two shirts. There was also a knife and an ax that he found by the fire. He looked in the pockets of the clothes and found about $80 US and Mexican Peso notes and coins. He bundled everything into a shirt.

He would have to leave in the morning and get on his way by himself. The attendant at the store would be looking for the three men to come back for the car. H. Patel was not going back to the car in the morning. He would abandon the car and ride the train, the Chihuahua al Pacifico, from Creel to the north and then figure out what he would do from there.

H. Patel threw the keys for the Ford sedan into the cave.

***

After five days had elapsed since the three men parked their car behind the store and began their hike up the mountain, the attendant from the store sent a Tarahumara Indian up the trail to find the men. The Indian reported that he found the cave and the spirits of two men who were recently burned to death. The Indian said the two men both died in great pain. The ghosts of the men told the Indian they were unable to scream because the pain was so intense. The Indian also said he found the tracks of a third man that traversed from the cave, down the mountains to the railroad tracks and then headed for the tourist train. He also gave the attendant a set of keys for the Ford sedan.

The attendant did not consider the story about the two spirits to be credible. No one had seen anyone come off the mountain matching the descriptions of the three men. So to the mind of the locals all three of the men had gone hiking and disappeared into the woods. The attendant had offered them a guide but they were foolish foreigners and they were lost. That data was what made up the content of the official report. Eventually that report made its way to Cancún and to the Chief of Police.

The chief sent his Lieutenant of Detectives to the town of Creel with photographs of Anthony, Winston and H. Patel. The attendant positively identified the three men in the photographs to be the men in the Ford sedan who were lost on the mountain. The attendant told the Lieutenant of Detectives about the abandoned car. The Lieutenant then traced the Ford sedan back to a car lot where the car was sold to Anthony in Chichachia, México. The car dealer identified Anthony but did not remember the other men. The car salesman gave the Lieutenant of Detectives the name of the driver who brought the men to the car lot. The driver, who gave the men a lift to the car lot, also identified the photographs of Anthony, Winston and H. Patel.

Backtracking, the detective returned to Chihuahua, where he learned of the mystery C-47 cargo plane that was found in the desert and the discovery of a body wrapped in a tarp at the edge of the desert in the salt flats. The medical examiner identified the body as being that of Judge Lucius.

The lieutenant also notified Rick's insurance company of the existence of the C-47 airplane.

The lieutenant brought all of this information to the Chief of Police.

The chief closed his file on the four fugitives. The file was marked: "Deceased."

Chapter 65

Rick Ibn and Anna Hernando wanted a spring wedding, but they could not delay the ceremony. Rick had settled with the insurance company. The insurance company had convinced the Mexican Government in Chihuahua that they had a claim to the C-47 air plane that was purchased by Winston Grey. The insurance company paid the government authorities $5,000 US for the government's costs for storing the C-47 and then settled with Rick for $30,000 US and also transferred the title to the C-47 to Rick. Rick intended to use the plane in a commercial cargo business. His first customer would be the air conditioning installation enterprise that his future wife was managing in Belize City in a suite of rooms above the medical clinic. She continued to practice medicine but closed the funeral home. Rick continued to work for TACA and also TAN when they needed the help of an expert mechanic for emergencies, such as when a plane flew through a flock of birds on takeoff.

The pair was very industrious and Anna Hernando was very pregnant.

Tom was invited to the wedding and he brought Darlene. They were dating seriously, but neither one was ready to give up the single life. They did form a union. They combined their law practices. Tom still worked as a consultant for businesses from the States that wanted to take his chances in Central America. It was the Wild West. You never knew if you would make a million or lose your shirt. It was a good territory for a lawyer/consultant who knew the locals and knew when it was no longer worth it to stay in the game. Darlene moved her practice out of the townhouse condominium to Tom and Roger's office. She wanted to concentrate on impossibly difficult criminal cases that involved allegedly innocent people who had been found guilty by a jury of their peers. There seemed to be no end to those cases. They had also invited Andrew Prince Jr., the son of the former Solicitor General, to form an association that would allow the firm a law office in Central America in Belize City.

The wedding was nice, so far as weddings go. They spent a lot of money at the Fort George Hotel. Really, it would have been better at the beach.

And so, after the wedding, Tom asked Darlene if she would go with him to Cancún for a vacation from the vacation. She agreed. They flew from Belize City to Cancún. Tom rented a suite with separate bedrooms at the top of the fanciest hotel on the beach. They went out to Isla Mujeres and went deep sea fishing but they caught few fish. They also planned to take a trip to the Mayan ruins at Palenque, Chiapas, México. Rick offered to fly them into the nearest airport at Tenoseque de Pino Suary, but when Tom and Darlene took a look at Rick's C-47 they opted out. Darlene said she really just wanted to look at the ocean and lay on the beach and so they went to the beach at Cancún.

On the next to last day of the vacation Darlene suggested they go to Tulum to swim and see the ruins. Tom asked the doorman if the ruins had been affected by the hurricane which had blown through some five months past. The doorman said the ruins were in good shape.

"What about the fishing village at Punta Rosa?"

"You can only get there by boat or sea plane. The village was wiped off the map except for the Ships Store, but the store's entire inventory has been stolen. Did you know Felix and his family? Such a tragedy," said the doorman.

"No, I did not meet Felix or his family," said Tom.

"If you need a car to go to Tulum, I could rent you one," said the doorman.

"That would be good."

Tom went back to the room and reported to Darlene what the doorman said about Tulum. She said she would like to see the ruins at Tulum.

"Then we will go. Take extra clothes. The ruins are said to be in good shape – not affected by the hurricane, but there is nothing else there, not even a restroom. Oh, I rented a car."

"A nice car I hope." When they were on the Isla, Tom rented a car that had no front windshield. It was a convertible so Tom said it didn't matter that it had no front windshield, it also had no top.

"Of course it's a nice car," said Tom, who had no idea what he was renting.

***

The trip to Tulum was bumpy. Darlene talked away as Tom avoided pot holes. Each one he hit caused a clang in the right front wheel well. The suspension system was done. You didn't know it on a nice flat road but it was obvious once you hit a bump and heard the clang.

The weather was delightful. Clear blue sky, warm but not hot, it was breezy, perfect.

They were the only ones at Tulum, except for workmen who were building a tiki hut bar with a palm roof.

Tom was talkative and so while Darlene swam in the warm surf he button holed the foreman of the construction crew. What Tom could get out of him was that the eye of the storm had blown through and washed away the bar. What was left of the bar was over to the west somewhere in bits and pieces. After the storm someone stole all the bottles of booze that had not been broken. The owner went bankrupt and the new owner had moved the location of the bar farther up from the beach and closer to the ruin where the elevation was higher. Apparently the ruins had very few visitors since the tiki hut bar was destroyed. The government was anxious for the bar to be rebuilt so there was someone responsible who was watching out for the ruin and providing a restroom for visitors.

Their conversation was in English.

"Are you an American?" asked Tom.

"No, I'm East Indian."

"Your English is very good," said Tom as he tried to get more information from the foreman. The foreman, though, tried to ignore Tom. He kept looking at his men, avoiding eye contact with Tom. Tom was surprised that the man was bald. He seemed too young.

Tom saw Darlene waving to him and he walked back toward their blanket on the sand. Darlene was in a powder blue swim suit. She was really beautiful, thought Tom.

"Will you marry me?" asked Tom.

"If I decide to marry you, I will ask," said Darlene.

Tom was left totally flummoxed by the response. "Well, you didn't say, 'no'."

"That's true," said Darlene.

They stayed on the beach the whole day. Swimming and resting, talking about nothing in particular.

Tom thanked Darlene for helping him save his business and his license.

"You were my best client," said Darlene.

End of Book ll of La Florida

Maps and Illustrations

YUCATÁN PENINSULA

Map 1
Central America

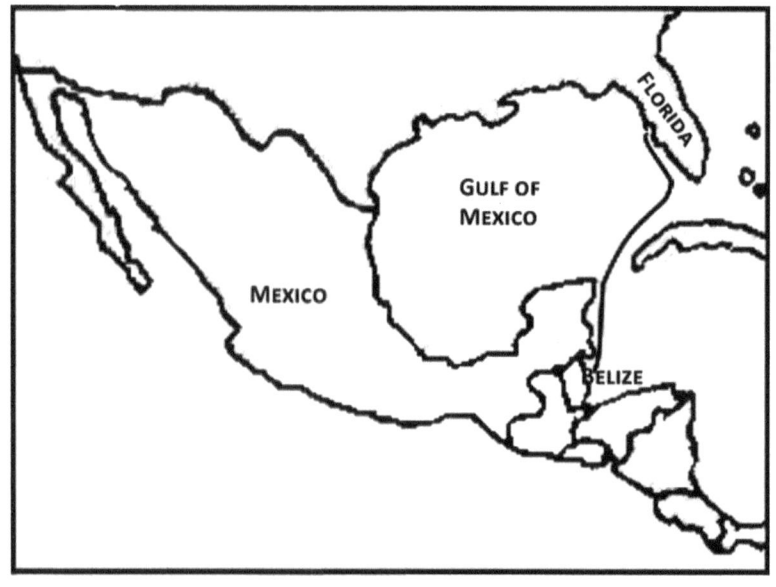

Map 2
Route from Tampa to Punta Rosa

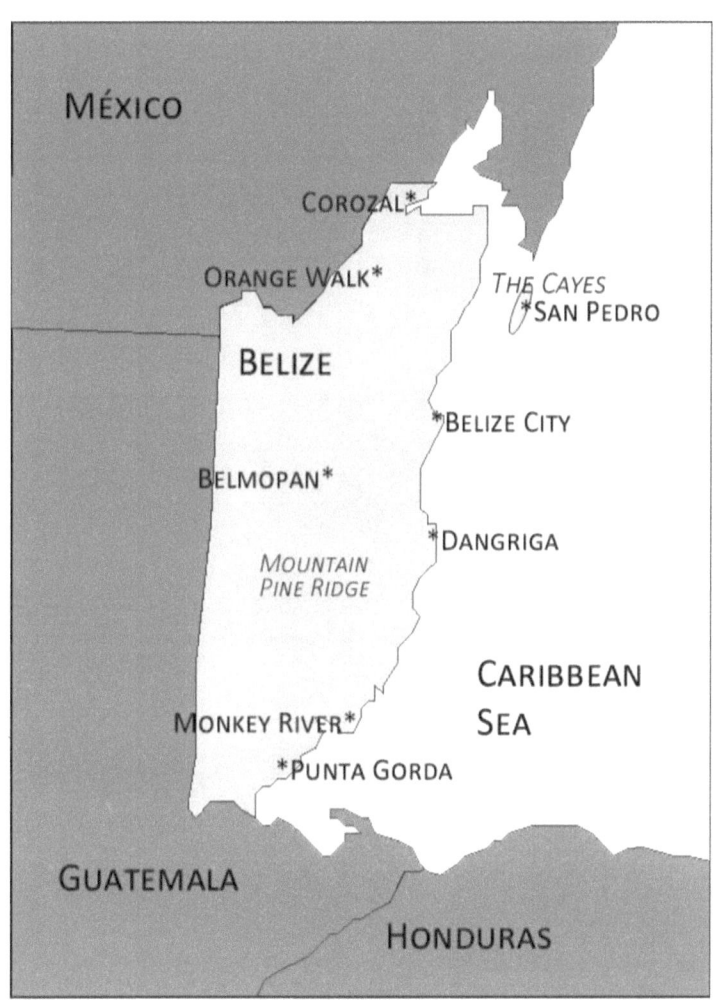

Map 3
Belize

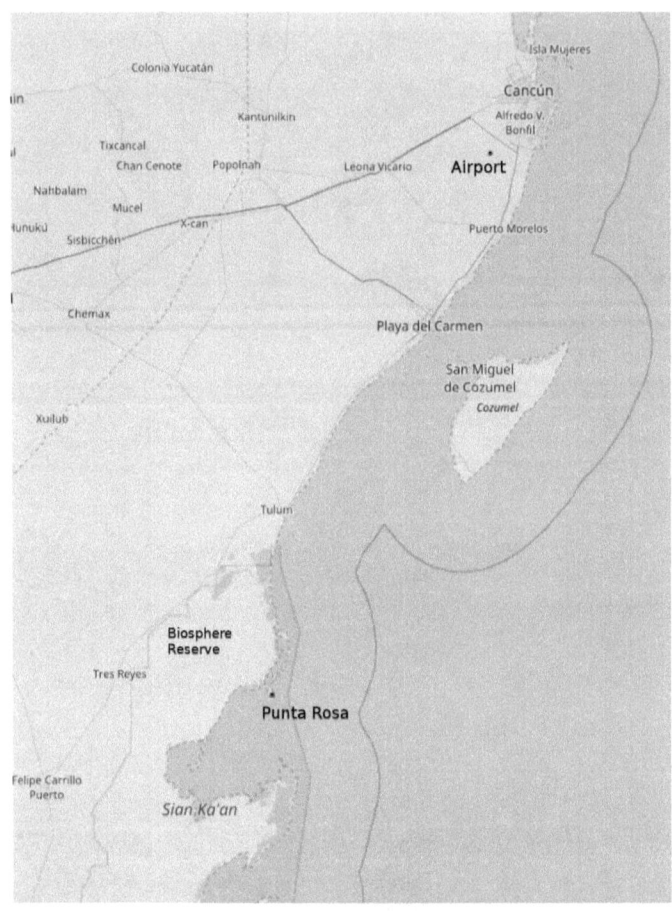

Map 4
Yucatan Peninsula

Appendix

BELIZE

Belize should have been called "Florida" because Belize is always in bloom. It has two seasons – wet and dry. In the dry season, the weather is more humane because it is less humid, but it is still hot.

The small country is nestled below Mexico on the Yucatán Peninsula. It is east and north of Guatemala. Belize is about the size of Vermont; in 1970 it had about 300,000 people and about 70,000 people lived in Belize City.

Belize borrowed its bureaucracy and parliamentary system with its prime minister and appointed cabinet from the British. In 1964 Belize claimed it won its independence, but in my opinion the British had wrung the country dry and the British abandoned Belize as a colony. Belize remained a Protectorate of Britain. Through the agreements that flowed from the Protectorate, the British had what they wanted – a military foothold in Central America that allowed the English to arrive in an hour by Harrier jet to its other interests in the Caribbean. The British Air Force has a base at the International Airport in Belize City.

I feel the multinationals abandoned Belize when it gained independence. For a hundred years, chicle, a product produced from the resin of the Zapota (aka, sapodilla) tree, was processed into chewing gum, but chicle had been replaced by a synthetic. The markets for virgin pure stumps and naval stores were still viable but weak. The last large tropical timbers in the jungles, that were privately owned, had been cut by the Mennonites, who established a colony in the highlands in the west near Guatemala in the land known as the "Spanish Lookout". Some timber taken from government lands was last processed at the steam sawmill on the Belize River near the airport in the 1960's. The saw mill is now abandoned. The workers left the large factory building throwing their wrenches and tools to the ground. When I visited the steam sawmill the tools still lay where they were thrown. There was a caretaker at the sawmill who now herded goats on the property and so its ten acres was strewn with black goat pellets. The only multinational who maintained its operations was a confectioner, which had a forest of cacao trees. This operation was serviced by a village that the company supported.

When the multinationals left Belize, they sold their rights and licenses to harvest natural resources that were granted by the government. The multi-nationals sold the licenses for mere pennies on the dollar, so long as the assignment of the license contained a clause that relieved the multinational of any responsibility it had to Belize for the right to strip the country of its resources.

When Belize gained its independence, the country had high unemployment, but unemployment statistics were skewed to the downside because a Belizean who worked at all, even cutting a yard on a regular basis for a few Belizean dollars, was counted as among the ranks of the employed.

Although there was high unemployment, the people of Belize City all acted like they were employed. At 8:00 a.m. Central Time, it seemed the entire population got out on the streets and mingled with the few cars and trucks on the road. The unemployed marched into the city's core with the people who were employed, and then the unemployed loitered on the streets. Some hawked a few meager items to tourists – post cards, a carved mahogany dolphin. The citizens looked for the opportunity to earn a few pennies. Though they had no jobs, everyone seemed to have a place to sleep and there was fruit in the trees, so they lived. Everyone had support from family.

When a commercial plane arrived, a mass of entrepreneurs with their wares – carvings and food stuffs – mostly tamales – swamped the few visitors as they were assaulted by the heat and humidity after leaving the air conditioned Customs house. Most of the arrivals were business people, but there were a few tourists who arrived to tour the Mayan ruins or to visit the Cayes, (the name for the barrier islands off the coast). Canadians had recently discovered an extensive system of Mayan ruins and a few tourists from Canada had heard about the discoveries and they visited. Divers and fisherman flew in and then went to the Cayes. A few knew about and visited Blancaneaux Lodge in the Mountain Pine Ridge. Otherwise, in the 70's tourist venues had not yet been established.

To be a tourist destination, the venue would necessarily have to be safe and therefore the government would have to separate the tourists from the locals and provide a secure walled environment. Most tourists do not desire to see beggars plying their disease or deformity for profit. The beggars' solicitation was not mailed in a clean envelope from a non-profit agency. Pleas for money came with the rap of the stump of an elbow to your back while you were stopped to observe an Indian without legs seated on a mat who had grasped your ankle. The beggars, though, were being run out by the drug addicts who were more troublesome because they had a good pair of legs and you were unable to gain any distance from them by walking away. You had to listen to their pleas as they followed behind. "Man, I am hungry. I am sick. I need a meal. I will work for you. I will come with you. I will stay at your doorstep." They said, "I will be your slave for a dollar."

A tourist venue would necessarily avoid the city dump in Belize City that was established behind the grave yard. The pickers and the diggers and the dead all vied for space and peace. A tourist wouldn't shop at a hut on the road that has little inventory and a strange mix of merchandise – hair picks, a lipstick, moon pies, syrupy pink colored drinks, Coke, rum and the local beer. The shops were an excuse for the beer named "Belikin", which was quite good.

In Belize City, tourists wouldn't walk on the roads because the road was the sewer and the fish market near the swing bridge smelled putrid.

In fact, to establish a tourist venue in Belize, you would necessarily have to avoid Belize City. You would need to bus the tourists from the airport to a location outside the city to a walled enclave with private police. You would have to satisfy government officials with gifts and offer minimal work to the locals and closely monitor them. The optimum would be to build a private pier out into the sea as a dock for an ocean liner or use vessels to transport tourists from ship to shore. The tourists would then pass through a duty free bazaar with crafts and tobacco and rum that led to a transfer facility. The tourists would then be bussed to a tourist activity. You had to lure tourists from the liner with a safe experience; tourists would not pay for the experience of the native Belize. In the 70s, few people in the civilized world knew Belize existed. Some may have heard of it when it was called British Honduras. But they would as soon believe it was in Africa as that it was in Central America, and they had no reason to visit.

I avoided all the un-pleasantries of Belize City by renting a car or hiring a cab and driver. Each time I came to Belize City the harassment on the streets by the addicts was worse so that now when I am in the city I take private transportation even if I only have to go a block. This was true except in the early morning. To get a grip on myself and free my mind I get up at dawn and run from the hotel out to the light house along the sea to the river, then past the Belize City sawmill to the airport and then reverse this route. The trip is 5 miles and takes 50 minutes. I am back in time for a shower and breakfast at 7:00 a.m. When I ran, no one was on the street. The addicts were huddled back under the stilts of the buildings as I jogged by. Later at, 8:00 a.m., the citizenry was on the streets and I was in a car.

Most of the core area of Belize City is at or below sea level. It seemed that any ground that was not paved was home to hordes of large fiddler crabs. They were black with one large bright orange pincher claw. The city straddled the Belize River which ran into the sea. There was a harbor at the mouth of the river, but it was very shallow and filled with sediment. Larger boats and ships had to launch their cargo or passengers from out at sea and deliver them to the harbor. Had the country maintained and repaired the dredge it owned, the harbor would be deep and accessible. But the dredge was a wreck.

Housing in the city was generally built on stilts.

Most living areas were 8 to 12 feet off the ground, stacked on concrete pilings. The living quarters were built of a poor quality wood which the locals called Baltique (or Batik) that looked like mahogany when it was first cut but had no resin and faded quickly and rotted away unless the surface of the wood was covered with varnish or paint.

Few citizens painted their houses so they began to rot immediately from the sun and rain.

The coast of Belize was susceptible to violent low

pressure storms. Most of those storms, though they were as strong as hurricanes, were unnamed. Hurricane Hattie was the exception. The storm was named and notable for causing great death and destruction. Most of the population lived in Belize City at the time and 2,000 souls and most of the housing in the city was lost in this storm. Afterward, a decision was made to leave the coast and move the city inland to Belmopan.

A new capital was constructed in Belmopan on the plateau west of the center of the country. Belmopan did not grow after the capital was reestablished. The ministry buildings and offices for the bureaucrats were constructed and the office of the Prime Minister and the Parliament were completed and there were well designed, modern two bedroom, one bath houses that were occupied by the bureaucrats and the business people who serviced the government. But the people from Belize City did not follow. The people remained in Belize City. As a result, the government maintained its old offices in Belize City – maintaining two sets of government buildings was difficult. The buildings in both centers fell into disrepair. I believe much of the construction of the government facilities was funded with loans from the World Bank. The loans were expensive and the terms dictated by the World Bank forced concessions from the government to conduct its affairs in accordance with its dictates – essentially – the country was to renounce Communism.

Belize had little money to repay the loans from the World Bank. It had natural resources that were of value but there was little competition for the resources. It had no heavy industry; it had no significant agricultural products for export – and therefore it had no collateral and it could not borrow from international banks. The country could not afford an infrastructure. Belize seemed to become like its beggars. The Japanese engineered and rebuilt a bridge that had collapsed. The Canadians brought portable water to households in sections of the city. Otherwise, if not donated by the world, the people did without and poached what little the British had left behind.

In my opinion the country was the perfect partner for drug trafficking. It was close to production centers in Columbia, Ecuador and Peru. The country was situated on the flight paths of small overloaded drug planes. The planes would load fuel and make repairs to the transport planes before flying on to the USA. Belize was not the primary player in the industry but it was a participant and the industry was like honey, ensnaring Belizians in its sticky goo.

The drug industry was a corrupter of countries large and small. The U.S. dollar was openly used as the primary medium of exchange in South and Central America and even though there were laws against it, local currency was openly traded for dollars. And as a result, the local currency collapsed in value against the dollar on the street and the local currency was not used in any transaction that involved more than the cost of the purchase of a beer.

In my opinion it was probable, more likely than not, that any businesses transaction funded in dollars was at least tainted by drug money and that any income received by a citizen of Belize was directly earned from or was subsidized by the drug industry. In this way, economically, drugs corrupt all human activity in Belize.

Belize was close to demand centers in the U.S. and Canada and Europe, and could transfer the product to those markets easily. So Belize, by its location and the weakness of its government, became a prime distribution link for the narcotics industry.

And even though the country was awash in U.S. dollars, the infrastructure of the country was non-existent and decrepit, because the government could not directly tax the drug industry without recognizing it and legalizing it. If the government legalized the industry, the government would become a pariah. It would lose its loans from the World Bank and its contacts with legitimate banks. The government did obtain tax revenue from the drug industry by taxing the goods imported with drug money. But imports were smuggled into Belize because the citizens involved in the import of legitimate trade goods did not want to reveal their new found wealth, as the wealth would cause suspicion that the person was involved in illegal activities. So, the citizens did not share their wealth with the country, but instead established private bank accounts in Miami, Panama, the Caymans or the Netherlands Antilles.

The drug industry is a waste. It fails to produce a life sustaining product. It ultimately provides pain and death. Sad to say, I indirectly represented those involved in the drug industry, if only in relation to their legitimate operations. In other words, we are like the criminal lawyer who would represent a bank robber, but would refuse to take his fee in cash wrapped in a bank wrapper because the cash was too recently stolen. The fee had to age a bit. It had to be laundered through another legitimate business before I would touch it.

/s/ Tom Night

Preview of The Oar House

PART I

Justice and Truth are usually only found in a Court of Law by accident.

Chapter 1

Tom Night received the urgent call at 3 a.m. None of Tom's clients had an emergency while he was having a second cup of coffee while sitting at his desk at the office. It was always at a god awful time when he was deep in sleep.

Tom was 47 years old, married, no children and heterosexual. In the 1970's everyone was heterosexual or pretended to be same. Tom was early to bed and early to rise. He was hard working and a successful lawyer and business man. He was tall (6'), a bit over weight, but fit and athletic, and enjoyed a simple life and life's routine.

The emergency call at 3:00am was from Francis, the wife of his law clerk. His clerk, Alphonse Alesse, had been arrested earlier in the night. Tom was stunned by the call regarding his clerk. The police had held him incommunicado for five hours and he finally was allowed to call his wife who called Tom. Alphonse was a nice kid. He was in his last year of law school at Stetson University. Tom was an alumnus of Stetson some 25 years ago and Tom hoped Alphonse would come on with his firm after he graduated.

Although it was early September, the weather was temperate and about 65 degrees at 4:00 a.m.

Tom's wife and law partner, Darlene Street, rolled over in bed, looked at the time and went back to sleep.

Tom pulled on his trousers and threw on a knit shirt and light jacket (London Fog), stepped into his penny loafers (no socks) and kissed his wife and headed out the door to the police station. The building was about ten minutes away. He parked his 250 SL Mercedes Benz convertible and walked down the ramp to the intake office of the holding facility. There were a number of small holding cells across the back wall of the jail. Each cell had a combination toilet and water fountain. Who thinks these things up? thought Tom. A combination toilet/water fountain? Bizarre.

The jailer greeted Tom. He was well liked. To the police most attorneys were stuck up bastards.

"Can I speak to Mr. Alesse in a private room?" asked Tom.

"No problem," said the jailer.

"I need you to turn off the recorder," Tom emphasized. "I want privacy so I can speak confidentially with my client."

"No problem. The detectives are through with him."

"Has he been charged?"

"The detectives want to speak to John Hale the State Attorney first."

"What was the arrest for?" asked Tom.

"Aggravated Battery, I think."

"Is there a bond set?"

"$10,000," said the jailer as he led Alphonse out of the cell. He was in cuffs and the cuffs were attached by a chain to leg irons. He was shackled at his ankles. The shackles pulled him down so he appeared shorter than his six feet in height. Besides the cuffs and shackles the City of St. Petersburg had provided Alphonse with an orange jump suit and flip flops and taken his civilian clothes.

"What's this with all the iron and the orange suit?" asked Tom.

"I'm the only one here this morning," said the jailer. "I'm not having a prisoner rabbit on me."

"Ok. I don't want to argue. Let me just talk to him," said Tom to the jailer. "And would you call Billy so we can get started on posting the bond?"

"You ought to wait to talk to your law clerk before you spend money bailing him out. He may be guilty."   The jailer guided Alphonse into the small interrogation room. Tom reached in his pocket and pulled out a small portable radio. He flipped it on to a hillbilly station and turned it up. The room filled up with a lot of twang.

"I told you I would turn off the tape recorder," said the jailer.

"Yes, that's what you said." Tom nodded. He didn't believe the jailer. "The music adds to the flavor of the jail." The music would also drown out Tom's conversation with Alphonse. The recording system the police used in the interrogation room would pick up the music and not record the conversation between the men.

Alphonse saw Tom and he dropped his head. Embarrassed, he told Tom he was sorry to bring him out so early. He said he had tried to get the police to let him call his wife as soon as he was brought into jail but the detectives kept trying to talk to him and ask him questions. He said he kept repeating that he wanted to talk to his lawyer. Alphonse said he did not make a statement to the police.

"What do the police think you did?" asked Tom.

"They said I assaulted an exotic dancer."

"Where did the assault allegedly occur?"

"The best I could get from them was that this dancer was assaulted in her apartment by two men. One man was tall and the other was short. I guess I am supposed to be the tall man," said Alphonse.

"What was the nature of the assault?"

"The woman was cut on her face and body, is what they said."

"Why were you arrested?"

"They said the woman identified me going in a store last night."

"Were you with anyone in the store? You know, a short man."

"No, but the police said they had arrested another man who was supposed to be my co-defendant. That arrest was some time back, a week or two ago."

"When did they say the assault occurred?"

"The detective said it was early morning 17 days ago. I figured it out," said Alphonse. "That would have been August 7th, if I have the date right. I was home alone that night. My wife had gone to visit her mother in Jacksonville."

"Where did the detectives say you were identified?"

"The police said I was going in a Quick Mart to buy a pack of cigarettes and the woman was in the store and saw me and called the police."

"Did you see the woman in the store?" asked Tom.

"There was a woman in the Quick Mart with bandages on her face. She caught my attention because it is unusual to see a person, particularly a woman with bandages. I did look at her and she seemed to notice me."

"Did you recognize her?"

"No."

"Where did the detective say she worked?"

"At a bar called The Oar House."

"Have you ever been to The Oar House?"

"No," said Alphonse.

Tom began to read the Complaint, (A Complaint is paperwork given to the prisoner explaining why he was jailed.) "The Complaint says the victim's name is Lori Schaefer. Do you know anyone with that name?"

"No," said Alphonse.

"That's enough for now," said Tom. "I am going to have to speak to Billy the bondsman and see if he can bond you out. Unless you have a spare $10,000 that you can put up in cash you will need to pay a bondsman 10% and the insurance company Billy works for will post the bond."

"We have a little in savings and my wife's mother has a house that she would put up as collateral," said Alphonse. "My wife and I talked about it already, we all agreed."

"Well, talk to Billy and see if you can get out of jail and we will talk in depth once you are out of jail and back in the office. In the meantime, don't talk to anyone about the case or your arrest. In particular, don't talk to any of the prisoners. Do you understand?"

"Yes," said Alphonse.

"Can I call anyone for you?"

"No," said Alphonse and then he added, "Don't you want to know if I did it?"

"Well, did you do it?" asked Tom.

"No," said Alphonse.

Criminal clients always want to tell their lawyer they are innocent, thought Tom.

Chapter 2

Alphonse was at his desk at the office by 7:00 a.m. the morning of his arrest. He was working on legal research that had been assigned to him by Roger Adams, a partner and civil trial lawyer with the firm. Alphonse did not know what was going to happen to him since he had been arrested. Was he going to be fired?

It was touchy when a lawyer is arrested. The attorney is still accorded the presumption of innocence. But still, the firm had to be realistic. The law firm's clients would not appreciate it if they were left alone in a room with a lawyer who was out on bail for a heinous crime. Alphonse knew the chance he would have a job at day's end was slim.

Tom, Roger and Darlene had a meeting of the partners of the firm over coffee and donuts to determine the fate of their law clerk. The fact that a lawyer might be charged with a crime was not unusual, Tom had not only been charged but convicted of a felony charge two years earlier. His situation was different from Alphonse's in that Tom was charged with a criminal contempt involving a procedural rule. However, he had been convicted and sentenced to six months in jail.

Lucky for Tom, his wife, Darlene, had successfully represented him. Not only was he exonerated, but his accuser, a local judge who brought the contempt charge had been determined to have set Tom up. The last they heard of the judge was that he was in prison and was later placed in a witness protection program after testifying against numerous criminals in a drug cartel.

A lawyer friend had heard the Judge testify in Miami in a drug conspiracy trial. The Judge testified in court as a State witness. To protect the judge's identity, he was seated behind a screen and his voice was disguised, but the lawyer was convinced that the person testifying was Raymond Barrow, the former circuit judge of Bushton, Summer County, Florida. Bushton was an agricultural town a two hour drive north of St. Petersburg, Florida.

Judge Barrow testified that he had provided favors for drug defendants. He would reduce bonds; rule favorably on motions that freed defendant's such as motions to dismiss on stipulated fact (They are called: C4 motions.) and motions to suppress confessions and evidence. These rulings by Judge Barrow allowed the defendants to go free. In return the judge was paid handsomely. Tom was unaware Judge Barrow was a crook.

Tom's attitude toward the presumption of innocence had changed after he was incarcerated. Before his arrest he didn't see its importance-- how vital the presumption was to protect a person who was not yet convicted of a crime. Darlene had felt empathy for Tom when he was arrested. However, his partner, Roger was only able to last a day before he was ready to throw Tom to the wolves. He wanted Tom to resign as a partner in the firm and retire his license to practice law. Even Tom's faith in himself was shaken. He began to question whether he should resign for the good of his clients. Even Darlene was affected emotionally by the criminal conviction. They realized that without the presumption of innocence the accused had little chance of successfully fighting a criminal charge.

Alphonse was asked to join the meeting of the partners. He was offered a donut and coffee. He declined. His stomach was in a knot and he felt ready to retch. Alphonse had worried himself into a small bald spot that was on the top of his head. For sure he would go totally bald from worry now with his arrest.

Tom asked Alphonse if he wanted to stay on as a clerk. Alphonse admitted that it would probably hurt the firm and might have a detrimental effect on their clients if he was employed while the charge of assault was pending. The partners agreed that he could face recriminations from their other clients, all that is, except Darlene's clients who were most likely in jail and awaiting a decision on their appeals.

The agreement they reached was that Alphonse was to continue his assignment as a clerk. The firm would write a letter to all of its present clients advising them of the arrest and that if there was any question they should call Tom and he would talk to them and try to assure them that the firm stood by Alphonse and would give him the benefit of the doubt and let the case play out in the court system. The staff at the firm had already been advised of the arrest by Darlene and none of the other clerks and secretaries were openly concerned about the arrest. To a person, no one who knew Alphonse believed he was guilty of the charge, Aggravated Assault, but they were not aware of exactly what the facts of the charge were. They might change their minds if they knew the facts.

***

Anyone arrested for a felony charge in Florida had a right to a preliminary hearing. The purpose of the preliminary hearing was to determine if there was sufficient evidence for the arrest. In Florida in the late 1960's and early 1970's, Justices of the Peace (JPs) handled Preliminary Hearings and decided if there was sufficient evidence to hold an accused for trial. At trial, guilt would be determined by a jury. The jury had to find guilt beyond a reasonable doubt. The prosecutor could avoid a preliminary hearing by filling a charge by Information. However, even though the prosecutor could file an Information to avoid the preliminary hearing, the DA had reasons to hold the hearing. The prosecutor could test the strength of the charge by letting the Justice of the Peace hear the evidence, normally the testimony of the victim of the crime, and the JP would make a decision whether the witness' testimony was strong enough to prove all of the elements of the charge. If there was enough evidence to convince the JP that there was a prima facia case, the accused would be bound over for trial.

If the evidence was inconclusive or unbelievable, the JP could release the defendant. The JP could also find there was only sufficient evidence for a lesser offense (For example: The JP finds a theft was proven but the value of the property was less than $100.00, so the defendant was bound over on the offense of petty theft and not grand theft).

The defendant could waive his right to a preliminary hearing, but that made little sense because the defense attorney got a look at the prosecutor's witness and listened to the witness and was able to cross examine the witness. The defendant never put on testimony, or at least Tom in his 25 years of practice had never heard of any defense attorney putting on a defense at a Preliminary Hearing.

Preliminary Hearings were held on Friday mornings. Alphonse's case was last on the docket two days after his arrest (Swift justice.) Alphonse's head was swimming.

***

There were two prosecuting attorneys representing the State of Florida this particular Friday. John Hale, the State Attorney was present which was unusual. Hale's chief assistant was also present. Tom Night and John Hale had known each other for many years. John had personally prosecuted Tom for Contempt of Court. There was no love lost between the two of them.

Preliminary Hearings were held on the main floor of the courthouse in Courtroom A. The court room was crowded with every person who had been arrested in the circuit in the last week. The court was a cattle call. Some defense attorneys had taken a retainer and only agreed to represent a client through the preliminary hearing and they and their client were still negotiating the fee if the JP bound the defendant over for trial.

Other attorneys were trying to use the opportunity of being before the court and the State Attorney to cut a deal. If they could work out the plea to a misdemeanor offence or to probation, the defendant would be sentenced on the spot and the case would be over. (Sweet.)

There were the usual glitches. Most often the problem was the absence of a witness. Each case had a lead detective and it was his job to produce the witnesses. If the witness did not show up for court, the case had to be continued or the assistant prosecutor would cut a deal and dump the case for a plea to a misdemeanor. It really upset John Hale if he was forced by the lack of a witness to reduce or dismiss a change. He felt the defendant was getting away without paying adequately for the crime particularly if the reason for the plea deal was that the lead detective was too lazy to keep tabs on the witness.

John Hale was really upset today. He was not going to be able to produce Lori Schaeffer, the victim of the assault in the case against Alphonse Alesse because the lead detective, Richard Cook, could not find her.

The Clerk called Alphonse's case.

John Hale stood up and was red faced.

Tom knew John. A red face meant John had witness problems.

The men approached the bench for a conference. John did not want the court reporter to record the sidebar.

"No," said the Justice of the Peace as he motioned the court reporter to come forward to record the conference. "I want a record. Mr. Hale, I assume you have a witness problem. Is that true?"

"Yes," said Hale. "We need some time."

"I am not inclined to grant extra time. I continued the case against this defendant's alleged partner in crime last Friday. You couldn't produce the victim last week and now this is the second time she is a no show," said the Judge.

"We want a continuance," said Hale. "And we want to increase the amount of the bond."

"You want to increase the bond and you cannot produce the victim?" The Judge was incredulous. "I am not going to do that."

"You need to look at this photograph, Judge," said Hale who was pushing an 8 by 10 inch glossy print under the judge's nose.

Tom objected. "What is the point of the photo? It has to be authenticated by the victim. The victim isn't here. The photo is therefore inadmissible. Mr. Hale is trying to prejudice the Court against my client."

"I know what he's trying to do, Tom."

"The detective can authenticate the photo," said Hale as he handed the photo to the Judge.

Criminal attorneys are accustomed to seeing gruesome images. But this photo of the upper torso and face of a young woman caused the Judge to grimace. Tom tried to act professionally when the Judge handed the photo to him to view but Tom also averted his eyes. There were wounds carved into the woman's body, some appearing to be letters or initials, "D" and "K".

Tom began to object but the Judge cut him off. "Look, fellas. I don't have time for this. I'm going to put this off for one week. Mr. Hale, you have until next Friday to be prepared for a hearing on the charges. I will hold the hearing for both of the defendants who have been arrested for this crime or you can file the assault charge directly by an Information. Mr. Hale. You have been the State Attorney for many years. You know the rules."

"What about the bond?" asked Hale as the Judge returned his gaze to the photo. "Mr. Alessi belongs in jail."

The Judge looked at Tom. "Mr. Alesse is your law clerk? Is that true?"

"Yes."

"I expect you to have Mr. Alesse here next Friday," said the Judge. "He is your responsibility."

"Ok," said Tom.

"If he doesn't show up you have to answer to me."

"I agree," said Tom. "Judge, one other thing, I need a copy of the photo that Mr. Hale introduced to the court."

"I didn't introduce the photo," said Hale.

"I'm afraid you did, Mr. Hale," said the Judge. "Give Tom a copy of the photograph."

On the way out of the courtroom Tom saw John Hale talking to Richard Cook, the lead detective. Tom thought he would hate to be the lead detective. There would be a ton of pressure on the detective to get a conviction in this case. Tom wondered what Hale was saying to the detective. He would like to be the fly on the wall.

After the hearing, Alphonse thanked Tom. He promised he would appear for the hearing once Tom explained what the Judge required.